I0885569

EBURY PRESS

FIRST FLOOD

Kalki Ramaswamy Krishnamurthy (1899–1954) was a pioneer of modern Tamil literature, whose active involvement with India's freedom struggle inducted him into journalism. A liberal humanist and true-blue Gandhian, he had a passion for his mother tongue and took pride in his pan-Indian heritage. Krishnamurthy was a fiery, often controversial, crusader for political freedom, social reform and cultural revival. He adopted the pseudonym 'Kalki' after the apocalyptic avatar with the avowed intention of destroying repressive regimes and creating a new era with radical writings.

Kalki's prolific output includes essays, fiction, travel writing, art critiques, songs, poems and even a screenplay or two. He is lauded for his mesmerizing storytelling, conversational style, lyricism, wit and trademark humour. The serialized historical romances that made Kalki a cult figure appeared in the eponymous nationalist weekly he founded in 1944. His magnum opus *Ponniyin Selvan* remains a bestseller in the Tamil-speaking world.

Gowri Ramnarayan is a writer, translator, journalist, playwright, theatre director and educator. Formerly deputy editor of *The Hindu* and vocal accompanist to the legendary Carnatic musician M.S. Subbulakshmi, she has authored children's books, a biography of M.S. Subbulakshmi and profiles of iconic Indian artists. The 2017 collection *Dark Horse* anthologizes her original plays. Gowri has translated Kalki Krishnamurthy's short stories, his award-winning novel *Alai Osai* (The Sound of Waves), a two-volume biography by M.R.M. Sundaram titled *Kalki Krishnamurthy: His Life and Times*, as well as two plays by Marathi playwright Vijay Tendulkar. She is the chairperson of the Rukmini Devi Arundale Trust, senior associate editor at *Sruti* magazine and adjunct faculty at the Asian College of Journalism. Gowri has served as a member of the International Federation of Film Critics (FIPRESCI) juries at film festivals and holds a PhD in comparative aesthetics from the University of Madras.

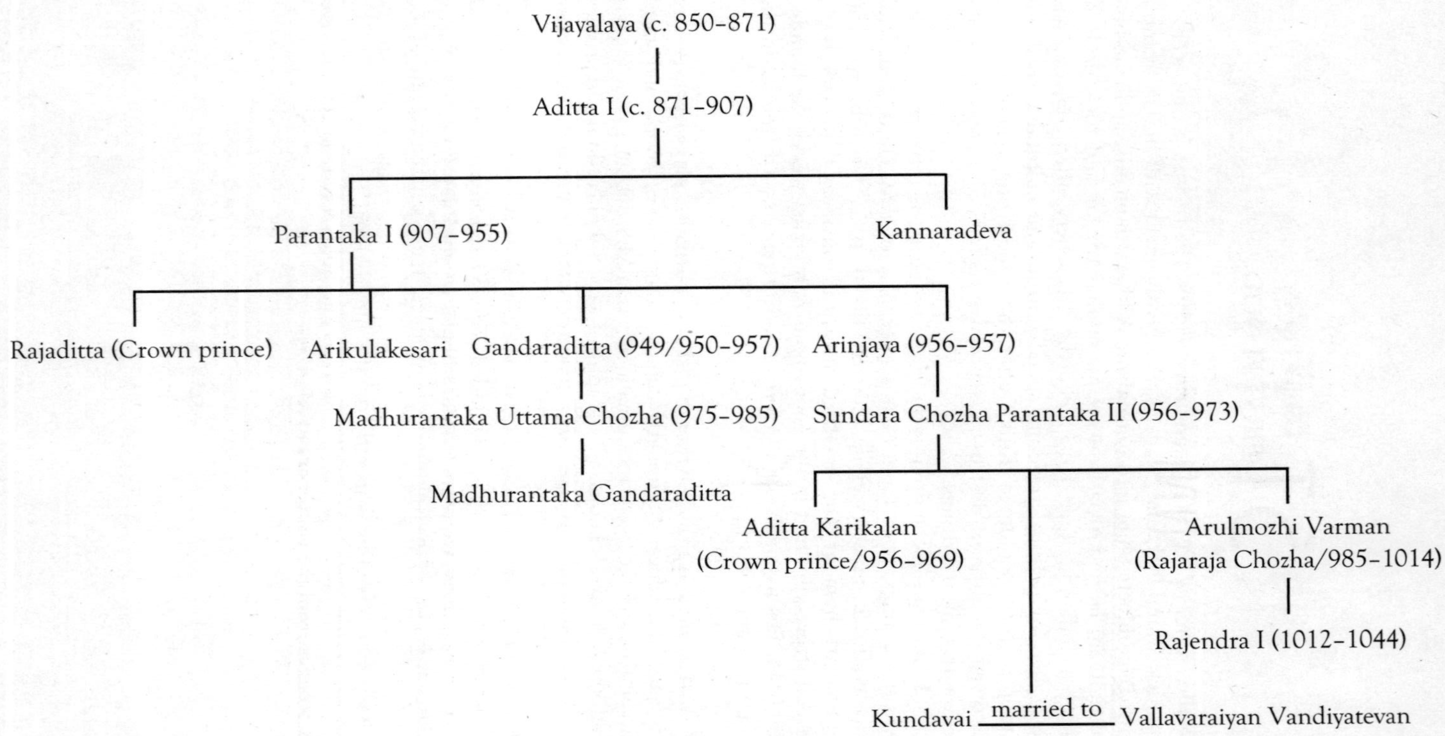
Vijayalaya (c. 850–871)
Aditta I (c. 871–907)
Parantaka I (907–955)
Kannaradeva
Rajaditta (Crown prince)
Arikulakesari
Gandaraditta (949/950–957)
Arinjaya (956–957)
Madhurantaka Uttama Chozha (975–985)
Sundara Chozha Parantaka II (956–973)
Madhurantaka Gandaraditta
Aditta Karikalan
(Crown prince/956–969)
Arulmozhi Varman
(Rajaraja Chozha/985–1014)
Rajendra I (1012–1044)
Kundavai
married to
Vallavaraiyan Vandiyatevan

FIRST FLOOD

PONNIYIN SELVAN 1

KALKI

Translated from the Tamil by Gowri Ramnarayan

EBURY
PRESS

An imprint of Penguin Random House

EBURY PRESS

Ebury Press is an imprint of the Penguin Random House group of companies whose addresses can be found at global.penguinrandomhouse.com

Published by Penguin Random House India Pvt. Ltd
4th Floor, Capital Tower 1, MG Road,
Gurugram 122 002, Haryana, India

Penguin Random House India

First published in Tamil as a series *Ponniyin Selvan* in *Kalki* magazine 1950–54
Published in Ebury Press by Penguin Random House India 2024

Translation copyright © Gowri Ramnarayan 2024

All rights reserved

10 9 8 7 6 5 4 3 2 1

This is a work of fiction. Names, characters, places and incidents are either the product of the author's imagination or are used fictitiously and any resemblance to any actual person, living or dead, events or locales is entirely coincidental.

Please note that no part of this book may be used or reproduced in any manner for the purpose of training artificial intelligence technologies or systems.

ISBN 9780670099924

Typeset in Goudy Old Style by Manipal Technologies Limited, Manipal
Printed at Thomson Press India Ltd, New Delhi

This book is sold subject to the condition that it shall not, by way of trade or otherwise, be lent, resold, hired out, or otherwise circulated without the publisher's prior consent in any form of binding or cover other than that in which it is published and without a similar condition including this condition being imposed on the subsequent purchaser.

www.penguin.co.in

FSC www.fsc.org MIX Paper | Supporting responsible forestry FSC® C010615

Translator's Note

My first acquaintance with *Ponniyin Selvan* is the stuff of family lore. As a toddler, annoyed that my grandfather was nowhere to be found, I tore the handwritten pages he had left on the desk to shreds. They were brand new chapters of *Ponniyin Selvan*, serialized in 'Kalki' Krishnamurthy's eponymous Tamizh weekly, ready to be dispatched for typesetting. My uncle, K. Rajendran, found me playing with the torn scraps. His yells brought my grandfather to the room. Scooping me up as though I had done something splendid, Kalki told my uncle, 'Raja, piece and glue the scraps together and get them to the press.'

The same uncle, who went on to be editor-in-chief of *Kalki* after his father's demise, has never quite gotten over his vexation at having to clean up my mess. But it was he who read aloud all five volumes of *Ponniyin Selvan* to me when I was nine years old. I was obsessed with books even then, but I think it was with *Ponniyin Selvan* that I saw for the first time how the imagination can transport the reader across space and time, to claim experiences far beyond your age and ken as your very own.

You will ask, 'As a translator struggling with the text, did you lose that freedom?' True, translation is a Sisyphean task. But strangely enough, I found that transposing Kalki's Tamizh into English freed me. I was no longer a reader, subjectively identifying myself with the characters and stories in my mother tongue. I was experiencing the text as the 'other', through a language that remains foreign for all its familiarity and whose ambience offers a stark contrast to the Indian world view. My job was to find a way to overcome this deep cultural divide.

I also found that I could not be a *translator*, I had to become a *writer*.

To do that, I had to know not only *what* Kalki wrote but *why* he wrote it. My first question was 'Why did Kalki write historical fiction?' No Tamizh writer had focused on this genre before him. What a burden the research must have been, especially for someone who was grappling with editing his own magazine and writing most of its pages, from political analyses and reformist promotions to music/dance/film critiques, travelogues, satirical essays, and even the occasional poem.

The year was 1953. As certified by the Audit Bureau of Circulations, *Kalki* had reached the largest circulation among all newspapers and periodicals in every language published in India.* The singular force behind this phenomenon was Kalki the writer. His political opinions ignited debates, his reformist tracts triggered changes in mindset, and his reviews of music, dance and films made and unmade reputations. But it is Kalki's historical fiction, a genre that he pioneered in Tamizh—and arguably one in which he remains unsurpassed—that has mesmerized four generations of readers. Starting with

* Audit Bureau of Circulations, 1953.

the exploratory *Parthiban Kanavu* (Parthiban's Dream, 1941), Kalki went on to write what many deem his most compelling novel, *Sivakamiyin Sapatham* (Sivakami's Vow, 1944). Both are set in medieval south India and chronicle the Chozha thirst for freedom from the Pallavas, and the Pallava-Chalukya wars. In 1950, Kalki started writing about the imperial Chozhas in *Ponniyin Selvan*, the last novel he would complete before passing away at age fifty-four. Kalki himself considered *Alai Osai* (The Sound of Waves, 1948), which brings alive the turbulent decades of India's freedom struggle and received the Sahitya Akademi Award, to be his best work.

Born in 1899 in a tiny village in Tanjavur district, Tamizh Nadu, Krishnamurthy grew up in a family with limited means. After managing to get a scholarship to join high school in Tiruchi town, he left midway to answer the Mahatma's call for non-cooperation with the British government. His writing career began as a clerk and pamphleteer in the local Congress office, where he drew the attention of leaders like T.S.S. Rajan and C. Rajagopalachari (Rajaji). With their encouragement, he turned into a scribe. He continued writing for the nationalist cause, undeterred by three prison sentences and the loss of a secure job.

In 1941, with support from fellow activist T.S. Sadasivam and his wife M.S. Subbulakshmi (who funded their project with her earnings from a film role), Krishnamurthy launched *Kalki*, the weekly named after him. It gave him the freedom to follow his head and heart without making compromises. In life, as in his writings, Kalki did not blindly conform to conventions but stood his ground against opposing—often populist—currents several times.

You may be amazed to know that the author travelled with his illustrator—in India and Ceylon (Sri Lanka) for the medieval locations, and from Karachi to Kolkata, and old Delhi to the old Madras Presidency, for his pre-Partition settings. He also wrote news stories and travelogues from those places.

Kalki's historical novels drew accolades from critics as well as the general public. Historians marvelled at the way he wove fiction without distorting history. A fellow scribe called him, not without envy, 'the matinee idol among writers'. Old-timers recount how they fought each week to be the first to grab the current issue of *Kalki* from the postman. Sometimes, the winner was generous enough to read the chapters aloud to other equally eager family members. To avoid acrimony, some households subscribed to two issues of *Kalki*. Small-town residents waited regularly at news stands and train stations for the '*Kalki* parcels' to arrive, and read the chapters standing on the platform or walking home. Readers belonged to every stratum of society. A retired chief justice recalled that he, his mother, wife and children read every issue, after which their cook read it aloud to the maid, watchman and gardener. Even today, fan clubs continue to conduct tours following protagonist Vandiyatevan's trail.

As Kalki recreated the art and culture of the Pallavas and Chozhas for clamouring twentieth-century audiences, the glories of this heritage were brought to bear on contemporary Tamil self-fashioning. His mesmerized fans, then and now, sometimes have trouble in sifting fact from fiction. Even today, the tour guides at Mamallapuram (Mahabalipuram) will swear, 'This is exactly where Sivakami danced for Mahendra Pallava in the seventh century.' Last year, a priest in an out-of-the-way Tanjavur temple solemnly assured me that the resident goddess was a mute woman from Sri Lanka who had been buried at the sanctum with a dagger still plunged in her breast. She had sacrificed her life to save King Sundara

Chozha (956–973 CE). Though his novels featured plenty of historical figures, the dancer in *Sivakamiyin Sapatham* and the 'mute woman goddess' in *Ponniyin Selvan* were fictional, figments of Kalki's imagination.

There were very few published accounts of ancient Tamizh history in Kalki's time. The books he collected on the subject were stashed in a trunk beside his desk for ready reference. *The Colas* by K.A. Nilakanta Sastri was one and *Pirkala Chozhar Charithiram* (The History of the Later Cholas) by Sadasiva Pandarathar was another. Kalki's copy of the latter has sentences heavily underlined, along with notes on the margins such as 'useful information', 'suitable material for the novel', 'mere guesswork' and 'my inference'.

Let us look at an example to show how history became the springboard for Kalki's spiralling imagination. Pandarathar writes: 'Princess Kundavai was given in marriage to Vallavaraiyan Vandiyatevan, who must have belonged to the southern Chalukya dynasty in the Vengi realm'. Kalki's margin notes say, 'He could have been a prince of the Vaanan clan.' *Voila!* Kalki's five-part novel has its protagonist in the brave, quick-witted, resourceful, loyal Vallavaraiyan Vandiyatevan. 'Our hero', as Kalki often describes him, is the one constant in a 2500-page epic novel with criss-crossing threads of love, war and political intrigue. It begins and ends with him.

All that history records about Vandiyatevan would hardly amount to ten pages. Literature provided a necessary corrective to history. At the time of writing *Ponniyin Selvan*, Kalki recalled how, years ago, a Tamil aficionado recited three short verses about the kings of the Vaanan clan, Vandiyatevan's ancestors. At his request, the friend sent those poems by post. Readers will see how adroitly Kalki quotes them in strategic moments to establish his hero's background and character. That is how he found 'evidence' to establish Vandiyatevan as the descendant of the Vaanan clan of Tamizh (and not of Chalukya) origin. This gave Kalki the freedom to fashion his character. With no one to call his own and nothing to claim for himself, Vandiyatevan had to live by his wits and military training.

We cannot but ask–in a panoramic novel about an imperial dynasty, why would Kalki choose an orphaned, destitute nonentity as his protagonist? Kalki's political and reformist writings show that, though a staunch Gandhian, he had socialist leanings, believing that independent India would be best served by the Praja Socialist party on the opposition bench. While his allegiance to nationalist Congress leaders was unfaltering, he placed his faith in the ordinary citizen as an arbiter of the nation's destiny. He passionately believed in the equality of all human beings, irrespective of class, creed and gender, which meant empathy towards the underdog. Spoiler alert! In *Ponniyin Selvan*, he also turns a gardener into a king and a fisherwoman into a queen.

In fact, Kalki would have never written a single word if he had not been convinced that the pen could weed out retrogressive customs, create a new era of well-being for the nation and make the world a better place. Replying to the charge that he preferred propaganda to literary worth, Kalki begins with a glowing description of spring, reminiscent of the poet Kalidasa, which somehow ends up as the Gandhian appeal to wear khadi in the hot months and always. 'Don't expect writings of lasting literary value from me,' he tells his critics. 'Expect them from hundreds and thousands of writers who will appear hereafter. Let me be what I am, an old campaigner incurably set in his ways.'*

---

* M.R.M. Sundaram, *Kalki Krishnamurthy: His Life and Times*, trans. Gowri Ramnarayan (Kalki Biography Project 2022).

I asked myself—does Kalki's trademark 'propaganda' seep into his swashbuckling historical romances? As a boy, Krishnamurthy had found Walter Scott, Alexandre Dumas and Victor Hugo irresistible. As an author, he found their genre to be best suited for his purpose. His people had been plagued by the insecurities and inferiorities bred by long years of colonization. His writings had to inspire them to stand up for their rights, fight for independence and abolish the social evils riddling their society. The historical romance could remind the Tamizh people of their glorious heritage, restore their pride and strengthen their resoluteness. He wrote about the past thinking of the immediate present.

India's freedom struggle ran not only on political wheels but on philosophical and spiritual fuel, such as the idea of *satyagraha.* It was not enough for those engaging in the freedom struggle to be rebels and reformists. They had to make the force of *satya* (truth), *dharma* (righteousness), *ahimsa* (non-violence) and *tyaga* (sacrifice), the core values of the Indian way of life, their own. They needed role models to inspire them. So Kalki proceeded to create them.

In his epilogue to *Ponniyin Selvan,* Kalki openly admits that he wrote his mammoth novel to highlight the act of sacrifice by a man he visualized as possessing unimpeachable rectitude and integrity. That is why, though Vandiyatevan is the protagonist, the novel is named after Prince Arulmozhi Varman, who performed his most exceptional act, not on the battlefield, but in renouncing the throne for ethical reasons. He becomes the Pole Star to guide his people. In *Ponniyin Selvan,* you can see in Arulmozhi Varman shades of Rama, who never deviates from satya and dharma; Arjuna, named Bibhatsu for being repelled by anything that smacked of dishonour; and Gautama Buddha and King Asoka, who epitomized ahimsa and tyaga.

The novel is also a meditation on leadership. Only those who are not interested in power should assume power. A nation's economic prosperity and political strength depend on its leaders respecting all sects and creeds in the realm, and preventing religion from invading politics. Waging war in Sri Lanka, Arulmozhi Varman not only protects the civilians there but also restores their battered Buddhist monuments. *Ponniyin Selvan* acclaims those who prevent war and violence from endangering the civilian population. Here is where Arulmozhi Varman scores over Crown Prince Aditta Karikalan. Karikalan does not possess foresight, compassion or wisdom. He invites tragedy because he cannot control his mind. Kalki is also convinced that art and culture can foster this wisdom, promote liberal values, and develop compassion among those who govern and those who are governed.

Kalki championed women's empowerment. In *Ponniyin Selvan*, Princess Kundavai is acclaimed not only for her beauty but for her outstanding intelligence as well. She is depicted as the most astute member of the royal clan. Antagonist Nandini is as brilliant as she is bewitching. Poonkuzhali, the fisherwoman, has tremendous physical and mental strength, as well as an artistic bent. Dowager Queen Sembiyan Mahadevi is universally revered for shunning the material life, her goodness and wisdom. Manimekalai captures our empathy with her mental agility and selfless love. No, Kalki never underestimated women. His female characters drove the narrative forward.

Among the many nuances I spotted as a translator is that Kalki communicated his most profound, ethical and humanitarian convictions through his fictional characters Nandini and Mandakini. Both mother and daughter face unmerited injustice and rank cruelty. They are abandoned, cheated, exploited and victimized by those whom they loved and trusted. Orphaned Nandini is the target of jealousy and disdain among the entitled royals. Mandakini is forsaken and left to deal with her own traumas.

Kalki makes them respond to the same maltreatment in diametrically opposite ways. Nandini's rage fuels her thirst for revenge. She wants to assassinate the man who abandoned her to the wolves and uproot his entire clan. But mute Mandakini claws her way out of shock and despair with the power of forgiveness. She showers affection on the son of the man who deceived her and finally sacrifices her life for him.

Not for nothing did Kalki follow the Mahatma who believed in returning hate with love.

* * *

Let me share some of the difficulties I faced in translating *Ponniyin Selvan*. I have already mentioned the cultural and political divide between Tamizh and English. I use Kalki's favourite image to add that there were times when I felt like someone 'battling with hurricane-tossed waves on a limitless ocean'.

The architectonic of this novel is as mind-boggling as the Mahabharata. It has a maze of incidents and a superfluity of characters across generations with names totally unfamiliar even to native Tamizh speakers. To add to the confusion, many have two names each–Arulmozhi Varman–Ponniyin Selvan, Azhvarkadiyan–Tirumalai, Periya Velar–Bhooti Vikramakesari, Chinna Pazhuvettaraiyar–Kalantaka Kantan, Poonkuzhali–Samudra Kumari and so on.

Kalki was squeezing his writing of the chapters between innumerable tasks and calls on his time as a magazine editor, who also wrote editorials, opinion pieces and art reviews in every issue. Often, the weekly chapters were brought to the press by the office boy, page by page, before the ink could dry, even as they were being penned at the desk. Obviously, editing was out of the question. Nor could Kalki spare much time to revisit the pages before they were published as books. And yes, the books have their share of anomalies. Sometimes, characters contradict what they said before. Facts appear different. Again, some situations are left undeveloped. These lapses may escape the page-turning reader, but the translator has to make hard decisions in dealing with omissions and contradictions.

Having translated Kalki's short stories and a novel set in the contemporary milieu, I thought I knew all about his style. The term *kalkitamizh* had already been coined for this distinct style, best described by Rajaji as resembling the tone of a friend chatting with you, his arm around your shoulder, as you strolled along without a backward glance. However, I soon discovered that the man had created something wholly new for *Ponniyin Selvan*. The liquid flow was very much there, but now it had echoes from old bardic lays and folk ballads intoning tales about clans and heroes. Also, there were tonal shifts reminiscent of ancient and medieval classics.

Translators are all too familiar with the basic hurdles they must cross. The surge of emotion in the original can slide into the maudlin, charged descriptive analogies may make the narrative flag and strikingly poetic metaphors sink into corny hyperbole. The Peruvian writer Mario Vargas Llosa once explained that Spanish has its own temperature and pace, proceeding as it does in a splendid cavalcade of diverse characters surrounded by the panoply of drums and attendants. I knew that I had to be intuitive and resourceful in transferring the Tamizh 'cavalcade' into a language from another hemisphere that resists flamboyance and heat. I had to be sensitive to the ways in which each language conducts its business, and the possibilities of imagery and nuance in both. I had to be the author's ally, as Italo Calvino describes a translator's role. Above all, I had to prioritize Kalki's own method of conversing with the reader as with a friend. Otherwise, the translation would not stand on its own.

In Kalki's case, I had to be extremely alert to the stylistic contrasts he sets up. Take this chapter in *First Flood* where the action is set in a forest that has grown over an old battlefield. Kalki begins by delivering a factual lesson in history about how the outcome of that battle had changed the fate of kingdoms. Next, shifting to the present tense, the authorial voice adopts the rolling periods of oral narration declaiming mythological tales to describe the carnage of long ago. After that, the secret agent hiding and waiting to spy on the conspirators launches a philosophical harangue, 'O stars in the sky! You've seen rivers of blood flow and piles of corpses grow, why won't you laugh at human beings bent on decimating one another?' Finally, we are in a noir thriller, where the conspirators hatch their gory plots.

Humour is often a casualty in translation. Kalki's trademark humour, from satire to farce, spewing puns and jokes, should have been the toughest challenge for the translator. Luckily, though the puns and wordplay are lost, English is a language that thrives on humour, particularly self-deprecating irony.

However, the real difficulty came from the verses that Kalki quotes from sources bewilderingly varied—Sangam poetry, hymns of the sixth to eighth-century saint poets, random verses, verses from the Buddhist canon, folk songs and songs he had specially composed. Having heard my mother sing every one of them as she read *Ponniyin Selvan* aloud, I realized that to the Tamizh reader, they are not frills but integral to the narrative. They amplify the situation, throw light on the characters and indicate their state of mind. You cannot paraphrase them in prose. You have to ride on their lilts and rhythms to enter the world of Kalki's period romance.

I am no scholar of ancient Tamizh. Nor am I a poet. Anyway, these songs would not fit into any contemporary free verse mode of spare, jagged phrases or abrupt line breaks. I requested the poet Arundhathi Subramaniam to translate a crucial song for this book. (This is the plaintive song that Kalki wrote to introduce Poonkuzhali in the second volume. It is also the song that he asked his daughter to sing for him just hours before his death.) I took Gopal Gandhi's permission to use his translation of the Tirukkural. Then I prayed to the poets and did my best with the rest, hoping to *convey the intention and purpose of the novelist*.

In 2023, a scholar said testily, 'Ban *Ponniyin Selvan*! Obsessed fans don't realize that Kalki has written other, more substantial works.' It is true that many readers remain strangers to the rest of Kalki's oeuvre, but their allegiance to *Ponniyin Selvan* is genuine, even fierce. They claim it as their own legacy, as a Tamizh work highlighting Tamizh history, Tamizh language, Tamizh culture and Tamizh identity. After seeing it in English, I have come to believe that *Ponniyin Selvan* is as Tamizh as *Les Miserables* is French, *Anna Karenina* is Russian and *One Hundred Years of Solitude* is Spanish–which is to say, they go beyond their language and milieu. They belong to the world.

I hope the readers of this translation will see how Kalki's 'Tamizh' vision is eclectic and inclusive, and has a national sweep and international relevance. It continues to raise questions about politics and ethics, state and citizen, society and individual, gender and class, privilege and marginalization, and history and cultural revisionism.

Six months before his death, in his keynote address at the Tamil Writers' Conference, Kalki spelt out his credo:

> The test of good writing is whether it aids the unification of the human community or promotes discord . . . Any writing that militates against the ethical principles of love, empathy, justice and truth will bring harm to humanity. And any evil sprouting in any section of society will have an irreversible impact on the whole world.

Kalki Krishnamurthy wanted to be that good a writer. In him, the activist inflames the writer, the poet coexists with the propagandist and the creative mind informs the crusading spirit.

Kalki may not have read T.S. Eliot, but he knew exactly what the English poet meant when he insisted:*

> *Time present and time past*
> *Are both perhaps present in time future,*
> *And time future contained in time past.*
> *What might have been and what has been*
> *Point to one end, which is always present.*

Kalki Krishnamurthy knew just why he was following the footfalls of the historical past in a language flavoured with

* T.S. Eliot, 'Burnt Norton', *Four Quartets* (New York: Harcourt, Brace and Co., 1943).

resonances from old myths and romances. It was to invoke the present, quivering on the brink of the future. Therefore, to him, the act of writing was the fulfilment of the writer's responsibilities towards stimulating self-awareness in the community and enriching the world as best he could. He was claiming his basic human right to be empowered by imagination, to soar at will and to assert his freedom.

1

Aadi Festival

Along the flooding tides of time without beginning or end, we invite our readers to join us for a short while on a boat of fantasy. Sailing with ease at the speed of a century per second, we arrive at an age in the past, nine hundred and eighty-two years before our time.*

A lake as vast as the ocean lay in the southern part of Tirumunaipadi, between the Chozha and the Pallava regions. This was the Veeranarayana Lake, measuring some fifteen miles from north to south, five miles from east to west, and located at a distance of some twenty miles from the temple town of Chidambaram. The passage of time has corrupted its name to Veeranam, as it is known today.

On the eighteenth day of the month of *Aadi*,† a young warrior was riding on horseback along the shore of this mammoth lake in the early hours of the evening. Vallavaraiyan

* Kalki wrote this in 1950. Hence, nine hundred and eighty-two years.

† Aadi is the fourth month in the Tamil Calendar and falls between mid-July and mid-August.

Vandiyatevan belonged to the Vaanan clan, renowned for its valour in the annals of Tamizh history. Enthralled by the panoramic waterscape, he hardly heeded the fact that his travel-worn horse was moving at a slow trot.

The rivers of the Chozha land were generally in full spate on the eighteenth of Aadi. The lakes into which they overflowed were tossed by waves as the water brimmed over their banks. The river Kollidam rushed into the Veeranarayana Lake through Vadavaru, its tributary, transforming it into a turbulent sea. Bursting through its seventy-four canals, these fresh floods supplied abundant water for irrigation in the surrounding region far and wide.

On that day, peasants, both men and women, were singing in glee as they ploughed the lake-nurtured earth and planted seeds in the paddy fields stretching as far as the eye could see. Listening to them, Vandiyatevan was content to maintain a leisurely pace without spurring his fatigued mount. He had been counting the canals from the time he reached the lakeshore, checking to see if they were indeed seventy-four in number. He had reached the count of seventy by the time he crossed some fifteen miles.

What a gargantuan lake! Massive in length and breadth! How could the lakes built by the kings of the Pallava realm appear to be anything but puddles and ponds in comparison? How astonishing that Prince Rajaditta, son of King Parantaka, should have come up with the idea of channelling the waters of the river into a lake as vast as the ocean! What a genius he must have been to have transformed his vision into reality! Moreover, could anyone equal Rajaditta in valour? Did he not ride full tilt on his elephant into the battle of Takkolam? Did he not fight on until his chest was gored by the enemy's spear? Did he not ascend to the warrior's heaven hailed as the 'braveheart who perished on the elephant'? Amazing indeed are these kings of the Chozha dynasty. As valiant as they are righteous. Their faith is as great as their valour.

Vandiyatevan mused on as he reached the southern end of the lake where he beheld the Vadavaru branching off from the Kollidam and flowing into the lake. Between the shore and the lake lay a strip of arable land, where karuvela and vila* trees had been grown to prevent the river from flooding the banks. Naanal reeds† clustered beside the shore.

From the southwest, the tree-fringed river shaped a mosaic of many hues as it flowed into the lake.

Other scenes enhanced the gaiety and charm of the landscape.

Men, women and children from the surrounding villages were arriving in droves, dragging little chariots made of ivory-coloured palm fronds behind them, to celebrate the day of the fresh floods rising in the month of Aadi. They were dressed in new clothes and adorned in many different ways. The women wore bunches of tazhampoo, sevanti, senbagam, malli, mullai and iruvatchi‡ flowers in their hair. Families came in batches, carrying picnic lunches of rice seasoned with different spices. Some stood in the shallow waters of the lake as they ate off areca palm leaves. The more daring crossed to the other side and ate their lunch standing in the river. Children threw their used 'plates' into the lake, clapping their hands in glee as the leaves raced through the tunnels. Daring young men plucked flowers from their lovers' braids, dropped them into

---

* Mesquite and wood apple trees.

† Bulrush grass.

‡ Screw pine, chrysanthemum, champak and vaieties of jasmine.

the waters and rejoiced to see them floating to the other side of the tunnels.

Enchanted by these sights, Vandiyatevan halted for a while. He drank in the sweet strains as the women sang of boating, dancing and fresh floods rising in the rivers.

The Vadavaru swells along!
Friends, come and see!
The Vellaru rushes along!
Friends, enjoy the fun!
The Kaveri rolls along!
Friends, take a look!

Others sang of the glory of the Chozha kings. Some of the women sang a ballad about the saga of Vijayalaya Chozha, who fought thirty-two wars and bore ninety-six wounds on his body. One of the women described how Vijayalaya's brave son, Aditta Chozha, built sixty-four temples for Siva from the headwaters to the estuary of the Kaveri. With great zest did another enthusiast serenade the glory of Aditta's son Parantaka, who conquered the Pallavas, Pandyas and Cheras, and sent an army to Ilankai* to plant the flag of victory on the island. Each balladeer was surrounded by a group of listeners, voicing their appreciation with cries of delight.

An elderly woman noticed how the young man on horseback was taking it all in. 'Son!' she called out. 'You seem to have travelled a great distance. You look worn out. Get down. Come, share our meal.'

Several young girls took a close look at our young traveller. They whispered their comments about his appearance to one

* Sri Lanka.

another and burst into loud giggles. Vandiyatevan was torn between elation and embarrassment. He pondered whether he should accept the old woman's invitation. If he did, the giggling girls would surely surround him and make fun of him. So what? Was it so easy to find so many pretty girls in a single spot? Their teasing and laughter would sound like the music of the gods. To Vandiyatevan's youthful eyes, every girl on the lakeshore appeared to be a celestial nymph.

And yet, what he saw on the river in the south-westerly direction made him hang back. Like swans with their wings outspread, seven or eight barques with billowing sails of white were skimming swiftly across the waters.

On the lakeshore, folks enjoying fun and games stopped to gaze earnestly at the approaching barques.

One of the vessels swung ahead of the others to reach the spot where the shore took a northward turn. Burly soldiers stood on it, flashing their sharp, pointed spears.

Some of the soldiers leapt down to drive the people away. Giving them little opportunity for bullying, the people picked up their belongings and began to hasten away from the shore.

Vandiyatevan was puzzled. Who were these soldiers? Who was riding on the barques with multiple sails? Some member of the royal clan?

Vandiyatevan approached an elderly man holding a staff and showered him with questions. '*Ayya,*[*] to whom do these soldiers belong? Who commands these barques? Why are the people being driven away? Why should they clear out?'

'*Tambi,*[†] don't you know? Look at the flag on top of the barque at the centre! What do you see?'

---

[*] Sir.
[†] Brother.

'Looks like the image of a palm tree!'

'It *is* a palm tree. Don't you know that the palm tree is the emblem of the Pazhuvettaraiyar clan?'

Startled, Vandiyatevan exclaimed, 'The great Pazhuvettaraiyar himself? Here?'

The old man said, 'Must be. Who else would dare to raise this flag?'

Vandiyatevan's eyes widened in amazement as he stared at the barques. He had heard a great deal about the Pazhuvettaraiyars. From Ilankai in the south to Kalinga in the north, was there anyone at all who did not know the two brothers, Periya Pazhuvettaraiyar the elder and Chinna Pazhuvettaraiyar the younger? Their native town was Pazhuvur, on the northern side of River Kollidam, close to Uraiyur. The Pazhuvettaraiyar clan had been famous from the time of Vijayalaya Chozha. Several marriage alliances bound them to the Chozha kings. This, along with the hoariness of their clan and their reputation for valour, had given the privileges of royalty to the Pazhuvettaraiyar family. They had the right to raise a flag of their own.

Periya Pazhuvettaraiyar had taken part in twenty-four battles and was known as the invincible warrior of the Chozha realm in his time. He had held some of the highest posts in the Chozha government, and was the Chancellor of the Exchequer who was also in charge of the departments of food and agriculture. The treasury and the granary were under his control. Additionally, he was the Supreme Income Tax Commissioner who could levy and collect taxes as he thought fit, according to the needs of the state. He had the prerogative to fix the amount to be collected every year from feudal chieftains, heads of provinces, districts, village conglomerates and clan leaders. Therefore, after King Sundara Chozha, the most powerful man in the Chozha empire was none other than the senior Pazhuvettaraiyar.

Vandiyatevan felt an overwhelming desire to see the grand warrior who wielded such immense strength and power. But he remembered what Prince Aditta Karikalan had impressed upon him when he spoke to him privately in the newly built golden palace in Kanchi city.

'Vandiyatevan, you are a man of true valour. But it is my faith in your sagacity that makes me entrust you with this responsibility. You must hand over my missives to my royal father, and to my sister. No one must know anything about them. I hear all kinds of rumours about the highest-ranking officials in the Chozha kingdom. Even the most important functionary should not suspect that you carry a message from me. Mind you, no brawls along the way. You must not retaliate even if someone tries to drag you into a fight. I know how brave you are. You will not lose face if you avoid a fight. Above all, be on your guard with the Pazhuvettaraiyars and my uncle Madhurantakan.'

These instructions had been given by the crown prince of the Chozha kingdom, the supreme commander of the northern army. Remembering how the prince had repeatedly advised him on how he was to conduct himself, Vandiyatevan suppressed his desire to take a closer look at Periya Pazhuvettaraiyar. He spurred his horse, though the travel-worn animal could move only at a flagging pace. Vandiyatevan decided to spend the night at Sambuvaraiyar's palace in Kadambur. After all, his best friend Kandamaran was the son of the chieftain of the Sambuvaraiyar clan. He would resume his journey on the morrow with a fresh horse.

2

Azhvarkadiyan Nambi

As he descended from the banks of the lake and turned his horse on to the path going south, Vandiyatevan's heart danced like a boat bobbing on the waves. There was an upsurge of elation which had lain dormant until then. Some instinct told him that the time had come for him to go through incredible experiences as no one had ever before.

If approaching the Chozha realm was enough to trigger such euphoria, what would it be like to cross the Kollidam and see the water-rich bountifulness of the land? What were they like, the people—and the young women—who lived there . . .

How many rivers it had! How many pools! Brooks running crystal clear! What about the Kaveri, lovingly called Ponni, the subject of poems and epics! The punnai, konrai and kadamba trees on its banks, bursting with blooms! How delightful to be beckoned by smiling lilies—blue and white—and welcomed by the red lotuses! What about the magnificently carved temples, built along the banks of the Kaveri by the kings of the Chozha dynasty, devout worshippers of the god Siva!

Ah! Pazhaiyarai city! The capital of the Chozha kings! Pazhaiyarai city that had reduced Poompuhar and Uraiyur to little hamlets! With its domed mansions, high towers, market streets, military encampments, and intricately designed Siva and Vishnu temples of stone!

Vandiyatevan had heard that the hymns rendered in those temples by sweet-voiced musicians enthralled listeners. Soon, he was going to have the privilege of hearing that music. That was not all. He was going to meet the emperor face to face—Parantaka Sundara Chozha, as valiant as Velan, the warrior god, and as handsome as Manmatha, the god of love. He was going to see his darling daughter Kundavai, the incomparable lady of the land.

Hopefully, he would encounter no hurdles along the way. What if he did? He had a spear in his arm, sword in its sheath, armour on his chest and grit in his heart.

Hoping to reach Kadambur before sunset, Vandiyatevan found himself near the Vishnu temple of Veeranarayana town. It was the day of the Aadi festival.* The surrounding groves were packed with pilgrims and holidaymakers.

Vendors selling jackfruit slices, sugarcane strips, bananas and various other snacks had put up their stalls everywhere. Some were selling flowers for women to wear and lotuses to be offered in worship. Others had heaped coconuts, tender coconuts, incense, sandalwood, betel leaves, jaggery and puffed rice for sale. Different kinds of entertainment were also being

* Celebrated in Tamizh Nadu on the eighteenth day of the Aadi month (July), the festival coincides with the annual rising of the water levels in the rivers, heralding the onset of the monsoon. The festival pays tribute to water's life-sustaining properties with prayers in riverside temples and picnics by the river.

showcased. Nor was there any lack of astrologers, palmists, interpreters of omens and dispensers of poison cures.

Vandiyatevan ambled along until he noticed a group of men huddled around a noisy altercation. He felt an uncontrollable curiosity to know more. Leaving his horse on the roadside, with a pat to indicate that it should wait for him, he dismounted and pushed himself through the throng. He was surprised to see that only three men were engaged in the debate. However, each drew boisterous support from different sections of the crowd.

Vandiyatevan began to pay attention to the subject under dispute.

One of the polemicists was a Vaishnava, a devotee of Vishnu. He was short, bulky and brawny, with a staff in hand, his body streaked with sandalwood paste, and a tuft on his head.

The other was a Saiva, a votary of Siva, covered all over with thick stripes of ash.

The third was a saffron-clad monk with a shaved head. A follower of neither Siva nor Vishnu, he was a philosopher, a proponent of the non-dualistic advaita doctrine.

The man of the Siva faith said, 'O Azhvarkadiyan Nambi! Answer me! Didn't Brahma and Vishnu fail to find the head and feet of Siva, who has neither beginning nor end? Did they not surrender to him? Therefore, how can Vishnu be greater than Siva?'

Swinging his staff menacingly, Azhvarkadiyan Nambi thundered, 'Stop it! Didn't your Siva shower the demon Ravana with boons? Weren't those boons reduced to dust by Rama, the avatar of Vishnu? How then can your Siva be greater than our Vishnu?'

The saffron-robed monk interposed to say, 'Why do you argue in vain? No debate, however long it may be, can resolve whether Siva or Vishnu is the greater god. But the Vedanta philosophy has an answer to this question. You fight over Siva and Vishnu only so long as you remain at a low level in the path of devotion. The path of *jnana* or knowledge is higher than *bhakti*, devotion. Beyond jnana lies the state of *jnasa*, where Siva and Vishnu cease to matter and everything is understood to be the ultimate reality beyond earthly phenomena. Everything is understood to be the ultimate reality beyond earthly phenomena. What Sri Sankaracharya says in his commentary on the Brahma Sutra is this–

Azhvarkadiyan broke in to exclaim, 'That's all very well! But do you know what your Sankaracharya said after writing his commentaries on the Upanishads, the Bhagavad Gita and the Brahma Sutra? He said, "O foolish mind! Chant the name of Govinda! Chant the name of Govinda! Chant the name of Govinda!" He said it thrice because he was addressing brainless wonders like you!'

The crowd burst into applause, with cheers and mocking laughter.

But the monk was not silenced. '*Adey*!* Nambi! You are absolutely right. I am indeed brainless to talk to a man whose staff and head are both made of wood!'

Nambi's faction began to roar as he raised his staff and announced, 'Yes, a wooden staff! Perfectly capable of cracking your bald pate!'

'Stop!' said the monk. 'Keep your staff to yourself! Even if you use it to thrash me, I will not be angry or retaliate in kind. Brahmaan, the ultimate reality, is omnipresent. He who hits,

* A form of 'hey you!', a threatening exclamation addressed to another man.

and he who is hit, are both part of that transcendent reality. Hit me, and you hit yourself.'

'Here! Take a good look!' Nambi hollered as he brandished his staff and approached the monk. 'Brahman is going to thrash brahman! I am going to thrash myself!'

Vandiyatevan, who had been watching the proceedings, now felt impelled to snatch the staff and give Nambi a sound drubbing.

But the monk had disappeared into the crowd. This made the Vaishnava faction erupt into noisy demonstrations of support.

Swivelling to face Bhattar, the Saiva debater, Azhvarkadiyan said, 'What say you? Are you going to turn tail like the monk?'

'Do you think that I am your Krishna? After all, your Krishna was soundly beaten when he stole butter from the *gopis*!'*

Before Bhattar could finish, Nambi advanced towards him. 'Why? Have you forgotten that your Siva was slammed on the back as he carried a load of sand to earn a few sweets?' he asked.

Azhvarkadiyan was a burly man. Bhattar was all skin and bone. Their supporting factions began to prepare for a free-for-all.

Vandiyatevan had a mind to stop that senseless fight.

He stepped forward to say, 'Why are you fighting? Don't you have anything better to do? If you have the urge to fight, why not go to Ilankai where a huge war is taking place?'

Turning towards Vandiyatevan, Nambi demanded, 'Who the hell are you to settle the dispute?'

---

* Cowherdesses among whom the god Krishna, the avatar of Vishnu, grew up in childhood.

Vandiyatevan's good looks and gallant demeanour drew some of the onlookers to his side. 'Tambi, go on! Tell it as it is! We are here to support you!'

'I will tell you what I think. Siva and Vishnu don't seem to be fighting each other. They seem to be good friends. Why should this Nambi and Bhattar quarrel?' Vandiyatevan's comments aroused much laughter.

Bhattar said, 'This youngster seems to be intelligent. But can jokes settle disputes? Let him state whether Siva or Vishnu is the greater god!'

Vandiyatevan said, 'Both are great. Worship the god of your choice. Why get into fights?'

'How can you say that? Can you prove that Siva and Vishnu are equal in glory?' Azhvarkadiyan demanded aggressively.

'Proof? I will give you proof,' Vandiyatevan said. 'Last evening, I was in Vishnu's abode. Siva was there too. They were seated at the same level. They were both the same height. Still, to be absolutely certain, I measured them with my own hands.'

'*Dei!** Are you mocking us?' Azhvarkadiyan roared.

The crowd hollered, 'Go on, tambi, go on! We are with you!'

'I did not stop with that but asked the gods themselves to answer this question. Do you know what they said? "Siva and Vishnu are one. Those who don't know this are undone," said they and gave me a fistful of sand for those ignorant fools.' As he spoke, Vandiyatevan dribbled the sand in his fist to the ground.

Everyone began to grab fistfuls of sand and throw them on Nambi and Bhattar.

Shouting insults, Azhvarkadiyan flailed his staff as he pounced on the crowd. A brawl seemed imminent.

---

* A threatening exclamation addressed to a man.

Fortunately, a commotion broke out at a little distance. 'Make way for the warrior of warriors, champion of champions, he who fought twenty-four wars and bears sixty-four wounds, the exterminator of the Pandya forces, the lord of the treasury and the granary of the Chozha empire, the superintendent of taxes and revenues! Make way for Periya Pazhuvettaraiyar! Make way! Make way!'

The heraldic criers came first, followed by drummers and bearers of the palm tree flag. Then came a company of soldiers, marching proudly, spear in hand. Behind them came a dark man of majestic mien, mounted on a splendidly ornamented elephant, like a dusky cloud resting on a mountain peak.

Vandiyatevan joined the crowd that had assembled on both sides of the road. He guessed that the man on the elephant was Pazhuvettaraiyar himself.

A silk-curtained palanquin followed the elephant. Before Vandiyatevan could wonder about its occupant, an extremely fair hand emerged from inside to part the screen a little. A woman's luminous face appeared, like the moon shining in all its splendour after the clouds had passed.

Vandiyatevan had eyes that rejoiced at the sight of feminine beauty. And yet, though the face he glimpsed was as lustrous as the full moon, somehow it inspired no joy in him.

Something beside him drew the woman's intent gaze. He heard a piercing shriek. The screen fell back into place.

Something told Vandiyatevan that the woman had closed the curtain because she had seen something–or someone–close by. He looked around to see what it could be. Behind him, Azhvarkadiyan Nambi stood, leaning against a tamarind tree.

3

The Vishnu Temple

At times, a trifling incident sets off events of great significance. Such an incident occurred in Vandiyatevan's life at that very moment.

Vandiyatevan had been standing by the street and watching Pazhuvettaraiyar's retinue go by. The last few troopers happened to catch sight of his horse, standing at a little distance.

One of them exclaimed, 'Dei! Look at that horse!'

A jester among them quipped, 'First of all, make sure whether it is a horse or a donkey.'

'We will,' said another as he approached the horse and tried to mount it. Recognizing that the man was not his master, the intelligent animal bucked and shied, refusing to allow the stranger to get on its back.

'Cranky beast! He will allow only a member of an ancient royal clan to mount him! In that case, Tanjavur Mutharaiyan will have to return to ride this horse!' This wisecrack drew much laughter as the Mutharaiyan clan had been extinct for well over a century. The Chozha flag with its tiger emblem flew over Tanjavur now.

Another gagster interposed, 'Tandavaraya! Make sure that he's a real horse and not the dummy horse from the temple festival!'

'Let me check it out,' Tandavarayan retorted as he twisted thc animal's tail. The horse kicked its hind legs and galloped away.

'He is running! A real horse after all!' The men's cries incited the horse to run faster through the crowd of pilgrims gathered for the temple festival. A stampede ensued as people tried to save themselves from being trampled under the horse's hoofs. But a few people did get hurt as the animal ran amok in a wild frenzy.

All this happened in a twinkling. From the look on his face, Azhvarkadiyan guessed that the horse belonged to Vandiyatevan.

'Tambi! See what the Pazhuvur louts have done! Why don't you show them the bravado you showed me?

Vandiyatevan was roused to fury but managed to keep it under control. The Pazhuvur men were large in number. It would be foolish to attack them. Nor did they wait to engage with him. They moved on, guffawing over the runaway horse.

Vandiyatevan followed the horse in the direction it had taken. He knew that it would come to a halt after a short sprint. But the thought impressed itself firmly on his mind that, one day, he should teach a sharp lesson to the arrogant men of Pazhuvettaraiyar's company.

He found the horse standing sadly all by himself in a deserted tamarind grove. The animal neighed at him in reproach. 'Why did you abandon me to face this trouble?'

Vandiyatevan led it back to the road with a comforting pat. Several voices upbraided him, 'Why did you bring this wild horse into the crowd? It kicked so many people to the ground!' Others tried to mollify the accusers by saying, 'What can this young man do, or the horse for that matter, when the mishap was caused by the Pazhuvur men?'

Azhvarkadiyan was still waiting on the street. Vandiyatevan scowled in exasperation, thinking, 'What a pain! Why won't he leave me alone?'

'Where are you going?' Azhvarkadiyan asked.

'I? Well, I go west, take a turn to the south, go around to the east, then move along to the southwest.'

'All I want to know is, where are you spending the night?'

'Why do you want to know?'

'I have something to do in Sambuvaraiyar's mansion at Kadambur, in case you are planning to stay there.'

'Are you a magician? How do you know I am going to the Kadambur palace?'

'You don't need magic to know that! Guests from many different places are bound for Kadambur today. Why, Pazhuvettaraiyar and his retinue are going there.'

'Is that so?' Vandiyatevan exclaimed in surprise.

'Didn't you know? The elephant, palanquin and other gifts of honour have been dispatched from the Kadambur palace to welcome Pazhuvettaraiyar.'

Vandiyatevan fell into a reverie. To lodge anywhere with Pazhuvettaraiyar as a fellow guest was by no means an everyday occurrence. He might even find a chance to get acquainted with the great warrior. However, he could not get over his bitterness in his encounter with the Pazhuvur troopers.

'Tambi! Will you do me a favour?' Azhvarkadiyan pleaded.

'What can I do for you? I am new to these parts.'

'I am not asking for anything you cannot do. Take me with you to the Kadambur palace today.'

'Why? Is some Saiva to be found there with whom you can argue about whether Siva or Vishnu is the greater god?'

'No. Don't think I am interested only in wrangling. A grand dinner will be served at the Kadambur palace tonight. Various entertainments will be showcased after dinner. I want to see the *kuravai koothu*[*] performance!'

'But how can I take you with me?'

'Say I am your servant!'

With mounting suspicion, Vandiyatevan said, 'No one will believe me. I don't need a servant like you. Moreover, after listening to what you have said, I am beginning to wonder if I can manage to get into the fort today.'

'Aren't you an invited guest?'

'In a way, I am. Sambuvaraiyar's son Kandamaran is a close friend of mine. He has given a standing invitation to visit him if and when I travel in this region.'

'Is that all? In that case, you are going to have your own problems today.'

They walked on in silence.

'Why are you following me?' Vandiyatevan asked.

'I can ask you the same question. Why are *you* following me? Why don't you go your way?'

'Because I don't know the way. Nambi, where are you going? To Kadambur perhaps?'

'No. Didn't you say that you can't take me? I am going to the Vishnu temple.'

'To the Veeranarayana temple?'

---

[*] An ancient traditional dance performance in Tamizh Nadu where the performer may sometimes go into a trance and make prophecies.

'Yes.'

'I want to go to the temple and pray to the deity.'

'I wondered if you would enter a Vishnu temple. Ishvaramuni, the priest, is a great soul.'

'I have heard of him. But why are the temple precincts so crowded today? Anything special?'

'Today is the birth anniversary of the poet Andal. And it coincides with the eighteenth day of Aadi.'

They reached the Veeranarayana temple.

* * *

It was Parantaka I, the grandson of Vijayalaya Chozha, the 'conqueror of Madurai and Ilankai', who laid the foundation for the Chozha empire. He was renowned in history as the king who had roofed the Chidambaram temple with gold. Many honorific titles lionized him, including Parakesari, Chozha Sikhamani, Soora Sikhamani and Veeranarayana.

In Parantaka's time, the Rashtrakuta kings had gained power in the north. Since Parantaka expected them to invade his country, he stationed a colossal army in Tirumunaipadi with his firstborn, Rajaditta. As the soldiers had nothing to do but wait for the war, Rajaditta came up with the idea of employing those thousands of men under his command to perform a stupendous task for public welfare.

The superabundant water of River Kollidam was draining into the ocean. To utilize those waters purposefully, Rajaditta had his soldiers construct a lake as vast as the ocean and named it after his father. He built a town of the same name beside the lake with a Vishnu temple, whose deity was also named Veeranarayana. Since Vishnu, or Narayana, was the god who slept on the water and was considered to be the embodiment of water, it was customary in those times to safeguard reservoirs by building a shrine to Vishnu beside them.

As soon as they reached the temple sanctum, Azhvarkadiyan began to sing the hymns of the poet Andal, followed by those of Nammazhvar.

Glow! Glow! Glow!
Gone is the curse of life, crushed are the torments of hell
No place here for the god of death.
The age of Kali ends, all ills fade away.
As you will see! For here they are,
Lovers of the sea blue lord.
See them sing and dance and rejoice.

We've seen! We've seen! We've seen!
We've seen what's sweet to the eye.
All of you who serve, come, join us,
To pray, and pray.
As bees swarm around his tulsi garland
See! His heavenly troops descend
To sing and dance in his praise
All across the earth!

These thousand and ten songs,
Hailing the glory of the lord
By Karimaran Satakopan, of Kurukur,
The town of lush fields,
Cleanse the dross from the heart

As he sang, tears streamed from Azhvarkadiyan's eyes and ran down his cheeks. Vandiyatevan listened attentively. Though he did not shed tears, he was deeply moved. He changed his mind about Azhvarkadiyan and began to believe he was a man of profound faith.

Among the listeners were Ishvaramuni, his little son and the temple officials. When Azhvarkadiyan finished singing, the child said something to his father. Ishvaramuni wiped his eyes and said, 'Ayya, they say that Nammazhvar has composed a thousand songs. Do you know them all?'

'I am not so fortunate. I know only a few verses.'

'Please teach whatever you know to this child,' Ishvaramuni said.

In the future, this town was going to be celebrated for many achievements. The tender child with the glowing face who stood listening to the songs of Nammazhvar was going to be hailed as Nathamuni, the first in the line of the eminent preceptors of the Vaishnava doctrine. His research would result in the compilation of a thousand poems of Nammazhvar, which his disciples would sing and propagate across the land.

Nathamuni's grandson Alavandar would perform miracles.

On his pilgrimage to the birthplace of these two luminaries, the great savant Ramanuja would be inspired by the Veeranarayana Lake with its seventy-four canals enriching the land. He would appoint seventy-four preceptors of his Vaishnava philosophy to facilitate the flow of divine compassion into the hearts of all living beings.

Let us leave these stupendous events to be narrated by the history of the Vaishnava gurus, and turn to Vandiyatevan once again.

When they emerged from the temple after the puja, Vandiyatevan said to Azhvarkadiyan, 'Nambi! I had no idea that you were a man of exemplary devotion and scholarship. Forgive me if I said anything amiss.'

'I will. But now, will you do me a favour?'

'Did you not accept the fact that I cannot oblige you?'

'This is about something else. I will give you a note. If you get to stay in the Kadambur fort, you must hand it over at the right time.'

'To whom?'

'To the woman in the palanquin in Pazhuvettaraiyar's retinue.'

'Whom do you take me for? How did you imagine that I'd do such a thing? If anyone else had asked me . . .'

'Tambi! Don't get into a flap! It is perfectly all right. But if you had helped me now, my assistance would have come in useful to you at some other time. Never mind! Farewell!'

Vandiyatevan would tarry no more. He jumped on his horse and galloped away to Kadambur.

4

The Kadambur Palace

Rejuvenated after getting some rest, Vandiyatevan's horse reached Sambuvaraiyar's palace within half an hour.

Senkannar Sambuvaraiyar was one of the great clan elders of the Chozha realm. The gateway to his palace resembled the portals of a huge citadel. Massive walls rising on both sides curved and stretched like the ramparts of a fort.

Commotion reigned in the front yard, teeming with elephants, horses and bullocks, their handlers, carriers of fodder and water, torchbearers, and those who fed the flares with oil. Armed with spears, soldiers stood at the gateway like the sentries of the underworld. Vandiyatevan was filled with apprehension. Why had he arrived just as some big event was about to take place? At the same time, he hankered to know exactly what the event was all about.

The gallant youth decided that he would be stopped if he dithered. He should clear the gates with confidence. But what a disappointment! As soon as he reached the gates, two men crossed their spears to stop him. Four others rushed to grab the reins. One thrust a torch near his face as another stared at him.

Vandiyatevan cried out in fury, 'Is it the custom in your town to stop guests at the door?'

'Cocky, are we? And who may you be?'

'You want to know who I am? My name is Vallavaraiyan Vandiyatevan! My birthplace is Tiruvallam in the land of the Vaanan tribe. Once, the warriors of your land were proud to inscribe my ancestors' names on their chests!'

'Why didn't you bring a herald with you to make this grand announcement?' demanded the guard. The men laughed.

The chief guard declared, 'Whoever you may be, you cannot get in now. All the invited guests have arrived. Our master has ordered that nobody should be allowed in.'

The contretemps attracted other soldiers. One of them exclaimed, 'Dei! Looks like the horse we chased away at the festival.'

Another interposed, 'Donkey, you mean!'

'But see how proudly the man sits on the donkey!'

As soon as he heard these remarks, Vandiyatevan knew what he must do.

'Let go!' he said. 'I am turning back.'

The guards slackened the reins.

With both his feet, Vandiyatevan kicked the horse in its belly, as hard as he could.

At the same moment, he drew his sword from its sheath. Like the discus wielded by the god Vishnu, his sword dazzled the eye as he swirled it around at lightning speed. The horse galloped into the fort. This unexpected manoeuvre sent the guards tumbling down and scattering in all directions.

Several things happened at once. The doors of the fort clanged shut. Shrieks of 'Seize him!' mingled with the clamour of spears and swords. The drums boomed to signal danger.

Some thirty to forty guards surrounded the horse. Vandiyatevan leapt down. He cried out as he twirled his sword, 'Kandamara! Kandamara! Your guards are murdering me!'

His cry halted the guards and made them step back.

A voice thundered from the balcony above, 'Stop the din!' Some seven or eight men looked down.

A guard shouted from the ground, 'Master! A man has broken into the fort! He is calling out the young master's name!'

The thundering voice said, 'Kandamara! Go and see what the racket is all about.' Vandiyatevan guessed that the voice belonged to Senkannar Sambuvaraiyar.

Everyone including Vandiyatevan stood still, waiting.

'What's all this?' a young voice called out. The guards made way for a youth to come through. Looking at Vandiyatevan, who stood twirling his sword like a god who had destroyed a demon, he shouted in excitement, 'My dear friend! Is it really you?' and hugged him.

'Kandamara, I came to your house because you had invited me so many times! This is the welcome I get!' Vandiyatevan said, indicating the company of guards.

'Fools! Get lost!' Kandamaran dismissed them. Then, grabbing Vandiyatevan by the hand, he took him along with a skipping gait and a leaping heart.

Is there anything more enthralling than friendship in the years of youth? Oh yes, there is that thing called love. But in love, there is more grief and pain than joy and elation. But no shadow of grief mars the exhilarating friendship of the young ones.

As they made their way in, Vandiyatevan asked, 'Kandamara, all this tumult and surveillance! Why?'

'I will explain later. When you and I were at the camp beside River Pennai, didn't you keep on saying that you wanted to see Pazhuvettaraiyar, Mazhavaraiyar and a host of others? You can see them all, right here, today,' Kandamaran said, as he took his friend to the hall upstairs where the guests were seated. Leading him to his father, Kandamaran said, 'Appa! This is my friend Vandiyatevan. He belongs to the Vaanan clan. Haven't I talked to you about him many times?'

Vandiyatevan folded his hands before the elderly man and bowed. But Sambuvaraiyar hardly appeared to be pleased.

'Is he the one who made a racket at the palace gateway?'

'The racket was caused by the fools we have appointed as guards. Not by my friend.'

'He need not have made such a late and disorderly entry.'

Kandamaran winced. He did not wish to argue with his father. He took Vandiyatevan away and introduced him to Pazhuvettaraiyar, who occupied a high seat at the centre. 'This is my dear friend Vandiyatevan. He belongs to the royal Vaanan clan. When we were at the army camp by the River Pennai, he would keep on chanting, "I must see Periya Pazhuvettaraiyar, the greatest of warriors! Does he really bear sixty-four battle scars on his body?" I would reply, "Why don't you see for yourself one day?"'

'Tambi, is that so? You won't believe in my scars unless you count them yourself? Do you think that no one can be as brave as the members of your own Vaanan clan?'

The two friends were startled. They had not expected their flattery to be misconstrued.

Vandiyatevan was overcome with indignation. He concealed it to say, 'Ayya, who am I to doubt the valour of the Pazhuvettaraiyar clan, celebrated as it is from Kanyakumari to the Himalayas?'

'Good answer! Smart boy!' Pazhuvettaraiyar said.

The young men escaped with relief. Sambuvaraiyar signalled to his son and whispered, 'Make sure your friend is fed quickly and given a quiet place to rest. He must be worn out by his long journey.'

Kandamaran took his friend to the women's quarters. It was crowded. Vandiyatevan bowed to Kandamaran's mother and guessed that the young girl hiding behind her must be Kandamaran's sister. His eyes scanned the group, searching for the woman he had glimpsed on the palanquin.

5

Kuravai Koothu

They had just left the women's quarters when a voice called out, 'Kandamara! Kandamara!'

'Mother is calling me. Wait here,' said Kandamaran, and went in again. Vandiyatevan could hear women's voices firing a series of questions and breaking into laughter at Kandamaran's faltering replies.

He was disconcerted by the thought that they might be laughing at him. Kandamaran came out, grabbed Vandiyatevan by the hand, and dragged him off to tour the palace with its vast terraces, marbled chambers, domed halls, high towers, granaries, stables and performance stages for music and dance.

Vandiyatevan asked, 'Kandamara, there was a great deal of tittering when you went into the women's chambers again. Such mirth at meeting your friend?'

'They were indeed delighted to meet you. Mother and the others seemed to like you. But their laughter had nothing to do with you.'

'What was it about?'

'Periya Pazhuvettaraiyar has recently married a young girl. He has brought her with him in a palanquin but locked her up in his chamber instead of sending her to the women's quarters. They were laughing at the description of her beauty by a maid who had caught sight of the woman peeping through the window. They were debating whether the girl is from the Sinhala, Kalinga or Chera land. Don't you know that Pazhuvettaraiyar's ancestors came to Tamizh Nadu from the Chera region?'

'I do. Why, it is you who told me about it. Never mind. Kandamara! How long has Pazhuvettaraiyar been married to this mystery maiden?'

'Three years or so. It seems he never leaves her alone. Wherever he goes, he takes her along in a palanquin. There is some chaffing about it all over the country. After all, an old man's obsession with a young girl is bound to provoke ridicule.'

'That's not it. Shall I give you the real reason? In general, women are prone to jealousy. Don't think that I am faulting the women in your family. They have a dusky beauty. Pazhuvettaraiyar's young wife is extremely fair and has a golden sheen. That's why these women make fun of her, though they make up other stories to disguise it.'

'How odd that you should know anything at all about her "golden sheen"! Have you seen her? Where? How?'

'I was standing by the street, quietly observing Pazhuvettaraiyar and his retinue passing through Veeranarayanapuram when . . . Is it true that the elephant, horses, palanquin and other gifts of honour were sent from your side to welcome him?'

'Yes. So what?'

'So, nothing. I compared it to the way I was received.'

Kandamaran gave a short laugh. 'We offered him the welcome due to the supreme commissioner who levies taxes. You had a true warrior's reception. One day, by god's grace, if you become the son-in-law of this household, we will welcome you as a bridegroom,' he said and added, 'But we digress. How did you know that Pazhuvettaraiyar's favourite wife was fair?'

'Pazhuvettaraiyar was riding on the huge black elephant from the Kadambur palace, like the god of death on a buffalo. All my attention was focused on him. As I stood fantasizing about how, one day, I too would grow to be like that great man, a curtained palanquin came by. I wondered who could be within, when a hand moved the curtain slightly, and a face came into view. Both the hand and face were extremely fair. From what you have told me, I surmised that the girl must be Pazhuvettaraiyar's favourite wife.'

At that moment, *jalli, karadi* and *udukku* drums began to reverberate along with the flute.

'What's that?' Vandiyatevan asked.

'That is the prelude to the kuravai koothu. The performance is about to begin. Do you prefer early dinner and bed or do you want to see the koothu?'

Vandiyatevan remembered Azhvarkadiyan's reference to kuravai koothu. 'I definitely want to see it,' he said. As they took a few steps and turned a corner, they saw the performance stage, with the audience gathering before it.

The kuravai koothu stage had been built in a courtyard covered with white sand and surrounded by the high walls of the fort. Designs of cocks, peacocks and swans were painted on the stage. Silvery puffs of roasted paddy, turmeric-steeped millet grain, flowers of many colours and coral bean seeds were used to decorate the stage. Flares and long-stemmed lamps strove to banish the darkness. However, the lights were dimmed by the smoke from the flares and incense fumes. Seated beside the stage on one side, musicians were playing their instruments with compulsive force. Their reverberations mingled with the scent of flowers and incense. Vandiyatevan's head began to spin.

When the distinguished guests assembled, nine women entered the stage in tight-fitting costumes, ornaments securely fastened, bells around their ankles, and tresses adorned with kanni, kadambam, kantal, kurinji and the crimson alari flowers dear to the god Murugan. They had also twined long strings of those flowers around themselves. Some of them were holding beautiful parrots made of sandalwood and painted green.

The women bowed to the audience and began to sing and dance, extolling the god Murugan. They sang of his grace and his valour in beheading the demons with his victorious spear. They sang of how though sought in marriage by celestial nymphs, he nevertheless came down to the earth and into the Tamizh realm, to marry Valli, a woman of the hill tribe, who was guarding the millet fields.

Song, dance, drum and flute combined to intoxicate the viewers. The performance ended with the prayer, 'May hunger, sickness and hostilities cease, may the rains, prosperity and wealth increase.'

The women left the stage. Now Tevaralan and his partner Tevaratti came to perform the dance of the god Velan, also known as Murugan. They wore blood-coloured garments and garlands of bright red oleander. Their foreheads were generously smeared with red paste, their mouths dyed blood-red by chewing betel leaves and areca nuts. Their eyes were as red as the scarlet gourd.

The dance was calm to begin with. They danced apart and with their hands held together, their movements gaining manic intensity as time passed. Tevaratti picked up a spear and tried to prevent Tevaralan from grabbing it. With a jump that shook the stage, Tevaralan seized the spear from her. She exited in fear.

Alone on the stage, Tevaralan began to dance in frenzy. Demon Chief Sooran and all his cohorts were smashed to the ground. Velan's rage mounted and sparks flew from his eyes as Sooran went on sprouting new heads as fast as they were cut off. Finally, the demon fell dead. Tevaralan dropped his spear.

Now all the instruments ceased playing. Only the udukkai drum throbbed on. Every cell vibrated in Tevaralan's body. The assembled men whispered to one another, 'He is in a trance!'

Presently, the priest looked at the tranced man and prayed, 'Vela! Muruga! Kanda! General of the gods! Exterminator of the demon! Speak words of grace to your devotees!'

'I will. Ask me what you want!' shrieked the man.

'Will rains fall? Waters flow? Lands prosper? Wishes come true?'

'Rains will fall! Waters will flow! Lands will prosper! Wishes will come true! But you have not offered worship to my mother! Mother Durga demands sacrifice. The goddess who destroyed the demon demands sacrifice!'

'What sacrifice?'

'Will you give her what she wants?'

'We will. We swear we will.'

'She wants royal blood. She demands royal blood from a thousand-year-old clan,' the man squealed in a terrifying voice.

Pazhuvettaraiyar, Sambuvaraiyar, Mazhavaraiyar and others seated before the dais looked at each other. Their reddened eyes signalled to one another.

Sambuvaraiyar looked at the priest and gave a nod.

The priest stopped beating the udukkai. Tevaralan crashed to the ground like an uprooted tree. Tevaratti rushed in and carried him away.

The assembly dispersed. From afar came the sounds of foxes screaming together.

Unnerved by what he had seen, Vandiyatevan glanced in that direction. What he saw was a head on the wall, Azhvarkadiyan's decapitated head placed on the outer wall. For a split second, he found himself overwhelmed by terror. He blinked. The head vanished. Vandiyatevan was embarrassed to have been duped by a mere hallucination.

6

Midnight Conference

Physically fatigued and mentally agitated as he was, Vandiyatevan could not enjoy the grand feast after the performance. Kandamaran proudly identified the assembled guests by whispering their names as he unobtrusively pointed them out to his friend: Mazhapadi Tennavan Mazhavaraiyar, Kundrathur Perunilakizhar, Mummudi Pallavarayar, Tantongi Kalingarayar, Vanangamudi Munaiyar, Devasenapati Poovaraiyar, Anjadasinga Muttharaiyar, Irattaikudai Rajaliyar . . .

It was customary to suffix the honorific 'araiyar' to the names of royal chieftains and others of equal distinction. They were also referred to by the name of their hometown.

That was the age when royalty was not merely a matter of birth. Nor did royals luxuriate in the opulence and comforts of the palace. Only those who proved their might on the war front could continue to retain the throne. Most chieftains and clan elders acquired their fame–and their scars–on several battlefields. Presently, all of them had accepted Sundara Chozha's sovereignty and exercised authority within their feudatories. Some held high posts in the Chozha government.

Somehow, Vandiyatevan was not as thrilled as he should have been to see so many important dignitaries of the Chozha empire in a single place. The question of why they had assembled under the same roof nettled him and filled him with vague suspicions.

It was with these troubling thoughts that Vandiyatevan retired to the space allotted to him. With so many guests in the palace, all he could get was an open *mandapam** in a corner of the terrace. Kandamaran left him there saying, 'You are washed out. Sleep in peace. I will come and sleep right beside you after taking care of the other guests.'

Sleep engulfed Vandiyatevan the moment he turned in. But what was the use? The mind cannot be brought under control, not even by the goddess of slumber. When the body lies inert and the eyes are shut, thoughts buried deep within morph themselves into dreams, unfolding incidents and experiences that defy sense and reason.

From somewhere far away came the high-pitched cry of a fox. The lone fox multiplied itself into ten, hundred, thousand foxes, all screaming together, their eyes glowing like embers as they came closer, and closer, and closer . . .

Vandiyatevan tried to run in the opposite direction—only to see some ten, hundred, thousand hounds barking in unison as they leapt towards him, their eyes glinting like burning coals.

Terror-stricken at the thought of being trapped between foxes and hounds, Vandiyatevan ran through the open doors of a temple he spied ahead and locked himself in. It was a Kali temple. The sculpted figure of Mother Kali loomed before him, her mouth hideously open. A priest emerged from

* Pavilion.

behind her, holding a ghastly sickle in his hand. He came nearer, and nearer, and nearer . . .

'Tell me the truth! How old is your clan? How long have your ancestors ruled the land?'

'The Vallavaraiyars of the Vaanan clan have ruled for three hundred years. In my father's time, we lost our kingdom to the Vaidumbaraiyars.'

'Beat it!! You are not noble enough to be sacrificed.'

Suddenly, Mother Kali turned into the god Krishna. Two girls danced with garlands in their hands as they sang the verses of Andal. Vandiyatevan's rapture was interrupted by a song that came from behind him. He turned to see Azhvarkadiyan Nambi singing a hymn. Not the man himself. It was his severed head that sang from the top of the sacrificial altar.

Repelled by the sight, Vandiyatevan turned away and crashed into a pillar. The dream broke. His eyes opened.

What he saw before him melded dream and reality.

Directly in front of him was a head on top of the rampart encircling the Kadambur fort. Azhvarkadiyan's head. This time, it was neither dream nor illusion. The head remained stationary, and it could be easily surmised that a body was attached to it, supported by the two hands gripping the edge of the wall. Moreover, Azhvarkadiyan was staring intently at something within. What could it be? Some treacherous motive must have brought the man there to perform some wicked deed. As Kandamaran's friend, was it not Vandiyatevan's duty to stop him? How could he remain idle and not prevent his kindly host's household from coming to harm?

Vandiyatevan jumped up. He armed himself with the sword he had left beside the bed and proceeded towards the head.

From the corner of the terrace where he had been sleeping, Vandiyatevan had to make his way across and around several domes, platforms, pillars and spires. He was arrested midway by the sound of voices. He stopped, held on to a pillar, stood hesitantly behind it and peered below. Some ten or twelve persons were seated in a narrow courtyard, with high walls surrounding it on three sides, cutting the half-moon's beams from slanting down. But an iron lantern fixed to the wall threw some light on them.

Vandiyatevan realized that he was looking at the dignitaries he had met at the feast that night, the feudal lords and government officials of the Chozha kingdom. They must have gathered at midnight to confer among themselves on a matter of crucial importance. Azhvarkadiyan must be standing on the rampart, intent on discovering what they were talking about. The man had cleverly stationed himself in a spot from where he could not see them very well but could hear them very clearly, while he himself remained unseen. But all his cleverness was not going to save him from Vallavaraiyan Vandiyatevan of the Vaanan clan! He would catch the fraudster red-handed . . .

But how? Vandiyatevan could not approach Azhvarkadiyan without attracting the attention of the men below, which could spell danger for him. He remembered Sambuvaraiyar remarking, 'He need not have made such a late and disorderly entry.' The dignitaries were here to discuss something important. Clearly, they did not want others to know of their plans. Vandiyatevan's sudden appearance would arouse their suspicions and end in misconceptions. Before Vandiyatevan managed to offer any explanation, Azhvarkadiyan would have jumped down and vanished. Moreover, what could Vandiyatevan say if he were asked, 'How did you land up here when you were supposed to be in bed?' Kandamaran would be embarrassed.

There! Kandamaran was seated in a corner. He seemed to be a participant in the cogitations. Surely, he would explain everything in the morning.

Vandiyatevan's attention was drawn to the curtained palanquin placed beside the assembled company. The same palanquin that had followed Pazhuvettaraiyar's elephant . . . Where in this vast palace was the woman who had been inside, the woman who parted the curtain to be seen for an instant?

The old codger hadn't sent her to the women's quarters. This is the problem with old men marrying young girls. Suspicion gnaws at them. Not even for a moment can they leave their young wives alone. Perhaps, even now, Pazhuvettaraiyar's wife was in the palanquin. What a fate for the greatest of warriors! Trapped and enslaved at his age, by a young woman!

But Azhvarkadiyan's infatuation was equally strange! This palanquin might be the reason for his hanging out here! What could be the relationship between him and this woman? Was she his sister, or . . . his lover? Pazhuvettaraiyar may have forcibly carried her off! He would be perfectly capable of such a deed. And Azhvarkadiyan was wandering around restlessly, just to find an opportunity to speak to her . . .

But why should he, Vandiyatevan, concern himself with these matters? Why not go back to bed?

Just as the young man came to this decision, he heard his name mentioned below. At once, he began to pay attention.

'Where is your son's friend? He must know nothing of our discussions. Remember that he serves Aditta Karikalan. No one must know about our plan until it is confirmed and carried out. This boy must not be allowed to leave the fort if there is the least suspicion of his having learnt anything about it. It would be best to finish him off once and for all.'

Readers may imagine Vandiyatevan's feelings on hearing these remarks. And yet, he did not move away. He decided to hear their entire conversation.

He heard Kandamaran say, 'Vandiyatevan is fast asleep in a far corner of the terrace. He will not be able to hear anything. Nor is he the kind of man who pokes his nose into things that do not concern him. Even if he were to get an inkling of our talk, I guarantee that no harm will come of it.'

Pazhuvettaraiyar said, 'I am happy to know that you trust him so much. I warned you only because he is a stranger to us. What we are about to discuss is a matter concerning the right to the throne of a great empire. All of you must remember that a single careless word can bring about terrible consequences.'

7

Laughter and Fury

Vandiyatevan made up his mind as soon as he heard Pazhuvettaraiyar referring to the right to the throne. What were these people going to say about it? What right had they to discuss it? He *had* to know what was happening in that conference. He would stay where he was. He could not hope to find a better location. Best to let Azhvarkadiyan go. Why bother about him?

Even earlier, Vandiyatevan had had a hunch that something untoward was about to occur that day. His suspicions had been roused by Azhvarkadiyan's contradictory statements, the insolent behaviour of the sentries at the gateway, Sambuvaraiyar's half-hearted welcome and the impassioned utterances of the man in a trance. Why should he let go of this fortuitous opportunity to know the truth?

By this time Periya Pazhuvettaraiyar had begun to speak. Vandiyatevan sharpened his ears.

'I am here to make an important announcement to all of you. Sambuvaraiyar has organized this conference for this very purpose. Maharaja Sundara Chozha's state of health has become a matter of grave concern. My private enquiries have resulted in the royal physicians admitting that he has little hope of recovery. We must now deliberate on what has to be done in the immediate future.'

'What do the astrologers say?' someone asked.

Another replied, 'Why should we ask the astrologers? Is it not enough that the comet has been visible in the late evening for quite some time now?'

'We have asked the astrologers. They merely postpone the date of what is to happen,' Pazhuvettaraiyar replied. 'In any case, we must think about who is in the line of succession.'

A husky voice interjected, 'What is the point of thinking about it when Aditta Karikalan has been designated crown prince two years ago?'

'True enough. But I would like to know if any one of us was consulted before that decision was taken. Each of us belongs to an ancient clan whose members strove for over a hundred years and through four generations to heighten the glory of the Chozha empire. My greatgrandfather died in the battle at Tirupurampiyam, my grandfather met his death in the battle of Vellur. My father sacrificed his life in the battle at Takkolam. Similarly, your ancestors have given their lives to establish the glory of the Chozha realm. Young men in our families have died on the battlefield. Even today, our boys are fighting in Ilankai. And yet, the maharaja did not ask any one of us before nominating his heir apparent. Even King Dasharatha consulted his ministers, administrators, generals and chieftains before inducting Rama as the crown prince! Not Emperor Sundara Chozha!'

'It is true that our counsel was not sought, but it is not right to say that no one was consulted. Can Pazhuvettaraiyar deny that Queen Sembiyan Mahadevi and

Princess Kundavai were both asked for their advice?' The jibe sparked some laughter.

'Ah! I cannot imagine how you can find it in you to laugh! My stomach burns, my blood boils. I wonder why I must live on in shame. Today, that man in a trance announced that Mother Durga demands human sacrifice. She wants blood from a thousand-year-old royal clan. Sacrifice me! My clan goes back to more than a thousand years. Take your sword and strike me in the neck, each of you! Mother Durga will be appeased. My soul will be at peace.'

Pazhuvettaraiyar raged on like a man in a trance. This frenetic outburst was followed by a silence that was broken only by the soughing of the west wind and the rustling of the trees beyond the ramparts.

Sambuvaraiyar spoke with deep feeling. 'Our lord of Pazhuvur must bear with us for indulging in inadvertent raillery and laughter. You are our supreme leader! Each of us is ready to follow where you lead and obey your command. Please forgive us.'

'You too must forgive me for losing my composure. But think about this! Exactly three hundred years ago, Vijayalaya Chozha defeated the Mutharaiyars and conquered Tanjavur. He stood by the Pallava forces in the battle of Tirupurampiyam and annihilated the Pandya army. Since then, the Chozha kingdom has been expanding its territories day after day. Not even in the age of the legendary Karikal Valavan had the kingdom attained such glory. Today, the Chozha empire stretches from Kanyakumari in the south to the rivers Tungabhadra and Krishna in the north. The realms of Pandya, Nanjil, Tondaimandalam, Bhagi, Gangapadi, Nulambapadi, Vaidumba, Cheetpuli, Perumpanapadi, Kudagu the birthplace of the Kaveri, and also the recently conquered Chera territories, are all under Chozha suzerainty. They pay tribute to the empire. The Chozha flag flies over them all. By this time, Ilankai in the south, and the Rashtrakuta and Vengi kingdoms in the north, should have all come under our control. You know very well why they have not done so.'

'Yes. We do know there are two reasons why Ilankai and Vengi have not been subjugated—the first is Prince Aditta Karikalan, supreme commander in the north, and the second, his younger brother, Arulmozhi Varman.'

'I agree with Mazhavaraiyar. In the last hundred years, army commanders were appointed under a system that was very different from what we have today. Only mighty veterans were appointed as commanding generals and squadron leaders. But now? The older brother is the supreme commander of the forces in the north. What is he doing? Instead of invading the Rashtrakuta and Vengi kingdoms, he dawdles in Kanchi city, building a palace of gold. All of you belong to old and mighty clans. I ask you, has any king of the Tamizh realm, at any time, built a golden palace for himself? Not even the late Parantaka Chozha, the world-renowned conqueror of Ilankai and Pandya territories, had done so. He put up a roof of gold for the Chidambaram temple. But Prince Aditta Karikalan is building a golden palace for himself. It seems that none of the royal palaces where generations of Pallava rulers had dwelt in is grand enough for him! Not even a single copper coin has been sent to the royal treasury from all the wealth garnered from his conquests of Gangapadi, Nulambapadi and Kudagu!'

'Has the palace been fully built?'

'Yes. My trusted spies have confirmed it. Moreover, Maharaja Sundara Chozha has received several letters from his darling son, requesting him to visit this brand new palace of gold.'

'Is the maharaja going to Kanchi?' one of the men enquired anxiously.

'No. I am taking care of it. Then, there is my younger brother, Chinna Pazhuvettaraiyar, the commander of the fort. No one can enter the Tanjavur Fort without his permission. Nor can anyone meet or hand over any message to the maharaja without my knowledge. I have stopped such messages twice or thrice.'

This was greeted by cheers hailing Pazhuvettaraiyar's courage and astuteness.

'Listen! There is more!' said Pazhuvettaraiyar. 'Prince Arulmozhi's methods of waging the war in Ilankai are stranger than those of his brother, the crown prince. What do we know about the code of warfare? What are the rules our ancestors have followed through the centuries? All the food required for our armies must be obtained from the countries where they are making war. Our soldiers must be paid from the wealth captured in those lands. Anything left over must be sent to the state treasury. But what does Prince Arulmozhi do? He demands that his army must be supplied with food by us, from here! For a year now, ten times have I shipped food to Ilankai.'

Shouts of 'Strange!', 'Inconceivable!', 'Insufferable!' greeted him.

'Listen to Prince Arulmozhi's rationale for this bizarre demand. "Seizing food for our army from the land where we are at war would incur the displeasure of the native populace," he says. "Our war is with the rulers of Ilankai, not with the subjects of that country," he says. Therefore, we must not make them suffer in any way. After defeating the ruler, we should govern the land with heartfelt support from the people. So food and money must be sent from here to conduct the war in Ilankai.'

One of the men in the group exclaimed, 'Until now, we have never heard of any battle strategy stipulating that nothing must be seized from the people of the land we have invaded; on the contrary, we must grovel before them!'

'Thanks to these strategies of the two princes, the treasury and the granary are continually depleted. Therefore, I am compelled to increase your tax. You have appointed me as the supreme commissioner of income tax for this very purpose! But for my commitment to the Chozha realm, I would have resigned from this post long ago!'

'Ah! Never! Our safety depends on you! Have you not tried to inform the maharaja about these transgressions?'

'I have. Several times! All the reply I get is "Ask Sembiyan Mahadevi! Ask Kundavai!" Haven't I told you that the maharaja has completely lost the power to think for himself? Nor does he consult us on important issues. To him, his aunt Sembiyan Mahadevi's words have scriptural authority. His other suggestion is to take counsel from his darling daughter Kundavai. Greybeards like us who have grown old in the nation's service must go to that chit of a girl for advice! How's that? Never before in the annals of the Chozha empire have we heard of women interfering in matters of state. How long can we endure this humiliation? If you all agree, I will give up my official responsibilities and the problem of levying taxes to fill the state's coffers, and go back to my native place.'

Sambuvaraiyar exclaimed, 'No! No! Warriors in their thousands have shed their blood for the Chozha empire! If the lord of Pazhuvur abandons us, this kingdom will be destroyed in an instant!'

'In that case, it is you who must tell me what I must do in the present situation. It is you who must find a solution to deal with this shame of being ruled by women.'

8

Who is in the Palanquin?

After this, the men became involved in general discussions. Vandiyatevan could not distinguish anything in the medley of voices.

Then Sambuvaraiyar broke in loudly. 'No point in chattering among ourselves. It is well past midnight. There! The moon has come up! Should we not answer the Pazhuvur lord's question?'

'I have a doubt. Others may share it. I hope the Pazhuvur lord won't get angry if I bring it up,' said the husky voice which had spoken before.

'Is it not Vanangamudiyar who speaks? Please get up and come under the light,' Pazhuvettaraiyar said.

'Yes. It is me! And yes, I am here, under the light.'

'I show my anger on the battlefield. To foes, not to friends. You are free to ask me anything,' Pazhuvettaraiyar said.

'Then I will. Many accuse Pazhuvettaraiyar of the same fault that he finds in Maharaja Sundara Chola. I don't believe it, but I would like to get this cleared up all the same.'

'What is that? You must explain.'

'We all know that the Pazhuvur lord married a girl a few years ago.'

Sambuvaraiyar broke in angrily. 'We object to Vanangamudiyar's raising this issue. It is totally wrong to ask such impertinent questions of our chief guest, our great leader.'

'I request Sambuvaraiyar to be patient,' Pazhuvettaraiyar interposed. 'Let Vanangamudiyar feel free to ask his question. It is better to come out in the open than to let it fester within. I have never declared myself to be the Rama of kaliyuga. I fell in love with a girl when I was fifty-five years old. She returned my love. I married her according to the traditional rites of our Tamizh country. What's wrong with that?'

Several voices called out, 'Nothing wrong!'

'Nor did I find any fault with the marriage. Who among us is committed to monogamy? But . . . But . . .' Vanangamudiyar paused.

'But what? Don't hesitate to ask.'

'Some people say that Pazhuvettaraiyar follows his young queen's advice. They say that he seeks her counsel even in matters of state. They say that he takes her with him wherever he goes.'

A crack of laughter broke through the assembly.

Sambuvaraiyar jumped up, drew his sword and roared, 'Who dares to laugh? Let him come forward and explain himself!'

'Don't get worked up! It was I who laughed,' Pazhuvettaraiyar disclosed, and added, 'Is it a crime to take my lawfully wedded wife with me wherever I go? It is true that I do so. But it is not right to say that I consult her on matters of state. Never have I done so . . . '

'In that case, may I ask you to clear just one more doubt? Palanquins belong to the women's quarters. Why is one here among us during our discussions? Is anyone inside? If not, where did the sounds of throat-clearing and tinkling bangles come from?'

Vanangamudiyar's question brought a strange silence. No one had the nerve to contradict him because the same question had been on their minds. No words escaped Sambuvaraiyar's lips beyond a murmur.

Pazhuvettaraiyar's words tore sharply through the silence. 'A good question. I am bound to answer it. I will clear your doubt before this meeting ends. Do you trust me enough to wait for ten more minutes?'

Several voices shouted, 'Yes. Yes! We have complete faith in Pazhuvettaraiyar!'

Vanangamudiyar said, 'No one need think that my faith and devotion to Pazhuvettaraiyar are in any way less than theirs. I asked this question only because he gave me leave to speak my mind. I am ready to obey his orders. At his bidding, I am ready to give up my life at this very instant!'

'I know Vanangamudiyar's mind. I know that all of you have faith in me. First, let us take a decision about the issue which has brought us together today. May Maharaja Sundara Chozha rule this country forever! However, if something were to happen to him, if the physicians' words should come true, if the trailing comet brings ill luck, we must decide who has the right to succeed to the throne.'

'We request you to give your opinion. None of us will oppose it,' Sambuvaraiyar said.

'That is not right. Everyone must express his considered opinion. In this context, I wish to recall some facts from the past. Twenty-four years ago, King Gandaraditta, the great warrior, wise savant and noble soul, passed away unexpectedly. His son Madhurantakan was but an infant then. Before his death, Gandaraditta had announced that his younger brother Arinjaya should be king. Fate decreed that Arinjaya should not occupy the throne for long. In the best interests of the kingdom, ministers, councillors, feudal rulers, heads of cities and towns decided to crown Arinjaya's firstborn Parantaka Sundara Chozha, who was then just twenty years old. No need to regret that choice! Until two years ago, the maharaja ruled the land with irreproachable rectitude. He gave us due respect and consulted us in governing the state. Therefore, the kingdom grew in extent and prosperity. But now the state of his health arouses anxiety. In such a situation, who has the right to claim the throne after him? Gandaraditta's son Madhurantakan is now an adult, capable of ruling the kingdom. His intelligence, education, character and piety make him suitable to be crowned king. Sundara Chozha's son Aditta Karikalan is now the supreme commander of the army in the north. Between the two, who should inherit the throne? What would be the right thing to do according to the conventions of the tribe, law and justice, and the ancient tradition of the Tamizh realm? Should Madhurantakan, the son of the elder brother, take the throne? Or should it go to Aditta Karikalan, the grandson of the younger brother? Each one of you must share your frank opinion.'

Sambuvaraiyar declared, 'Madhurantakan would be the honourable, ethical and proper choice for the throne.'

Each member of the assembly repeated in turn, 'I agree!' 'I think so.'

'I hold the same view,' said Pazhuvettaraiyar. 'The throne belongs to Madhurantakan. But is each and every one of us ready to go all out to establish that claim? Are we ready to sacrifice our possessions, our flesh, blood and soul in the struggle? Are we ready to take an oath of allegiance to this effect before the mother goddess?' Pazhuvettaraiyar's voice rang with passion as never before.

Silence pervaded the assembly. Sambuvaraiyar broke it to say, 'We are ready to take such an oath in the presence of the goddess. But before we do so, you must make this clear. What is Prince Madhurantakan's view? We have heard that Gandaraditta's son has spurned the material world and is totally immersed in godly pursuits; he has no interest in the kingdom. We also hear that his mother, Sembiyan Mahadevi, is entirely against her son being crowned. Is he ready to ascend the throne and bear the responsibility of ruling the kingdom? We want to know the truth from you.'

'Good question. You have asked it at the right time. I am duty-bound to answer it. Forgive me for not having spoken of this earlier.' With this prelude, Pazhuvettaraiyar continued. 'The entire country knows that Sembiyan Mahadevi wanted her son to be free from the ambition to rule and follow the path of devotion. Taking his mother's wish as a divine command, Madhurantakan too had been striving to cultivate detachment and immersed himself in Siva worship. However, his mind has slowly begun to change. The thought that it is his duty to protect the kingdom, which rightfully belongs to him, has taken root in his mind. He is ready to acknowledge this in public if he is sure of your support.'

'Any proof for this . . . ?'

'I will give proof that will satisfy you, right now. If I do, are you ready to take the oath of allegiance?'

Many voices rose to say, 'Yes!'

'Any doubts left in anyone's mind?'

'No! No!'

'Here is the proof then. I will also clear Vanangamudiyar's doubt at this time,' Pazhuvettaraiyar said. He turned to the palanquin and spoke again. 'Your Royal Highness! Please push the curtain aside and grace us with your presence. All the great warriors in this assembly are ready to sacrifice their body, soul and all their possessions for you!'

Concealed behind the pillar on the terrace, Vandiyatevan had been avidly drinking in every word. He now looked down gingerly.

A hand parted the palanquin's screen. Vandiyatevan realized that what he had mistaken for a bangle was a cuff bracelet worn by royal princes. In the next moment, a face as luminous as the full moon was revealed. A form as handsome as the god of love emerged from the palanquin and stood smiling.

Ah! So this was Gandaraditta's son, Prince Madhurantakan! Vandiyatevan checked to see if Azhvarkadiyan, who had made the same mistake as he had in assuming that a curtained palanquin had to be occupied by a woman, was still standing on the wall, with his head thrust forward. But a tree had cast its shadow there.

Passionate slogans were being raised below. Men were shouting with upraised swords and spears: 'Hail Prince Madhurantakan!' 'Hail Crown Prince!' *'Vetrivel!' 'Veeravel!'**

Realizing that to tarry any longer would invite danger, Vandiyatevan left quickly and went back to lie down once again.

* Victorious spear! Valiant spear! (the Chozha war slogan).

9

Chatting on the Way

Having spent all his life in the dry regions north of the River Palar, Vandiyatevan did not know how to swim. While he was on sentry duty on the banks of the north Pennai, he once stepped into the river to bathe, only to be sucked into a whirlpool. The currents whipped him round and round, and tried to drag him underwater. In no time at all, he was drained of all his strength. By god's grace, just as he began to despair of ever being able to escape death, he found himself free. The current had saved him by pushing him to the shore.

He relived that experience when he went to bed that night. He felt that he was unwittingly trapped in the political conspiracies of a vast empire. Could he escape from these spiralling machinations as he had done from the whirlpool?

All that he had learnt from the midnight conference in the Kadambur palace left him flabbergasted. Only a few years ago had the Chozha empire become free of its enemies beyond the borders. Prince Aditta Karikalan, who was not only a redoubtable warrior but also a past master in the art of warfare and political strategy, had harnessed his own ingenuity and the army's combat skills to destroy the power of Krishna, the Rashtrakuta king. The external enemy was finally quelled. But now plots and conspiracies were burgeoning from within. These internal discords posed dangers greater than assaults from without. What would their consequences be?

Worst of all, these frightful attempts were being made by the renowned warriors, ministers, feudal lords and administrators of the Chozha empire. How powerful and influential the Pazhuvettaraiyar brothers were! Nor were the others assembled in Kadambur any less famous, influential or powerful. Could this be their first meeting? What an advantage his marriage to a young woman had turned out to be for Pazhuvettaraiyar in carrying out his stratagems!

Until then, Vandiyatevan had never questioned Aditta Karikalan's right to the throne and never dreamed of any rivalry in the matter. He knew about Gandaraditta's son, Madhurantakan. He knew also that the son was as devout as the father. Never had he heard that Madhurantakan had any idea of staking his claim or fighting for the throne. Both princes seemed to have justice on their side. If they were to compete, who would win? What was Vandiyatevan's duty?

'Ah! I had built so many castles in the air when I started on this journey from Kanchi! So many pipe dreams! Hoped to gain high posts in the Chozha empire by pleasing the crown prince! In time, even regain the old kingdom of the Vaanan clan! But the very foundation of all these hopes has turned out to be shaky.' These musings kept Vandiyatevan awake for a very long time. It was close to dawn when he finally managed to fall asleep.

The next day, Vandiyatevan did not stir even when the sharp rays of the sun fell upon him until Kandamaran's tap startled him awake.

Kandamaran made the customary query, 'Did you sleep well?' He added, 'I came to see you after the other guests retired to rest. And there you were, snoring away.'

Suppressing his seething thoughts, Vandiyatevan said, 'All I remember is tumbling into bed after the kuravai koothu . . . Why, it is so late! I must leave at once. Kandamara! Please ask your attendants to get my horse.'

'Certainly not! What's the hurry? You must stay here for at least ten days before you leave.'

'No, my friend! My uncle in Tanjavur is in poor health. I got a message saying that he might not survive. I must go right away to be able to see him alive.'

'In that case, you must stop here for a few days on your return journey.'

'Why not? We will see about that when the time comes. Give me leave to depart now.'

'Don't be in such a hurry. You can leave after breakfast. I will accompany you up to the Kollidam river.'

'How can you? You have important guests here.'

'No one is more important than you,' said Kandamaran and broke off abruptly. He added, 'Yes, the guests are important. But my father is there to take care of them. The palace officials are there too. I hardly spent any time with you last night; I won't be happy unless I get to chat with you along the way.'

'I have no objections. Suit yourself.'

Half an hour later, the two friends left Sambuvaraiyar's palace on horseback. The horses maintained a slow trot. The ride was pleasant. So lost were they in recalling old memories that they did not even notice that the winds were intermittently showering them with dust from the road.

After some time, Vandiyatevan said, 'Kandamara, I am happy to have stayed in your house even if it was only for one night. But I do have a regret. When we did our military service on the banks of the Vadapennai, you had described your sister effusively. But all I could get was a partial glimpse of her face when she cast a glance at us from behind your mother. Your sister seems to have a greater share of modesty and shyness than what we generally find among women.'

Kandamaran's lips twitched as if to say something. But no words came.

'Never mind! After all, you have asked me to visit you again when I return. I could meet her then. By that time your sister too might have shed some of her bashfulness. Kandamara, what is your sister's name?'

'Manimekhalai.'

'What a sweet name! If she is as sweet and beautiful as her name . . . !'

'My friend! I beg of you, forget my sister. Forget everything I told you about her. Don't ever mention her again!'

'Kandamara! What's this? Why, even last night you hinted that I was to become the son-in-law of your family!'

'Yes, I did. Things have changed since then. My parents have decided to get my sister married elsewhere. Manimekhalai too has given her consent.'

It was with inward relief that Vandiyatevan greeted Manimekhalai's decision. It was not difficult for him to guess to whom Manimekhalai was to be given in marriage. It had to be the man in the palanquin—Prince Madhurantakan.

'Oh! So you decided to wed her to one of your wealthy guests. Kandamara, I am neither surprised nor disappointed. In fact, I expected it.'

'Why?'

'Who will give any girl to a poor orphan like me? Which girl would agree to marry a man who has neither a home nor a hometown? How does it matter that once upon a time, my ancestors had been rulers with a kingdom of their own?'

'My friend! Enough! Stop. Don't think so meanly of me or my family. It's not what you think. I cannot say anything more now. You will surely understand when you get to know all about it at the right time.'

'Kandamara! What's this? You sound mysterious today!'

'Please forgive me. This is something so momentous that I cannot talk about it, even to you. Believe me, it will not affect our friendship in any way. When the time comes, you will be the first person to be told. Trust me until then. Believe me, I will never leave you in the lurch.'

'Thank you. Only, I cannot imagine why I should be left in the lurch. Nor am I the kind of person who depends on others. Kandamara, I depend only on my sword and spear!'

'The opportunity to use that sword and spear may come sooner than later. Then we will both fight shoulder-to-shoulder, on the same side. Your wishes will be fulfilled . . . '

'Why? Do you think war is imminent? Or is it that you intend to join the war in Ilankai?'

'Ilankai? You will be astonished to hear about how the war is being waged there! Food and provisions are being sent to Ilankai from the Chozha realm. Disgusting! I am talking about something else altogether. Bear with me! Don't try to make me spill my guts now!'

'All right! All right! You don't have to say anything! There! The Kollidam!' Vandiyatevan said.

They saw the river running in full spate. In a few minutes, the two friends had reached the riverbank.

Vandiyatevan gazed in astonishment at the overflowing river, blood-red in hue, shaping circular patterns as it whirled and swirled and roared on, trying to smash the banks on both sides as it raced tumultuously towards the deep sea.

A ferry bobbed at the wharf. A man who looked like an ardent Siva devotee was already seated on it. Two ferrymen with long oars stood in readiness.

Seeing them, a ferryman asked, 'Are you taking the ferry?'

'Yes, he is,' Kandamaran said.

The two friends dismounted. Vandiyatevan said, 'How thoughtless of me! What about the horse? Can it be ferried across?'

'No need. One of the two men who followed us will take your horse back to Kadambur. The other will come with you and get a new horse for you on the other shore.'

'Such forethought! You are a true friend indeed!' Vandiyatevan exclaimed.

'You would not have known that, unlike the Palar and Pennai rivers, you cannot take a horse across the Kollidam.'

'True! Forgive me for underestimating the rivers of your Chozha land. What a river! It billows like the ocean!'

The two friends embraced and took leave of one another.

Vandiyatevan walked to the jetty and got into the ferry. One of Kandamaran's men got in with him. The ferrymen started plying their oars. The boat began to move.

Suddenly, they heard a shout, 'Stop! Stop! Stop the boat!'

The man who had called out reached the shore in double-quick time. Vandiyatevan recognized him at once. It was Azhvarkadiyan Nambi.

When the Saiva in the boat realized that the approaching man was a Vaishnava, he hollered, 'Go! Go! I will not ride in the same boat with that charlatan! Let him take the next boat!'

But Vandiyatevan told the boatman, 'Wait! Let him come. After all, there is plenty of room!'

Vandiyatevan wanted to find out a great many things from Azhvarkadiyan about the happenings of the previous night.

10

The Astrologer of Kudantai

In the Tamizh realm, River Kaveri is known as Ponni, 'the golden lass'. Born and nurtured in the Kudagu region, when Ponni reached the age of youth, she wished to join her lord, the ocean king. She was overcome by all the exhilaration of a bride approaching her groom as she raced across the hills, forests, rocks and chasms. Coming closer and closer, she threw out two arms to embrace him. But they were not enough to express all her teeming ardour and anticipation. Soon, she multiplied those two arms into ten, twenty, a hundred . . .

How ravishingly did her foster mothers of the Chozha realm adorn Ponni, as she skipped along in the full bloom of her youth! They draped her in garments of green, decked her in blossoms of myriad hues and sprinkled her with sumptuous fragrances. The punnai and kadamba trees lining her banks showered their pearly white and ruby red flowers on her.

O River Ponni! Which young woman would feel anything but delight at the sight of you dressed in bridal finery? Is it not natural that they should seek you with all the eagerness of nubile maidens hurrying to surround the bride?

Arasalaru is one of the arms that the river Ponni extends to embrace her beloved spouse. It flows to the south of the main river, hidden by a dense wall of trees. Newcomers to the region will never know of its existence unless they are told about it. 'This dainty river may be described as a royal maiden who has never stepped outside the confines of the palace.

Ignoring the protocol that denies intrusion into women's quarters, our readers may join us as we push through the dense foliage to reach the maiden river.

What an enchanting scene! Where beauty enhances beauty and nectar sweetens nectar!

Who are these charming girls seated on a splendidly carved sailboat, shaped like a swan? Who are these celestial maidens, whose songs waft along the river's course? Who is that dazzling young woman, seated in their midst, like the full moon surrounded by the stars, like an empress born to rule the seven worlds? And who is the serene beauty seated beside her, playing the veena? One may never tire of gazing at her fingers dancing on the strings, slender as flame lilies.

How sweet their music! The river ceases its burbling to hear their song. On the trees, the parakeets and cuckoos sink into silence. Any wonder then that those who are lucky to be born human and blessed with the faculty of hearing should be mesmerized by that heavenly song!

In a garb of flowers
Bright and fair
Haunted by bees
Humming their songs
Your dark eyes darting
Like fish in the waters
You glide and sway
As you walk along

Your lord's sceptre
Unbent, upright,
Empowers you
To stroll along
So I've learnt.
Hail Kaveri!

The peacock struts
In the flowery dell
The cuckoo sings
Its notes of glee.
Your garlands sway
As you wend your way.
The lance of your lord
With all its might
Empowers you
To glide along
Your garlands sway
As you saunter along.
So I've learnt.
Hail Kaveri!

We are familiar with these lovely verses from the *Silappathikaram*.* However, rendered by these women, they become alluring as never before. As soulmates of the river, they meld lyric, melody and sentiment in an outpouring of enthralling bliss. By no means can this be art; it is witchcraft!

---

* 'The Tale of an Anklet', a tragic Tamil saga (circa 2 century CE) of love, betrayal and the heroine's marital fidelity, rooted in the more ancient Tamil bardic tradition, and attributed to Ilango Adigal, a prince turned Jain monk.

The boat reaches a cove. Two women disembark. One of them has the bearing of an empress born to rule the seven worlds. The other is the girl whose fingers drew melodious notes from the veena strings.

Both are dazzling in their beauty but strikingly dissimilar in appearance and impact.

The former possesses the regal splendour of the pink lotus, the latter is endowed with the delicate loveliness of the blue lily. If one is the full moon, the other is the morning crescent. One has the flamboyance of the dancing peacock and the other, the sweetness of the songbird. One has to be Indrani, the queen of the heavens, the other is Rati, the beloved spouse of the god of love. One is the hurtling Ganga, the other the gliding Kaveri.

Let us not test our readers' patience by keeping them in suspense any longer.

The woman with the commanding presence is Princess Kundavai, the beloved daughter of Maharaja Sundara Chozha, and the older sister of Arulmozhi Varman, the prince who is to be renowned in the annals of history as Rajaraja. This valiant and illustrious woman of the Tamizh realm, in times to come, would establish the monumental glory of the Chozha empire. She would raise Rajendra, Rajaraja's son, to become the warrior of warriors and the king of kings.

The other is a princess of Kodumbalur, a Chozha feudatory, who has sought the privilege of serving Kundavai as her companion. A woman of modesty, sweetness and serenity, she is destined for unparalleled good fortune in the future.

As soon as they got off the pleasure boat, Kundavai turned to the girls and said, 'Wait here. We will be back in half an hour.'

All those girls were princesses raised in the palaces of several vassal kings in the Tamizh realm. They had come to Pazhaiyarai for the privilege of serving Kundavai as her companions. Their eyes expressed jealousy and disappointment to see Kundavai getting down, accompanied by only one among them.

A chariot, harnessed to horses, stood waiting on the riverbank. 'Vanathi, get in,' Kundavai said and entered the chariot after her. The chariot began to move at a swift pace.

'*Akka*!* May I know where we are going?' Vanathi asked her.

'We are going to Kudantai to see the astrologer.'

'Why? Won't you tell me?'

'Why not? I want to ask him about you. For the past few months, haven't you been losing weight and walking around in a daze? I want to know when you will recover and improve in health.'

'Please, Akka! I beg of you. I am perfectly all right. No need to make any enquiries about me. Let us return.'

'No, my dear, no. This is not about you. I am going to make enquiries about myself.'

'What can you learn about yourself from the astrologer?'

'I am going to ask him if I will ever get married or remain single all my life.'

'Akka! Why go to an astrologer for something that you should ask yourself? All you have to do is to give the nod! The princes of the fifty-six kingdoms, from the Himalayas to Kanyakumari, will come running to compete for the honour! Why, they will come from lands across the sea as well! It is you who must decide which prince should have the privilege of taking you by the hand.'

---

* Elder sister.

'Vanathi, even if you are right, there is a problem here. If I marry any of those princes, I will have to accompany him to his kingdom. I have no wish to leave this Chozha land where the Ponni flows. I have made a vow never to move elsewhere.'

'No problem! Any prince who marries you will fall at your feet and remain your slave. He will be ready to stay here with you.'

'Ah! Are you asking me to bring a prince from another land to settle in our country? That's like letting a rat into the house!'

'But every woman has to get married someday.'

'No shastra says so. Vanathi, what about Avvai?* Did she not remain unwed to live long as a great poet?'

'Unlike you, by god's grace, Avvai attained old age in her green years.'

'All right. If I do decide to get married, I will choose a poor warrior from the Chozha land. He will have no kingdom to take me to, he will remain right here.'

'Akka! You will never leave the Chozha realm?'

'Never. Not even to become the queen of paradise.'

'Now I am at peace.'

'Why?'

'If you go away, I will have to accompany you. I cannot be separated from you. But I don't have the heart to leave this Chozha land.'

'But you will have to leave it when you get married!'

'I am not going to marry.'

'What about the advice you gave me?'

---

* Avvai, the poet of yore was celebrated for her wisdom. Legend has it that she was granted the boon of old age in her youth, to devote herself to god and poetry.

'Am I like you?'

'You scamp! I know it all. Do you think you can deceive me? You have no special regard for the Chozha land. The Chozha land you adore has gone off to Ilankai, with sword and spear! You think I don't know your secret?'

'Akka! Akka! Am I such a fool? Can the dewdrop dream of the sun?'

'The dewdrop is tiny, insignificant. The sun is huge, radiant. And yet, doesn't the dewdrop capture the sun within itself?'

Vanathi asked eagerly, 'Are you saying that even a dewdrop can reach the sun?' But despondency took over, 'The dewdrop dreams . . . It captures the sun. But what is the use? It is punished all too soon. It dries up and vanishes without a trace.'

'Wrong, Vanathi! The sun sees the dewdrop's ardour and absorbs it within himself, because he does not want anyone else to espy it. But in the night, he releases the dewdrop. Doesn't it appear once again?'

'Akka! You say this to comfort me.'

'Admit then that you need cheering up. Didn't you swear that it is not so?'

'What is the use of going to the astrologer about it?' Vanathi heaved a big sigh.

* * *

The astrologer's house was beside a Kali temple in a secluded corner of Kudantai town. The ease with which the charioteer avoided the town as he drove through its outskirts to reach his destination suggested that he had taken that route several times before.

The astrologer stood waiting at the threshold with his assistant. He welcomed the princesses with great deference.

'Your Royal Highness! You are the embodiment of the goddess of wealth and the goddess of learning! This poor hut is indeed fortunate to welcome you once again!'

'Are you sure that no one else will come looking for you at this time?' the princess asked.

'No, Amma! Nowadays, I hardly have any clients. People seek the astrologer only when the world is full of hardships. But now, under the reign of your blessed father Sundara Chozha, everyone leads a happy and prosperous life. Why would anyone come searching for me?' said the astrologer.

'Are you saying that I am here because I am in trouble?'

'No, Your Highness, not at all! Only a blind man will imagine that the cherished daughter of the emperor, whose kingdom overflows with abundance and prosperity, faces hardship of any kind. However, in this trouble-free world, the poor astrologer is beset with troubles. No one pays any attention to him. You are here like a goddess who has come to put an end to my troubles. Please grace this hut with your presence. It would be an offence to keep you waiting outside,' said the sagacious astrologer.

Kundavai said to the charioteer, 'Wait beside the temple under the shade of the banyan tree.'

Then, led by the astrologer, she entered the cottage with Vanathi.

The astrologer said to his assistant, 'Young man! Be vigilant. Don't let any chance visitor in.'

The room within had been spruced up to receive the princess. A picture of the mother goddess hung on the wall, strung with flowers. Two seats had been placed in readiness. The long-stemmed lamps had been lit. Here and there, *kolam*[*] patterns were drawn on the floor. Palm leaf manuscripts and wooden boards inscribed with charts were scattered around.

The astrologer sat down after the women had taken their seats.

'Devi, please tell me what you wish to know,' he said.

'Can't you discover it from your charts?' Kundavai asked him.

'All right,' said the man and chanted mantras with his eyes closed.

Then, he opened his eyes and said, 'You have come here principally to consult me about this young girl's horoscope. That is what the goddess tells me. Am I right?'

'Ah! Wonderful! What can I say about your skills? Yes. I am here to ask you about this girl. She came to the Pazhaiyarai palace a year ago. For a few months, she was full of zest. She was the most convivial, playful and animated among my girls. But something has happened to her in the last four months. She has bouts of despondency and blankness. She has forgotten what it is to laugh. She says there is nothing wrong with her health. But if her parents were to come and ask me about her, I don't know how to answer them.'

'Amma, is she not the daughter of Siriya Velar, the younger lord of Kodumbalur? Isn't her name Vanathi?' the astrologer asked.

'You seem to know all about her!'

---

[*] A decorative traditional art form where a design of lines, dots, curves and loops is drawn on the floor with rice flour, mingling aesthetics with the ritual propitiation of the gods for prosperity.

'I have her horoscope with me. Please wait,' said the astrologer, as he opened an old box and riffled through its contents. He picked out a horoscope and began to study it attentively.

11

Barging In

In the age when our story takes place, the town whose name found its place even in the English dictionary as *kumbakonam*,* was known as Kudantai. The pilgrimage centre's reputation was enhanced by its resident astrologer as well.

At a little distance from Kudantai, the domed palaces and temple towers of Pazhaiyarai town, the erstwhile Chozha capital, loomed high in all their stateliness.

The astrologer of Kudantai had collected the horoscopes of every member of the royal family residing in the Pazhaiyarai palace. That is how he was able to find the Kodumbalur princess' horoscope among them.

After scrutinizing the horoscope for some time, the astrologer raised his head to look at Vanathi's face. Then he turned to the horoscope again. He repeated these actions several times but did not open his mouth.

---

* In old English dictionaries, kumbakonam was a term for chicanery.

Finally, Kundavai asked him, 'Well, are you going to say anything at all?'

'Amma! What can I say? How can I say it? Quite by chance, I happened to glance at this horoscope once before. I couldn't believe what I saw. I put it away doubting what it implied. Now, seeing this young woman's face and the horoscope together, I am dumbfounded.'

'All right! Take your time to get over your astonishment and give us some specific details.'

'This horoscope spells extraordinary good fortune. I have never seen anything like it. If you will not mistake me, I will say that it is superior to yours.'

Kundavai smiled. Vanathi felt bashful and said, 'Akka! He says that someone as unlucky as I am is the luckiest woman in the world! Is this all he can do?'

'Amma! What did you say? I will give up my profession if I am proved wrong!' the astrologer declared.

Kundavai interposed, 'No! Don't do that! Go on saying agreeable things to people! But you have been making sweeping statements without getting to the specifics. That is why this girl doubts you.'

'You want me to be specific? All right. Four months ago, an incident occurred which appeared to be inauspicious. But actually, it was not so. In fact, it was the beginning of this great lady's good fortune.'

'Vanathi! See! What did I tell you?' Kundavai asked.

'You must have already told him all about it,' Vanathi replied.

'Look at her!' Kundavai exclaimed.

'Let her say what she likes today. Once she marries the king of kings . . . '

'That's right! Go on! Young girls will listen to you only if you talk to them about marriage!'

'I did want to speak of it. But if I plunged headlong into the subject, you would think that the old man has lost it.'

'What about her husband? Where and when will he appear? Anything that marks him out? Can you deduce all this from the horoscope?'

'Ah! Why not? I can certainly do that,' said the astrologer and began to scrutinize the horoscope once again, or at least, made a pretence of scrutinizing it. Finally, he looked up to say, 'Devi, her spouse does not have to come from afar. In fact, he is someone who is close by. And yet, right now, that great warrior is not in this country. He has gone beyond the seas.'

Kundavai looked at Vanathi. Vanathi tried to suppress her delight. But her face gave her away.

'Who is he? To which family does he belong? Any signs to identify him?'

'Yes, indeed. The lucky man who weds this girl will have lines on his palm, tracing the conch and the discus, representing Vishnu, the divine protector of the universe.'

'In that case, wouldn't there be something similar in her hands as well?'

'Amma, have you ever seen the soles of her feet?'

'What are you saying? Are you saying that I should clasp her feet?'

'No! Of course not! But someday, queens, empresses, princesses and any number of noble ladies will yearn for the privilege of touching this lady's feet!'

'Akka, the old man is making fun of me. Did you bring me here for this? Please get up, let us go!' Vanathi said in genuine anger.

'Why are you upset? Let him say what he will.'

The astrologer cut in to say, 'I am not speaking "at will". I speak of what I find in this horoscope. Poets use the term "lotus feet" as an embellishment. Ask this girl to show the soles of her feet to you. They will definitely have lines depicting the lotus.'

'Enough!' Kundavai said. 'If you say anything more, this girl will grab my hand and drag me away. What about her spouse?'

'Ah! The man who takes her by the hand will be the bravest of the brave. He will be on the frontline in hundreds of battles and win them all. He will be the king of kings. He will be hailed by a thousand kings and enjoy a long reign.'

'I don't believe you! How can it be?' Kundavai's face reflected an agitated blend of eagerness, delight and doubt.

'The man spouts nonsense. He thinks that these words will please you,' Vanathi said.

'Never mind!' said the astrologer. 'You may not believe me today, but one day, you will. On that day, don't forget this poor old man!'

'Akka! Can we go?' Vanathi asked again. Tears shone at the corner of her dark eyes.

'Let me tell you just one more thing before you leave! The man who marries this princess will face many dangers and threats. He has several enemies.'

'*Ayo!*'*

'But in the end, they will all disappear. His enemies will be utterly routed. He will overcome every obstacle to reach the pinnacle of glory. Amma, I am an old man. I may speak without embarrassment. Please take a look at this girl's abdomen one day. I will give up my profession if you don't find lines representing the banyan leaf on it.'

'What is so special about that?' Kundavai enquired.

---

* An exclamation signifying fear, dismay.

'Don't you know about the god who sleeps on the banyan leaf? A son will be born to her with the attributes of the god Vishnu. Her husband will face hurdles, impediments, dangers and threats. But the son born to this girl will be a stranger to hurdles. He will achieve everything he desires. Every attempt of his will meet with success. Whatever he touches will turn into gold. The tiger flag will fly wherever he goes. Amma, like the fresh floods of River Ponni, the armies he leads will march on with nothing to impede them. The goddess of victory will serve him at his command. The fame of the land of his birth will spread across the three worlds. The name of his clan will endure as long as the earth exists.'

Her eyes riveted on the astrologer, Kundavai drank in every word until she was startled by Vanathi calling out feebly. 'Akka! I feel . . . ' she gasped, and slumped down in a swoon.

'Quick! Water!' Kundavai told the astrologer and took Vanathi's head on her lap. She sprinkled some of the water he brought on her face.

'Don't worry, Amma! She will be all right,' The astrologer assured her.

'I am not worried. This happens quite often. In a few minutes, she will open her eyes and wonder whether she is on earth or in heaven,' Kundavai said. She continued in a low voice, 'I came to consult you about something important. There are rumours flying across the land. Do they have any significance? Do they pose any danger to the kingdom? Any imminent threat or major change?'

'Amma! Please don't ask me about such things. There are no horoscopes for kingdoms or matters of politics. No predictions can be made about them. Savants, seers and yogis may have the foresight to make such prophecies. But stars, horoscopes and the science of astrology remain powerless to make forecasts about the affairs of the state.'

'That is just clever talk. You don't have to make predictions about the kingdom. But you can examine my father's and brothers' horoscopes, and make some predictions about them, can't you? And that would be tantamount to making predictions about the state.'

'Let me do it at leisure on another day, Amma! On the whole, these are times of danger and disruption. Everyone must remain watchful.'

'I have been greatly perturbed since my father left Pazhaiyarai and went to Tanjavur.'

'Have I not said this before? The maharaja has some great peril looming ahead. Your family has many dangers to face. But everything will be resolved by the grace of Durga, the mother goddess.'

Vanathi's voice broke in faintly. 'Akka! Where are we?' Her eyelids opened slowly, quivering like the wings of a bee.

'Darling! We are still earthbound. No celestial aircraft has come to take us to the heavens. Let us return to the palace on our horse-drawn chariot! Get up!'

'Did I faint?' asked Vanathi as she raised herself.

'No. You took a nap in your Akka's lap. Did you not hear me singing a lullaby?'

'Akka, don't be annoyed with me! My head began to spin.'

'If this man had said to me what he said about you, my head would have started spinning too.'

'That's not it, Akka! As if I believed what he said!'

'I don't know whether you believe it or not! But you scared this man out of his wits. I should never take someone faint-hearted like you anywhere with me.'

'Didn't I tell you that I would not come to the astrologer's place?'

'My fault! Get up! Let's go. Can you walk or should I carry you?'

'I can walk very well.'

'Please wait, Amma! Please accept the offerings made to the goddess before you leave,' the astrologer interposed as he started tying up the horoscopes.

'You talked so much about me. But you haven't said anything at all about Akka,' Vanathi remarked.

'I have already told her everything. What more do you want?'

'The greatest of all warriors who is to wed Akka–'

Kundavai cut in, 'The invincible champion–'

Vanathi continued, 'Undoubtedly! The most valiant prince–'

'Endowed with all the thirty-two ideal attributes–as wise as Brihaspati, the guru of the gods, as skilled as Sarasvati, the goddess of learning, as handsome as Manmatha, the god of love, as valiant as Arjuna, the mythic hero!' Kundavai laughed.

'When and where will that prince charming appear?'

The astrologer said, 'He will come. Certainly he will, and very soon!'

Kundavai scoffed, 'How? On horseback? Mounted on an elephant? Will he stroll in? Jump from the sky and tear through the roof?'

'Akka! I hear hoof beats!' Vanathi said with some trepidation.

'You hear what others don't!'

'I'm not joking. Listen!'

The sound of cantering hoofs became audible.

'Is it not normal for horses to go trotting through the streets of Kudantai town?' Kundavai remarked.

'It sounds as if the horse is coming here.'

'You have odd fancies. Get up, let's go.'

Just then, a fracas broke out beyond the threshold.

'Is this the astrologer's residence?'

'Yes. Who are you?'

'Is the astrologer at home?'

'You can't go in!'

'I will.'

'Won't let you.'

'I must see the astrologer.'

'Come later!'

'No. I'm in a hurry!'

'Dei! Dei! Stop! Stop!'

'Let go! I will kill you if you don't!'

'Ayya! Ayya! Don't go in!'

The door opened with a bang.

A young man barged in. Another gripped his shoulder and tried to drag him away. The young man shook him off, crossed the threshold and stepped in.

By now, readers would have guessed who the young man was. Yes, none other than our brave lad, Vandiyatevan.

The eyes of all the three persons within the house became riveted on him.

Vandiyatevan too saw them. No, he saw just one of them.

He did not see Princess Kundavai fully but only her radiant face. No, not even the whole face. He saw her coral lips, parted a little in surprise. He saw her large eyes, filled with stateliness, astonishment and roguish mirth. He saw her forehead of ivory hue. He saw her cheeks, dimpled and rosy, her neck as smooth as a conch. He saw them all discretely and wholly. They became distinctly imprinted on his mind.

All this took place within a few seconds. Turning swiftly to the attendant, he shoved him out of the doorway saying, 'Why on earth did you not tell me that there were ladies inside? If you had, would I have barged into the house?' With that he made his exit, but not before turning to take a backward look at Kundavai again.

'Oh my goodness! A storm rages and subsides!' Kundavai remarked.

'Listen! It is not over yet,' said the princess of Kodumbalur.

Outside, Vandiyatevan and the attendant were still squabbling.

'Who is he?' Kundavai asked.

'Don't know, Amma! Seems to be a stranger from some other town. Quite a ruffian.'

Struck by a sudden thought, Kundavai burst into loud laughter.

'Akka! Why are you laughing?'

'Why? Because I remembered we were discussing whether the man who is to wed me would appear on horseback, on an elephant or jump through the roof from the sky!'

Now Vanathi too could not control her laughter.

Their pealing laughter stifled the sounds of the dispute outside.

Lost in pensive silence, the astrologer offered *kumkumam** to the princesses and accompanied them as they rose and left the house.

---

* Powder with turmeric, slaked lime and other substances used in ritual worship, and to mark the forehead decoratively but with a religious significance to promote prosperity.

Vandiyatevan was still hanging back near the doorway. As soon as he saw the women, he said in a loud voice, 'Please forgive me. This smart fellow did not tell me that there were ladies within. That is why I barged in.'

Her eyes brimming with mischief, mockery and self-assurance, Kundavai turned a bright face to take a quick look at Vandiyatevan. She gave no reply, but linking arms with Vanathi, she walked to the chariot waiting under the shade of the banyan tree.

They heard Vandiyatevan shouting loudly, 'Looks like the women of Kudantai town are strangers to civility. A man takes the trouble to address them. Should they not have the courtesy to respond?'

The charioteer had the horses harnessed in readiness.

He took the front seat after the women got in.

The vehicle began to move swiftly towards Arasalaru.

Vandiyatevan stood looking at the chariot until it disappeared from view.

12

Nandini

We had left Vandiyatevan on the ferry on the river Kollidam. Should we not explain how he landed up at the astrologer's house in Kudantai at the time he did?

As soon as the ferry began to move, the Saiva elder who had objected to Azhvarkadiyan's entry into the boat turned to Vandiyatevan and said, 'Tambi, it is for your sake that I allowed him to get in. He must not mention that eight-syllabled name on this boat.'

'Nambi! Did you hear?' Vandiyatevan asked.

Azhvarkadiyan retorted, 'I will refrain if he avoids that five-syllabled name.'

The Saiva roared, 'Who is he to stop me from chanting *Nama sivaya*?* That is the mantra to save you even if you are tied to a stone and dropped into the sea!'

Azhvarkadiyan began to sing loudly, 'I sought him again and found his name—*Om namo narayanaya*.†

---

* 'I bow to Siva', the sacred five syllabled invocation.

† The eight-syllabled invocation of the god Vishnu.

'Siva! Siva! Siva!' chanted the Saiva, shutting his ears with both hands. He removed them only after Azhvarkadiyan stopped singing.

Azhvarkadiyan looked at Vandiyatevan and said, 'Tambi, this Saiva finds it painful to hear Vishnu's name. Why don't you remind him that this Kollidam river washes Vishnu's feet as the god slumbers in Srirangam? Doesn't Siva perform his penance standing in this river precisely because its waters have been purified by flowing over Vishnu's blessed feet?'

Before Azhvarkadiyan finished what he was saying, the outraged Saiva pounced on him. Vandiyatevan and the ferrymen had to forcibly separate them to prevent the boat from capsizing.

'O venerable men of faith! You seem to think falling into the floods will take you straight to heaven. But I have a few things left to do in this world,' Vandiyatevan told them.

'Don't know if falling into the Kollidam takes you to heaven, but it is sure to take you straight into the crocodile's belly. Look there!' said a ferryman, pointing to a crocodile with its jaws hideously open.

'I don't fear crocodiles, not in the least! The omnipresent god who saved the elephant from the crocodile's jaws is here too,' Azhvarkadiyan scoffed.

'There he is, hiding behind the girls in the woodlands of Brindavanam,' the Saiva sneered.

'Or it may be that Siva has got into difficulties as before! And Vishnu has gone to save him yet again, as he has done before!'

'This man doesn't remember how his Vishnu was humiliated when Siva killed the Tripura demons!'

'Why on earth do you keep on fighting? Why not be content with worshipping the god of your choice?' Vandiyatevan said.

At this point, it may be pertinent to explain just why the Saiva elder and Azhvarkadiyan were fighting on the boat as they had done in Veeranarayana town before.

For nearly six hundred years, Buddhism and Jainism had gained ascendancy in the ancient Tamizh realm, bringing several benefits to the land. Sculpture, painting, poetry, literature and the other arts flourished. Then came the *azhvars*[*] and the *nayanmars*,[†] who made Saivism and Vaishnavism thrive. Their propagandist strategies were exceedingly powerful. They harnessed sculpture and music to poetry. The *tevarams*[‡] of the Saiva poets and the *pasurams*[§] of the Vaishnava poets were set to sublime music and sung everywhere. Eulogized by their poetry, the temples of Siva and Vishnu gained greater fame and sanctity, which in turn stimulated the efforts to rebuild the shrines of brick and wood with rock and stone. Such restorations were carried out from the time of Vijayalaya Chozha by the kings and other members of the royal Chozha dynasty.

In the same era, a special event occurred in the Kerala realm. A great soul was born in a village named Kaladi. Renouncing

---

[*] 'The immersed', the twelve Tamil saint poets (5 CE–9 CE) who extolled Vishnu as the lord supreme, pioneers of the pan-Indian bhakti movement.

[†] 'The Hounds of Siva', sixty-three saint poets (6 CE–8 CE), contemporaries of the Azhvars, who worshipped Siva as the ultimate reality and pioneered the pan-Indian bhakti movement.

[‡] The devotional poems on Siva by some of the Nayanmars, the medieval saint poets. Among them are the three most important poets: Sambandar, Appar and Sundarar, quoted in *Ponniyin Selvan*.

[§] Songs of praise addressed to the god Vishnu by saint poets of the Vaishnava faith, particularly by the woman saint poet Andal.

the world in his youth, he evolved the philosophy of *advaita*,* based on the Upanishads, the Bhagavad Gita and the Brahma Sutra. A past master in Sanskrit, he travelled widely across the subcontinent and established eight monasteries in eight different places. The monks who followed his philosophy of non-dualism travelled everywhere and promoted his doctrines throughout the country.

At the time in which our story takes place, religion was undergoing a great upheaval, throwing up some baneful elements as well. Adherents of Siva and Vishnu sprouted everywhere. They engaged in needless polemics in random places. The advaita monks joined in the fray. Their debates over faith sometimes ended in fisticuffs.

The mutual antagonism between the Saivas and Vaishnavas in those days is perfectly illustrated by this story.

A Vaishnava from Srirangam was walking beside the outer wall of the Siva temple in Tiruvanaikaval town. Suddenly, a small stone hit his head and drew blood. The Vaishnava looked up and saw that the stone had been dislodged by a crow swooping down to perch on the wall. Overcome by elation, he forgot his wound and pain, and hollered, 'O brave Vaishnava crow! Demolish this Siva temple!'

As we proceed with this story, it may be well for readers to know that, in those days, religious bigotry was an endemic part of life.

* * *

* Non-dualism—a path of philosophy, spiritual discipline and experience propounded by Adi Sankara (700–750 CE) where the brahman or oversoul is singular and omniscient, and all individual souls are a part of that whole. Illusion or *maya* prevents the recognition of this basic truth.

When the ferry reached the other shore, the Saiva elder departed after hurling a curse at Azhvarkadiyan, 'May you be damned forever!'

The guard accompanying Vandiyatevan went to find a horse for him from the town nearby. Azhvarkadiyan and Vandiyatevan sat under a peepal tree by the shore. Hundreds of birds trilled their sweet notes on the branches above them.

Both wanted to prise information out of one another. They began with some discursive small talk.

'Tambi, so you went to the Kadambur palace without me!'

'I found it extremely difficult to get in.'

'Is that so? How did you manage? Perhaps you didn't go at all?'

'Oh, I did. I did. No hanging back after making a decision. The sentries stopped me. I spurred my horse. Those who stopped me fell to the ground. My friend came to take me inside before they could get up and attack me again.'

'That's what I thought. You have a great deal of gumption. What happened next? Who else was there?'

'So many dignitaries! I don't even know their names. Pazhuvettaraiyar was there. So was his young wife. Oh my god! How can I describe her beauty!'

'Did you see her?'

'Of course! How could I not see her? Kandamaran took me to the women's quarters. I saw her there. She stood out among them all. Her face shone like the full moon among all those dusky women. Even the celestial nymphs must be ranked after her!'

'You are really going overboard! What happened next? Kuravai koothu?'

'Yes. It was excellent. I thought of you.'

'I was unlucky. What else?'

'Tevaralan and Tevaratti danced in a frenzy.'

'Did they go into a trance? Did they make any prophecy?'

'Oh yes. They said that wishes will come true, rains will fall and crops will grow.'

'Is that all?'

'Tevaralan spoke of political matters. I paid no attention.'

'Is that so? Tambi, you are young. You appear to be strong and brave. You should pay attention to any discussion about state matters.'

'You are right. I had the same thought this morning.'

'Why in the morning?'

'My friend Kandamaran and I were chatting as we rode to the riverbank. It seems that last night after I went to sleep, the guests met and discussed important matters concerning the state.'

'What did they discuss?'

'That I don't know. Kandamaran made some innuendos and wouldn't say anything outright. Something was about to happen, he said, and he would inform me when it did. Mysterious! Do you know anything about it?'

'About what?'

'Everywhere, people are talking about the comet in the sky, about imminent changes regarding the throne and so on. These rumours have reached even Tondaimandalam. It seems that great men are meeting often to discuss who should be crowned next. What do you think? Who will succeed to the throne?'

'I know nothing about these things. What have I to do with state affairs? I am a Vaishnava. A humble servant of the devotees of Vishnu. I roam from town to town singing the songs I know,' said Azhvarkadiyan and began to sing.

Vandiyatevan broke in. 'Stop, for god's sake!'

'Why are you stopping me from singing this divinely beautiful Tamizh song?'

'Azhvarkadiyan Nambi, I have a doubt. Shall I tell you what it is?'

'Do!'

'You won't hoist your staff and pounce on me?'

'On you? Could I hit you?'

'I suspect that your devotion, these physical marks of faith and hymn-singing are all an act!'

'*Ayyayyo!** Blasphemy! Blasphemy!'

'Not at all. You disguise yourself to hide your craze for women. I have seen others like you. Don't know what you see in them!'

'Tambi! There are people who are obsessed with women. Don't count me among them. I am no imposter.'

'Why then did you ask me to carry a message to the woman in the palanquin? Should you be thinking of a married woman at all? Didn't you want to come to the Kadambur palace for the sake of meeting her? Don't deny it!'

'No, I won't deny it. But your reasoning is wrong. There is another reason, a valid reason. That's a big story.'

'Doesn't look as if the horse is going to come anytime soon. Why not tell me that story?'

'It is not a made-up story; it is a real one. You still want to hear it?'

'Yes, if you'd like to tell me.'

'All right, I will. If I ask for your help some other time, will you agree to give it to me?'

'If it's a fair demand, yes, I will. But you don't have to say anything you don't want to.'

---

* Exclamation signifying deep disturbance.

'But I must. The young wife of that demon to whom I asked you to take my letter, well, her name is Nandini. Her story will astound you!'

With this preamble, Azhvarkadiyan launched into Nandini's story.

* * *

Azhvarkadiyan was born in Pandya country, in a village by the river Vaikai. His family was steeped in the Vaishnava cult. One day, his father found a female infant lying in a grove beside the riverbank and brought her home. Since the child was charming and winsome, his family raised her with care. They named her Nandini. Azhvarkadiyan cherished her as his own sister.

As Nandini grew, so did her devotion to the god Vishnu. The whole neighbourhood began to believe that she would turn into another Andal and bring redemption to the entire community of devotees. Azhvarkadiyan had believed this with all his heart. After the death of his father, he took on the responsibility of taking care of Nandini. Both went from town to town, promoting the Vaishnava cult by singing the verses of the azhvar poets. Those who heard Nandini rendering the hymns, wearing a garland of tulsi leaves around her neck, became intoxicated by her singing.

Azhvarkadiyan decided to go on a pilgrimage to Tirupati but his return was delayed. That was when Nandini met with misfortune.

The final and crucial battle between the Pandyas and the Chozhas took place near Madurai. The Pandya forces were utterly routed. Wounded in every limb, their king Veerapandiyan had fallen on the battlefield. Some of his personal attendants found him and tried to save his life. They brought him to Nandini's house that very night. Moved by his plight, Nandini nursed the king. But very soon, the Chozha soldiers managed to find him. They surrounded Nandini's house and left with Veerapandiyan as their captive. On beholding Nandini, Periya Pazhuvettaraiyar became infatuated with her beauty and forcibly abducted her.

All this had happened three years ago, after which Azhvarkadiyan was unable to see Nandini. He had been trying to meet her at least once and to take her away if she wished to be free. He had not met with any success.

Vandiyatevan's heart melted when he heard this account. For a split second, he felt impelled to disclose the fact that it was not Nandini but Madhurantakan who had been the occupant of the palanquin in the Kadambur palace. But something stopped him. He wondered if the entire story was a figment of Azhvarkadiyan's imagination.

Just then, at a little distance, he saw the guard approaching them with a horse.

'Tambi, will you do me a favour?' Azhvarkadiyan asked.

'How can I help you? Pazhuvettaraiyar has the power to control the entire kingdom. I am a single man with no influence at all. What can I do?' Vandiyatevan spoke guardedly. Then he said, 'Nambi, are you saying that you know nothing of political matters? Can you not tell me who would succeed to the throne if something were to happen to Maharaja Sundara Chozha?'

'What do I know? Tambi, if you ask the astrologer in Kudantai, he might be able to tell you something about it!'

'I see! Is the man really so astute?'

'Yes, indeed! He can make astrological forecasts. He can also make predictions based on his understanding of the ways of the world.'

From the dawn of time, human beings have been obsessed with the desire to know what the future holds for them. Kings and paupers, intellectuals and imbeciles, have all been motivated by the same fascination. No surprise then that our daring young warrior, who had undertaken his journey at great risk, became susceptible to the same delusion. Vandiyatevan made up his mind to see the astrologer in Kudantai before he continued his journey.

13

The Waxing Moon

When the royal chariot disappeared from view, the astrologer took Vandiyatevan into the house. The young man took a quick look around the room. The astrologer sat down and invited Vandiyatevan to take a seat. Then he looked him up and down before asking, 'Tambi, who are you? Where did you come from?'

Vandiyatevan chuckled.

'Why do you laugh?'

'Well, you are such a famous astrologer! Can't you find out who I am and why I have come to you?'

'I see! Why not? But I can't help wondering who will pay me if I make predictions for myself.'

It was with a smile that Vandiyatevan asked him, 'Sir, who are those people who were here before me?'

'O! *Those* people! I know just whom you mean. You mean those people who got into the chariot and rode away spewing dust behind them,' said the astrologer, resorting to circumlocution.

'Yes, yes! Just so.'

'You can certainly ask me about them! Why not? They are women. Two women.'

'I am not blind. I can see the difference between men and women. I can even recognize a man disguised as a woman.'

'Then why do you ask?'

'I want to know who they are, their lineage . . .'

'Oh! Is that what you want to know? There are four categories of women, called Padmini, Chittini, Gandharvi and Vidyadhari–'

'Oh god!'

'What is it, my son?'

'Why do you respond when I call upon god?'

'What is wrong with that? You don't seem to have had the benefit of the company of elders. Don't you know that god is omnipresent? God is within me. God also resides in the attendant you dragged into the house earlier.'

'Enough! Enough! Please stop!'

'God asked me to speak all this while. It is god who asks me to stop now.'

'Sir! I asked you to tell me the name, place and lineage to which the girls who just left belong. If you can answer without beating around the bush . . .'

'What will you give me if I tell you?'

'My thanks.'

'Keep your thanks to yourself. Tell me if you will pay me.'

'Do you promise to tell me if I pay you?'

'Only if it is something that can be told. Tambi, listen to me. Many visitors come to an astrologer's home. Their identities may not be disclosed. I will not speak of those who left just now. Nor would I breathe a single word about you if anyone asks me.'

'Ah! What Azhvarkadiyan Nambi said about you is entirely true.'

'Azhvarkadiyan? Who's he?'

'Don't you know him? He spoke of you as if he knew you very well.'

'I may know the man but not his name. Describe him if you will.'

'He is short and burly with a tuft on his head. His clothes are secured firmly around his little potbelly. His body is smeared with sandal paste in upward strokes. He picks a fight with any Saiva he meets. He brandishes his staff at advaita monks. Did you not say just now that god is in you and me? If Azhvarkadiyan were to hear you, he would say, "God attacks god" and thrash you with his staff.'

'Tambi, I think this must be Tirumalai.'

'Does he go by multiple names?'

'He has a different name in each town.'

'So, he changes his guise according to the person he meets!'

'He assumes the guise that would be suitable for the occasion.'

'Would what he says be somewhat false and fictitious?'

'Yes. But it may also be somewhat true.'

'A scamp, then!'

'Not quite. He is good to the good and bad to the bad.'

'So you can't believe anything he says?'

'Depends on what he says.'

'For example, his saying that you make helpful predictions–'

'Didn't I say that what he says may be somewhat true? This belongs to that category.'

'In that case, say something about me. Be quick! It is getting late. I have to hurry!'

'Why are you in such a hurry?'

'Can't you discover that in your charts? I came to ask you where I should go, where I should not go and if my task will be fulfilled . . .'

'My friend! There must be some basis for making forecasts. A horoscope. The date and the reigning star at the time of birth. At least the name of the client and his birthplace.'

'My name is Vandiyatevan.'

'Ah! Of the Vaanan clan?'

'Yes.'

'Vallavaraiyan Vandiyatevan?'

'Indeed!'

'Tambi! Why didn't you tell me this before? I think I have your horoscope. I will be able to find it if I search for it.'

'I see! But why do you have it at all?'

'What else do you think we fortune tellers do? We collect and store the horoscopes of boys and girls belonging to illustrious clans.'

'But I was not born in any illustrious clan!'

'What are you saying? So many great poets have sung about your Vaanan clan! Perhaps you have not heard any of those verses.'

'Why don't you recite one? Let me hear it!'

Is there
Any mouth that does not hail Vaanan's glory?
Any chest not inscribed with Vaanan's name?
Any staff that does not bear his flag?
Any kingdom not under his sovereign rule?

When the astrologer sang, it became clear that he was no musician. When he finished the poem he asked, 'How's that?'

'Good. But it is I who will have to raise my own flag.'

'This is your situation today. Who knows about tomorrow?'

'I am here because I thought you would know.'

'Tambi, like everybody else, I am a mortal being. But the stars and planets speak of what is to happen tomorrow. Whatever I discover by studying them, I share with those who come to me.'

'Ayya, what do the stars and planets say about me?'

'They say that each day will witness your growth.'

'As it is, I had to duck to enter your house. What is the use of growing higher and higher? Don't speak in general terms, say something specific.'

'Ask me something specific and I will answer.'

'I am going to Tanjavur on a mission. Will I succeed?'

'Yes. That is, if the mission is personal in nature. Right now, the planets are aligned to augur great success for you. But if it concerns others, their horoscopes will have to be examined before any forecast can be made.'

Vandiyatevan placed a finger on his nose and shook his head as he said, 'Ayya! I have never seen anyone as smart as you!'

'Don't flatter me, Tambi!'

'All right. I will ask in very clear terms. I wish to see the emperor in Tanjavur. Will I?'

'There are two astrologers in Tanjavur who are greater than me. You must ask them.'

'Who are they?'

'One is Periya Pazhuvettaraiyar, the other is Chinna Pazhuvettaraiyar.'

'They say that the maharaja's health is deteriorating. Is it true?'

'People spread all kinds of rumours. Don't believe them. And don't talk about it.'

'Who will get the throne if something were to happen to the maharaja?'

'Neither you nor me. Why worry?'

'I guess we are lucky!' Vandiyatevan remarked.

'True, tambi. Claiming the throne is no ordinary matter. It is extremely dangerous.'

'Ayya, what does fortune have in store for Prince Aditta Karikalan, now in Kanchi?'

'I don't have his horoscope with me. I have to check it before I can say anything.'

'What about Madhurantakan?'

'A very strange horoscope, similar to a woman's, always under someone else's control . . .'

'They say that, even now, the Chozha kingdom is being ruled by women. Things are worse here than under Alli, the legendary queen.'

'Who says so? Where?'

'In the north, beyond the Kollidam.'

'They must be talking about the authority wielded by the young queen of Pazhuvur, whom Pazhuvettaraiyar married recently.'

'I heard something different.'

'What?'

'They say that it is the maharaja's daughter Kundavai Devi who rules the country.'

The astrologer stared at Vandiyatevan's face, trying to gauge whether he had recognized the woman who left the house earlier as Kundavai Devi. But he could find nothing to suggest that it was so.

'Completely wrong. Tambi, Maharaja Sundara Chozha is in Tanjavur. Kundavai Devi is in Pazhaiyarai. Moreover . . .'

'Moreover what?'

'They say, "Look around before you speak during the day and hold your tongue at night." But it should be all right to say this to you. What power does the maharaja have now? The Pazhuvettaraiyars have it all!' said the astrologer and looked hard at Vandiyatevan once again.

'Ayya, I am not Pazhuvettaraiyar's spy. You need not have doubts on that score. A little while ago, you referred to my own clan as you talked about the impermanence of kingdoms and dynasties. Please tell me the truth. What does the future hold for the Chozhas?'

'I say this with absolute conviction. At the end of the month of *Aani,*[*] fresh floods rush into the Kaveri and its tributaries. Those who dwell by the riverbank know that these floods will continue to increase through the following months of Aadi, *Avani* and *Purattasi.*[†] Only in the months of *Kartikai* and *Margazhi*[‡] will the waters start to subside. Today, the Chozha empire is comparable to the fresh floods swelling day after day. The sweeping flood will grow higher and vaster in the hundreds of years that are to come. The Chozha empire is like the waxing moon now. There are many days to go before the moon becomes full. In the same way, more and more will the Chozha empire continue to grow and flourish . . .'

---

[*] The month of June in the Tamizh calendar.

[†] August and September.

[‡] November and December.

'Thank you. Please tell me one more thing if you can. I have long wanted to board a ship and sail across the seas . . .'

'That wish will certainly come true. *Sakata yoga*[*] reigns over your fortunes, ordaining wanderlust. Your itchy feet will make you wander day in and day out. You will walk, ride horses, mount elephants, board ships . . . Very soon, you will undertake a voyage across the sea.'

'Ayya, what do the stars and planets say about Prince Arulmozhi Varman, who is presently conducting the war in Ilankai?'

'Tambi, voyagers sailing on ships use a magnetic tool to find the cardinal directions for navigation. Lighthouses are also useful for this purpose. But more than all these devices, do you know what provides the best guidance to the sailors at sea? It is the pole star in the north. Other stars and planets are subject to constant shifts as they move along their course. The seven stars of the *saptarshi*[†] constellation deviate from their path, but the pole star stays motionless in its allocated spot. Maharaja Sundara Chozha's youngest son, Prince Arulmozhi Varman, resembles the pole star. He has unwavering resolution and undeviating strength. He excels as much in might and valour as in rectitude and the spirit of sacrifice. He has both formal learning and knowledge of the world. A man of irresistible charisma, he is the darling son of the goddess of good fortune. Just as sailors see the pole star as their beacon, it would be most advisable for young people like you to set their course in life with Arulmozhi Varman as their leading light.'

---

[*] Sakata yoga signifies instability in one's fortune, like the carriage/cart which is constantly in motion due to its rolling wheels. Sakata means cart/carriage.

[†] Ursa Major or the Great Bear.

'Oh my goodness! You have so much to say about him! You describe Arulmozhi Varman like a lovelorn girl waxing eloquent on her beloved.'

'Ask anyone on the banks of the Kaveri and they will say the same things.'

'Many thanks, Ayya! When the time comes, I will follow your advice.'

'I spoke to you as I did only because I know that the planets augur the height of good fortune for you.'

'With heartfelt gratitude, I offer what I can. Please accept it,' said Vandiyatevan as he placed five gold coins before the man.

'The generosity of the Vaanan clan has not diminished,' said the astrologer as he took the coins.

14

The Crocodile on the Riverbank

When Vandiyatevan left Kudantai, he made his way to the riverside first. Along the way, he was wonderstruck by the scenes unfolding before him, exceeding by far all that he had heard about the beauty of the Chozha country. Appearing before him in quick succession were greening fields of paddy, copses of ginger and turmeric, orchards of sugarcane and plantain, groves of coconut and areca palm, pools, brooks and canals . . . Water gushed through the conduits. The little streams were filled with lilies. The ponds made a dazzling display, covered as they were with lotuses red and white, lilies blue and pink. White cranes flew above, flock after flock. Red-legged storks stood in the waters, engaged in meditation. Tillers were ploughing the fields, their black soil enriched by the blend of manure, mulch and leaf mould. In the fields thus prepared, women were transplanting seedlings, singing sweet folk songs as they worked.

Beside the sugarcane orchards were the mills where the ripened crops were chopped and juiced. The nostrils were assailed by the tangy smells of sugarcane being pressed and boiled to make jaggery.

Between the palm groves were thatched huts and tiled houses. In every village, all the houses had their front yards washed and swept until they shone like sheets of glass. On some of those yards, paddy had been spread out to dry. Cocks and hens wandered in and out to peck at the grain. But the children guarding the grain did not drive them away. They continued to play their *sozhi* and *pallankuzhi* games, ignoring the fowl with this thought, 'After all, how much can they eat anyway?' Smoke rose from the stoves through the thatched roofs, mingled with the mouth-watering aroma of paddy being parboiled, millet being roasted and meat being fried. Like most soldiers of his time, Vandiyatevan was a meat-eater.

From the smithies located here and there on the roadside came the clangour of iron slabs being hammered. Their furnaces flamed and glowed. Ploughs, spades, pickaxes and other agricultural implements lay in piles, along with swords, shields, bows and spears. Farmers and soldiers waited patiently and fought to buy them.

Gongs, drums, mantra chants and tevaram hymns resounded from the little temples in the small villages. Carrying Mariamman and other village deities in processions, priests beat their drums and danced with the *karagam** pots on their heads, performing celebratory rituals with offerings of paddy.

There were cattle with bells round their necks, taken out to graze by the boys. Fatigued by their hard labours through the day, the field workers relaxed under the trees and entertained themselves by driving their rams to fight.

---

* Ancient folk dance performed with pots balanced on the head, as entertainment and ritual.

Peahens called from the rooftops. Making a tremendous effort, the peacocks managed to raise their heavy tails and fly up to perch beside them. Doves fluttered here and there, moving their pretty heads this way and that.

The caged parakeets and mynahs made sad music.

Vandiyatevan slowed his horse down and jogged on. His eyes were fully engaged and his mind gladdened by the varying sights. However, deep within his heart, he could constantly see a woman's face, veiled by mists. He thought to himself, 'Ah! What would she lose by opening her rosy lips and speaking a few words to me? Who can she be? Whoever she may be, should she not have shown me some courtesy? Do I appear to be someone who can be so easily dismissed? That old fortune teller thwarted me by refusing to disclose her identity. He is clever. Extremely clever. How well he understands what goes on in other people's minds! His words are informed by his experience of the world. True, he did not foretell anything of significance. He evaded commenting on state affairs. He managed the situation adroitly by merely repeating what everyone knew. But he did say that the planets were positioned at their best to bring me good fortune. May things go well for him!'

As he reached the banks of the Arasalaru and moved further down, Vandiyatevan heard the sounds of tinkling bangles and women's laughter. The dense trees hid them from sight. He advanced in the direction from where he could hear the voices. All at once, he heard a cry for help, 'Ayo! Ayo! Crocodile! Crocodile!' He spurred the horse to a gallop until he saw the women through the gap between two trees. Many of them appeared to be scared out of their wits. How strange! Among them were the two women who had left the astrologer's house before him.

Vandiyatevan grasped all this within a split second. He saw something else. Under the dark shadow of a big tree, camouflaged by the roots, lay a crocodile with its mouth gruesomely open, half in and half out of the water. Only recently had Vandiyatevan seen a similar sight on the Kollidam river. He had also heard about the beast's savagery. He shuddered to see the creature with open mouth and jutting jaws, lying so close to the women. All it had to do was to make a single movement to make an end of its victims. Nor could they hope to escape by running away, for the trees clustered thick behind them.

However, his agitation did not make his resolution falter. It took him only a second to decide on his course of action. Aiming with great care, he flung his spear with all his might. It whizzed away to plunge deep into the crocodile's thick hide. Part of the stem could be seen sticking up from the creature's back. Then Vandiyatevan drew his sword from its sheath and ran towards the crocodile to finish it once and for all.

The women broke into peals of laughter. He froze in astonishment. Why were they laughing in the face of danger? He looked at their faces. They held no trace of fear or alarm. On the contrary, what he saw was mockery and amusement. He could not believe that they were the same women who had screamed in panic-stricken voices just a few moments ago. One of the women he had seen earlier admonished the others, 'Girls! Stop it! Why are you laughing?'

Having leapt towards the crocodile with his sword upraised, Vandiyatevan now halted in uncertainty. He stared at the crocodile. Then he turned again to take another look at the women's faces. He was assailed by a doubt that made him recoil in shame.

By this time, the woman he had seen earlier came forward and stood before the crocodile as if to protect it.

'Ayya,' she said, 'we thank you. But it was not necessary for you to have taken all this trouble.'

15

Vanathi's Ruse

Now we must know what the young women on the yacht did after Kundavai Devi and the Kodumbalur princess Vanathi took the chariot to Kudantai.

One of the girls said, 'Taraka! Just look at this Kodumbalur woman's luck! Why does our Kundavai Devi favour her so much?'

'That's not true! For the last four months, this girl has been fainting so often and looking as if she has gone mad. Our Kundavai Devi is worried because she feels responsible for this girl who has neither a father nor a mother. That is why she has gone to the astrologer to make enquiries about Vanathi's health. Who knows? She may be possessed by a ghost or a ghoul. The evil spirit must be exorcised by some mantra or the other,' Taraka replied.

'Ghost? Ghoul? Nonsense! Why should any ghoul try to possess her when she herself is capable of driving a hundred ghouls away!' Varini exclaimed.

Another girl said, 'All this fainting is nothing but pretence! Vanathi thinks that she can trap the prince with these stratagems!'

'Niravati is absolutely right,' Varini agreed. 'That is not all. How on earth did she manage to drop the tray with all those lamps, on that day Prince Arulmozhi took his leave? It was a move calculated to draw attention to herself. How could a tray held with both hands manage to slip and fall? Is our prince a wild beast to have frightened her out of her wits?'

'How cunning she must be to pretend to swoon!' Niravati exclaimed.

'The real joke is that our prince and princess were taken in by her tricks!' Sentiru fumed.

'The times favour fibbers, frauds, tricksters and cheats!' Mandakini sighed.

'The prince actually came back to see this Vanathi after taking his leave to go to war. What more do you want? See how successful her ruse proved to be!' Varini said.

Taraka interposed, 'Nonsense! Our prince is so noble! Would he leave without making enquiries about a girl who had tumbled down in a swoon? You need not misinterpret his actions!'

'What you say about Prince Arulmozhi is absolutely true. Can we find a nobler man in all the seven worlds? No legend or epic can provide his equal. What I am saying is entirely different. This girl–this Vanathi . . . do you know why she swooned? You don't have to go to a fortune teller, I can tell you what kind of fainting fit it was,' Varini said.

'So, what is it? Tell us!' Sentiru begged her. Varini whispered in Sentiru's ear.

Niravati asked, 'What did she say?'

'She says that it was a "lovesick swoon".'

The girls broke into shrieks of laughter. The birds on the trees by the riverbank flapped their wings and took flight.

Niravati said, 'When our prince returns from Ilankai, this girl will try her tricks again. We must watch out for it and stop her.'

Taraka announced, 'If Vanathi is not reduced to a gibbering lunatic by the time the prince returns, I will change my name from Taraka the star to Tataka the demoness!'

'Let it go. Come, should we not carry out Kundavai Devi's orders before they return?' Mandakini said.

The girls now removed the wooden plank at the bottom of the boat. A crocodile stuffed with cotton and fibre lay in the hollow space below. Rowing to the shore, they placed the dummy crocodile on the roots of a tree which had snaked down to spread across the waters. It appeared lifelike and gruesome. To prevent the dummy crocodile from drifting away, they fastened a rope around one of its legs, plunged the rope into the water, and tied its other end to the tree.

Taraka asked, 'Tell me, Mandakini, why has Kundavai Devi asked us to put this dummy under this tree?'

'Don't you know? To make Vanathi get over her fears and gain some courage! Vanathi is such a coward!'

'Looks like Kundavai Devi has decided to get Vanathi married to the prince,' Niravati exclaimed.

Envious, Varini said, 'Just you wait! Any such move and I will poison Vanathi!'

'No need for you to get so worked up! Who is going to give this Vanathi a second glance when the kings of Rashtrakuta, Vengi and Kalinga, even the emperor of faraway Kanauj, are all waiting to give their daughters in marriage to our prince?' Mandakini said.

'You may be right! But the prince says that if at all he decides to marry, he will only marry a girl from the Tamizh realm.'

Taraka declared, 'This simplifies things. Each one of us will have to show our skills! After all, why can't we do what Vanathi has done? Don't we have all the wiles that she seems to possess?'

At this point, it becomes necessary to tell the readers about the incident that gave rise to this discussion among these young women.

16

Arulmozhi Varman

Some nine hundred and eighty years ago, Parantaka Sundara Chozha reigned in south India. He ascended the throne fifteen years before our story began. The Chozhas had been growing stronger through the hundred years preceding his coronation and had extended their kingdom in all directions. However, their enemies in the north and south had also gained power. Sundara Chozha's predecessor was famed as 'Sivagnana' Gandaraditta, for his profound faith in Siva. He was uninterested in expanding the kingdom. His brother Arinjaya, who succeeded him, reigned only for a year. It was after his death that Parantaka Sundara Chozha ascended the throne.

Sundara Chozha had all the attributes of a great king. Skilled in warfare, he invaded the Pandya kingdom in the south soon after becoming king. A great war took place between the Pandyas and Chozhas in Sevur. Mahinda, the Sinhala ruler, sent a large army to support Veerapandiyan, who was then the Pandya king. The vast Chozha battalions defeated the Pandya and the Sinhala forces. Losing his crown and army,

Veerapandiyan escaped from the battlefield. He managed to keep himself alive by hiding in a cave in the wastelands of the Pandya realm.

The Sinhala forces were almost completely wiped out in Sevur. Those who escaped death shed their fame and valour on the battlefield to run away to their island home.

It had become the practice of the Sinhala kings to butt into the wars between the Chozhas and the Pandyas by sending their troops to assist the latter. Sundara Chozha wished to stop this once and for all. Therefore, he sent a Chozha army under the command of Chiriya Velar, the younger brother of the Kodumbalur chieftain Periya Velar. Unfortunately, due to the lack of ships, the entire army could not reach the island at the same time. The first batch made a foolhardy advance without forethought. Under the command of Mahinda's general, Sena, the Sinhala army surrounded the Chozha forces. In the terrible war that ensued, the Chozha commander Chiriya Velar proved his valour by losing his life. His name found its way into historical inscriptions as 'Chiriya Velar who died in Ilankai'.

When this news reached Veerapandiyan in his hiding place, he regained his courage and emerged to collect a big army and engage in war once again. This time not only was the Pandya army massacred, but Veerapandiyan too lost his life. In this war, Sundara Chozha's eldest son, Aditta Karikalan, performed incredible deeds of valour and was acclaimed for beheading Veerapandiyan.

Not only Sundara Chozha but the military commanders, generals and soldiers of the Chozha kingdom were determined to teach Mahinda a sound lesson. A huge army was gathered again for this purpose. The choice of the commander posed a question.

At that time, Sundara Chozha's firstborn, Crown Prince Aditta Karikalan, was quartered in Kanchi, the old capital of the Pallavas, striving to defeat and repel the Rashtrakutas who had been exercising their authority in Tondaimandalam and Tirumunaipadi. He was also making preparations to invade the north.

The situation fostered fierce competition among the military generals of the Chozha empire. Each wanted to be appointed supreme commander of the army invading Ilankai.

This rivalry bred jealousy and complaints. For in the ancient Tamizh realm, it was rare indeed to find anyone who wanted to escape from conscription. It was their eagerness to enrol that sparked envy and hostility among the rivals.

Sundara Chozha's younger son, Arulmozhi Varman, came forward to end this rivalry in a way that would satisfy them all. He said to his father, 'Appa! I have been cossetted for far too long by aunts and grandmothers. Time for me to get out of the palace. Let me lead our forces to Ilankai!'

Arulmozhi was only nineteen years old. He was Sundara Chozha's youngest child, his much-indulged son. He was the darling of all the queens who dwelt in the Pazhaiyarai palace. In fact, he was the pampered son of the entire Chozha realm.

Sundara Chozha was a handsome man. Infatuated by her beauty, Arinjaya, his father, had married Kalyani, a princess of the Vaidumbaraya clan. They named their son Parantaka. But his extreme good looks made the people call him 'Sundara' Chozha, the handsome king, until it virtually became his name.

All his children had inherited Sundara Chozha's good looks, but Arulmozhi outdid them all. As a child, the queens of the Chozha family would kiss his cheeks again and again until they became red. His elder sister, Kundavai, doted on him. Though she was merely two years older than Arulmozhi, Kundavai was convinced that she was solely responsible for raising him. Arulmozhi's affection for his sister equalled hers for him. He would never do anything against her will. All she had to do was to give the word. Arulmozhi would not disregard it even if the gods urged him to do so. To him, his sister's word was law.

Fixing her earnest gaze on her brother's face, not only in his waking hours but also when he was asleep, Kundavai would muse, 'This boy has some divine power in him. It is my responsibility to set it alight.' While he slept, she would often pick up his hands and fancy that the lines on his palms shaped the images of the conch and the discus.

Ah! He is born to rule the world!' she would sigh. But there was no possibility of even thinking about his wearing the Chozha crown when there were two older claimants to it. But who knew god's will? The world is a vast place. So many countries, so many kingdoms! Epics and legends spoke of so many people migrating from one land to another and establishing kingdoms with their own strength of arms! Didn't a prince from the land where the Ganga flows sail to Ilankai and reign over that island? Hasn't his Sinhala dynasty ruled for a thousand years!'

Kundavai was lost in such endless reveries. She came to a decision when a debate arose over who was to lead the Ilankai invasion.

'Tambi, Arulmozhi, even a brief separation from you will be hard to bear. And yet, the time has come for you to leave. It is you who must lead our forces to Ilankai,' she said.

The prince gladly agreed. He had been waiting to escape from all the mollycoddling in the palace. His dear sister herself had asked him to go! What could stop him now?

Nothing was impossible in the Chozha kingdom when Kundavai set her mind to it. The young prince Arulmozhi became the supreme commander of the Chozha military forces in the south. He went to Ilankai. But the war would not end quickly. His methods of conducting the war were vastly different from those of others. Moreover, the authorities in his motherland would not replenish armaments and provisions according to his needs. He had to make a trip home to speak to his father and make the necessary arrangements before returning to Ilankai.

Kundavai arranged an auspicious send-off ceremony for her beloved brother in the Pazhaiyarai palace. Drums and conches resounded in the courtyard. Victory slogans rose to the sky.

All the mothers in the Chozha clan blessed their darling child, smeared sacred ash on his forehead and made the customary gestures to ward off the evil eye.

At the entrance of the palace, on the steps of the threshold, Kundavai's companions stood holding trays with lighted lamps. There was nothing commonplace about those companions. Each belonged to some celebrated royal clan in the feudatories of the Chozha kingdom. They had come to the Pazhaiyarai palace for the privilege of waiting on Queen Sembiyan Mahadevi and serving Kundavai as her companion. Among them was Vanathi, the daughter of Siriya Velar, the younger brother of the chieftain of Kodumbalur.

Every girl in that group became flustered when the prince approached the doorway. As he came nearer, they circled the tray in the customary manner. Suddenly, Vanathi began to tremble all over until she dropped her tray with a clang. 'What a bad omen!' was the thought that gave rise to anxiety in every heart. But everyone was mollified to see that the flame was still burning on the fallen tray. The elders insisted that this augured good fortune.

Arulmozhi Varman smiled at the girl who had dropped the tray in needless alarm before he walked on. As he passed her, the thought of what she had done made Vanathi shrink and slump down in a swoon. As directed by Kundavai, the other girls picked her up and put her on a raised platform in a room within. Without waiting to see her brother depart, Kundavai rushed to nurse Vanathi. Arulmozhi, who had seen the girl fall, sent an attendant to enquire about her before he mounted the horse. Kundavai sent the man back, asking the prince to come in once again before he left. The prince, who always deferred to his sister, re-entered the palace. He was moved to see his sister holding Vanathi against her breast and trying to revive her.

'Akka, who is this girl?' he asked.

'She is the daughter of Chiriya Velar of Kodumbalur. Her name is Vanathi. She is timid by nature.'

'Ah! Now I know why she fainted. Didn't her father die on the battlefield in Ilankai? She must have recalled it,' said the prince.

'Perhaps. Don't worry, I will take care of her. May you return victorious! Keep me informed.'

'I will,' said the prince. 'Please do send word about things happening here.'

At this moment, perhaps due to the charm of his gentle voice, Vanathi began to regain consciousness. Her eyes opened slowly and widened to see the prince standing before her. Her face bloomed. The smile on her lips brought dimples to her cheeks. She got up bashfully and saw that Princess Kundavai was holding her. She was mortified. With tears in her eyes, she said, 'Akka! What have I done?'

Before Kundavai could respond, the prince said, 'Don't worry about it, Vanathi. Anyone can make a mistake. Moreover, you had a reason for it. That is what I was telling my sister.'

Vanathi began to doubt her eyes and ears. The prince who never glanced at women . . . was he actually speaking to her? Comforting her? How could she take in this good fortune! Why, she was getting gooseflesh. She was feeling dizzy once again . . .

The prince left after saying, 'Akka, I take my leave of you. Take good care of this girl who has lost both her father and mother. When you send me news, do let me know about her state of health.'

From the balcony and window, Kundavai's companions watched and heard it all. They began to burn with jealousy.

From that day onwards, Kundavai began to single out Vanathi with affection and concern. She taught her all the skills that she had acquired from the education she had received and the arts she had trained in. She made Vanathi accompany her everywhere. She took her to the palace garden and exchanged confidences. She shared all her dreams for her brother's glory. Vanathi listened with rapt attention.

After that incident, Vanathi had four or five giddy spells. Each time, Kundavai nursed her, only to see Vanathi bursting into sobs as she regained consciousness. 'Silly girl! Why are you weeping?' Kundavai would admonish her. Vanathi would say, 'I don't know, Akka! Please forgive me.'

Then Kundavai would hug Vanathi, kiss her on the forehead and calm her down. All this made the girls feel even more jealous.

With these events on their minds, was it not natural for Kundavai's companions to talk as they did when they saw their royal princess setting off for Kudantai with Vanathi as her sole companion?

17

The Horse Sprang

Kundavai had decided that Vanathi was the most suitable bride for her brother, Prince Arulmozhi Varman. But Vanathi had a major failing–she was timid. How could anyone who was to marry an outstanding warrior and give birth to the monarch of the world, be so timorous? Kundavai wanted to transform fainthearted Vanathi into a woman of courage. It was with that intention that she had set up the scene with the stuffed crocodile. But Vanathi passed the test with flying colours.

When they returned from the astrologer's house in Kudantai, Kundavai and Vanathi got into the swan-shaped pleasure craft which took them to the spot where Kundavai and the girls indulged in water sports.

As soon as everyone got down, one of the girls pointed to the other side of the tree and squealed, 'Ayo! Crocodile!' It set off everyone shrieking and running helter-skelter.

But even though everyone followed Kundavai's instructions in pretending to be terrified, timid Vanathi showed no trace of fear. When she saw the crocodile close by, with its mouth wide open, all she said was, 'Akka! Tell the girls not to be afraid. A crocodile is strong only as long as it is in water, it is powerless on land.'

'What a humbug you are! Someone must have told you that this is a dummy!' the other girls said.

'I am not afraid of crocodiles. But lizards and cockroaches terrify me,' Vanathi said.

It was at that moment that Vandiyatevan arrived to save the girls from the monstrous creature. He sprang down from the horse and flung his spear at it.

And that was when the woman of regal mien came to stand before the crocodile and addressed him. All the chagrin he had felt at being ignored by her at the astrologer's house vanished. But why did she say that he should not have bothered about the crocodile? He began to have vague misgivings about why the crocodile was lying inert, and for so long.

The young woman went on, 'Ayya, you apologized for having barged into the astrologer's house. We left without responding to you. You must have thought that the women of the Chozha land are devoid of courtesy. Please don't come to that conclusion. I was somewhat distraught because my companion had suddenly fainted. That is why I did not answer you.'

'Oh! What a delectable voice! Why is my heart pounding? Why am I choking? No flute, lute, tabor or war drum has ever intoxicated me as much or shaken me to the core like this! Why am I not able to respond? Why does my tongue cleave to my palate? Why has the wind stopped blowing? And this crocodile . . . ! Why does it lie still?'

His heart continued to palpitate. The woman's voice went on, as if in a dream. 'You believed that you were saving helpless women from the crocodile. It is indeed rare to see a spear thrown with such speed and accuracy!'

The girls laughed again. The sound dispelled Vandiyatevan's amorous fantasy. The spell was shattered. He stared at the crocodile once again. He walked up to it without paying any attention to the girls. He shook the spear still embedded in its back and drew it out. Blood did not spurt out of the wound. Cotton wool and plantain fibre did.

Once again, the girls broke into wicked laughter. This time, they sniggered and chortled loudly.

Vandiyatevan blenched in flesh and spirit. He had never been so shamed before. 'Such humiliation! Before so many women . . . ! Are they women at all? No. No. They are ghouls. I must not stay anywhere near them. I must not even cast a look at them. *Chee*!* My precious spear! Did you have to go through this ignominy? How can I ever wipe you clean?' All these thoughts raced through his mind. If those who had dared to laugh had been menfolk, the scene would have been transformed into a war zone. They would have lost their lives instantly! Their blood would have turned the flowing waters of the Arasalaru crimson. But they were women! What could anyone do to them? The only option was to run away.

Without a single backward look, even at the woman who had enthralled him, he leapt to the riverbank. His horse was waiting there. It neighed. Vandiyatevan thought that even the horse was laughing at him. Directing all his anger towards the poor animal, he whipped it hard, twice. The horse bounded away on the path by the river.

Kundavai gazed at the disappearing horse until the dust raised by its hoofs settled down. Then, turning to her

---

* An exclamation of disgust.

companions, she said, 'You don't seem to have any sense of decorum. You should not have laughed. When we are alone, you can be as high-spirited as you please. But should you not show some restraint in the presence of a stranger? What kind of impression have you given that young man about the women of the Chozha realm?'

18

Idumbankari

We had left Tirumalai, alias Azhvarkadiyan Nambi, at a jetty on the Kollidam. Let us now turn our attention to him.

As he watched Vandiyatevan mount a horse and ride to Kudantai, Tirumalai said to himself, 'This young man is a scamp. He manages to be one-up on me all the time. I am unable to discover whom he serves, where he is going and why. Nor is it clear whether he was a member of the cabal in Kadambur. It is good that I told him about the Kudantai astrologer. Let me see if the astrologer discovers what I could not.'

'Swami! Are you talking to yourself or the peepal tree?' Azhvarkadiyan turned to see who was addressing him. It was the attendant from Kadambur who had fetched a fresh horse for Vandiyatevan.

'Are you talking to me?' Azhvarkadiyan asked. 'I was talking neither to myself nor to the tree. A phantom lives on this tree. I had a brief chat with it.'

'Oh! Is that so? Is the phantom a Saiva or a Vaishnava?'

'Exactly what I was asking the phantom. But it disappeared when you spoke. Never mind. What is your name?'

'Why do you ask, swami?'

'Did you not save me from drowning? Should I not remember the name of my benefactor?'

'My name . . . my . . . name . . . is . . . Idumbankari, swami!' the man drawled.

'Oh! Idumbankari? I think I've heard it before!'

Idumbankari did something odd. Placing his palms one above the other, he wiggled his thumbs and stared at Azhvarkadiyan.

'What are you doing? I don't understand what this gesture means . . .' Tirumalai said.

'I? But I didn't do anything!' Idumbankari said.

'You did, my man, you did. I saw it. You made a gesture that signifies Vishnu's first avatar in the Bharatanatyam dance vocabulary.'

'What is Vishnu's first avatar?'

'Don't you know? The avatar in the form of a fish.'

'Fish?'

'Yes, fish.'

'Swami! You see strange things! You see a phantom on a tree. You see fish in my hands! Perhaps the swami is overfond of fish?'

'Chee chee! Don't say such things! Never mind! Did you see where the Saiva who came with us happened to go?'

'To the same place where I went to buy a horse. He was cursing you all along the way.'

'What did he say?'

'He said that if he ever saw you again he would shave your head–'

'He knows the barber's trade, does he!'

'He was going to erase the *namam** streaks on your body and smear you all over with the sacred ash.'

'In that case, I must certainly see him again. Do you know his hometown?'

'He said it was a place called Pullirukku Velur.'

'I will make it a point to see him again. Are you going in the same direction?'

'No, no. Why should I? I am going to cross the Kollidam again and return to Kadambur. My master will yank my eyes out if I don't.'

'All right. Go. There! The ferry is about to leave.'

Idumbankari saw that Azhvarkadiyan was right. The boat was indeed about to leave.

'Right, swami! I'll get going,' said Idumbankari and walked briskly to the jetty.

Halfway down the path, he sneaked a backward look. But before he did, Azhvarkadiyan had done something peculiar. He had jumped on the tree and climbed up to hide himself in the thick branches above where Idumbankari could not see him.

Idumbankari reached the jetty. The ferryman asked him if he was taking the boat. 'No, you may go. I am taking the next one,' Idumbankari replied.

'Is that so? I stopped the boat when I saw you hurrying,' said the boatman and started rowing.

Azhvarkadiyan had concealed himself very well by then. He began to speak to the invisible phantom. 'So! My guess turned out to be right. He is not getting into the boat. He

---

* Red and white vertical streaks painted on the forehead, emblematic symbol of faith in Vishnu.

is coming back. I must see where he goes next. I saw his hands making the sign of the fish very clearly. What does it mean? Fish! What does fish stand for? Ah! The Pandya emblem. Could it be . . . Let me see. Let me be patient. With patience, you may rule the earth. Impatience lands you in the wilderness. But as things stand, wilderness may be the better option. In any case, let me see what patience can achieve.'

Very soon his guess was proved right. The boat left without Idumbankari. Idumbankari turned to stare at the peepal tree. Then he sent penetrating glances in every direction. Deciding that Azhvarkadiyan was not around, he came back to the same tree and settled himself under it. His eyes continued to scan every direction as if expecting something or someone. But he did not look up. Had he even done so, he could not have caught sight of Azhvarkadiyan, who remained well and truly hidden.

Some twenty-five minutes passed. Azhvarkadiyan's limbs became numb. He could not stay on the tree any longer. Nor did it look as though Idumbankari was going to get up any time soon. But how could he escape? However gingerly he may slide down on the other side of the tree, he could not do it in total silence. And Idumbankari had a sharp dagger tucked at his waist. How could Azhvarkadiyan be sure that Idumbankari would not plunge it into him?

What else could he do? Should he shriek like a banshee and jump down on the man below? Would Idumbankari faint in fear, or cut and run, believing that he was attacked by the phantom? Azhvarkadiyan could then seize the opportunity to escape. Just as these thoughts chased one another in Azhvarkadiyan's head, it looked as if his test may be over soon.

A man was striding down the Kudantai highway from the southwest. Azhvarkadiyan's instinct told him that Idumbankari had been waiting for him.

Idumban got up when he saw the newcomer. The newcomer made the gesture that Idumban had made earlier. Placing one hand on the other, he wiggled his thumbs to make the sign of the fish. Idumban repeated the gesture.

'Your name?' the newcomer asked.

'Idumbankari. Yours?

'Soman Sambavan'

'I was waiting for you.'

'I came searching for you.'

'Which way should we go?'

'Westward.'

'Where do we go?'

'To the enemy's sepulchre.'

'Near Tirupurampiyam?'

'Don't speak so loudly. Someone may overhear.'

'No one is here. I checked.'

'No chance of anyone hiding nearby?'

'None.'

'Then let's go. I'm not sure of the way. You go ahead. I will follow you.'

'Not an easy path. All woods and knolls, rocks and thorns.'

'All right, all right. Get going! Even though our trail goes through the woods, if we spy anyone, we must hide at once. Got it?'

'Got it. Got it.'

Idumbankari started walking towards the west, along the Kollidam shore. Soman Sambavan followed a little behind.

Having seen and heard it all, Azhvarkadiyan stayed put on the tree until both men disappeared from view.

'Aha! These are evil times! Unexpected things are happening. By god's grace, I have the opportunity to unravel a baffling mystery. Success depends on how smart I can be. I was able to get only an inkling of this matter at the Kadambur palace. This time I must not allow myself to be hoodwinked. The enemy's sepulchre at Tirupurampiyam . . . It must be the memorial shrine for King Prithvipati of the Ganga dynasty. A hundred years have passed since it was built. It lies in ruins now, with a tangled forest around it. The village is far away. Why are these two going there? If there was something to be settled between the two of them, they would have finished it here. No need to walk ten miles through the forest! So it is certain that a few more will join them there. Why? Why should one of them refer to Prithvipati's memorial as the "enemy's sepulchre"? To whom is Prithvipati "the enemy"? So, my surmise must be true . . . Well, these people are taking the Kollidam trail. Let me go by the Manni River, even though the forest is thicker on that route. What do I care about forests and knolls, rocks and thorns? It is they who should fear me!'

Murmuring these thoughts to himself, Tirumalai got down from the tree and went southward until he reached River Manni. From there he followed it to the west.

Trekking through the dense undergrowth, devoid of any trace of human presence, Azhvarkadiyan reached the sepulchral shrine in Tirupurampiyam as the sun began to set.

19

The Forested Battlefield

In the ancient Tamizh realm, it was the custom to consecrate a stone slab to memorialize great warriors who lost their lives on the battlefield. Such a memorial was known as a *nadukar koil*, or a consecrated stone. When the memorial stone was walled in with a deity installed beside it, it came to be called *pallipadai*, or a tomb which was also a shrine.

On the northern bank of the river Manni, five miles to the northwest of Kudantai town, there was a pallipadai near Tirupurampiyam village. It was raised to commemorate Prithvipati, a ruler of the Ganga dynasty who had lost his life in the great war that had taken place. Those who are acquainted with world history will know how some battles like those at Waterloo, Panipat and Plassey changed the course of history. The Tirupurampiyam battle holds the same significance for the Tamizh realm. This battle took place some hundred years before our story begins, and it is essential for the Tamizh people to know its history.

The glory of the Chozhas was eclipsed for nearly six hundred years after the many-splendoured age of the ancient

Chozha kings–Karikal Valavan, Perunarkilli, Ilanchetchenni and Toditotchembian. The Pandyas of the south and the Pallavas of the north grew powerful and threatened the Chozhas from both sides. When the pressure became unendurable, the Chozhas were compelled to leave their long-term capital Uraiyur and shift to Pazhaiyarai near Kudantai.

Among the kings ruling from Pazhaiyarai, Vijayalaya earned matchless fame for his valour in the many battles he had fought. Several court poets of later times hailed him as the 'victorious hero ornamented with ninety-six battle scars'.

His son, Aditta Chozha proved to be his father's equal, earning his reputation on the battlefield.

When he reached a ripe old age, Vijayalaya crowned his son and retired from active service. That was the time when the enmity between the Pandyas and the Pallavas grew intense and instigated several wars. Most of these wars between Varaguna Varman the Pandya king, and Aparajita Varman the Pallava king, took place in the Chozha realm. The citizens of the Chozha land found themselves trapped like a little bantam chick between two battling elephants. However, Vijayalaya took up arms again and turned these combats to his advantage by taking his small troops to fight alternately on one side or the other. Though victory and defeat came by turns, the Chozha realm saw the growth of martial skills by leaps and bounds.

The Chozha country is enriched by the Kaveri and its many tributaries flowing south of the great river. Among them, the river Manni, branching off from the Kollidam, flows between the Kollidam and the Kaveri.

It was on the northern bank of Manni near Tirupurampiyam village that the final test of power between the Pandyas and the Pallavas took place. The armies on both sides were more or less equal in size and strength. Prithvipati of the Ganga realm had come to support the Pallava king, Aparajita Varman. Aditta Chozha too joined Aparajita Varman's side.

Compared to the Pandya and the Pallava armies, the Chozha troops were quite small. But Aditta knew that if the Pandyas won this time, the Chozha dynasty would be exterminated. That was the reason why he had merged his small troop with the colossal Pallava army, like a small river melding into the ocean.

The four kinds of troops—chariotry, elephantry, cavalry and infantry—were engaged in fierce combat spreading across a vast terrain. Like clashing mountains, gargantuan elephants slammed into each other and set the earth quaking in all the cardinal directions. The spears of their riders flashed lightning streaks when horses leapt on horses like colliding cyclones. Chariots crashed and splintered into shards that went flying everywhere.

Three days of relentless fighting had transformed the battleground into a sea of blood. Dead horses and elephants lay in mounds, and pieces of shattered chariots floated like the planks of a ship wrecked on the sea. The dead lay everywhere in their thousands and ten thousands.

After three days of brutal combat, only a small portion of the Pallava army remained. Those survivors were completely exhausted. Blessed with inexhaustible energy, the brave Pandya soldiers continued their hammering attack. A council was held in the Pallava king's tent, where the three kings, Aparajita Varman, Prithvipati and Aditta, decided that continuing the attack would be out of the question. Retreating to the northern bank of the Kollidam was the practical solution.

That was when a miracle took place. Vijayalaya, debilitated by old age, bearing ninety-six scars on his body, unable to stand due to the crippling wounds inflicted on his legs, somehow managed to come to the war front. He knew that if the Pallava army retreated to the north beyond the Kollidam, the Chozhas could never raise their heads again for ages to come.

The old lion's roar put new hearts into the few men left in the Pallava army.

'An elephant! Give me an elephant!' he bellowed.

'Our elephantry has been completely routed. Not even a single elephant has escaped death,' they said.

'A horse! Bring me a horse!' he cried.

'Not a single horse has survived,' they answered.

'Are there two men, brave and true, among the Chozhas? If so, come forward!' Vijayalaya hollered.

Not two but two hundred men came forward.

The dauntless warrior said, 'Two men! Two men with hefty shoulders and staunch hearts! Come, take me on your shoulders. The others should follow me in pairs. If the warriors bearing me should fall, the pair following close behind should replace them.'

Two warriors as burly as the legendary Bhima came forward and took Vijayalaya on their shoulders.

'Go! Go to the frontlines!' the king thundered.

Fighting was still going on in a corner of the battlefield where the intrepid Pandya warriors were making the Pallava soldiers pull back.

Riding on the shoulders of the two volunteers, Vijayalaya rushed into the thick of the battle. He held two long swords in both his hands and began to twirl them like the discus of the god Vishnu. No one could stop him. Wherever he went, foes dropped dead on both sides.

The fleeing soldiers returned to marvel at this spectacle. At first, they stood still, dazed by Vijayalaya's superhuman valour. Then they began to motivate each other and to fight again.

That was all. The goddess of victory began to shower her grace on the other side.

The Pallava commanders abandoned their plan to withdraw to the north of the Kollidam.

The three kings entered the fray, surrounded by their troops. Soon, the Pandya soldiers began to fall back. They stopped only when they reached the borders of their own kingdom.

King Prithvipati of the Ganga clan performed great deeds of valour, established his fame on the battlefield and ascended to the warriors' haven.

A memorial stone was placed on the battlefield to commemorate him. Later, a shrine was built over it.

For a long time, the site of that ghastly war remained barren. No grass or weed would grow there. No one would go anywhere near it. Slowly, it was covered by undergrowth. A forest grew around the sepulchral shrine. Foxes came to live in the bushes. Owls and bitterns made their homes on the dark branches of the trees. As time went by, people stopped going to the tomb. It began to split and crack. At the time of our story, it lay in ruins.

Azhvarkadiyan reached this ruined shrine as dusk began to fall. The guardian ghouls sculpted on the top edge of the mandapam tried to scare him. But our Vaishnava was made of a different mettle. He jumped up to the top of the shrine and hid himself under an overhanging branch. His eyes had the power to tear through the darkness. His ears were sharp enough to hear the least sound.

Half an hour . . . another half hour . . . an hour and a half . . . The surrounding darkness smothered him and tried to suffocate him. Now and then he could hear the trees rustling. There! A civet cat was climbing a tree. Fearing the civet, a bird flapped its wings as it flew up to a higher branch. An owl screeched. A bittern called from the other side. There! The foxes had started screaming.

A sound came from above. A squirrel, lizard or some other small creature had leapt on the branch.

A small patch of the sky could be seen through the gap between the branches from where the twinkling stars looked down. As the darkness intensified his loneliness, Azhvarkadiyan felt that the stars claimed him as a friend. He spoke to them in a low voice.

> O stars! Today you seem to be winking, mocking and laughing at the imbecility of the people of the earth. And you have cause enough to laugh. You saw the huge war that took place here. For a long time after that, you saw blood swamping the ground. You wondered why human beings should be so hostile to one another! You wondered why human blood had to be shed in surging floods. This tomb is still identified as the enemy's memorial. A man who has been dead for over a hundred years continues to be 'the foe'. A meeting is to be held beside this enemy's tomb. Why? To make plans to torment the living in the name of the dead. O stars in the sky! Why won't you laugh? Go on! Have your fill of mirth!
>
> Lord! Is this going to be a waste of time? Is the night going to pass in this manner? Are the men not going to turn up as expected? Did I hear it all wrong? Have I been negligent? Have those who made the sign of the fish changed their minds and gone elsewhere? How disappointing! If I have been fooled today, I cannot forgive myself. Ah! A

light in the distance! What's that? Gone! It appears again. No doubt about it. Someone is approaching with a flaming torch. No, two men are coming. The waiting has not been in vain.

The two men crossed the sepulchre to reach a little clearing in the middle of the tangled forest. One sat down. The man with the torch looked around. It was clear that he was expecting someone. A little later, two men arrived together. They must have come to that particular spot before. Otherwise, how could they have found it in the dense forest and the darkness?

Those who came ahead spoke to those who joined them. But Azhvarkadiyan could not hear anything.

Then two more turned up. They talked among themselves. The last man to arrive had a bag in his hand. He opened it and emptied its contents on the ground. Coins of gold shone brilliantly in the torchlight.

The man who spilled the coins laughed like a maniac. 'My friends! We are going to destroy the Chozha kingdom with gold from the Chozha treasury. How amusing!' he said and guffawed again.

'Ravidasa! Don't shout! Speak softly,' another warned him.

'Why not? Only foxes, civet cats and owls can hear us. Luckily, they will not repeat what they hear,' Ravidasan said.

'Still, it is better to lower the voice.'

The men began to speak in low voices. Azhvarkadiyan thought that it would be pointless to remain where he was. He simply had to get down, go up close to the men and eavesdrop on them. He had to overcome the dangers such a manoeuvre could precipitate. As Azhvarkadiyan put his thoughts into action, he brushed against a branch. It made a rustling sound.

Two of the men jumped up at once and hollered, 'Who's there?'

Azhvarkadiyan's heart stopped beating. He had no choice but to run. But running would mean more rustling. The men would catch up with him all too soon.

Just at that moment, an owl opened its wings and flapped them loudly. It broke into a piercing screech.

20

The First Enemy

Azhvarkadiyan greatly appreciated the owl for coming to his rescue at the right time.

When they saw the owl shrieking and flapping its wings, the conspirators concluded that the bird had been responsible for the sound they had heard.

One of them said, 'This owl has managed to scare us! Chop it down!'

'No. Save your swords for worthy tasks. Keep them razor-sharp to decimate our enemies. Owls and bitterns are our friends. When the world sleeps, they stay awake with us,' Ravidasan said.

As Ravidasan was speaking, Azhvarkadiyan advanced with slow, silent steps and reached a massive maruda tree. The hundred-year-old tree had a small cavity below, over which long buttress roots ran in all directions. He stood between two such roots in that hollow space, his back pressed against the tree.

'As long as the Tanjavur treasury exists, we have no dearth of what we need. What we need most is the gumption to finish what we have undertaken and the strength of mind to maintain secrecy until the task is completed. We must divide ourselves into two groups. One group should go to Ilankai at once. The other must go to Tondaimandalam and wait for the right time to perform the mission. Both tasks must be performed around the same time. Any delay after finishing off one of the enemies would alert the others into adopting safety measures. We must not give them that opportunity. Understand? Now, who is ready to go to Ilankai?' Ravidasan asked.

Several voices rose simultaneously, 'I will go!' 'I must go!'

'Let us decide that at our next meeting. There are other matters to be settled now,' Ravidasan said.

'Which is the best route to Ilankai?' one of the men enquired.

'You can go via Kodikkarai. It is a good spot for crossing the sea. But it is difficult to make your way to Kodikkarai from here. There are enemies all along the way. And spies in several places. Therefore, it may be best to cross the sea at Rameswaram and disembark near Mathottam. Those who go to Ilankai must know how to row a boat, steer a catamaran and swim. Who knows swimming?'

Several voices rose to say, 'I do! I do!'

'You must first meet Mahinda, the king of Ilankai, before starting your work. At least one of the men going to Ilankai must know the Sinhala tongue. Why is Soman Sambavan not here yet? Has anyone seen him today?'

'Here I am,' a voice called out from somewhere very close to Azhvarkadiyan, who pressed himself even more against the tree, sighing, 'How mortifying that this stupid body should have become so fat!'

Two newcomers joined the group. Azhvarkadiyan cautiously thrust his face a little forward and confirmed that they were the two men he had met by the Kollidam shore.

'Come! Come!' Ravidasan welcomed them. 'I was afraid that some danger might have kept you away. Which path did you take?'

'We came by the Kollidam river. On the way, we were surrounded by foxes. We got delayed in having to escape from them.'

'It makes sense to be afraid of lions and tigers. But what can you achieve if you are scared by a fox?' one of the men who had arrived earlier scoffed.

'Don't say that! A fox is worse than a lion or a tiger. The lion and the tiger come singly to pounce on you. You can manage to fight them. But foxes come skulking in groups. And that is why they are stronger. Our king, who was second to none, lost the battle and his life only because the Chozha foxes came in huge numbers to attack him. How else could it have happened?'

'We will massacre the entire tribe of foxes! We will rout them until they vanish without a trace!' Soman Sambavan shouted in fury.

'Here are the tools to accomplish that,' said Ravidasan, pointing to the heap of gold coins.

Picking up a few coins and examining them, Soman Sambavan said, 'Ah! A tiger on one side, a palm tree on the other!'

'Chozha gold. Pazhuvettaraiyar seal. I have accomplished what I undertook. What about you? Idumbankari must have some news!' Ravidasan said.

Idumbankari began to speak. 'At your command, I joined the Kadambur palace staff as an attendant. Only last night did this ploy bear fruit. A grand dinner was held at Sambuvaraiyar's palace. Periya Pazhuvettaraiyar, Vanangamudi Munaiyar. Mazhapadi Mazhavaraiyar and others were the guests for whom kuravai koothu and velanattam were performed. Everyone thought that his young queen had accompanied Pazhuvettaraiyar in the covered palanquin. Pazhuvettaraiyar declared that Maharaja Sundara Chozha's health was not good and he would not live for much longer. Everyone decided unanimously that his successor should be Madhurantakan and not Aditta Karikalan. Some of them asked if Madhurantakan would agree to this plan. "I will ask him to tell you in his own words," Pazhuvettaraiyar replied. As he drew the curtain, Madhurantakan emerged from the palanquin and declared that he was ready to take the throne.'

So! They are going to crown the gallant hero who puts on a woman's guise! Excellent! Things are going according to our expectations. Internal chaos in the Chozha kingdom is an advantage for us. Whatever happens, no one will suspect us. Idumbankari! The information you have brought is extremely valuable. But how did you get the opportunity to learn all these things? Ravidasan asked.

'They asked me to stand guard at their midnight council and prevent anyone from approaching anywhere near. I did my sentry duty with my eyes and ears open.'

'Did you learn anything else?'

'Yes. A stranger was watching all the proceedings of this midnight conference from the top of the wall around the fort.'

'Who was he?'

'A Vaishnava with a tuft on his head.'

'Ah! So it was he! What did you do? Did you not capture him and take him to Sambuvaraiyar?'

'No. I thought he might be one of us. I wondered if you had sent him.'

'You have made a grave mistake. He does not belong to our group. He is short and burly. Always ready to pick a fight. His name is Tirumalai. He calls himself Azhvarkadiyan.'

'The same man! This afternoon I realized that I had been mistaken. I found out that he was not one of us.'

'How?'

'Yesterday, Kandamaran's old friend had also come to the Kadambur palace. It became clear that he had nothing to do with Pazhuvettaraiyar's council. This morning, knowing that my young master was going to accompany his friend up to the Kollidam shore, I kept on appearing before him until he asked me to go along. He returned to Kadambur after bidding me to cross the river and find a horse for his friend. I told him that I would visit my aunt in Kudantai before returning to Kadambur. That is how I was able to come here without giving rise to suspicion.'

'Good! Good! But how did you learn that the Vaishnava was not one of us?'

'He got into the ferry at the last minute. From his exchanges with Kandamaran's friend, I thought he could be one of us. Moreover, it appeared as if he was waiting on the other bank of the Kollidam for me. I showed him our secret sign. But it made no sense to him. I decided that he did not belong to our group.'

'You made a huge mistake. Never make our sign before strangers. Friends! Listen to this! Our work is in Kanchi and Ilankai. Our principal adversaries are in those places. But more than those two, our most alarming opponent, our primary foe, is none other than Tirumalai, who traipses around under the false name of Azhvarkadiyan. He is capable of wrecking us and our mission. He is trying to abduct the lady who is our matchless leader. The next time any one of you sees him anywhere, in any state, plunge your weapon into his breast and kill him at once. If you don't have any weapon on hand, grab him by the neck and squeeze him to death. Or tip him into the flood to be consumed by crocodiles. Use any trick of the trade to take him up the cliff and push him down. Kill him without mercy, just as you would kill a snake or a scorpion. As long as he remains alive, he will prevent us from fulfilling our mission.'

'Ravidasa! From what you say, it looks as if he must be quite a shark! Who is he?'

'He is a monstrously clever spy. He is chief minister Aniruddha Brahmarayar's man.'

'Ravidasa, are there others like him?'

'There is an astrologer in Kudantai. I have my doubts about him. He makes forecasts to all and sundry, and makes them spill a great deal of information. None of you must ever go anywhere near him. If you do, you will surely be hoodwinked.'

Azhvarkadiyan was chilled to the bone. He sweated all over. He began to doubt if he could escape with his life.

At that very moment, as bad luck would have it, he had an uncontrollable urge to sneeze. He tried to muffle the sneeze by covering his nose with a piece of cloth.

The wind had stopped blowing. The trees had stopped rustling. Faint as it was, the conspirators could not but hear Tirumalai's sneeze.

'I hear something behind that maruda tree. Take the torch and check it out,' Ravidasan said.

The man holding the torch approached the tree. The light grew brighter and brighter as he came nearer and nearer. There! He was about to reach the tree. The torch was going to shine on Azhvarkadiyan's face. What was going to happen now? Survival would be nothing short of rebirth!

Tirumalai's heart beat fast. He looked around to see if there was any hope of escape. No. He looked up. A monstrous bat hung upside down on the branch of the tree. Something flashed in his head. He raised his hands swiftly, grabbed the bat and kept it ready. The moment the man turned to face the tree, Azhvarkadiyan threw the bat at his face. The torch fell and its light dimmed. The man shouted incoherently. Azhvarkadiyan began to run. In no time at all, he had disappeared into the forest.

21

The Rustling Curtain

Can two minds function simultaneously within a single body? On that day, from his personal experience, Vandiyatevan learnt that they could.

He was riding through the most fecund region in the fertile Chozha realm. It was the season when fresh waters surged and overflowed in the rivers. Water gushed noisily into the fields through sluices, canals and ducts. Water, water, everywhere! As he reflected on the aptness of describing the Chozha country as the land of abundance and the Chozha king as the dispenser of plenitude, Vandiyatevan also recalled all the dangers that threatened that very land and its king. What was his duty in this situation? Should he decide that his duty was completely discharged when he handed over Prince Karikalan's missive to the maharaja? Why should he get involved in the fratricidal feuds of the royal clan?

His musings continued. 'How does it matter to me who among the rivals for the Chozha throne wins? The Chozhas had been the foes of the Vaanan clan. Didn't the Chozha, Ganga and Vaidumba rulers combine to destroy Vaanan's rule, leaving me without a kingdom? Can Prince Karikalan's affection for me today erase all those iniquities? Yet can the actions of those old kings be called unjust? Isn't it the norm for kings to make war? What is the use of the loser raging against the victor? When my ancestors had power, did they not unleash unholy terror on other kings? Did they not try to wipe them out? Ah! I remember . . . There was a poem about it . . . What did it say?

Mulching the war field
With massacred foes,
Drenching the land
With their crimson blood,
As stampeding elephants
Mangle their flesh
To enrich the sludge,
The Vaanan king,
Lordly and proud,
The monarch of bards,
Seized the crowns
Of three great kings,
And planted them deep
Into the soil.

'My ancestors too indulged in gory deeds on the battlefield. The loser's fate is always desperate. Can every king be as compassionate as the legendary Rama and Dharmaputra? They were exiled to the forest precisely because they possessed this attribute. They had to undergo great suffering even though they were strong men, supported by brave warriors. Politics accommodates no mercy. In fact, it is evident that the men of the Chozha clan are not wholly devoid of compassion. They do try to turn their foes into friends. And to that end, they enter into marriage alliances with members of other clans. Didn't Sundara Chozha's father Arinjaya marry Kalyani, the daughter of the Vaidumba clan? It was from the beauteous Kalyani that her son Sundara Chozha, and his children, inherited their amazing good looks. Ah! Talk of beauty and the woman by the banks of the Arasalaru comes to mind. No, she does not "come" to mind. She has been in my mind all the time.'

As Vandiyatevan's conscious mind pondered the beauties of nature and the political conspiracies in the Chozha land, his subconscious mind was immersed in thoughts of the woman he had seen. Now, as the conscious and the subconscious coalesced, the beauties of nature began to remind him of her form. The smoothness of the bamboo reminded him of her shoulders. The lilies in the pools became her eyes. He doubted if the lotus could be compared to her face. As bees hovered over the blooms clustering on the trees beside the river, he wondered if their humming could equal the lilt in her voice. 'Such metaphors are part of poetic usage.' He shrugged. 'But what are these scenes compared to her beauty? When I saw her I was thrilled to the core. Even now, as I think of her, my heart begins to soar. Can these bees and flowers arouse the same rapture . . . ! Whom did she resemble–the woman I saw in the astrologer's house . . . who spoke to me by the river . . . ? Could it be . . . ? No! This is madness, it can never be true! But why not? She may be Kundavai Devi herself! Did I behave like a barbarian before the lady whose fame pervades the land from the Vindhya hills to the Ilankai island? How can I face her again with the letter from the prince?'

Vandiyatevan travelled along the Kaveri with these random thoughts until he reached Tiruvaiyaru. The splendour of the town stole his heart. He made enquiries to verify that it was the same town he had heard so much about. Surely those reports had underestimated its grandeur. 'You can never see such trees in Tondaimandalam. Or such giant fruit hanging from the jackfruit trees. Somehow, monkey troops manage to find these verdant regions. Look at the agility with which they jump from branch to branch! What did the poet Sambandar say? "Women dance on the stage in the street corners of Tiruvaiyaru. The drums synchronize with the beats of their songs. Mistaking the drumbeats for cracks of thunder, monkeys clamber to the topmost branches to see if the rains are coming."

'This is so true even today! Monkeys are scampering up the trees! Sweet medleys of song and dance waft from the town. The chimes of the anklets mingle with the instruments—*yazh, kuzhal, tannumai* and *muzhavu drums*. This is not the kuravai koothu of Kadambur. This is the classical genre of Bharatanatyam, accompanied by sophisticated music. There! You hear not only the tinkling of the dancers' anklets but also the tap of the conductor's baton.'

As batons twirl to lead their moves,
Bangles tinkling in their arms,
The smiling girls dance on and on,
Their darting eyes like gliding fish,
As arching eyebrows rise and fall.
Arrayed in all their finery
They trip the light fantastic toe
. . . This is Tiruvaiyaru.

'Ah! The poet Sambandar was a great devotee of Siva. More importantly, he was a fine connoisseur. Why, even today, Tiruvaiyaru appears to be exactly as he had pictured it. I must enjoy these shows of music and dance, and offer worship to the god and goddess at the temple. Ah! Look at the crowds of devotees praying on the banks of the Kaveri! How bright the streaks of sacred ash on their bodies! At times, their cries of the mantra 'Nama sivaya' drown the sounds of music and dance. There! Someone is singing a tevaram verse in such an appealing voice! Surely, this place has been created by the Lord solely for music and the arts! I must certainly spend a whole day here to see all the sights.'

Something caught Vandiyatevan's attention just as he came to this decision. From the west came a palanquin on the path beside the Kaveri, with a few guards marching in the front and at the rear. A sudden suspicion stopped Vandiyatevan in his tracks. As the palanquin drew near him, he saw the palm tree emblem on its curtain. It had undoubtedly come from Kadambur but by a different route from the one he had taken. However, Pazhuvettaraiyar was not to be seen. He must have decided to break his journey elsewhere along the way.

The palanquin turned to the south, towards Tanjavur. Vandiyatevan dropped the idea of staying in Tiruvaiyaru. A lucky opportunity could present itself if he followed the palanquin. Surely, the bearers would put it down at some point, and Prince Madhurantakan would come out. Vandiyatevan would then be able to make his acquaintance. That might help him to enter the Tanjavur Fort and meet the emperor. He might have to indulge in some clever talk and role-play. But could he succeed in his mission without employing tricks and stratagems?

Vandiyatevan followed it at a distance. But he did not get the chance he hoped for as the palanquin crossed the four rivers between the Kaveri and Tanjavur without stopping anywhere. There! They were now near enough to see the

Tanjavur Fort and its portals. Once the palanquin entered the fort, he could say goodbye to his hopes. He must do something before that happened, something that demanded pluck. What would happen if he did? Would his head be cut off? So what? What was the use of returning without completing the mission he had taken up? Vandiyatevan was also motivated by the indignation he felt when he thought of Madhurantakan. He was impelled by a great urge to tear the curtain and expose the person inside; to show that it was no woman, but a grown man.

As Vandiyatevan wondered how he could accomplish this, he found one of the men in the retinue lagging behind and staring at him.

'Who are you? Why have you been following us from Tiruvaiyaru?' the man asked.

'Ayya, I am not following you. I am going to Tanjavur. Is this not the road to Tanjavur?'

'Yes. But this route is reserved for very important persons. There is a different road for others.'

'Is that so? I too am a very important person,' Vandiyatevan said.

The man smiled and said, 'Why are you going to Tanjavur?'

'My uncle lives in Tanjavur. He has fallen sick. I am going to visit him.'

'Does your uncle work for the government?'

'No, he is an innkeeper.'

'I see. All right. But why don't you go ahead instead of following us?'

'What pleasure do I gain from gazing at your back all the time? My horse is tired, Ayya!'

While talking, Vandiyatevan managed to come up close to the palanquin. That was when the idea that he had been driving his brain to discover came to him in a flash. He dug his spurs into the horse's flanks, yanked the reins and drove it straight at the men bearing the palanquin in the rear. They turned to look at him in dismay. Vandiyatevan yelled, 'Maharaja! Your palanquin bearers are attacking my horse. Ayo!'

The curtain screening the palanquin began to rustle.

22

The Velakkara Corps

The outer curtain of the palanquin, bearing the palm tree emblem, was drawn aside. Then the inner silk curtain started moving. A hand with the golden sheen that Vandiyatevan had seen before, came into view. He jumped down at once, realizing that it would be unseemly to remain mounted. 'Your Highness! Prince! Your palanquin-bearers . . . ' said he as he ran to the palanquin.

He looked up. He stared. He blinked. Then he stared hard once again at the dazzling sight. His tongue tied itself into knots. His throat ran dry. He began to babble, 'No . . . no! You are . . . Pazhuvur P-p-prin-s-s-s q-q-ueen! Pazhuvur Q-q-q-uee-ee-ee-cess-s-s-s . . . ! Your horse hit my pa-pa-lanquin!'

All this happened in the blink of an eye. The armed guards accompanying the palanquin now rushed to surround Vandiyatevan, whose hand instinctively reached for the sword at his waist. His eyes, however, refused to tear themselves away from the face that was shimmering with all the lustre of the moon.

Contrary to his expectations, what Vandiyatevan saw in the palanquin was the form of a woman. A real woman. But what a woman! Vandiyatevan had never imagined that such beauty could exist in the terrestrial world. It was beauty that could drive the beholder insane!

Fortunately, something clicked in his brain. A weird notion darted into his mind. He decided to put it to use.

Clearing his throat with a huge effort and forcing his tongue to regain its power of speech, he said, 'Please forgive me. You are the younger queen of Pazhuvur. It was to see you that I came all the way.'

A little smile played about the Pazhuvur queen's lips. The lotus bud, closed until then, began to unfold slowly and display a row of pearls. The magnetic power in that smile made our young man reel and totter.

Meanwhile, the men waited for orders from their mistress. A gesture sent them back to stand at a distance. Two men held Vandiyatevan's horse.

The woman in the palanquin looked at Vandiyatevan. Two sharp spear points pierced his heart. 'Yes, I am the younger queen of Pazhuvur,' she said.

Vandiyatevan wondered if there was some drug in her voice to make his head spin as dizzily as it did. Was it possible to blend in a woman's voice, the softness of silk, the intoxication of liquor, the sweetness of wild honey and the glitter of monsoon lightning?

She continued, 'What did you say? You complained about the palanquin-bearers . . . Did you say that they rammed the palanquin onto your horse?'

The mocking smile playing about her lips showed that she was thoroughly enjoying the joke. Taking heart from the smile, Vandiyatevan replied, 'Yes, great queen! That's what they did. My horse took fright.'

'You too seem to have taken fright. Go to the priest in the Durga temple. He will treat you with neem leaves to make you snap out of it.'

By this time, Vandiyatevan had overcome his trepidation and even begun to laugh.

The young queen's expression changed. Moonlight turned into flames of fire.

'No more games. Tell me the truth. Why did you stop the palanquin?'

This question had to be answered, and satisfactorily. If not . . . ? But luckily, Vandiyatevan had his answer ready. In a voice deliberately lowered to remain out of others' earshot, Vandiyatevan whispered as if he was sharing a secret, 'Devi! Nandini Devi! Azhvarkadiyan . . . Yes, Tirumalai himself . . . He asked me to meet you. Pardon me. I used this ruse for that purpose . . .'

As he was speaking, Vandiyatevan's eager eyes stared hard at Nandini, trying to gauge her response. He was throwing a stone at a fruiting tree. Would it hit the target? Bring the fruit down? Or bounce back to hit him on the head? Or initiate something more unpredictable?

The queen's dark eyebrows went up. Her eyes reflected surprise and doubt. She arrived at a quick decision.

'It is not safe to talk in the open street. Come to the palace tomorrow. We can discuss everything at length,' she said.

Vandiyatevan was overjoyed. Mission accomplished? But half measures were of no use; he had to go all the way. 'Devi! Devi!' he cried. 'They won't let me into the fort or the palace. What should I do?'

The Pazhuvur queen took her silken purse and drew out an ivory ring. 'Show this, and they will let you into the fort and my palace,' she said as she gave it to him. Vandiyatevan glanced at the ring with the image of the palm tree and looked up again to thank her. But the curtain had closed. 'Ah! The shadow creeps very slowly to eclipse the moon. But this moon has been swallowed whole in an instant!' Vandiyatevan sighed.

A voice soft as silk came from within the palanquin. 'Don't follow me anymore. It can be dangerous.'

The palanquin started moving. The men marched in front and at the rear as before. Vandiyatevan's eyes noted that the man who had talked to him earlier shot several backward glances at him.

Vandiyatevan's thoughts were circling the bewitching woman within the palanquin. He asked himself if what he had seen and heard in the past few minutes was true. Or, merely an illusion, a dream of fantasy. Could a woman of such spellbinding beauty exist in the world?

The legends spoke of the celestial maidens Rambha, Urvasi and Menaka. Their beauty had distracted even the sages from their meditation. But in the real world . . . ? The widespread gossip about Pazhuvettaraiyar being enslaved by this enchantress must be true. He was an old man, wrinkled and grey. She was a young and lovely woman. Surely, he would do anything for a single smile from her!

Vandiyatevan was lost in ruminations for a long time. Then he mounted his horse and rode slowly towards the Tanjavur Fort.

The sun was setting when he reached the fort's main gateway. The city lay widespread outside the fort with many market streets beside it, where a multitude of goods were being sold. They bustled with people going to and fro, buyers and sellers of goods, bullock carts and horse-drawn chariots. There were streets where people engaged in different professions lived. Vandiyatevan was eager to explore those streets in the new capital of the Chozha empire, and learn all about the citizens and their lifestyle. But he had no time for such excursions. First of all, he had to complete the task on hand. Only then could he think of sightseeing.

Vandiyatevan approached the main portals of the fort. The gigantic doors were shut. Sentries were regulating the crowds. Instead of going about their business, men, women, children and even senior citizens stood by the roadside as if eagerly waiting for some procession.

The space in front of the gateway had been cleared with only the sentries standing beside the doors. Vandiyatevan was curious to know more. But he did not want to give rise to an unnecessary row by accosting the sentries when everyone was standing away. His task was too important for him to get into meaningless spats. So, he stood in a corner from where he had a clear view of the gateway. The heady scent of jasmine rose beside him. He turned and saw a young man with ash streaks and *rudraksha** beads round his neck, standing with two baskets of flowers in his hands.

'Why is everyone standing away from the street? Anything about to happen?'

'Ayya, are you not from these parts?'

'No. I belong to Tondaimandalam.'

'Oh, that's why . . . ! It may be wise for you to dismount and stand beside the horse.'

---

* Dried seeds of the fruit of the utrasum bead tree, associated with Siva, strung and worn for protection and used as a rosary.

Vandiyatevan jumped down to converse more easily with the youth.

'Tambi, why did you ask me to dismount?'

'The Velakkara troop is about to come out of the fort after an audience with the maharaja. That is why these people are waiting.'

'To watch the spectacle?'

'Yes.'

'Why can't I watch it on horseback?'

'You can. But it would be a problem if the Velakkara soldiers saw you.'

'What problem? Will they carry my horse away?'

'Both horse and rider. They are dangerous men.'

'Will they be let off if they snatch a horse and man away?'

'How can they not be let off? In this town, the Velakkara troop's word is law. No questions asked. Even the Pazhuvettaraiyars do not interfere with the Velakkara men.'

A clamour rose from behind the gates. *Nagaras* boomed, *parai* drums throbbed and *kombu* horns blared, setting up loud echoes as they mingled with ceremonial slogans raised by hundreds of men.

Vandiyatevan knew all about the Velakkara troops. It was an important institution in the ancient Tamizh land, particularly in Chozha country. The Velakkaras were the bodyguards of the ruling king but were quite different from other security personnel. They were men who had vowed to risk their lives to protect the king. If the king lost his life due to their carelessness, their oath bound them to cut off their own head before the sanctum of the goddess Durga. It was natural for men who had taken such a bloodcurdling vow to be granted privileges denied to others.

The gates opened with a clang. First came two horseriders holding a flag in their right hand depicting bizarre images—a tiger and a crown, and beneath them, a sword and a severed head on the altar. The flag terrified the beholder.

Behind the flag-bearers came two massive bulls bearing large *bherikai* drums on their backs, with two men banging upon them. Fifty soldiers followed, beating the *siruparai*, *perumparai* and *tambattam* drums. Another fifty walked behind them with resounding kombus. Last of all came a company of soldiers thundering slogans. These cries brought goosebumps to everyone as they rose from a thousand voices and reverberated through the fort's massive portals. Many voices in the crowds took up the slogans.

Hail Emperor Parantaka Sundara Chozha!
Hail! Hail!
Hail king of Tanjavur!
Hail! Hail!
Hail vanquisher of Veerapandiyan!
Hail! Hail!
Hail conqueror of Madurai, Tondaimandalam and Ilankai!
Hail! Hail!
May the tribe of Karikal Valavan be ever victorious!
Hail! Hail!
May the great and glorious goddess Durga bring victory!
Hail! Hail!
May the tiger flag conquer the earth!
Hail! Hail!
Vetrivel! Veeravel!

The sound and fury continued through the entire spectacle of the Velakkara corps marching out of the gateway, proceeding through the street and disappearing into the distance.

23

Amudan's Mother

The Velakkara troops marched through the main market street. Some of the soldiers began to indulge in their own little shenanigans. One of them popped into a confectionery, grabbed a basket of sweets, distributed them among his companions and thrust the basket upside down over the shopkeeper's head. The soldiers and onlookers hooted with laughter. Another soldier snatched a basket of flowers from an elderly woman and started scattering them, announcing, 'Look! It's raining flowers!' His companions jumped, laughed and made a racket as they tried to 'catch' the flowers. One of the soldiers stopped a bullock cart, untied the animal and drove it away. The frightened bullock bumped into people and pushed them to the ground as it ran through the streets. This too was greeted with great big guffaws.

Watching these sports, Vandiyatevan thought, 'Ah! These men indulge in devilry just as Pazhuvettaraiyar's men do. Their games make trouble for others. Thank goodness I escaped unnoticed.' But he saw that there was a major difference between the two factions. The people did not object to the

Velakkara men's behaviour; in fact, they relished their hijinks and joined in the fun.

When Vandiyatevan turned to find out more from his interlocutor, he found that the boy had disappeared into the noisy crowd.

Vandiyatevan learnt that no one was allowed to enter the fort after the departure of the Velakkara troops. Only members of the royal family, ministers and squadron leaders could enter at any time of the day or night. Members of the Pazhuvettaraiyars' household too enjoyed that privilege. He changed his mind about getting into the fort before nightfall. He did not want to test the power of the signet ring. Better to spend the night seeing the sights outside and enter the fort the next day. In any case, there was no possibility of handing over his message to the king at night.

It was evening by then. Hundreds of street lamps had begun to light the streets. Vandiyatevan took his time to explore the streets circling the fort. His exhausted horse had to get some rest soon. Otherwise, it would be of no use the next day. He had to find some comfortable lodging.

Tanjavur was a new and growing metropolis. Its streets were packed with noisy crowds of people going about their varied businesses. Many had come from villages and towns and from regions recently absorbed into the Chozha kingdom. There were visitors from various kingdoms situated between the east coast and the west coast, and between the rivers Porunai and Palar. Here and there, men from beyond the Vindhya mountains could be seen along with those who had crossed the ocean from lands beyond.

The sweet stalls had customers swarming like flies. Bananas and other fruits lay in mountainous piles, while the heaps of mullai, malli, athi and shenbagam flowers were surrounded by women buzzing like the bees themselves.

As he passed the flower sellers, Vandiyatevan recalled the youth with the flower baskets. Just as he thought how convenient it would be if he ran into him again, he saw the youngster walking down the street. Vandiyatevan dismounted and approached him.

'Tambi, your baskets are empty. Sold all the flowers?'

'I don't sell flowers. I am going home after delivering them for the puja at the temple.'

'To which temple do you make this offering?'

'Have you heard of the Talikulathar temple?'

'Yes. Is it a big temple?'

'No. A small one. It is the Durga temple that has been famous for quite some time now. That is where worship, offerings, sacrifices and festivals happen on a grand scale. Members of the royal family and the Pazhuvettaraiyar household frequent it. The Talikulathar temple does not have the same draw. Not many people come to worship there.'

'Do you get a stipend for delivering flowers there?'

'Our family has received this stipend from the time of my grandfather, during the reign of King Gandaraditta. Now my mother and I perform this service.'

'Is the temple built of bricks and now rebuilt with stone?' Vandiyatevan asked. All along the way he had seen temples where bricks were being replaced with stones.

'Right now it is a structure of bricks. They say that, soon, it is to be rebuilt with stone. Queen Sembian Mahadevi of Pazhaiyarai wants to launch the restoration at once. But . . . '

'But what?'

'Why repeat idle rumours? Don't they say, look out before you talk during the day and stay dumb at night? This is a city square, with crowds milling around us . . .'

'Best place to share secrets. No one will hear us in this bustling crowd.'

The young man looked at Vandiyatevan with some suspicion and said, 'What secrets?'

'This boy is very bright. It would be useful to make friends with him. I can glean much information from him. But I must not make him suspicious,' Vandiyatevan thought and spoke reassuringly, 'Obviously, we have no secrets of any kind. Never mind. Tambi, I have travelled a long way and am thoroughly worn out. I must find a place to sleep in peace tonight. Where can I stay? Can you suggest a good place to lodge?'

'No dearth of lodgings in this huge town. So many inns! There are special inns for those who come from foreign countries. However, if you like . . .'

'Tambi, what is your name?'

'Amudan, Sendan Amudan.'

'What a wonderful name! Amudan! Nectar! I can taste nectar when I hear your name. Were you not going to say that I can stay at your house?'

'Yes! But how did you know that?'

'Sorcery! That's how. Where is your house?'

'My house is in a flower garden outside the city.'

'Ah! It must be your house for me. I cannot endure the din of the city through the night. Moreover, I would like to meet the good woman who bore a good son like you.'

'My mother is indeed a good woman but an unlucky one.'

'Why do you say that? Perhaps your father . . .'

'Yes, my father is dead. But that's not all. My mother was born unlucky. You will know why when you meet her. Come, let us go.'

In half an hour, they reached the garden outside the city. Vandiyatevan felt singularly and happily drowsed by the fragrance of the night flowers. The din of the city was barely audible.

There was a tiled cottage within the garden, with two huts beside it where the gardeners lived. Amudan asked one of them to tether and feed the horse.

Then he took Vandiyatevan inside. The moment he saw Amudan's mother, Vandiyatevan knew what her misfortune was. The lady could neither speak nor hear. But he saw compassion and affection on her face, along with the gleam of a sharp intelligence. Is it not one of the conundrums of life that people with a physical disability may possess exceptional intellectual attributes?

From Amudan's signs, the lady made out that his guest was an outlander. She welcomed him with an expression of kindness.

A little later, she served them dinner on plantain leaves. First came idiappam and sweet coconut milk. In his entire life, Vandiyatevan had never eaten anything so delicious. He finished ten or twelve idiappams and a good measure of coconut milk. Then came a dish prepared with cornflour accompanied by tamarind curry. All the gorging could not satisfy his hunger, though he did end his meal only after consuming a large amount of rice with a larger serving of curd.

As they ate, Vandiyatevan gathered several bits of information from Amudan.

He learnt that the palaces and the retinues of Periya Pazhuvettaraiyar and Chinna Pazhuvettaraiyar were in

Tanjavur. The royal treasury and granary were located in the city, along with the officials and accountants who maintained them. Chief Minister Aniruddha Brahmarayar, who had Sundara Chozha's trust and affection, and the officer who recorded the king's orders on palm leaves, were also within the fort. The sentries under Chinna Pazhuvettaraiyar's command, and hundreds of tax accountants under Periya Pazhuvettaraiyar's control, were all housed within the fort along with their families. Goldsmiths, silversmiths and gemstone traders were allotted quarters. The Durga temple was situated in a corner of the fort. Priests, temple dancers and others who served there lived close by.

'Are all the ministers within the fort now?' Vandiyatevan asked.

'How can they be? They will be in and out as they go about their tasks. Aniruddha Brahmarayar has not been in the city for some time now. It is rumoured that he has gone to the Chera land. Periya Pazhuvettaraiyar left four days ago. We hear that he went to the central region north of the Kollidam.'

'Would you know if he has returned?'

'This evening I saw the Pazhuvur queen's palanquin at the fort's entrance, but not Pazhuvettaraiyar. Perhaps he broke the journey somewhere along the way and may return tomorrow.'

'Tambi, doesn't Prince Madhurantakan also live within the fort?'

'Yes. His mansion is adjacent to Chinna Pazhuvettaraiyar's palace. After all, he is Chinna Pazhuvettaraiyar's son-in-law.'

'Is that so? I didn't know this until now.'

'Not many do. The wedding was conducted without fanfare in view of the emperor's poor health.'

'Is Madhurantakan in the fort now?'

'He must be. He doesn't go out much and the people don't get to see him too often. Reports say that he spends all his time in worship, prayer and meditation.'

'And yet he did get married after all this time.'

'Yes. It was a bit of a surprise. They also say that, after his marriage, the prince has undergone a complete change of mind. But what is it to us? Best not to talk about people in high places.'

Vandiyatevan was eager to know more, but he did not want to provoke suspicion by asking too much. Friendship with this innocent youth would prove to be of great help to him. He had been lucky to find such a lodging in Tanjavur. Why spoil things? Vandiyatevan was also fatigued by his long hours of travel. Staying awake through the previous night added to the fatigue. Sensing this, Amudan quickly made up a bed for him.

Just before sleep claimed him, the face of the younger queen of Pazhuvur came before his eyes. Such breathtaking beauty! Such radiance! Recalling how one look at her enchanting form had reduced him to unblinking paralysis reminded Vandiyatevan of another experience. In his childhood, he was once walking in the forest when, suddenly, he was confronted by a snake with its hood raised. Such irresistible beauty! Hypnotized by this spectacle, Vandiyatevan stood still, unable to blink or move. The hood went on swaying until his body began to sway along with it. Who knows how it might have ended but for a mongoose leaping in to pounce on the snake. They began to fight. Vandiyatevan made a run for it.

'Ugh! How stupid! Comparing the most beautiful woman in the world to a snake! One look at her tender face would make anyone forget hunger and thirst. How incredibly sweet the tones of her voice! How unique her beauty! And I am to see her tomorrow! But the other woman I saw in Kudantai? And beside the Arasalaru? Her face was refulgent and had a sparkling aura. But how different the two women were in their beauty! One had a face refracting majesty and nobility. The other's face is alluring and captivating.' Vandiyatevan's reflections on the two women were interrupted by a third woman. The omnipotent goddess of sleep brought him under her despotic rule.

24

The Crow and the Cuckoo

Having slept like a log all night, Vandiyatevan awoke well after sunrise. He had no mind to get up from bed. A sharp wind blew. The branches of the trees and shrubs rubbed noisily against one another. Aligned with their droning, a young man's melodious voice sang Sundarar's tevaram.

> Lord of the golden form
> A tiger skin at your waist
> The glistening konrai flower
> On your auburn locks . . .

Vandiyatevan opened his eyes. He saw konrai trees festooned with strings of golden flowers. He heard Sendan Amudan singing as he plucked them with a hooked pole. Amudan had bathed at dawn. His arms and forehead were smeared with sacred ash. He appeared to be the legendary Markandeyan, the devout young Saiva.

Vandiyatevan got up, ruing the fact that Amudan's mother could not hear her son's beautiful singing. Why couldn't he spend his life in bliss like Amudan, tending the garden and serving the lord? Why should he roam from place to place with sword and spear? Why should he be always ready to kill and to be killed? Soon, his thoughts changed. Was everyone in the world as good and high-minded as Amudan? What about thieves, thugs, scammers, double dealers and those who rejoice in tormenting the helpless? A governing regime was needed to subjugate them, and to maintain law and justice. The Velakkara corps was necessary to protect the state from harm. Agents like Vandiyatevan were needed to carry messages to kings. Yes. He must see Emperor Sundara Chozha without fail, on that very day. He had to accomplish this before Periya Pazhuvettaraiyar returned, or it would remain a pipedream.

Bathing in the lotus pond, Vandiyatevan dressed himself as best he could. How could he present himself to the emperor in everyday clothes? However, we cannot quite deny that the hope of seeing the young queen of Pazhuvur, rather than the emperor, goaded him in his anxiety to appear trim and well-groomed.

When Amudan left for the temple's morning puja, Vandiyatevan joined him. They walked; Vandiyatevan had decided not to take his horse. It must have its rest. Very soon, he might need to take the horse on a long journey.

He chatted with Amudan and acquired some more information. 'Don't you have any family apart from your mother?' he asked. Amudan replied, 'I do. My mother had a sister and a brother. The sister is dead. The brother serves the Kuzhagar temple at Kodikkarai. He is also the lighthouse keeper there. He has a son and a daughter. The daughter . . .'

'What about the daughter?'

'There is a strange streak in my family. Some of us are born dumb. Others sing well.'

'Your uncle's daughter is not dumb, is she?'

'No, no!'

'That means she sings well. Better than you?'

'What a question! It is like asking, "Can a cuckoo sing better than a crow?" When Poonkuzhali sings, the ocean stops breaking into waves and falls silent in order to hear her. Cows and goats and the wild beasts stand transfixed . . .'

'Poonkuzhali! Lovely name!'

'It's not the name alone that is lovely.'

'She must be lovely too. Otherwise, you wouldn't be so besotted.'

'The fawn and the peacock pale into insignificance before her. Goddesses will have to perform penances through many lifetimes before they can think of approaching anywhere near her in beauty.'

Vandiyatevan realized that Sendan Amudan's heart was not totally given over to his faith. 'Then she is the right bride for you. After all, she is your cousin. So, when is the wedding?'

'I will never say that she is right for me. I am unfit for her in every way. If they held a *swayamvaram** for Poonkuzhali to choose her groom as in the old days, the rulers of the fifty-six kingdoms would compete for her. Even the gods may come down from the world above as they did for the legendary Damayanti. Though this may not happen in this kaliyuga of ours . . .'

'So, you would reject her even if she wished to marry you?'

'What are you saying? If god appears before me and asks, "Do you want to go to heaven in your human form as the poet Sundarar did, or do you want to stay on earth with

* Self-choice ceremony mentioned in the epics, where a princess chooses her spouse from the invited guests of kings and princes.

Poonkuzhali?", I will certainly choose the latter. But what is the use?'

'What do you mean? If you agree, the marriage is almost decided. Does anyone bother about the girl's acquiescence? For example, would Pazhuvettaraiyar's marriage have taken place with the consent of the girl who is now his young queen?'

'*Anna!** Why should we talk about people in high places? I am going to warn you, seriously. You are entering the fort. Don't talk about the Pazhuvettaraiyars there. If you do, you invite danger.'

'Tambi! You are trying to scare me!'

'I speak the truth. The two Pazhuvettaraiyars rule this land. There is no authority higher than theirs.'

'Are you saying that the emperor does not have greater power?'

'The emperor is sick. People say that he never overrules the Pazhuvettaraiyars. He does not even heed his own sons' words in this matter.'

'Is that so? The Pazhuvettaraiyar influence must be great indeed! They did not have this power two years ago.'

'No. Since the emperor came to Tanjavur, the Pazhuvettaraiyars have acquired boundless authority. They say that Chief Minister Aniruddha Brahmarayar is so fed up that he has gone away to the Pandya country.'

'Tambi, do you know why the emperor shifted from Pazhaiyarai to Tanjavur?'

'I will tell you what I know. Three years ago, Veerapandiyan died in the war. At that time, the Chozha army perpetrated

---

* Elder brother, also used to address any older man with affection and familiarity.

great atrocities in the Pandya land. Well, that is the price we pay when we make war. Madurai was assimilated into the Chozha kingdom. But those who were close to Veerapandiyan have vowed to take their revenge somehow. The Pazhuvettaraiyars brought the king to Tanjavur, declaring that he could not be protected if he remained in Pazhaiyarai. The Tanjavur Fort is bigger, its fortifications and garrisons are stronger. Moreover, the physicians suggested that Tanjavur was better for the king's health.

'Everyone talks about Sundara Chozha's illness. But no one knows what it is.'

'The emperor had a stroke. Both his legs are paralysed.'

'Does it mean that he cannot walk at all?

'No. He cannot walk. He cannot ride a horse or an elephant. He is bedridden. He can only be carried on a palanquin, which is painful for him. That is why the emperor never leaves the palace. They say that his mind too has been affected for some time now.'

'How terribly sad!'

'You are not allowed to say that, Anna! The Pazhuvettaraiyars will call it sedition and ordain punishment.'

Vandiyatevan said to himself, 'Pazhuvettaraiyar! Pazhuvettaraiyar! Talk to anyone, anywhere and it is all about the Pazhuvettaraiyars! They may be mighty warriors, but the emperor should not have entrusted them with the royal granary, state treasury, the city's defence, the intelligence division and just about everything else. Acquiring all these powers has turned them into conspirators. Who knows what success their plots may achieve? I must make every effort to stop them from succeeding. If possible, I must warn the emperor . . .'

They had reached the entrance of the fort by then. Sendan Amudan left his new friend and went to the Talikulathar temple. Vandiyatevan approached the portals of the fort, his mind building its own castles in the air.

25

Inside the Fort

The morning hour saw vendors, accountants, government officials and others trying to crowd into the fort. The guards let them in one by one, after checking each and every one with a brash display of authority.

But the ring with the palm tree emblem proved to be as powerful as the magical rings of fiction. All our young man had to do was to flash it, and the guards instantaneously opened one of the big portals and ushered him in with great deference. Vandiyatevan entered the fort.

For a short while, Vandiyatevan remained lost in wonderment.

Kanchi, the capital of the old Pallava empire, had often faced military attacks. Its palaces, mansions and public buildings were old and falling to pieces. They had ornate sculptural embellishments, but most of them were lying in ruins. Like the last blooms on a dying tree, the mansions restored by Aditta Karikalan served only to highlight the city's state of dilapidation.

With its new mansions and new public buildings, Tanjavur offered a complete contrast to Kanchi. Between the gleaming white mansions, a few buildings of red brick shone like rubies embedded among pearls and diamonds. Their gardens had trees growing lush and thick in the rich, red soil. The luxuriant, multigreen foliage on the asoka, peepal, banyan and neem trees soothed the eye and invigorated the mind. Surely, this brand new city was constructed by no ordinary architect, but by a powerful magician. Entering it was to feel revitalized, joyful and inexplicably proud.

Having seen the crowds thronging outside the fort, and the strict rules and regulations for visitors' entry, Vandiyatevan had imagined that the streets within would be practically empty. But they were bustling. Horses and horse-drawn chariots made the ground quake. As elephants ambled by, the bells around their necks echoed across the city. The vendors' cries shattered the ear. The resounding *bherikai* drums, the bells pealing at every hour, and the medley of instruments and singing voices, all mingled to create a tumultuous and festive ambience. Well, here was a city! The capital of an empire that was expanding day by day!

Vandiyatevan thought that asking for directions would invite ridicule. 'New to the city, are you!' they would laugh. Anyone who wanted to be directed to the royal palace would be put down as a country bumpkin. It would not be impossible to find his way on his own.

Wherever he looked, he saw domed mansions with festoons and flags. Most of the flags sported tiger and palm tree emblems, and crackled as they were tossed by the sharp winds. A huge tiger flag flew above them all, seeming to touch the clouds. Guessing it to be the royal palace, Vandiyatevan walked towards it, thinking about what he had to do.

The first task was to hand over the missive to the emperor in person and convey Prince Karikalan's verbal message to him. It would not be possible to see the emperor without Chinna Pazhuvettaraiyar's permission. How could he get it? God helped him to enter the fort, but could he leave everything to divine guidance? He must come up with a strategy of his own. What could it be? After all, he had inherited his brain from a long line of Vaanan kings. Let it rise to the occasion now. Let it unleash its power of invention! For, the faculty of imagination empowered not only those who wrote poems and epics but also agents involved in matters of state, as he was.

As soon as he crossed the fort, Vandiyatevan asked a sentry at the gateway, 'Has Pazhuvettaraiyar returned?'

'Which Pazhuvettaraiyar do you mean? The younger brother is in the palace.'

'Don't I know? I meant the elder brother who had gone to the central region.'

'Oh! The central region? That I didn't know. The younger queen's palanquin returned last evening. The great chief has not yet come back. We have news that he may be here by nightfall.'

That was good news. Somehow, he had to hand over the letter to the emperor before Pazhuvettaraiyar's return. How? An idea dawned in his mind. The anxious look disappeared. His face was lit up by a mischievous smile.

He did not have to wander a great deal to find the emperor's palace. He went towards the tiger flag flying high above all the others and reached the entrance.

What a palace! Like the palace of the king of gods! Or the palace of the mythical Vikramaditya of Ujjaini city! Marvels of sculpture adorned the entrance pillars. Among them, two horses stood with their front legs raised high, as though they were about to leap.

There were several entrances to the palace, each guarded by sentries on foot and horseback. Many people carefully kept their distance from them as they went about their business. A few approached the gates, stared at the entrance and the flag flying above, and spoke softly to each other. The sentries dispersed the crowds that lingered overlong.

Vandiyatevan approached the sentries unhesitatingly, briskly and with a swagger. But two horses came to stand before him, with their faces touching one another, and the guards crossed their spears to bar the way.

Vandiyatevan showed his magic ring. That was all! The men shed their arrogance and pride. Three men examined the ring. 'All right,' one of them said. The spears swung back and made way for him. Vandiyatevan strode in boldly.

But who knew how many more barriers there would be? Where was Chinna Pazhuvettaraiyar? How could he find out? Whom should he ask? How could he discover the whereabouts of the ailing emperor in this vast palace all by himself?

Vandiyatevan noticed some ten to twelve men walking behind him. They came to a halt near the guards. They wore garments of costly silk, ear studs, strings of pearls and rich pendants around the neck. Some of them had smeared themselves with sacred ash. Others had streaks of *javvadu*, *kumkumam* and *chandanam** on their foreheads. Why, they must be poets! This surmise was confirmed when one of the guards announced, 'The poets are here! Make way!' Turning to his fellow guard, he said, 'Chinna Pazhuvettaraiyar is in the great hall. Take them to him.'

---

* Perfumed powder, red turmeric powder and sandal paste.

To the poets, he added, 'If you receive gifts, return by this route. If not, find another exit.' This wisecrack provoked guffaws among the men.

Vandiyatevan was happy that things were taking a good turn. The poets would take him to Chinna Pazhuvettaraiyar. After that, he would have to see how ingenuity and luck would carry the day.

Vandiyatevan followed the poets.

26

'Danger! Danger!'

Vandiyatevan entered the great hall before the poets did. He guessed that the man with the regal appearance on the high seat must be Chinna Pazhuvettaraiyar. Around him stood many men with their arms folded deferentially. One of them waited with a sheaf of documents. The accountant was ready to render the tally. The leaders of the security forces waited for their orders of the day. Servants hung about to do his bidding. A couple of attendants stood behind him, fanning him with whisks. A man stood by, holding a box of betel leaves.

Though Vandiyatevan was second to none in displaying style and aplomb, he approached Pazhuvettaraiyar with humility.

The younger brother seemed a cut above the elder in his commanding presence.

Brightening as soon as he saw our young man, he asked, 'Tambi! Who are you? Where do you come from?'

Chinna Pazhuvettaraiyar's grim face always lit up when he saw young warriors. He was eager to get all the brave youth of the realm into his security forces.

'Commander, I come from Kanchi. Prince Aditta Karikalan has sent a missive,' Vandiyatevan answered in a meek voice.

The word 'Kanchi' brought a hard look to his face as Chinna Pazhuvettaraiyar repeated his query, 'What did you say?'

'I have come from Kanchi with the prince's message.'

'Where is it? Give it to me!' Though he spoke carelessly, his voice betrayed some perturbation.

Vandiyatevan said with great deference, 'Commander, the missive is for the emperor.'

Chinna Pazhuvettaraiyar took the scroll nonchalantly, but he looked at it eagerly as he handed it to the man standing by to be read aloud. Then he muttered to himself, 'Nothing new.'

'Commander, the letter . . .'

'I will give it to the emperor.'

'No. I was asked to hand it over in person . . .'

'Is that so? I am not to be trusted? Did Prince Aditta Karikalan say so?'

'The prince did not say so. It is your brother's order.'

'What? What! Where did you see him?'

'On the way, I spent a night at Sambuvaraiyar's mansion in Kadambur. I met him there. It was he who sent me here with this ring.'

'Ah! Why didn't you tell me this before? You spent the night at Kadambur? Who else was there?'

'Dignitaries from Mazhapadi, Tirumunaipadi, Nadunadu and other places had gathered there.'

'Wait! Wait! Let us talk about this at leisure. Go and hand over this scroll to the emperor now. The poets will be there all too soon. They chatter endlessly . . .' said Chinna

Pazhuvettaraiyar, and added to an orderly, 'Take this boy to the emperor!'

Vandiyatevan followed the man into the palace.

The throne of the Chozha empire whose borders resounded on three sides with the tumult of the waves, had now turned into a sickbed. Emperor Parantaka Sundara Chozha was reclining on the throne. Though he had delegated the kingdom's administration to others and was undergoing treatment for his illness, there were a few occasions when, for the welfare of the kingdom, it became essential for him to be seen by others, such as ministers, generals and members of the Velakkara corps.

Vandiyatevan was struck dumb when he saw the emperor. The warrior famed for his invincibility on so many battlefronts, the king hailed in town and country as 'Sundara' Chozha, who rivalled the gods in beauty, now lay gaunt and emaciated, wasted by illness. Tears came to his eyes. He went closer to the emperor and handed over the scroll with reverence and devotion.

The emperor asked in a feeble voice, 'Where do you come from? Who sent this?'

'Your majesty, I come from Kanchi. The message is from Prince Aditta Karikalan.'

The emperor's face lit up at once. Looking at Empress Vanamadevi–the daughter of the feudal chieftain Malayaman of Tirukovilur–seated next to him, he said, 'Devi! A letter from your son!'

He read it and winced as he spoke again, 'Ah! Your son has built a palace of gold. He wants you and me to spend some time in it. Devi! See what your son has done! Emperor Parantaka, my grandfather, who was famed throughout the world, gifted all the gold accumulated in the palace to roof the

Chidambaram temple. None of our ancestors had ever built a palace of gold for themselves. They thought that building a temple was far more important than building a palace. But Karikalan! What penance can we perform for redemption from this sacrilege?'

The empress's face had brightened a little when she saw the letter from her son. Now it drooped again. She could not reply.

Gathering courage and confidence, Vandiyatevan managed to say, 'Your majesty! Your son's action is not so wrong after all. To a son, his father and mother are akin to the gods. Your son has done the right thing.'

Sundara Chozha said with a smile, 'Tambi, I don't know who you are. You seem to be very bright and intelligent. But even if a son regards his parents to be godlike, they are not gods to anyone else. A golden temple should be erected only for the god who is worshipped by everyone.'

'Your Majesty, to a son, his father is god. To his subjects, the king is god. Therefore, even from this point of view, building a golden palace for you is an appropriate thing to do.'

Looking at his queen again, Sundara Chozha said, 'Devi! See how quick-witted this boy is! We don't have to worry about our Aditta if he has such men around him. Nor need we be anxious about his brashness and recklessness.'

Then, turning to Vandiyatevan, he said, 'Tambi, whether it was right or wrong to have built the palace of gold, I cannot travel to Kanchi. Don't you see I am bedridden? I cannot undertake a long journey. It is Aditta who must visit me. I long to see him. Come again tomorrow. I will have the reply ready for him.'

Vandiyatevan realized that a crowd was approaching the royal chamber. The gang of poets! Perhaps Chinna

Pazhuvettaraiyar was accompanying them. Once they arrived, Vandiyatevan would not be able to say what he felt he had to say. Deciding that he had to encapsulate everything in a few brief sentences, Vandiyatevan said, 'Your Majesty! Please hear me out. You must leave Tanjavur at once. Here, there's danger all around you. Danger! Danger!'

As he was speaking, Chinna Pazhuvettaraiyar entered the royal audience chamber. The poets followed him.

The commander of the fort heard the last two words spoken by Vandiyatevan. His face flamed in anger.

27

The Court Poets

And now, let us salute the great company of the bards! Minstrels par excellence! Scholars who have dived into the unfathomable depths of Tamizh learning! Descendants of the mystic poet Agattiyar, past masters of *Tolkappiyam*,* old hands at *Tirukkural*,† specialists in *Silappathikaram*! Pundits who know the five great Tamizh sagas *and* all the *Sangam* works backwards. Poets themselves, they are also masters of the semantics of poetry. Their worth may be gauged from the fact that any collection of their original outpourings would keep zillions of termites alive and kicking through countless centuries.

The group of venerable bards came into the presence of the king. They showered their good wishes on him. 'Hail!

---

* 'Ancient Literature' (1 CE–4 CE), a treatise on grammar and poetics, presupposing the existence of literature far older.

† A classic Tamil text, universal and secular in content, comprising short aphoristic couplets (*kural*) on virtue (*aram*), wealth (*porul*) and love (*inbam*), attributed to Valluvar or Tiruvalluvar.

Hail! Hail Sundara Chozha, emperor of the seven worlds! Hail the beheader of Veerapandiyan! Hail the benefactor of bards! Hail the patron of poets! Hail the grandson of Parantaka, the great connoisseur king!'

The emperor did not much care for the noisy salutations. But, disregarding his illness and distaste for praise, he tried to stand up to welcome the visitors.

At once, Chinna Pazhuvettaraiyar came forward to say, 'Your Majesty! The bards are here to see you and offer their respects, not to trouble you. Please do not strain yourself.'

'Yes! Yes! Your Majesty! King of kings! We would not like to inconvenience you in the least,' said Nallan Sathanar, the leader of the group.

'I am delighted to see you after a long time. Please take your seat. You must recite some verses before you leave,' said the king, who was a great lover of the Tamizh tongue.

Everyone sat down on the plush carpet spread out on the floor. Seizing the opportunity, Vandiyatevan squatted down along with them. He did not have the heart to leave without telling the king what he had on his mind. Perhaps, if he waited, he would get another chance.

Chinna Pazhuvettaraiyar noticed this. At first, he wanted to dismiss him. Then he decided that it would be best to have the man under his watch. So he chose to ignore him. He decided that after the poets left, he would take him aside and find out exactly what he was saying to the maharaja. The words 'Danger! Danger!' continued to ring in his ears.

Meanwhile, emperor Sundara Chozha was telling the poets, 'It has been quite some time since I heard any Tamizh poetry. My ears yearn for it. Have you brought any new poems with you today?'

A bard stood up at once and said, 'Your Majesty! I am here from the Buddhist monastery in Ulagapuram which bears your name. Buddhists all over the Tamizh realm acclaim you, a Siva worshipper, for making donations to the Buddhist monastery. Ever since they learnt about your ill health, the monks have been anxiously praying for your well-being. Please allow me to repeat that prayer song.'

'Please do. I am waiting to hear it,' the emperor said.

The bard sang the verse.

May his majesty
The gracious Sundara Chozha
The Lord of Nandipuri
Providing shade and shelter
To the adherents of the Buddha
Grow in power, strength and beauty
Unsurpassed in the world.

(Pazhayarai, the erstwhile capital of Sundara Chozha, was also called Nandipuri, the name by which it was known when the Chozha lands were under Pallava dominion.)

'Well said!' 'Well said!' the bards exclaimed in appreciation. A staunch Saiva poet exclaimed, 'How surprising it is to find such gratitude among the Buddhists!'

'Yes. It is certainly surprising. The service I rendered to the Ulagapuram monastery is insignificant. Should it receive so much praise?' said the king.

One of the poets exclaimed, 'How can anyone who has received the emperor's largesse not acclaim him always and with gratitude? Why, even the gods Indra, Surya and Siva have benefited from your liberality!'

With a smile on his lips, Sundara Chozha enquired, 'What is this? Indra and Surya? And Siva too? Why should they be grateful to me?'

'Please permit me to recite a verse,' the bard said.

'Go on,' said the king.

The bard took up a palm leaf manuscript and began to read.

> To Indra, he gave an elephant.
> And seven horses to the Sun
> glowing red.
> A palanquin to Siva
> as a bridal gift.
> Can anyone in the world
> equal Sundara Chozha
> of Pazhaiyarai?

When the verse was finished, all the bards in the assembly nodded their heads and clapped their hands in joy.

With a beaming smile, Sundara Chozha asked, 'Can anyone expound the meaning of this poem?'

Many stood up at once. Then everyone sat down, save Nallan Sathanar who began to speak. 'Once upon a time, there was war between Indra, king of the heavens, and the demon called Vritra. When his elephant died in the clash, Indra became desperate to find a substitute as powerful as his own had been. He came with this request to King Sundara Chozha in Pazhaiyarai. The king took him to his stable saying, "I don't have an elephant like yours, but I have many that surpass it in might." Indra gazed in astonishment at the thousands of elephants there, not knowing which one to pick, until Sundara Chozha himself chose one and gifted it to him. Still, Indra was bemused because he had no weapon to control that elephant. Again, Sundara Chozha gave him a goad strong enough for that purpose.

'In a later age, a huge battle ensued between Surya, the sun god who lights up the world, and Rahu, the serpent demon. Rahu tried to swallow the sun. In the process, the demon spewed venom, killing the seven horses harnessed to the sun's chariot. Dismayed by the loss, Surya wondered how he could resume his journey. Seeing him in this state of consternation, Sundara Chozha took seven new stallions to the god and begged him to make use of them to protect the world. Surya greatly appreciated the timely help given to him by this Chozha emperor, a scion of Suryavamsha, his own clan.

'Still later, the marriage of Siva and Parvati took place on the Kailasa mountain. The bride's family had brought all the bridal gifts but failed to bring a palanquin. They were bemoaning the fact that there was no mount for the wedding procession except for Siva's bull, when Sundara Chozha reverently offered his pearl-encrusted palanquin. On this vast expanse of the earth, surrounded by the oceans, is there anyone who can be compared at all to the Great Emperor Sundara Chozha of Pazhaiyarai?'

Sundara Chozha broke into loud, gleeful laughter. This outburst from the king, whose illness had banished all laughter from his life for so long, brought some joy to his devoted wife Vanamadevi, as well as the serving maids and the palace physician.

Chinna Pazhuvettaraiyar, the keeper of the fort, who had been standing all the while, now folded his arms together and said, 'Your Majesty! I made a great mistake. Please pardon me.'

'Ah! Is it the general who speaks? What did you do? Perhaps you snatched the elephant and the white horses I gave Indra and Surya? Or grabbed the palanquin offered to Siva? You are certainly capable of doing that!' said the king and chortled again. The poets joined the king in his merriment. Vandiyatevan's guffaws were the loudest. Chinna Pazhuvettaraiyar glared at him. Then he quickly turned to the emperor again and said, 'King of kings! My mistake was this. Deferring to the advice of the palace physician, I barred the bards from visiting you. But their arrival has cheered you. Their words made you laugh. This has brought joy to the queen and her maids. I too became happy. Was it not a grave mistake on my part to have kept them away from you?'

'You are right, general! At least now you have realized your mistake. Now you know why I repeatedly told you not to follow the physician's advice and stop the poets from visiting me.'

The palace physician got up, folded his arms and began to speak. Ignoring him, Sundara Chozha turned his attention to the poets and asked them, 'Please tell me if you know who wrote this fine poem.'

Nallan Sathanar replied, 'Your Majesty, try as we might, our efforts have been in vain. We want to find him, honour him with the title of "The Emperor of Poesy" and take him on a procession in a palanquin borne on our shoulders.'

'This is no surprise. The great poet who has stuffed so many lies into a verse of four lines would naturally not want to come forward and reveal his identity.' These words left everyone stunned and speechless.

However, Vandiyatevan got up boldly and declared, 'Your Majesty! This must not be summarily dismissed as lying. If the common people say something untrue, it is a lie. If men involved in running the state do it, it becomes political strategy and diplomacy. When the poets indulge in it, it is creative imagination, literary embellishment, metaphor, poetic analogy . . .'

The bards shouted exuberantly, 'Well said!'

The emperor shot a keen glance at Vandiyatevan and said, 'Oh! You are the one who brought the scroll from Kanchi. You are a clever boy! You have worsted me.' Then, turning to the gathering, he continued, 'The verse is no doubt a fine one, but there is no need to make a huge effort to discover the man who wrote it or to confer the title of "The Emperor of Poesy" on him. I know the versifier who wrote this. He bears the heavy weight of the crown of the Chozha empire. He is already struggling under the burden of several titles, including "Emperor of the World", "Emperor of the Three Worlds" and "Emperor of the Seven Worlds".'

If we should declare that, on hearing this, the bards found themselves struggling to escape from drowning in the depths of stupefaction, our readers must not summarily dismiss the statement as false. They must accept it as the writer's creative use of poetic embellishment, analogy, image and metaphoric expression . . .

28

The Iron Grip

Once the poets recovered from their shock, Nandan Sathanar said slowly, 'Your Majesty! That means . . . the person who wrote . . . this verse . . . '

'Is Sundara Chozha, who is lying in bed before you with his legs paralysed.'

Exclamations of astonishment rippled through the assembly of poets. Some found themselves trembling in wonder. Others remained frozen, unable to comprehend their own state of mind.

Sundara Chozha continued, 'Once poets and scholars had come to the court in Pazhaiyarai. Some of you may have been in that assembly. Their verses eulogized the munificence of the Chozha clan. They also sang about my generosity. Once the bards left after receiving their gifts, Kundavai, who was a little girl then, acclaimed their songs. I made a wager to do better than them and rustled up this song for fun. "What about a reward for me?" I asked. The child climbed on my back and gave me two playful slaps. I remember it as if it were yesterday. But it happened several years ago.'

The poets expressed their elation with cries of 'Amazing!', 'Incredible!', 'Marvellous!' and 'Wonderful!'

Vandiyatevan felt a quiver running through his body when he heard Kundavai's name. He had heard so much about the peerless woman of the Chozha clan, her beauty, learning and intellectual attributes. The man before him had been lucky enough to have fathered such a matchless lady. Her mother was the lady beside the emperor. With what joy and pride the emperor spoke of his daughter! And with such warmth and tenderness in his voice!

Vandiyatevan's right hand stroked the silken pouch at his waist which held the letter for Kundavai. The hand froze. The mind was devastated. 'Ayo! What's this? The letter is not here! Where did it go? Did it slip down somewhere when I drew out the letter for the emperor? Where could it have fallen? In the great hall perhaps? Would it have fallen into Chinna Pazhuvettaraiyar's hands? Will that lead to danger? What a blunder! What a huge fiasco! How can I get out of this situation?'

Vandiyatevan was now on pins and needles. Once he realized that he had lost the scroll, he was unable to concentrate on any of the proceedings.

Meanwhile, Sundara Chozha went on speaking. 'Kundavai must have shared my little spoof with someone. He has leaked it and made it possible for the whole country to mock me.'

'Your Majesty! What if you had composed it? The verse is beautiful. Now, you are not only the emperor of the world but also the emperor of poesy,' Nallan Sathanar said.

'If I were to compose the same song now, I wouldn't have stopped with giving an elephant to Indra, horses to Surya and a palanquin to Siva. Did not Siva once deliver a kick to Yama, the god of death? Yama escaped, but his buffalo did not. I would have added that Sundara Chozha of Pazhaiyarai learnt about this loss and sent a replacement. It is on that beast that Yama is riding in all his grandeur as he comes searching for me. Not even Chinna Pazhuvettaraiyar, our commander of the Tanjavur Fort, can stop Yama, or his mount, can he?'

Tears began to rain down from Queen Vanamadevi's eyes. Many others began to sob aloud.

But Chinna Pazhuvettaraiyar did not lose his resoluteness. 'Your Majesty! I am ready to fight with Yama in your service.'

'I don't doubt that! But no mortal has the power to fight death. All we can do is pray to god for fearlessness in the face of death. Does anyone here remember the song sung by one of the great sons of the Tamizh land?' the emperor asked.

One of the poets stood up and recited the verse.

We are subject to none
We are unafraid of death
We will not suffer in hell
We have neither guile nor deceit
We are free from all afflictions–

The emperor cut in here with, 'Ah! Who could dare to sing this except a great soul who had seen god in person? Appar's severe stomach ache was cured by god's grace. That is why he says we are strangers to sickness. Stop eulogizing me and my bountifulness, and sing such words of grace. The poets Appar, Sambandar and Sundarar have composed thousands of devotional poems in exquisite Tamizh. How marvellous it would be to compile them all. A single lifetime would not be enough to benefit from them.'

'O king of kings! At your order, we are ready to start the work immediately,' Nallan Sathanar said.

'No. This is not going to happen in my lifetime . . . ' Sundara Chozha paused and became lost in thought.

The royal physician whispered something to Chinna Pazhuvettaraiyar. When he noted this, the king was jerked out of his thoughts and stared at the assembly with his eyes wide open.

'Your Majesty, you wanted to hear a poem from the Sangam anthology. Can they recite it and take their leave?' Chinna Pazhuvettaraiyar said.

'Oh, yes. I had forgotten. Not only my body, but my mind too is losing ground. Let's hear it now,' said the king.

Chinna Pazhuvettaraiyar signalled to Nallan Sathanar, who got up and said, 'Your Majesty! The most famous among your ancestors, Karikal Valavan, had planted the tiger standard on the Himalayan mountain. During his reign, Poompuhar was the capital of the Chozha empire. Many galleons came to dock there from many different foreign countries. A poet of the Sangam age depicts the wealth and prosperity of the city by describing the merchandise they brought from those lands.

Gems and gold from the northern mountains
Sandalwood and eaglewood from the western mountains
Pearls from the southern sea, coral from the eastern sea
Grain from the Ganga shores, the yields of the Kaveri
Food from Ilankai, merchandise from Burma . . .

At this point, the bard stopped at a sign from Sundara Chozha.

'General! This verse says that in Karikal Valavan's time, food came from Ilankai to the Chozha land. Didn't you invite these bards for me to know this?'

'Yes, my king!' This response from the keeper of the fort came in feeble tones.

'I got it. Now these men may depart with gifts.'

The commander told the bards that they may take their leave of the emperor. They left with slogans hailing the king.

Distressed by the loss of the missive to Kundavai Devi, Vandiyatevan mingled with the group of bards and positioned himself in their midst, hoping to slip away with them. In vain. As he neared the threshold, his wrist was caught in an iron grip. Vandiyatevan was extremely strong, but the power of that unassailable grip shook him from head to toe before immobilizing him.

He realized that the hand that held him in that iron grip belonged to Chinna Pazhuvettaraiyar. The bards left the royal chamber.

29

Our Guest

When the bards left, the physician brought a palliative potion. The queen, Malayaman's daughter, took it from him and gave it to her husband.

Chinna Pazhuvettaraiyar, who had waited patiently until then, now dragged Vandiyatevan forward.

'Your Majesty, any improvement with the new medicine?' he asked.

'The physician says so, and so does the queen. But I believe that all these efforts are useless. My fate is calling me. The god of death has gone to Pazhaiyarai in his pursuit of me. Once he knows I am no longer there, he will come straight here.'

'Your Majesty, you must not be disheartened. You must not break our hearts. Your ancestors–'

The king interposed, 'Ah! You are going to say that my ancestors were not afraid of death. If only I had the good fortune of dying on the battlefield as many of them did! I will not be afraid of such an end but embrace it eagerly. My uncle Rajaditta died fighting on his elephant mount. He established the valour of the Chozha dynasty on the battlefield, and became famous as the "king who perished on the elephant". What kind of reputation will I leave behind me as the "king who died on his sickbed"? His devotion to Siva freed my other uncle, Gandaraditta, from the fear of death. He went to the west coast on a pilgrimage. He died there and came to be known as the "king who passed away in the west". I am not a man of faith like him. Anyway, I am no longer fit to undertake any pilgrimage. How long will I lie in bed? How long will I be a burden to those around me? But something tells me that I will not linger long . . .'

'Your Majesty! The royal physician says there is no danger to your life. The astrologers say there is no danger of any kind. But this youngster thought it fit to warn you about some kind of danger . . .'

'Ah! He's the boy from Kanchi. Yes. He did mention something about danger. Why, tambi? Were you talking about my state of health?'

Vandiyatevan's mind worked at lightning speed. Any admission of having mentioned 'danger' would put him in danger. He had to get out of that tight spot. All right. He would try this gambit.

He immediately burst into speech, 'Your Majesty! Who am I to talk about *danger*? How can any danger come anywhere near you when we have the mighty Chinna Pazhuvettaraiyar as the commander of the fort, and the queen, who is goddess incarnate, beside you? All I did was make a humble appeal to you. I am a *stranger*, a stranger in this land. Today, I am the only surviving representative of the ancient Vaanan clan. I have been serving the great Chozha empire to the satisfaction of your valiant son. I beg you to bestow your grace on me and grant me a small part of the ancient kingdom that once belonged to my ancestors.

O king of kings! I am a *stranger* here, a stranger in this region. I come to you for shelter!'

This speech brought a scowl to Chinna Pazhuvettaraiyar's face. But the emperor's face brightened again. Her face brimming with compassion, the queen said, 'Surely, the goddess of learning must have blessed this boy at birth with the gift of eloquence.'

Seizing the moment, Vandiyatevan said, 'O mother! You must speak for me. I am an orphan. I have no one at all. I have to speak for myself. Please intercede with the emperor for me, as the goddesses Parvati and Lakshmi spoke to their divine spouses on behalf of the poor devotee. Ten villages from our old kingdom will be more than enough for me. I will be completely satisfied with that.'

Vandiyatevan's words surprised and gladdened Sundara Chozha. He said to Chinna Pazhuvettaraiyar, 'General! I like this boy very much. My queen's face tells me that she is ready to adopt him as her third son. Can we not grant his request? Will there be any difficulty in doing this? What do you think?'

'It is not for me to offer any opinion in this matter. But should we not know what Prince Karikalan has in mind?'

Vandiyatevan interposed, 'Your Majesty! The prince says that I must ask the lord of Pazhuvur. Now the lord of Pazhuvur says that I must ask the prince. Caught between the two . . .'

'Young man! Don't worry. We will work it out when they are together,' said the emperor and added to Chinna Pazhuvettaraiyar, 'General! This young man brought a missive from the prince. Adittan asks me to come to Kanchi as before. He wants me to stay in the golden palace that he has built, at least for a short while.'

'You wish is our command,' said the keeper of the fort.

'Ah! It may be so for you, but my legs refuse to obey my orders. It is not possible for me to travel to Kanchi. The very thought of travelling like a woman in a curtained palanquin is repugnant to me. A message must be sent to Aditta Karikalan, asking him to come here.'

'Would this be the right time for the prince to leave Kanchi? Our enemies are getting stronger in the north.'

'Partibhendran and Malayaman will take care of that. My instinct tells me that the prince must be by my side now. That is not all. A message must be sent to Ilankai to ask my younger son to come here at once. I want to make a crucial decision after consulting them both together. When Arulmozhi arrives, you can inform him about your objections to sending food to Ilankai.'

'Your Majesty! Pardon me. It is not I but the people of the Chozha kingdom who object to it. The last harvest has been a poor one. The people object to several shiploads of food being dispatched to Ilankai when they are on short rations. Their mutterings of today will soon turn into cries. Those cries will become so loud that they will penetrate the palace and affect your health.'

'Arulmozhi would never want to do anything against the will of the people. Anyway, let him come here on a short visit. Let us take a call on sending for him after Periya Pazhuvettaraiyar returns. When is he coming?'

'He will be here by tonight.'

'We can also send a missive to Kanchi tomorrow. Can't we entrust it to this boy?'

'This boy has come straight from Kanchi at full speed. Let him stay here for a few days and take a break. We can send the message through somebody else.'

'Do that. He can stay here until the prince arrives.'

Malayaman's daughter stood up. At once, Chinna Pazhuvettaraiyar said, 'Pardon me, I have troubled you for too long today. So long that Her Majesty had to warn me.'

'This boy is our guest. Please make sure that he has every comfort. If the emperor had been well, we could have hosted him in our palace,' said the queen.

'I will take care of him, Devi! I will take very good care of him.' As Chinna Pazhuvettaraiyar gave this assurance to the queen, his hand automatically went to his moustache and gave it a twist.

30

The Portrait Gallery

Chinna Pazhuvettaraiyar took Vandiyatevan with him to his great hall. He was not completely satisfied with Vandiyatevan's version of what he had told the emperor. He wondered if he had been wrong in sending the youth to the emperor by himself. It would have been logical to suspect any messenger from Aditta Karikalan. But there was no room for doubt here, as it was his brother who had sent Vandiyatevan with his signet ring. Ah! Was there any need for anyone to preach caution to his brother? And yet . . . Chinna Pazhuvettaraiyar remembered how the young man had faltered and goggled at him when he entered the royal chamber. He recalled hearing him cry 'Danger! Danger!' Could he have possibly misheard 'stranger' as 'danger'? All things considered, it would be best not to send the boy back immediately. Once his brother returned, he would consult the elder and take the right step. He should also try to absorb such a gutsy youth into his personal security forces. He would come in useful at the opportune moment. Why, a part of the boy's ancient kingdom could be restored to him. He was the kind of young man who would always be grateful, and serve his benefactor faithfully. If he turned out to be a foe, why, that too could be taken care of. Anyhow, he would wait for Periya Pazhuvettaraiyar to return.

As soon as they reached the great hall, Vandiyatevan began to scrutinize every corner with great concern. He stared again and again at the spot where he had handed over the scroll to the commander, to see if by some chance the other scroll was still lying there. He would be nothing but a rank imbecile if he could not recover it. He would never be able to see the princess acclaimed by the whole world. He would have left half the job undone.

Chinna Pazhuvettaraiyar said to one of the attendants, 'Take this boy to the guest wing and take care of his needs. Stay there until I come.'

When the attendant left with Vandiyatevan, another came forward and respectfully held out a scroll. 'This was lying on the way to the royal audience hall. The young man might have dropped it.'

The commander took it quickly, opened and read it. His eyebrows shot up alarmingly. His expression underwent a brutal transformation.

'Ah! A message from Aditta Karikalan, addressed in his own hand, to Princess Kundavai! *You had asked for a true warrior to perform confidential undercover tasks, someone who would succeed in fulfilling any mission he undertakes. You can place complete trust in the bearer of this letter and assign any task of the highest importance to him,*' Chinna Pazhuvettaraiyar said to himself. 'There is something fishy here! Does my brother know about this letter? I must be even more careful with this boy.' Then he whispered something to the attendant who had found the scroll. The man left at once.

* * *

Vandiyatevan was given royal treatment in Chinna Pazhuvettaraiyar's mansion. Every luxury was provided for him. He was given a bath and new clothes to wear. Vandiyatevan, who was a bit of a dandy, was so thrilled that he momentarily forgot all about the lost letter. He was fed on sumptuous royal fare. Ravenous as he was, he did more than justice to it. Then he was taken to Chinna Pazhuvettaraiyar's portrait gallery. 'Please enjoy these wonderful paintings until the commander comes,' they said and began to have their chit-chat over a game of draughts.

Tanjavur was renowned for its excellence in sculpture and painting. Just as the performing arts of dance and music flourished in Tiruvaiyaru, Tanjavur was home to the visual arts.

Vandiyatevan entered the celebrated painting gallery in Chinna Pazhuvettaraiyar's mansion. He gazed and gazed, entranced by the amazing murals on the walls, painted in glowing colours. He forgot himself. He even forgot his mission.

Most of the paintings were about the history of the Chozhas in the preceding century. Vandiyatevan was most attracted to the depictions of the Chozha kings and the key incidents in their lives.

At this juncture, we wish to briefly recapitulate the history of the Chozha kings who ruled from Pazhaiyarai and Tanjavur successively. This will be extremely useful to understand the episodes that are to follow in our story.

The Chozha kings alternately adopted the titles *Parakesari* and *Rajakesari*.* We have already talked about Vijayalaya Chozha, who bore ninety-six battle scars on his body. After 'Parakesari' Vijayalaya, his son 'Rajakesari' Aditta came to the throne, who proved to be a true son of his father. Firstly, he

* Supreme lion and Royal lion.

supported the Pallava faction in defeating the Pandya king. Then he stabilized his kingdom and made war against the Pallavas. He leapt on the elephant on which the Pallava ruler Aparajita Varman was seated, killed him there and then, and conquered his kingdom. Soon, Kongu land too came under his control. Aditta was a keen devotee of Siva. He built many temples for the god–from the Sahasya hill, the source of the Kaveri, to where the river meets the sea.

Rajakesari Aditta was followed by Parakesari Parantaka, who ruled for forty-six years. He was the greatest of the Chozha monarchs after Karikal Valavan, who planted the tiger standard on the Himalayan peak. Parantaka earned several titles: Veeranarayanan, Bhakta Vatsalan, Kunjara Mallan, Soora Sikhamani and conqueror of Madurai and Ilankai. Under him, the Chozha kingdom extended from Kanyakumari to River Krishna. This was the same king who had roofed the Chidambaram temple with gold. The Chozhas faced several threats during the last years of his reign. The Rashtrakutas of the north became mighty and challenged the Chozhas by invading their kingdom with some success.

Emperor Parantaka had three sons. The eldest was the extraordinary warrior Rajaditta. He set up camp in Tirumunaipadi with a vast army, expecting an attack from the Rashtrakutas. It was he who built the Veeranarayana Lake named after his father.

A brutal war broke out between the Chozhas and the Rashtrakutas in Takkolam, where, after massacring his enemies on the battlefield and earning great fame, Rajaditta lost his life and departed for the warrior's heaven. Like Aparajita Varman, Rajaditta too died fighting on an elephant's back. Stone inscriptions hail him as the 'braveheart who perished on an elephant'.

If Rajaditta had not died, it was he who would have ascended the throne after Parantaka. His descendants would have been crowned after him.

But since Prince Rajaditta died without being crowned, and without issue, his younger brother ascended the throne, according to his father's wishes.

Like his father and grandfather, Gandaraditta was filled with devotion to Siva and had a great love of Tamizh as well. Totally uninterested in ruling the kingdom, he spent all his time building temples and enjoying Tamizh poetry. Following the Saiva Nayanmar poets, he composed hymns to the god Siva. In the last of those songs, he referred to himself as a poet of the faith and went on to say that he, the king of Tanjavur, had poured out in the sweetest words, his praise of the lord who danced in the golden hall, whose attributes were as magnificent as they were indescribable. And those who chanted those verses wrought in the wondrous Tamizh tongue would achieve glory, fame and bliss in the world to come.

Since Gandaraditta was a ruler only in name, the administration was carried out by Arinjaya, his younger brother. Earlier, Arinjaya had stationed himself in towns close to Rajaditta's camp and assisted him. Very soon, he transformed the crushing defeat suffered at the hands of the Rashtrakutas into victory. He forced the Rashtrakutas to stop advancing into the south and halt beyond River Tenpennai.

Therefore, Gandaraditta proclaimed his younger brother Arinjaya as his heir and made a public announcement pronouncing him as his successor to the throne.

There was another reason for this decision. Gandaraditta's wife had passed away before he became king, and he did not remarry for a very long time. But Arinjaya had a son whose appearance, personal traits and military skills were all equally exceptional. He bore his grandfather Parantaka's name along with Sundara, the name given to him by the populace.

Gandaraditta decided that Arinjaya's son, Parantaka Sundara, should succeed his father. He made an open proclamation to that effect with the consent of his council of ministers, army commanders and the representatives of the people.

But after these decisions were made, an unexpected event took place in Gandaraditta's life. He happened to meet the daughter of the feudal chieftain, Mazhavarayar. Her beauty, modesty, purity and devotion won his heart, and he married her in his old age. In due course, a child was born to them. They named him Madhurantakan and nurtured him with love and care. But neither the king nor the queen wanted to change the earlier decision about the crown. Since they were both filled with devotion and detachment, they wished to raise their son in the same way. Convinced that any earthly kingdom was insignificant compared to the kingdom of god, they wanted their son to claim this other-worldly kingdom. Therefore, Gandaraditta confirmed his brother's and brother's descendants as the rightful rulers of the land.

That is how the crown passed from Rajaditta and Gandaraditta to Arinjaya and his descendants.

Parakesari Arinjaya did not long survive his brother. He left the world within a year of Gandaraditta's death.

The feudal chieftains, the administrative heads of the government and the people of the land gladly joined together to crown Sundara Chozha king. Rajakesari Sundara Chozha proved his skill and ability to be worthy of the supreme position that chance had bestowed on him. His wars at the beginning of his reign restored the Pandya and Pallava regions to the Chozha empire. He drove the Rashtrakutas away from the banks of the River Tenpannai.

Sundara Chozha's sons, Aditta Karikalan and Arulmozhi Varman, surpassed their father in going to the wars at a very young age and fighting on the frontlines. Wherever they went, the goddess of victory favoured the Chozha side.

31

'Thief! Thief!'

Vandiyatevan was delighted to see the lifelike portraits of the Chozha kings, from Vijayalaya to the reigning king known as Sundara Chozha. How mighty they were, each one of them! They had thought nothing of risking their lives to accomplish magnificent deeds. No myth or epic could boast their equals; they were peerless. The Chozha kingdom was fortunate indeed to be ruled by the kings of this dynasty. All the regions under their sovereign rule were equally fortunate.

Vandiyatevan noted an important detail in those depictions. Every Chozha king had received exceptional assistance and service from the chieftains of the Pazhuvur clan.

It had been a Pazhuvettaraiyar who first entered Tanjavur after laying siege to that city when it was under Mutharaiyar control. It was a Pazhuvettaraiyar who carried Vijayalaya on his shoulders when that Chozha king performed incredible feats on the Tirupurampiyam battlefield. A Pazhuvettaraiyar crowned Aditta Chozha and conducted his coronation. It was another Pazhuvettaraiyar whose shoulders served as the springboard for Aditta when he leapt on the Pallava king's elephant mount and killed him. Several Pazhuvettaraiyars had held the tiger flag aloft on the frontlines of the wars waged by Emperor Parantaka. When Rajaditta fell, it was a Pazhuvettaraiyar who took him on his lap and informed the dying prince that the defeated Rashtrakutas were fleeing. Many Pazhuvettaraiyars had executed valiant actions in the service of kings Arinjaya and Sundara Chozha.

These incidents depicted on the murals left Vandiyatevan speechless in wonder. Not for nothing did the Pazhuvettaraiyar brothers hold such sway in the Chozha kingdom of the present day. It was no surprise that Sundara Chozha sought their counsel before taking any action.

And now, undoubtedly, Vandiyatevan was trapped in a lethal quandary. Chinna Pazhuvettaraiyar had begun to doubt him. If the elder brother returned, the doubt would become a certainty. The secret of the signet ring would be out. Vandiyatevan would be damned and doomed. He had heard about the dungeons under Chinna Pazhuvettaraiyar's directorate of prisons. He could be thrown into one of them. Once you were impounded in those dungeons, it was practically impossible to get out. If you did, it would be as a witless idiot reduced to skin and bones.

By now our warrior had lost all interest in meeting the Pazhuvur queen. He would be happy just to escape the dungeons and slip out of the fort. How could he find a way to circumvent this grave peril? He had to come up with some subterfuge to decamp before the older brother arrived. Though he had lost the scroll, he could meet Kundavai Devi and deliver the message orally, in person. Let her believe him or not, as she pleased . . . But how could he break out of the Tanjavur Fort?

Vandiyatevan remembered the clothes he had worn before. Surely, he had been gifted with new garments so that his old ones could be inspected. The scroll to Kundavai must have been found by the commander. Now he knew why Chinna Pazhuvettaraiyar had held him in an iron grip. And why he had sent not one, but three guards with him. Ah! A feint! He had to discover one immediately. There! He found it! He would take up the challenge! Vetrivel! Veeravel!

Vandiyatevan peered through the window. Chinna Pazhuvettaraiyar was riding to the gallery surrounded by his retinue. This was the moment! No time for dithering.

The guards playing draughts at the doorway got up when they heard the sounds of Chinna Pazhuvettaraiyar's arrival.

Vandiyatevan went to them and asked, 'Brothers! Where are my old garments?'

One of them answered, 'Why do you need those dirty clothes? Our master has given you new ones of silk.'

'I don't need new clothes. Old ones will do. Fetch them at once.'

'They have gone for washing. They will be returned when they are ready.'

'No! You are thieves. I had kept some money in my old clothes. You have stolen the clothes to grab the money. Fetch them at once. Or else . . .'

'Or else . . . ! What will you do? Tambi, will you cut off our heads and dispatch them to Tanjavur? But remember, *this* is Tanjavur!'

'Dei! Will you or will you not fetch my clothes at once?'

'We can fetch them only if they are still here. We have thrown those soiled clothes into the Vettaru for the crocodiles. Can anything that has gone into a crocodile's belly ever be reclaimed?'

'Are you playing games with me? See! I will complain to your master,' Vandiyatevan shouted and started crossing the threshold. One of the guards went to stop him. Vandiyatevan landed a punch on his nose. The man fell down. Blood spurted from his nose.

Another came to wrestle with him, arms outstretched. Grabbing those extended hands, Vandiyatevan aimed a kick between his opponent's legs and gave a twist to the movement. The man screamed and crouched down. By this time, the third had come up close. Vandiyatevan kicked the man on the knee. He too crashed down with a scream.

All three scrambled up quickly and surrounded Vandiyatevan. This time, they approached him with caution.

By then, the horse had come to a halt at the threshold of the gallery.

Raising his voice to its highest level, Vandiyatevan shrieked, 'Thieves! Thieves!' and pounced on the men again. He shrieked over and over again as the men tried to stop him.

Chinna Pazhuvettaraiyar stepped into the gallery demanding, 'What's all this racket?'

32

The Examination

As soon as he saw Chinna Pazhuvettaraiyar, Vandiyatevan stopped fighting and strode up to him. Ignoring the guards who came running to grab him by the shoulders, he took a few more strides and released a flood of words. 'Commander! You came at the right time. Not only did these robbers steal my belongings, but they also tried to murder me. Is this the way to treat guests? Is this the way hosts customarily behave in Tanjavur? I am not only your guest. I am the emperor's guest. You heard what the empress said. I am the messenger who brought a missive from the crown prince. If these fellows can give me such cavalier treatment, what would they do to others? I am surprised that you have thieves in your employ. In our Tondaimandalam region, we impale such men on the stake.'

Chinna Pazhuvettaraiyar was filled with admiration for the brave youth who had singlehandedly brought three hefty soldiers to the ground. He became even more eager to assimilate the boy into his security guard. He therefore spoke in a calm voice. 'Wait, tambi. Wait. I don't think these men would do that. Let me question them.'

'That is all I ask for. Question them. And pass judgement. Make arrangements to have my clothes and belongings returned.'

'Dei! Release the boy. Come here. Why did you attack him?'

One of the men answered, 'Master, we followed your instructions. We gave him a fine oil bath, new garments and adornments. We fed him sumptuously. Then we took him to the art gallery. He spent some time happily gazing at the paintings. Then, all of a sudden, he demanded his old clothes and began to attack us.'

Looking at them with blood-red eyes, Chinna Pazhuvettaraiyar shouted, 'Three burly men beaten by a stripling!'

'Master, we hesitated only because he is a royal guest. Give us permission. We will finish him off.'

'Enough. Stop bragging. Tambi, what do you say?'

'I say the same thing. Give me leave. It has been a while since I fought Chozha enemies. My muscles are bristling. I will teach them a lesson on how to treat royal guests.'

Smiling broadly, Chinna Pazhuvettaraiyar said, 'Tambi! Keep your shoulders strong and taut to fight the enemies of the Chozhas. With the emperor being ill, all fighting is banned within the Tanjavur Fort.'

'In that case, ask them to return my belongings this instant.'

'Where are his things?' the commander asked his men.

'Master, we have kept them safe as per your orders.'

'Commander! See how they lie? They told me that my clothes had been sent for washing. Now they say you ordered them to be kept safe. Soon, they will accuse you of theft.'

Chinna Pazhuvettaraiyar said to his guards, 'Fools! All I told you was to give this boy new garments, nothing about his old clothes. Tambi! These fools are talking nonsense. Never mind. Why are you so concerned about your old garments? Have you kept anything of value in them?'

'Yes. Some gold coins for the journey–'

Before Vandiyatevan could continue, the commander said, 'Don't worry. I will give you all the gold you need for your travel expenses.'

'Commander, I am Prince Karikalan's messenger. I am not in the habit of accepting money from others . . .'

'All right. I will ask them to return your money and garments. Anything else . . .'

Chinna Pazhuvettaraiyar noted Vandiyatevan's moment of indecision before he said, 'There was something else tucked into my waistband. I hope your men have not tampered with it. If they have . . . they are doomed . . .'

'Ah! Your anger escalates! It makes you forget to whom you are speaking. I will forgive you because you are young. What is that "something"?'

'Commander, I cannot tell you. It is a confidential matter.'

'Within the Tanjavur Fort, there can be no confidential matter unknown to me.'

'It is a confidential matter entrusted to me by Prince Aditta Karikalan.'

'The prince is the supreme commander in the northern region. His authority prevails only in regions north of the River Palar. In this fort, the emperor's authority is supreme.'

'Commander, undoubtedly, wherever the tiger flag flies, the emperor's authority is supreme.'

'That is why, for the sake of the emperor's well-being, nothing within the fort can remain unknown to me.'

'Commander, the Chozha empire is indebted to you for your unremitting care of the emperor. Today, I heard the emperor commending you. Did he not say that it is fear of you that keeps even the god of death at bay? How true!'

'Yes, tambi. We don't know what kind of disaster would have occurred if we had not brought the king from Pazhaiyarai to Tanjavur. The mission of the Pandya conspirators may have been fulfilled.'

'Ah! To hear this from you! So, the rumours I heard must be true!'

'What rumours?'

'I heard that there was a conspiracy against the emperor and another against his sons.'

Chinna Pazhuvettaraiyar bit his lips. He realized that it was he who was getting the worst of it from the boy he had deemed gullible. He had more or less reached a stage where he was defending himself against the boy's accusations. He decided to end it.

'Why should you worry about it? We are here to blow up every conspiracy and protect the Chozha empire. Stick to things that concern you. You want your garments back, isn't that all?'

'My garments and whatever was in them.'

'You have still not told me what *was* in them.'

'I will if I must. You are responsible for my disclosure of what should have remained confidential. I had been given another missive by the prince.'

'Another? To whom? You never told me!'

'Because it was confidential. I am telling you now at your insistence. The prince gave a missive for Kundavai Devi in Pazhaiyarai.'

'Is that so? That means you cannot take the emperor's reply to Kanchi tomorrow. What exigency could have prompted the prince to send a message to Kundavai Devi, I wonder!'

'Commander, I don't read letters written to others. I have no objections to your reading this letter as you did the letter to the emperor. But the responsibility is yours. It is sufficient for me to have my gold and scroll restored to me.'

'You need not have any qualms on that score. I myself will restore them to you,' said Pazhuvettaraiyar as he walked away. Noting that Vandiyatevan was following him, he made a sign with his eyes. Five or six men blocked Vandiyatevan with their spears. Vandiyatevan decided that it was pointless to fight them.

After some time, Chinna Pazhuvettaraiyar returned with a man holding Vandiyatevan's belongings like gifts on a tray.

'Tambi, your garments. Be sure to check them properly.'

Vandiyatevan checked them. The scroll to Kundavai Devi was there, along with the gold coins. But there were more coins than before. Why? How did the lost missive turn up? It must have reached Chinna Pazhuvettaraiyar. He had read it before returning it to him. Why did he do this? Why had he added the extra coins? This was a man to beware of. Who knew how many more tests he was going to set? Vandiyatevan warned himself that he would have to be extremely alert in dealing with the commander to save himself from getting trapped.

'Tambi, is everything there? Your belongings, your gold . . . ?'

'Let me check,' said Vandiyatevan and counted the coins. He placed the extra coins before Chinna Pazhuvettaraiyar. 'I belong to the Vaanan clan. I am Prince Aditta Karikalan's messenger. I do not crave what belongs to others.'

'I appreciate your honesty. Yet you may keep this for your travel expenses. When do you want to leave? Today? Or would you like to spend a restful night here, meet my brother and depart tomorrow?'

'I would certainly like to spend the night here and pay my respects to Periya Pazhuvettaraiyar. But please tell your men not to touch my belongings.' As he spoke, Vandiyatevan took the extra coins and secured them in a pouch.

'Good! You will have no more trouble here. You may feel free to ask for anything you need.'

'Commander, I am very eager to go sightseeing. May I?'

'Certainly. These two men will take you around and show you everything. But don't go outside the fort. You cannot return when they close the gates in the evening. Explore anything you like within the fort,' Chinna Pazhuvettaraiyar said. Then he called two men and whispered something to them. Vandiyatevan could easily guess what he would have told them.

33

A Girl on the Tree

Vandiyatevan left to see the sights of the Tanjavur Fort. He had no doubt at all that the two escorts had been sent by the commander to prevent his escape. Nor was there any doubt about orders having been issued to prevent anyone from leaving the fort. And yet, it was imperative for him to do so. For, once Periya Pazhuvettaraiyar returned, it would be hardly possible to escape or to stay alive.

Therefore, as Vandiyatevan wandered from place to place enjoying the sights, his mind was brooding over the ways and means of escape. First, he had to shake off the two hellhounds who trailed him. Then he had to get clear of the fort. But . . . how . . . ?

Actually, it would be no big deal to get away from the guards. He could slam them to the ground in a split second and run away. But where could he run? The whole country knew how the Pazhuvettaraiyars had strengthened the fortifications. It was said that even the wind could not penetrate the fort without the Pazhuvettaraiyars' permission. That very morning, the emperor had maintained that even the god of death could not enter the fort. How could *he* get out of such a fort? A single movement would be enough for the two guards to raise the alarm. He would either lose his life or end up in the dungeons. Any direct attack would be useless. He had to deploy tricks. And after that, he still had to search for an exit from the fort. Even the strongest fort must have a secret underground passage. How to discover it? Who would know of it? Would those who knew it share the secret with him?

Bang in the middle of these cogitations came the thought of the Pazhuvur queen. If at all anyone could help him, it would have to be that lady. Of course, there was no certainty about it, but he could try to coax her by using Azhvarkadiyan's name. First, he would have to find Pazhuvettaraiyar's palace. Meanwhile, these scoundrels must not discover his intentions. They would inform Chinna Pazhuvettaraiyar at once, which would have disastrous consequences. Moreover, what if Periya Pazhuvettaraiyar turned up while he was in the palace to meet Nandini? Wouldn't he be putting his head into the lion's mouth?

Vandiyatevan's mouth was not idle, though his mind was busy. He continued to rain questions, 'What's that? What's this? Whose castle is it? Who owns this mansion? What's this building, that dome . . . ?' He was waiting to hear them say, 'This is Pazhuvettaraiyar's palace, this is the Pazhuvur queen's mansion.' His eyes darted everywhere. His mind registered that, though the main streets were wide and bustling, between them were any number of narrow alleys and lanes, and many gardens lush with trees. It would not be difficult to run through those lanes and hide in those gardens, even for a few days.

His getaway had to create the illusion of invisibility. And no one should search for him. Concealment was impossible if Chinna Pazhuvettaraiyar launched a manhunt. Of course, he could get into some house and plead for shelter. But who would give him shelter in the Tanjavur Fort . . . ? The Pazhuvur queen? He would have to use all his powers of persuasion to win her trust. But first, he must escape from the guards.

When they reached a cross street, he saw the chance he was waiting for. 'Ah! Slogans! Clamour! Procession! Lord, undoubtedly you are on my side!' The Velakkara troops were exiting the fort after their audience with the maharaja. What if he joined them? Could there be a better means of escape?

The guards would follow him. Nor would it be plain sailing to get out of the fort. The sentries at the gate were not blockheads. They would stop him. However, he had to make the attempt. He would be the world's greatest fool if he let slip this god-given opportunity.

Vandiyatevan asked the guards about the crowd. When they told him that it was the procession of the Velakkara corps, Vandiyatevan began to ask for more information. He declared that he wanted to go up close to the brave troop that he wanted to join. Suiting his actions to his words, Vandiyatevan mingled with the procession and moved ahead, expressing his desire to see the drummers marching in front.

He moved up, down and sideways through the procession, shouting slogans with greater exuberance than the Velakkara troopers. The troopers stared at him. Some of them thought he was deranged. Others concluded that he was tipsy. But no one stopped him or pushed him away.

Chinna Pazhuvettaraiyar's watchdogs did not dare to join the Velakkara procession. They followed at a little distance, sure of catching Vandiyatevan when he stepped out of the procession as he would have to, at some point.

A curd seller entered the street from a lane and stood waiting to let the procession go by. One of the troopers asked her, 'Will you give me some curds? I am thirsty.'

The girl replied cheekily, 'No. But I can give you a couple of slaps.'

The man approached her saying, 'Is that so? Let me have it then!' The curd seller began to run in fright. The trooper ran after her. Two men followed to bring him back. With all the noise and shouting, no one could make out what the fracas was about. They just thought that it was a bit of fun.

As he watched them run, Vandiyatevan decided to act. We have seen over and over again that, to Vandiyatevan, ever the man of action, execution invariably accompanied decision. Hanging back after making up his mind was foreign to his nature. So, he joined the other troopers as they pursued the curd seller, yelling 'Run! Run! Catch! Catch!' The girl ran on and disappeared into a narrow lane. The pursuers turned back. However, Vandiyatevan ran on through several lanes before he slowed down to a walk.

The Velakkara corps left the fort at sunset. Now the lanes were dark. Some of them had walls rising on both sides. Others had fences lined with trees and shrubs. Vandiyatevan walked on. He was not worried about losing his way. If he avoided the main streets and went through the lanes, he would eventually reach the fort's wall. Once he reached it, he would have the whole night to work out his plan of action.

He reached a blind alley. By this time, it had become so dark that he bumped into the wall. He could not gauge its height. It could be the wall circling the fort. He would know more shortly when the moon rose. Until then, there could be no better hiding place to sit and wait. By this time, his guards would have gone back and reported to Chinna

Pazhuvettaraiyar. He would have concluded that Vandiyatevan had exited the fort with the Velakkara troops.

'The search must be on, inside and outside the fort,' he surmised. 'Let them search. Let them search well. If I don't slip out of their hands and escape from this fort, my name is not Vallavaraiyan Vandiyatevan. Nor will I claim to be a descendant of the Vaanan clan. However, Pazhuvettaraiyar's men would find their job easy after moonrise. They may find this spot. Let them come! Who can find me if I hide in this dense grove?'

Vandiyatevan slumped down on the ground. Young as he was, he found that the ceaseless activities of the day were shutting his fatigued eyes. The trees shook and brushed against each other in the breeze in a soporific lullaby.

When Vandiyatevan awoke, the moon had come up above the horizon. Under the moonbeams slanting through the trees, the scenes around him appeared in blurred outlines. Vandiyatevan reminded himself of his plight. He was surprised that he had fallen asleep against the wall. He was even more surprised as he wondered what could have prodded him awake. A voice? Was it the voice of a human being, an animal or a night bird? Did he hear anything at all?

Vandiyatevan looked up. In the shadowy light of the moon, he could make out that the wall was steep, though not high enough to be the rampart of a fort. Could it be an inner fortification? Or the wall around a palace?

Suddenly, fear froze his heart. His insides rose up to stifle him. What was that thing on the branch above the wall? He remembered the stories he had heard about phantoms haunting trees.

But do phantoms speak? And speak in a human voice? In a woman's voice? What was it saying?

'What is this, Ayya! Did you fall asleep against the wall? How many times should I call you?'

Ah! This was no phantom. It was a female of the human species. A young girl sitting on the tree. Was this a dream? Or something real?

'Great! You have still not shaken yourself awake. Here, I am dropping a ladder. Come up. Watch out! Don't be stupid enough to fall.'

The girl dropped a bamboo ladder against the wall.

True, Vandiyatevan was all at sea. But would he let go of this rare opportunity that had dropped into his lap? He would risk the consequences and climb the ladder now. Once he reached the top, he could make all his enquiries at will.

When he was more than halfway up, the girl spoke again. 'What a sluggard you are! The young queen is waiting for you. And here you are, snoozing away!' The shock almost made Vandiyatevan slide off. Luckily, he managed to grab a stone jutting on the wall.

'Young queen! It had to be the young queen of Pazhuvur! How did she know I was crouching here? It had to be witchcraft. But why should she be so interested in seeing me? Perhaps . . . just perhaps . . . Have I climbed the ladder meant for somebody else? Whatever it may be, once taken, the step cannot be retracted. Anyway, everything is going to become clear soon.'

When he reached the top of the wall, the girl stretched out a hand and pulled him up. A moonbeam fell on her face. By this time, Vandiyatevan had lost the ability to be surprised. That is why, though her face resembled the face of the curd seller chased by the Velakkara troopers, he did not tumble off the wall. After this, all the shocks that may follow would leave no room for surprise.

'Hmm. Why are you sitting on the wall still blinking away? Hoist the ladder, put it inside and jump down. Hurry!' the girl said as she quickly climbed down from the tree.

Vandiyatevan did as he was bidden. He saw that he had jumped down into a large garden. At a little distance, a palace with domes and spires made a dream scene under the dim moonlight.

Vandiyatevan cleared his throat to ask, 'Whose palace is this?' But the girl shushed him, warning him with a finger on her lip, and walked on. Vandiyatevan followed her.

34

The Arbour

Vandiyatevan strode behind the young girl who darted along the footpath through the dense mango grove. It was not easy to negotiate his way in the dark without bumping into trees and bushes. When he stopped to avoid a tree, she glanced back to say, 'Forgot the way? But you can see in the dark, can't you?' Now Vandiyatevan shushed her by placing a finger on his lips as she had done earlier. They could hear noises on the other side of the wall as if people were moving about. When they resumed walking, Vandiyatevan gave a little laugh. The girl asked him, 'What makes you laugh?'

'Did you not hear the footsteps of those who are chasing me? I'm amused to think of their chagrin.'

She asked with some dismay, 'Chasing you? Why?'

'Why else would I have banged my head against the wall in this blinding darkness and waited there?'

At that moment, the breeze blew a branch aside. A moonbeam touched Vandiyatevan's face.

The girl looked at him in startled surprise.

'What are you looking at?' Vandiyatevan asked.

'I was trying to see if you are indeed you.'

'If I am not me, who can I be?'

'When you came last time, you had a thick moustache.'

'How can men like me who jump over walls survive if we don't frequently change the way we look?'

'But you look younger than you did.'

'Exuberance makes you younger.'

'What makes you so exuberant?'

'How can I not be exuberant when I have your maharani's favour?'

'No need to scoff. Today, my mistress is the younger rani. One day, she will surely become the maharani.'

'That's what I say.'

'Will you stop there? No. You will claim that it was your witchcraft that made her the maharani. You may even demand half the kingdom!'

Vandiyatevan had more or less learnt what he wanted to know. He stopped talking and plunged into serious reflection. 'Who am I going to see? The young queen of Pazhuvur? Or the daughter of Chinna Pazhuvettaraiyar, married to Prince Madhurantakan? I am to be introduced to her as a sorcerer. Whoever she may be, how do I put my best foot forward in her presence? O my heart! Don't lose your nerve. As long as you have fortitude, you can score victories. I have not failed in any challenge until now. Am I going to be undone by a woman?'

They reached a big mansion, but instead of taking him to the main entrance, the girl led him through the rear garden to an arbour. As they neared it, it could be seen that the arbour stretched into a vine-covered pergola between two huge palaces. The palace on the right was brilliantly illuminated. Sounds of good cheer came from within. The palace on the left remained unlit. Its walls loomed high under the moonlight. Darkness and silence dwelt within.

When they reached the arbour, the woman signalled to Vandiyatevan to wait. From where he stood, he inhaled the scent of flowers. Their overpowering fragrance pierced his nostrils, filled his head and made him feel bleary.

The voice of his guide could be heard within. Another voice replied, 'Ask him to come in at once. Why should you ask? You know I've been waiting all this time.' That heady voice indubitably belonged to the young Pazhuvur queen. In no time at all, he was going to find himself standing before her. How should he handle the situation? How would she react when she saw the man who rammed into her palanquin instead of the sorcerer whom she expected? With amazement? Anger? Perhaps . . . gladness? Or would she remain unreadable?

The girl who had led him now came out and made a gesture inviting him to enter the arbour.

Vandiyatevan approached and looked inside. In that split second, the vision before him etched itself on his heart. The flame burning on the golden lamp stand spread an aureate circle of light. It must have been filled with some rare, perfumed oil to produce such a dizzying impact on him.

A woman was reclining sinuously on an ornate couch scattered with flowers of many colours and scents. No doubt about it–she was the young queen of Pazhuvur. By day, in the palanquin, she had appeared beautiful. By night, in the light of the long-stemmed lamp of gold, she appeared to be the goddess of beauty herself. The scent of flowers, the fumes of incense and the Pazhuvur queen's mesmerizing beauty, all combined to stupefy Vandiyatevan.

'Vandiyateva! Beware!' his inner voice whispered. 'Once, when you drank liquor, you felt your brain getting addled.

You vowed that you would never drink again. Remember that, and do not lose your wits. This is way more intoxicating than the most potent wine.'

Seeing Vandiyatevan, the Pazhuvur queen parted her lips in surprise, giving a glimpse of her pearly teeth. Her inability to speak gave him the advantage.

He said, with a chuckle, 'Lady! Your maid had doubts about whether I was indeed the sorcerer. How do you think she expressed it? She asked me, "Are you . . . *you*?"' Vandiyatevan laughed again.

Nandini smiled. Lightning flashed before Vandiyatevan's eyes. It rained honey.

'She is often prone to such misgivings. Vasuki! Why are you still standing here? Go. If you hear any footsteps, bang the door shut,' Nandini said.

'Yes, Amma,' said Vasuki as she went down the pathway to the brightly illuminated palace and sat down in a dimly lit doorway.

Nandini lowered her voice. 'Did she suspect that you were not the sorcerer? Silly girl! Most men who claim to be sorcerers are fakes. *You* are the real magician. What kind of magic brought you here at this time?'

'Lady! It was not magic that brought me here. I climbed a ladder set against a wall to be here.'

'I can see that. I asked you what spells you used to trick this girl.'

'I gave her a smile under the moonlight. If it hadn't worked, I would have shown her the magic ring you gave me.'

'You have it safe, don't you? With that ring, you could have come here in broad daylight. Why did you have to sneak in like a thief at night?'

'The men employed by your brother-in-law, Chinna Pazhuvettaraiyar, are first-class thieves. At first, they tried to steal my garments and belongings. Then they would not leave me alone even for a moment. It was a huge challenge to shake them off. Slinking through bylanes and alleys, I was going round and round the walls of your palace, when I saw the ladder propped against the wall. I thought you had kindly placed it there for me. Forgive me, now I realize that I was mistaken.'

'There is no need for forgiveness.'

'How can that be?'

'You were not so wrong after all. Do you know why I sent for the sorcerer?

'No, rani. I know nothing of sorcery or clairvoyance.'

'You have been on my mind ever since I saw you last morning. I wanted to know why you hadn't come to see me. That is why I sent for the sorcerer.'

'I am astounded.'

'Why?'

'I too have been thinking of you ever since I saw you yesterday.'

'Do you believe that memories of previous births follow us in this lifetime?'

'You mean . . .'

'I mean, do the ties of blood and friendship continue from past lives to create new bonds in our present life?'

'Yesterday, I had no such thoughts. Today, I have come to believe it.'

Though Vandiyatevan was lying blatantly, he did have the woman in the astrologer's house in mind when he made this statement. But as Nandini had no way of knowing it, she assumed that he was talking about her.

'But it is not that belief which made you seek me. You mentioned something about a message from Azhvarkadiyan Nambi . . .'

'Yes, my lady. At first, I wanted to meet you only to convey his message. But once I saw you, I forgot everything else . . .'

'Where did you meet Azhvarkadiyan? What is his message to me?'

'I met Azhvarkadiyan Nambi near Veeranarayana town. With the help of his staff, he was trying to establish Vishnu as the greater god. That was when Pazhuvettaraiyar arrived with his retinue. Your palanquin came with it. Your fair hand pushed the curtain a little aside, perhaps to see what the racket was all about. Azhvarkadiyan recognized you and wanted to send you a message. Since I was staying in Sambuvaraiyar's palace that night, he sent it through me. But I could meet you only on the Tanjavur highway, not in Kadambur, and only because your palanquin bumped into my horse.'

Vandiyatevan could not gauge Nandini's response as she was gazing at something above them. But when she heard his last words, she turned and smiled bewitchingly as she said, 'Yes. My palanquin can be rather headstrong.'

35

The Sorcerer

From afar came the boom of the *bherikai* drum and *ekkalam* horn, and human voices raising cries of victory; along with sounds of horses and elephants pounding the ground, and the opening and shutting of the fort's portals.

Vandiyatevan saw that these sounds had claimed Nandini's attention. The startled maid came in to say, 'Amma! The master must have arrived.'

'I know. Get back to your place,' Nandini told her.

To Vandiyatevan, she said, 'The Lord Chancellor of the Exchequer has arrived. He will first make enquiries about the king's health, meet his brother and then come here. You must leave before that. What did Azhvarkadiyan say?'

'He claimed you as his sister. Is that true?'

'Why do you doubt it?'

'How can one believe the parrot and the monkey are siblings?'

Nandini laughed as she replied, 'In a way, it is true. We grew up in the same family, in the same house. He loved me like his own sister. Poor man! I brought great disappointment to him.'

'The message that Azhvarkadiyan has sent you is this. Lord Krishna is waiting for you. The community of Vaishnava devotees is waiting to celebrate your marriage to the divine Krishna.'

Nandini heaved a big sigh. 'Ah! He has still not given up that fancy. If you see him, tell him to forget me completely. Say that I am unworthy of becoming such a consummate devotee as Andal.'

'I don't agree.'

'Don't agree with what?'

'I don't agree that you cannot be another Andal. Andal had to sing hymns, string garlands, offer worship, sing and weep to prove her devotion before she could marry Krishna. You, on the other hand, do not need to take all that trouble. Krishna has but to catch sight of you. He will promptly abandon his wives and lovers, and seat you beside him on the throne.'

'Ayya! You are good at flattering people to their faces. I don't like it at all.'

'Lady, What is "flattering someone to their face"?'

'To look at someone directly as you praise them.'

'All right. Please turn your back to me. Then you cannot accuse me of flattery when I praise you.'

'You are a smooth talker.'

'Now you are flattering me to my face.'

'You too can turn your back to me!'

'Great queen, I never turn my back on the battlefield or before a woman. You are free to look me straight in the eye and flatter me.'

Nandini broke into a peal of laughter. 'You are a sorcerer all right,' she said. 'I haven't laughed so freely in a long while.'

'But lady, it is dangerous to make you laugh. The lotus smiled in the pool. The honey bee dropped down in a swoon.'

'You seem to be a poet too!'

'Yes, I am. But I sing before my enemies, hoping to kill them with words if not with arrows.'

'O lionhearted king of bards! You have still not disclosed your name.'

'My name is Vandiyatevan, Vallavaraiyan Vandiyatevan.'

'From a royal clan?'

'I am a descendant of the renowned and ancient Vaanan tribe.'

'Where is your kingdom now?'

'The sky above and earth below. I am now the sole and unrivalled emperor of the entire planet.'

Nandini looked at Vandiyatevan for a few moments.

'It is not impossible to regain your ancient kingdom.'

'How is that possible? Can anything that goes into a tiger's belly ever be recovered? Can the kingdom assimilated into the Chozha empire be reclaimed?'

'I can make that possible.'

'No! Please! I have never wanted to be king. Any ambition of that kind I may have had has vanished after seeing Emperor Sundara Chozha today. Better to be a man who doesn't know where he may get his next meal than an emperor who has to depend wholly on others.'

'I agree,' Nandini said, and continued as if she had recalled something, 'Why are Chinna Pazhuvettaraiyar's men pursuing you?'

'Like your maid, they had doubts about me.'

'What doubts?'

'Doubts about how the signet ring with the palm tree emblem came into my hands.'

A shadow of fear passed across Nandini's face. Startled, she demanded, 'Where is it?'

'Here it is,' said Vandiyatevan as he drew it out and showed her. 'Would I ever lose it?'

'How did he know that you had this ring?'

'I had long wanted to see Emperor Sundara Chozha. I made use of this ring to fulfil that ambition. The commander of the fort asked me how it came into my hands.'

'What did you say?' Nandini's voice expressed her consternation.

'I did not mention your name. I said that Periya Pazhuvettaraiyar gave it to me in the Kadambur palace.'

Nandini heaved a sigh of relief. 'Did he believe you?'

'I don't think he believed me entirely. That is why he has sent his men to follow me. He might have wanted to haul me before his brother and get at the truth.'

Nandini smiled again and said, 'You need not be afraid of Periya Pazhuvettaraiyar. I will make sure that he doesn't gobble you up.'

'Devi, the whole world knows your influence over the lord chancellor of the exchequer. But I have urgent work to do. I beg you to help me escape.'

'What urgent work?'

'There is so much I need to do. For example, I have to convey your reply to Azhvarkadiyan. What should I say?'

'Tell him to forget that he ever had a sister called Nandini.'

'I can. But it will be in vain.'

'What will be in vain?'

'Forgetting you. Having seen you just twice, I find it impossible to even think of forgetting you. How can someone who spent such a long time with you hope to forget you?'

Nandini's face shone in triumph. Her eyes pierced Vandiyatevan like spears.

'Why were you so eager to see the emperor?'

'What is surprising about my desire to see the emperor renowned for his extraordinary good looks? Usually, kings wish to see their kingdom expand, their fame spread, and their courage and virility grow. They ask their subjects to pray for these goals. But what are the attributes mentioned by the Buddhist monks in their prayers for Emperor Sundara Chozha? They pray for his good looks to endure along with his liberality and might. For a very long time, I too have longed to see the man who is as handsome as the god of love.'

'Yes. The emperor is proud of his looks. His darling daughter is even more conceited . . .'

'Daughter? Whom do you mean?'

'That vain and arrogant creature, Kundavai Devi of Pazhaiyarai . . .'

Vandiyatevan said to himself, 'Vandiyateva! You are a lucky man. The brainwave you were looking for has appeared out of nowhere. Make good use of it.'

Nandini, who had been reclining elegantly until then, sat up suddenly.

'Ayya! I will make a suggestion. Will you accept it?'

'Say the word.'

'Let us make a pact, you and me. I will help you. You will help me. What do you say?'

'Devi! You are the queen of the omnipotent Pazhuvettaraiyar. You have the wherewithal to accomplish anything you want. I have no influence at all. How can I help you?'

Nandini directed her sharp glance at him to discover whether he was paying lip service or speaking from the heart.

Vandiyatevan stood resolute, unflinching.

'I need a confidential assistant. If I secure a job for you in this palace, will you accept it?'

'I have already agreed to perform this service to another great lady. If she rejects me, I will come back to you.'

'Who is this great lady who sets herself up as my rival?'

'The woman whom you spoke of just now and with great fondness–Princess Kundavai Devi.'

'That is a lie! It cannot be. You are making fun of me.'

'Great queen! So many people have already read this scroll on the sly. It will be no loss if you too were to see it.' As he spoke, Vandiyatevan held out Aditta Karikalan's letter to Kundavai.

Nandini read it under the light of the lamp. When she finished, the lightning streaks flashing from her eyes reminded Vandiyatevan of a serpent's forked tongue. His body trembled involuntarily.

Casting a regal glance at Vandiyatevan, Nandini demanded, 'Ayya! Don't you wish to escape from this fort with your life?'

'Yes. That is why I seek your help.'

'I may help you on one condition.'

'Tell me.'

'You must bring me Kundavai's reply to this letter.'

'A dangerous stipulation.'

'Did you not boast about your fearlessness just now?'

'But there should be some reward for taking such risks.'

'Reward? You want a reward? You will get the reward that you have not even dared to imagine in your dreams. The reward that Pazhuvettaraiyar, the most powerful man in this Chozha empire, has been craving for years now,' said Nandini, and once again cast her ravishing spell on Vandiyatevan.

Poor Vandiyatevan's head started spinning. He told himself, 'O heart! Hold firm! O mind! Don't go to pieces!'

Exactly at that moment, as if to save him, the harsh call of an owl came from the garden–once, twice, thrice.

Vandiyatevan shivered. Nandini looked in the direction from where the call came and said, 'The real sorcerer has arrived.' Then, pointing to the side directly opposite to the one the maid had taken, she said, 'Go there and hide yourself in the darkness. I don't need the sorcerer anymore, but I will have a word with him anyway. He may be of some assistance in helping you escape.'

36

'Do You Remember?'

Nandini stood at the threshold of the bower and clapped her hands thrice. Whether her face was suffused with fear or shadowed by trees was beyond conjecture.

In the garden, the ancient trees stood tall in a tangle of winding creepers, a miasma of darkness looming behind them. Slitting the darkness, the sorcerer shoved the creepers aside as he advanced from behind one of them.

Nandini went back to seat herself on the flower-strewn bed. Her lovely face was now calm and serene.

The sorcerer entered the arbour. The golden lamp shed its light on his face.

A familiar face . . . ? Who was he? Oh yes, he was one of the men gathered beside the sepulchral shrine in the Tirupurampiyam forest at midnight. It was he who had dropped the jingling coins from a pouch. It was the same Ravidasan who had ordered the others to kill Azhvarkadiyan wherever they found him.

Ravidasan's face was burning in wrath. Seeing Nandini seated on the flower bed in a state of composure made his feline eyes blaze in fury.

Taking the seat that faced the couch, he glared at Nandini and began to chant, '*Om hreem hraam bhagavati chandikesvari . . .*'

'Enough! Enough! The maid seems to have fallen asleep on the front steps. Say what you have to say and quickly. Pazhuvettaraiyar has entered the fort,' Nandini said.

'Bitch!' Ravidasan hissed like a cobra.

'Whom do you mean?' Nandini asked with unperturbed composure.

Pointing his finger at her, Ravidasan said, 'Nandini, the ingrate! Nandini, the young queen of Pazhuvur. *You*!'

Nandini remained silent.

'Woman! You seem to have forgotten the unforgettable. Let me remind you!'

'Why bring up the old story?'

'Why? I will tell you why after I remind you,' Ravidasan said.

Realizing that it was impossible to stop him, Nandini sighed and averted her face.

'O rani! Listen to me! Once, at midnight, three years ago, a funeral pyre was burning by the Vaikai River, built with dry branches, twigs and withered leaves lying on the forest floor. No priest was there to perform the final rites. A corpse was brought out from behind a tree and laid on the pyre. The men set fire to it. The sputtering twigs began to blaze. Then they dragged you out of the tree shadows. Your wrists and ankles were bound, your mouth stuffed with rags. Your unbound tresses, now braided and adorned with flowers, swept the ground. The men wanted to burn you alive on that pyre. One of them said, "Let us wait till the flames rise higher." As your eyes and ears were not blindfolded, you could see and hear each man taking a terrible oath. Then they approached you. You, who had been motionless until then, rolled your eyes and tried desperately to make some signs with your bound hands. One of the men said, "She wants to say something." Another dismissed it with, "Must be the same old story. Fling her into the fire." A third said, "No. Let's hear what she has to say before we burn her." Since he was their leader, the men removed the gag from your mouth. Woman! Do you remember what you said at that time?'

Nandini did not reply. She did not turn to face him. Her countenance showed repulsion, terror and the inexorable determination of oath-taking. Two teardrops trembled in her black eyes.

'Woman! You refuse to speak. Never mind. I will do it. You said that you too would take the same oath of vengeance. You swore that you had a greater cause for taking revenge. You said that you would use your beauty and intelligence in the cause. You promised to do your best to help the others. You vowed to kill yourself the moment the mission was fulfilled. No one believed you. I did. I saved you from being thrown into the fire. *I saved your life.* Do you remember?'

'You ask me if I remember! Everything has been etched on my heart with flames.'

'Later, one day, we were going through the woods beside the Kaveri. We heard the clopping of hoofbeats. We decided that we would hide until the horsemen rode past. However, you stood in the open. The soldiers captured you. Pazhuvettaraiyar, their leader, was snared by your beauty. You married him. My colleagues trounced me for having trusted you. I did not lose sight of you. Somehow, I managed to find you alone. I wanted to plunge my knife into you. Once again, you begged for your life. You said that you had done the deed only for the sake of fulfilling our oath. You swore to help us from the palace. Is this true or false?'

'True, of course. Who denies it? But why are you repeating this again and again? Tell me what brings you here now.'

'No. Woman, you *don't* remember. You have forgotten everything. You have forgotten your oath in all the luxury and opulence of the Pazhuvur palace. You are a queen feeding on sumptuous fare, adorned in silks and jewels, lying on a silken mattress in the ornate *sapramanja* bed,* and riding in an ivory palanquin. How can you hold on to old memories?'

'Chee! Chee! Who wants this bed and mattress, these jewels and silks? Do I live for these paltry comforts? Never!'

'Or maybe you have fallen for the handsome face of a young wayfarer. This new-found craze might have made you forget all thoughts of revenge.'

Nandini was a little jolted. She controlled it at once to remonstrate, 'Nonsense! Downright lies!'

'If it is all nonsense, why did you not send the maid to the appointed place even though I had informed you in advance?'

'I did. But another man came up the ladder meant for you. That stupid girl brought him, mistaking him for you. Is that my fault?'

'What does it matter whose fault it is? One moment more and I could have lost my life. The guards who pursued him were about to capture me. I saved myself by staying underwater in the pond beside this palace until I was nearly asphyxiated. I came here dripping wet . . .'

'You deserve it. You washed away your sin in doubting me.'

---

* A bed carved in an age-old, traditional style of carpentry, a status symbol.

'Woman! Tell the truth! Did you not fall for that boy's good looks?'

'Chee chee! Does anyone even think of a man's beauty? It is in this shameless Chozha kingdom that a king is celebrated for his good looks. A man's beauty shines in his battle scars.'

'Well said! If you are speaking the truth, why did this young man come here?'

'Did I not tell you that Vasuki mistook him for you?'

'Why did you give him the signet ring you have never given me?'

'To get him here and talk to him. I am taking it back now.'

'Why did you bring him here? Why were you jabbering with him for ever so long?'

'This "jabbering" has brought a great advantage. He could prove to be tremendously useful in fulfilling our mission.'

'Wretch! Finally, you have proved that women are witless. You have disclosed our secret to a stranger!'

'Why are you jumping up and down? I told him nothing. On the contrary, I extracted a secret from him.'

'What secret?'

'He is taking a scroll from Kanchi to Pazhaiyarai. He showed it to me. You came just as I was telling him to bring me the answer to that message.'

'To hell with scroll and stylus! How do they matter to us?'

'Does your brain work at all? We have vowed to destroy the entire clan of tigers. But you men think of tigers alone. You have forgotten that a clan can grow through tigresses as well. That is not all. Who do you think is ruling the Chozha empire today? The feeble old codger lying in bed? The two princes in Kanchi and Ilankai?'

'Not at all. The whole world knows that it is the Lord Chancellor of the Exchequer, Periya Pazhuvettaraiyar, who has had the good fortune to gain you as his queen.'

'Wrong! That is what the world thinks. This old man is also duped into believing it. You too have been similarly taken in. In reality, it is the young tigress in Pazhaiyarai who rules this kingdom. That haughty woman sits in the Pazhaiyarai palace and holds the strings as she controls and manipulates all the puppets. I am going to use this young man to crush her arrogance.'

Ravidasan's face now showed signs of surprise and respect.

'You are a genius all right. But how can I be certain that all this is true? How can I trust you?'

'I will hand over the man to you. Blindfold him and take him out of the fort by the underground passage. Then wait for him near Pazhaiyarai. Bring him back with Kundavai's reply. If he tries to trick you or to escape, kill him at once.'

'No! No! You and he may get lost for all I care! Chinna Pazhuvettaraiyar's men are hunting him now. Soon they will launch a search outside the fort. It will be dangerous for me to accompany him. Let us talk about what I came for.'

'But you haven't told me what you came for.'

'Arrangements have been made for men to go to Ilankai and Kanchi. It is a tough task for those who go to Ilankai. They have to behave with great circumspection.'

'What are you asking me to do? Do you want more gold? Is there no end to your gold craze?'

'The gold is not for our personal use, but for the mission. Why else would we have left you here? Chozha gold coins are of no use to those who are going to Ilankai. Better to have Ilankai coins.'

'Why did you take so long to say this? I have it all ready for you, unasked,' Nandini said and bent down to pick up a bag. She gave it to Ravidasan. 'This bag is full of gold coins from Ilankai. Take it and go. Pazhuvettaraiyar will be here anytime now.'

As Ravidasan took the bag and was about to leave, Nandini said, 'Wait. Take that man out of the fort. He can make his way from there. I don't want to show him the secret passage.'

Nandini got up and looked at the palace shrouded in darkness. She could see nothing there. She made a sign with her hands. Then she clapped gently. No response.

Nandini and Ravidasan walked down the path and reached the entrance of the dark palace, but Vandiyatevan was not there. He was nowhere to be seen.

37

The Lions Clashed

The citizens of Tanjavur had a special regard for the Pazhuvur brothers. Didn't they bring new pride and fame to their old city?

A procession of elephants, horses and camels is always an enjoyable pastime for the populace. Crowds always gathered on both sides of the street to watch Periya Pazhuvettaraiyar leave and return to the Tanjavur Fort. They hailed him, wished him well, and threw flowers and auspicious rice flakes on him.

It was the younger brother's practice to welcome the elder at the portals on his return. Thousands of eyes were needed to fully relish the sight of their riding side by side, mounted on horse or elephant. When they put their arms around each other, it was as though the Podigai hill and the Nilgiri hill embraced one another.

Some compared the Pazhuvur brothers to the mythical demons Hiranya and Hiranyaksha, or Sunda and Upasunda. Others saw them as the loving brothers Rama and Bharata, or the valiant siblings Bhima and Arjuna.

But on that day, when Periya Pazhuvettaraiyar returned to the fort, though his retinue made the usual din, there were no joyful echoes on the street. Nor was Chinna Pazhuvettaraiyar there to receive him.

Periya Pazhuvettaraiyar disregarded his brother's absence and went to see him, thinking that something important must have come up. Perhaps the emperor's health had taken a turn for the worse . . . or . . . the 'big event' had taken place . . . This doubt took him and his retinue faster than usual to his brother's palace.

The younger brother looked perturbed as he waited at the entrance to receive him. He bowed to his elder and embraced him. After that, both men went into the conference chamber reserved for private discussions.

Periya Pazhuvettaraiyar asked his brother, 'Tambi! Kalantaka! Why do you look worried? What has happened? Is the maharaja doing well?'

Chinna Pazhuvettaraiyar, who was named Kalantaka Kantan,* replied, 'No change in the maharaja's condition. No improvement, no deterioration.'

'Then why do you look downcast? Why did you not come to receive me at the gateway? Why is the city devoid of its usual bustle?'

'Anna! A small incident took place. No big deal. I will tell you about it later. What about the task that took you away?'

'A thumping success. Every one of the invitees came to Kadambur. Everyone raised cries of victory as they unanimously agreed that your son-in-law should be the next

* He whose throat made an 'end' of the poison. A name of Siva who drank poison and arrested it in his throat to save the world from destruction.

king. Each one is ready to take up the sword and make war if Madhurantakan's claim is not accepted. Nothing can subvert our plan when even Mazhavaraiyar and Vanangamudi Munaiyar have agreed to it. Sambuvaraiyar is ready to offer his fort, fortifications, army and wealth for our cause. His son Kandamaran is equally enthusiastic. No worries at all about most of the other regions. The Chozha land is completely in our hands. Tirukovilur Malayaman, Partibhendra Pallavan and Kodumbalur Velar will oppose us. But the Kodumbalur chieftain is in Ilankai, not here. What can the other two achieve by themselves? We must inform the emperor as soon as possible and take a decision,' Pazhuvettaraiyar said.

'What you say about the feudal lords is absolutely correct. But the people? What if the people object?'

'Ah! Who is going to ask the people? Are the people consulted over the business of governing a kingdom? If the people dare to object, we must take measures to ensure that they never do it again. But I don't think it would be necessary. The people will pipe down if we say that this is the king's wish. Fortunately, Arulmozhi is in Ilankai. If he were around, the masses may get carried away by their blind adoration for him. But they have no great fondness for Aditta Karikalan. It would be easy to divert them into doting on Madhurantakan instead. He has already earned a name for himself as a man of devout and noble character. And you know that your son-in-law is better looking than the sons of Sundara Chozha. People are silly enough to believe that the face reflects the mind. It would surprise me only if they did not start hailing Madhurantakan as their emperor. In any case, why should you worry when I am in charge?'

'But the Velakkara corps? How to handle them?'

'The Velakkara soldiers have taken their oath to sacrifice themselves for Sundara Chozha, not his sons. And should they interfere, where are your battalions guarding the fort? All you have to do is to capture all the Velakkara men and throw them into the dungeons.'

'Anna! The opposition from Pazhaiyarai will be the most powerful. We don't know what kind of intrigue the dowager and the damsel will trump up together. We must tackle it with all our strength.'

'Tambi! Kalantaka! Are you suggesting that I should cower at the thought of what these two *women* may do? Don't worry. I have strategies to take care of all their tricks and tactics.'

'The emperor has ordered that we should bring both his sons to Tanjavur at once.'

'Aditta Karikalan will not come. Arulmozhi may obey his father's command. We will have to stop him. They can be allowed to step into the city only after Madhurantakan is established as the crown prince, invested with all the powers that go with the position. Leave it to me. But you did mention some niggling incident. What is it?'

'A youth came from Kanchi with letters to the emperor and Kundavai.'

'What did you do? Grab the scrolls and imprison him?'

'No, Anna! He said that he saw you in Kadambur and that you asked him to deliver the letter to the maharaja in person. Is it true?'

'Ah! Nothing but a lie. A young man had come to Kadambur uninvited, claiming to be Kandamaran's friend. I had my doubts as soon as I saw him. Were you fooled by him?'

'Yes, Anna! I was. I was fooled because he mentioned your name.'

'Dei! Idiot! What did you do? Give the letter to the emperor? Did you check to see what it said?'

'I did. Nothing in it. Just an invitation to visit Kanchi. After handing it over, the young man said something to the maharaja about danger.'

'At least then did you suspect him and imprison him?'

'I suspected him but did not imprison him.'

'What did you do?'

'He said he wanted to see the sights. I sent him with two guards. He tricked them and disappeared. I did not come to the fort's gateway to welcome you because I was making arrangements to search for him. I have issued a warning to the people.'

'Chee! Are you a man? You allowed yourself to be duped by a boy who doesn't have hair on his chin? I must blame myself for naming you Kalantaka Kantan, the warrior who trounces death itself. I deserve this for making you the commander of the fort. Aren't you ashamed to say that a scoundrel used my name to hoodwink you?'

'He did not merely mention your name. He showed me your signet ring. Did you give it to him?'

'Never. Am I a simpleton like you?'

'It is true that he had the signet ring with him. He showed it to me. He entered the fort by showing it to the sentries. If it did not come from you, there is only one quarter from where he could have obtained it.'

'What do you mean?'

'Can't you guess? I mean the young queen.'

'Chee chee! Beware! I will cut off your tongue!'

'You may cut off my tongue. You may chop off my head. But I will tell you what I have been wanting to say for a very long time. You are fostering a poisonous snake in your bosom because it is beautiful. One day, it will certainly bite. It is going to destroy us all. Don't keep it! Drive her away before you do anything else.'

'Kalantaka Kanta! Today, I too will tell you something that I have long wanted to say. You can express your frank opinion on any subject. You are free to criticize any action of mine if you disapprove of it. But if you say a single word demeaning the woman whose hand I have taken in marriage, I will kill you with the same hands that raised you. I, who taught you to hold the sword, will snatch *your* sword and cut you dead. Beware!'

The war of words between the two brothers raged on like the clash of roaring lions. Their confidential exchanges in the conference chamber resounded like blasts of thunder portending some dreadful catastrophe. Those who heard them from the outside trembled in fear.

38

Nandini Sulks

It was well past midnight when Periya Pazhuvettaraiyar returned to his palace. Thoughts clouded and stifled his mind like a dust storm. He felt apologetic about having had to upbraid his dear brother so sharply. After all, it was his brother's boundless affection for him that had made him speak as he did.

But why should he blame Nandini unnecessarily? True, Kalantaka Kantan was suspicious by nature. It was also human nature to blame others for one's own mistakes. Why should his brother adopt this shameful course?

How can blaming a woman, his sister-in-law to boot, be reconciled with his valour and manliness? Especially after letting the boy slip through his fingers? Never mind. No need to think about it any more. After all, his younger brother had repented and begged for forgiveness.

Periya Pazhuvettaraiyar continued to ruminate. 'And yet, could there be an atom of truth in what he said? Have I started lusting for women in my old age? For the sake of a woman found in the wilderness, should I have reprimanded my brother, who has supported me in a hundred battles, and saved me from threats and dangers? After all, what is so special about her? I know nothing of her antecedents. At times, her speech and behaviour do give rise to suspicions. Chee chee! My brother's words have addled my brain. How unfair! She loves me with all her heart. She galvanizes me in my work! At times, she even helps me with suggestions. Should I not consider the fact that she dared to marry an old man, well past the age of sixty? Her beauty would arouse envy even among the heavenly *apsaras*.* If a swayamvaram were to be held for her to choose her partner, the king of heaven would rush to attend it. Why, what would have happened if Sundara Chozha had caught sight of her! How absurd to doubt her in any way! We have heard of how old men who marry young girls ruin their lives with baseless suspicions. We have seen such people in real life too. Should I allow myself to be universally ridiculed?

'And yet, I must talk to her and clear some doubts. Why does she ask for my signet ring from time to time? Why does she frequent the arbour in the garden, alone? Who is the sorcerer who visits her? She has admitted that he comes at her bidding, but what is she going to learn from him? Whom does she want to control with mantras? Worst of all, how long is she going to keep me at arm's length even though we are man and wife? She talks of some vow, some rite, all vague and undefined. Doesn't this appear to be like the manipulative tricks played by sirens in stories? I must not allow for this kind of thing to go on. Tonight, I must talk to her firmly and put an end to this issue.'

---

* Celestial nymphs.

When Pazhuvettaraiyar reached his palace, his other wives, maids and attendants were waiting at the entrance to welcome him. His eyes searched for the young queen he wanted to see. But she was absent. He was informed that she was in the arbour. 'What does she have to do in the arbour past midnight?' was the question that fuelled his doubt and indignation at being ignored by her.

As he walked to the arbour, he saw Nandini coming towards him. She stopped when she saw him and turned to stare at the dark garden. The maid had halted a little behind her.

Nandini did not look at Pazhuvettaraiyar even though he came up close to her. He, who had arrived intending to admonish her was reduced to placating her and striving to mitigate her annoyance.

'Nandini! My darling! Why are you angry? Why do you turn away from me?' he asked and placed his hand of iron gently on her shoulder.

With a hand as delicate as a flower, Nandini pushed his mighty arm away.

The victor of a thousand battles begged her, 'Dear life! It is my good fortune, my privilege, to be pushed away by a hand as soft as silk. You have done what the bravest of the brave from the Trikona hills to the Vindhya mountains cannot do. But should you not tell me why you are vexed? My ears yearn to hear your sweet voice!'

'How long have you been away from me? Four full days!' said Nandini with a sob. Pazhuvettaraiyar's heart, which could not be pierced by swords and spears, melted like wax in a flame.

'Is this the reason for your anger? You could not bear four days' separation from me? What will you do if I go to war? We will be separated for months.'

'Do you imagine that I would stay away from you for months altogether? Forget it! I will follow you to the wars like a shadow.'

'Madness! How can I fight with you beside me? Darling! My chest has borne the attack of innumerable weapons. The world hails me for the sixty-four battle scars I bear. But my heart will break if a small thorn pricks your tender foot. How can I take you to the battlefield? I am unable to bear the fact that you have been standing for so long on this hard floor. Come! Take your seat on your flower bed. Let me look at your lovely face. Don't imagine that you were the only one to suffer in these four days. Every moment I don't see you is an age to me. Let me gaze at your face now and assuage my longing,' said Pazhuvettaraiyar as he took Nandini by the hand and made her sit on the flower-bedecked couch.

Nandini wiped her eyes and looked up at Pazhuvettaraiyar. He saw her pearly smile glowing in the golden light of the lamp and wondered, 'Ah! All three worlds may be given away for this single smile! All I can do is to sacrifice my body, soul and all my possessions. But she demands nothing from me.' All thoughts of questioning and rebuking Nandini vanished. On the contrary, he was now ready to do her bidding in a state of abject surrender. Though every kind of slavery is despicable, nothing reduces a man to imbecility as being enthralled by a woman.

With a sidelong glance, Nandini said in mock anger, 'All right, you spent four days away from me. But why didn't you come straight here on your return? Your brother has become more important to you than me.'

'My darling, that is not true. I wanted to come straight to you like an arrow. But I had to stop by my brother's house to check if Madhurantakan, that silly boy, had made his way back safely through the secret passage.'

'Ayya! I care about every task you take up. I want all your efforts to be successful. And yet, I do feel unhappy about a man travelling in my palanquin. People everywhere believe that you take me with you wherever you go.'

'Do you think it makes me happy? Not at all. But I bear it for the sake of the task I have undertaken. Besides, have you forgotten that it was your idea? It was you who suggested that I should take Madhurantakan with me in your palanquin. It was you who suggested that he could enter and leave the fort through the secret passage.'

'I did nothing but my duty. I shared the little idea that I had. Is it not the wife's duty to support her husband in his work?'

'Was that your only contribution? This boy, Madhurantakan, wore rudraksha beads and sacred ash, chanted *om namasivaya* all day long, and talked about nothing but temple and pilgrimage, proving himself to be his mother's true son. Though all of us tried our best to interest him in ruling the kingdom, we met with nothing but resistance. You had two conversations with him. And he was transformed beyond belief. Now his fantasies have stretched his kingdom from earth to sky, from Ilankai to the Himalayan mountains. He has become far more impatient than all of us and cannot wait to ascend the Chozha throne. Nandini! I don't know what spells you cast on that boy. When you yourself are such a magician, why do you need a sorcerer? Giving rise to unnecessary . . .

'My king! If anyone gossips about it, it is your responsibility to cut off their tongue and teach them a lesson. I have already told you why I need the sorcerer. It is only to drain the venom from that female cobra in Pazhaiyarai. As men of valour, you confront other menfolk on the battlefield. You dismiss women as weak and insignificant. Though you would be ashamed to fight with a woman, a single woman can cause more havoc than a hundred men. You cannot even imagine the schemes that Kundavai can come up with. I can. You may have forgotten how she humiliated both of us. Not I. In the presence of a hundred women, she asked me, "That old lecher has lost his mind on his deathbed. Why did you lose yours? Why did you marry the old codger?" How can I forget her saying, "You shine like a celestial nymph. Any prince would have been happy to marry you and make you his queen. Why on earth did you marry this old buffalo?" As long as I am alive, I cannot forget these taunts.' Nandini burst into sobs. Tears streamed down her cheeks and drenched her breasts.

39

The World Spun Around

Pazhuvettaraiyar knew that there had been a great deal of gossip about his marrying in his old age. He had heard that Kundavai Devi was among those who derided him. But no one had repeated her actual words of censure to him. When he heard them now through Nandini's mouth, his heart turned into a furnace. His breaths came like the hissing of the bellows. Nandini's tears added fuel to the fire.

'My darling! Did that harpy say this? Did she call me an old buffalo? Wait. She . . . She . . . See what I do to her. I will crush her like a buffalo that crushes the lily creeper. And . . . I will . . . I will . . .' Pazhuvettaraiyar stuttered as he struggled to deal with the towering rage that blocked his speech. His face became indescribably grotesque.

Nandini tried to calm him down. She interlocked her slender fingers with his hand of steel.

'I know that you cannot bear the humiliation I endured. And yet, the lion, which has the power to tear off the hide of an elephant and drink its blood, is unable to pounce on a puny cat. It is with sorcery and spells that Kundavai is forcing everyone to dance to her tunes, and controlling this entire Chozha kingdom according to her will. Only with counter-spells can she be outsmarted. Tell me if you don't like it. I will leave this palace today,' said Nandini and began to whimper again.

Pazhuvettaraiyar's fury abated, only to be replaced by the mounting fever of desire.

'No. No. Call a thousand sorcerers if you like. Please don't leave me. You are as dear to me as life itself. No, you *are* my life. What can the body do if life departs? As it is, though I am alive, it is killing me that you are keeping me away from you. You know so many spells. Can't you teach me one?'

'Dear one! Why do you need spells when you have a sword and spear? Leave witchcraft and sorcery to helpless women like me. You don't need them.'

'Darling, desire sends tremors through my body when you open your coral lips and say, "Dear one"! Passion makes my mind spin when I see your fair face. It is true that I hold a sword and spear. I can use them on the battleground against foes. But how can they serve me in this bower of creepers? I don't have any weapons to ward off the arrows of the god of love. You ask me why I need spells. Only to extinguish the fire that is burning me up, body and soul. Give me a spell to deal with it. If not, grant me the privilege of caressing your body, delicate as a blossom. Save my life! Darling, it has been two-and-a-half years since you and I were wedded before the world according to the rites of faith. And yet, we have not begun to lead the conjugal life of a married couple. You keep me at arm's length pleading about vows and rituals. You torture the man who has taken your hand in marriage. Give me poison with your own hands and kill me.'

Nandini covered her ears with her hands and said, 'Ayyayyo! Don't speak such cruel words. Or I will drink poison and die. Then you can be at peace, free from suffering.'

'No. No. I will not say such things again. Forgive me. How can I be at peace if you drink poison and die? I am half mad now. If that happens, I will go completely mad!'

'Dear husband! Why should you go mad? On the very day we held hands and were married, our two bodies found a single soul. My life has merged into your life. My heart has become one with your heart. Every beat in your heart finds its echo in mine. Every thought dawning in your mind is reflected in the mirror of my mind. A twitch in your flesh vibrates in mine. Now that our souls are one, why bother about the worthless flesh? This body is made of the earth. One day, it will be burnt to cinders and mingle with the earth.'

Pazhuvettaraiyar shrieked, 'Stop! Stop! Your words scorch my ears.' Without allowing her to speak, he continued, 'Did you say that your body was made of the earth? That is an outright lie. Don't tell such an outright lie with your mouth as sweet as honey. There are any number of women in the world whom Brahma, the creator, might have made of earth, stone, lime or even coal and ash. But do you know how he shaped you? He collected the mandara flowers raining down from the tree in heaven. He came to this Tamizh realm and picked lotuses. He soaked them together in a golden vessel filled with the nectar of paradise. He infused the rays of the moon into it. He invited the bards of the ancient Tamizh land and asked them to play the harp. He poured their music into the miraculous mixture with which he shaped your form.'

'Dear one! You talk as if you saw all this standing beside the creator! But should you single me out for these outpourings? There are so many high-born women of royal blood in your palace. You have enjoyed many years of matrimony with them. It has hardly been two and a half years since you met me . . .'

Pazhuvettaraiyar interceded before she could finish, as though he wished to find a verbal outlet for the seething floods of passion in his heart or to put out the conflagration within by this rain of words.

'Nandini! You mentioned the women in my palace. I married them only to ensure the continuance of the old Pazhuvur race. Some of them proved to be barren. Others gave birth only to girls. I made my peace by deciding that it was god's will. For a long time, I had given up all thoughts of women. I was wholly focused on the work of governance. There was no place in my heart for anything but the welfare of the Chozha empire. Then the war with the Pandyas took place. I was unable to stay away even though there were many young leaders in the army. Anyway, our victory would not have been so all-encompassing without me. After planting the flag of victory in Madurai, I went to the Kongu land. As I was returning alongside the Kaveri, I saw you standing in the wilderness. At first, I didn't believe that you were real. I blinked my eyes. You were still standing there. I approached you thinking that you were a forest spirit and would disappear when I reached you. But you did not vanish. I thought that you must be one of those celestial beings afflicted by some curse and forced to descend to the earth. You would not know any human tongue. But I did ask, "Who are you?" You replied in excellent Tamizh, "I am an orphan. I seek shelter. Save me." As I brought you home on the palanquin, my mind encountered thoughts that it had never known before. I believed that I had seen you before but just could not recall where and when. Then, suddenly, the veil slipped. Truth dawned. I had seen you—not in this lifetime—but in many lives before. I was swamped by a tumultuous rush of all those memories from previous births. You were born on earth as Ahalya. I was Indra, king of the gods. I abandoned the heavens and dared to risk a sage's curse as I came seeking you. Then I was born as King Santanu. I saw you, the river Ganga, who had assumed a human form when I went hunting beside the river and fell in love with you. In another age, you and I were born in Poompuhar city as Kovalan and Kannaki. I was deluded into forgetting you for a while. When that illusion broke, I came to my senses and took you to Madurai city to sell your anklet. I lost my life due to malice. Then I saw you in this present life as I was returning from Madurai after wiping out the Pandya clan. I realized that you were the Kannaki from whom I parted hundreds of years ago.'

Nandini was looking away and not at him when Pazhuvettaraiyar narrated these stories. Therefore, he was unable to note the changing expressions flitting across her face. If he had, he might not have continued speaking.

When he paused for breath, she turned to look at him, bright-faced and smiling as before, and said, 'Dear husband, none of these references seem particularly suitable. In fact, they are rather unpropitious. If you like, call yourself Manmatha, the god of love, and call me Rati, his consort.'

Pazhuvettaraiyar's face shone in pride and joy. Even the ugliest man on earth cannot but rejoice to be called the god of love by the woman he adores. However, he spoke as if he disdained such praise. 'Darling! It would be perfect to call you Rati. But to call me Manmatha . . . You do so because of your inordinate love for me.'

'In my eyes, you are Manmatha. The beauty of a man lies in his valour. The whole world knows that no warrior in the realm can equal you. Also, a brave man's beauty is found in his compassion for the destitute. I am living proof of your compassion. You gave shelter to me, a poor orphaned woman whose birthplace and background were unknown. You gave me love and support. I will not make such a person wait for too long a time. My vow will soon come to an end.'

'Darling, please tell me exactly what it is. I will make sure that it is fulfilled as quickly as possible.'

'The descendants of Sundara Chozha, the man who gloats over his good looks, must not ascend the throne in Tanjavur. Kundavai's arrogance must be crushed.'

'Nandini! You can take it that these two wishes have been fulfilled. Neither Aditta nor Arulmozhi will get the crown. All the chieftains of the land have accepted Madhurantakan as the heir to the throne.'

'Is it true? Has everyone agreed?' Nandini asked sharply.

'Yes, with two or three exceptions. Kodumbalur Velar, Malayaman and Partibhendra Pallavan will never join us. We need not worry about them.'

'But should we not take every precaution until the job is done?'

'Undoubtedly. I *am* taking every care. Any error would be due to other people's foolishness. Even today, there has been a mishap. A young man from Kanchi has duped Kalantaka Kantan, met the emperor and delivered a missive.'

'Ah! You are always full of praise for your brother. But haven't I told you that he lacks astuteness?'

'He has certainly been foolish in this case. He says that the young man showed him our royal signet ring.'

'Those who get fooled will always try to get away with some excuse. Any efforts to catch the young man?'

'Yes. The hunt is on, inside and outside the fort. They will capture him. But this will not affect our task in any way. After the emperor's death, Madhurantakan's enthronement is a certainty.'

'Dear one! The time has come for me to tell you about my vow.'

'Darling! All along I have been asking you to tell me what it is.'

'My vow will not be fulfilled if Madhurantakan, that fool of a boy who drools over every woman he sees, comes to the throne.'

'Tell me your wish. I am here to fulfil it.'

'Lord! When I was a child, a famous astrologer examined my horoscope. He said that I would face many hurdles until I turned eighteen.'

'What else did he say?'

'He said that once I was eighteen, things would take a new turn. I would be elevated to an incomparable position.'

'He spoke the truth. Tell me who he is. I will shower him with gold.'

'Dear one!'

'Darling!'

'Shall I tell you one more thing that the astrologer told me?'

'Of course. You must.'

'He said that the man who married me would wear the crown and sit on the throne of a vast empire, hailed and served by the kings of the fifty-six kingdoms. Will you make that prediction come true?'

Pazhuvettaraiyar saw Nandini and her flower bed twirling before him. Steeped in darkness, the whole garden began to gyrate. He found the tops of the trees shimmering in the moonlight as they revolved around him. Even the stars in the sky wheeled above him. The palaces on both sides were spiralling in circles. The whole world seemed to be spinning around him.

40

The Palace of Darkness

Let us now see what happened to Vandiyatevan who had vanished from view. We last saw him hiding near the dark palace, half-heartedly trying to overhear the conversation between Nandini and the sorcerer without much success. Now he realized that when he talked to Nandini, he had felt a kind of inebriation blunting his brain. Best to escape without meeting her again as it seemed more dangerous to be caught by her than by the Pazhuvettaraiyars. Before them, his brain functioned well, his physical strength was reinforced and he retained a firm grip on the sword. But before this siren, his mind was drained of power. His hand lost its grip. Who knew what would happen if he were to find himself before her again? Moreover, she had a sorcerer for her associate. Who knew the spells they could conjure together?

How virulent and vindictive she was towards Kundavai Devi! Fire spurted from her eyes when she spoke of the princess. Women were known to be fickle and wayward, he thought. Nandini might change her mind and hand him over to Pazhuvettaraiyar after all. Best to escape from her unscathed. But how? He would have to find his way through the garden and jump down from the wall. But what if his pursuers were waiting by the wall?

'Vandiyateva!' he said to himself. 'What happened to the luck that helped you all these days? Prod your brain! Use your eyes. Look around. Why is this palace seeped in darkness? What could it contain? Where would its door on the other side lead to? Should I explore it anyway? Who knows, one day it might come in useful. But how to get in? What a mammoth door! What a massive lock! Ah! There seems to be a door within the door. It opens when I touch it. This is luck indeed! Well, I will have to take my chance!'

Vandiyatevan entered through the small door within the big door and shut it behind him because he did not want Nandini to discover his whereabouts. The darkness increased by several degrees. The colonnade he had seen by the half-open door was now invisible in the unimaginable pitch blackness. He braced himself with the thought that darkness was intensified when one came in from the light. A little later, the eyes would adjust themselves to see. Why fear the dark when he knew this from experience? He could use his tactile sense to explore. The pillar he had seen earlier could not have disappeared into thin air.

Vandiyatevan took a few steps blindly, hands outstretched. He touched a pillar. What a pillar! A huge column of black granite. He went around it to feel another. But he could see nothing. Had he turned blind? What madness! How can one turn blind all of a sudden? He decided to go forward. No colonnade there, but he had the sensation of going down. Ah! A step. Good thing he didn't trip. Vandiyatevan felt a stab of fear as he wondered how long he would have to continue this sightless walk in the dark. He could not go on.

He had to get back to the arbour. Better to meet Nandini again and follow her advice than to drown in this darkness. He could promise her anything and manage to get out of the deal when the time came.

Vandiyatevan turned back, but was he going in the direction from which he entered? How could he be certain? Now his hands moved in the empty air. Where did the granite pillars go? Would he ever find the door? Would he have to wander in the dark forever? God! What a calamity!

Ah! What was this noise? A sputtering noise. Bats dwell in darkness, and this must be the fluttering of their wings. No. There were footsteps. Human footsteps? Or . . . Vandiyatevan's throat dried up. His tongue cleaved to his palate. He gathered all his strength and threw a mighty punch. Only to feel the agony of a hand being cut off. He stretched the other hand and found that he had not only banged himself on a pillar but punched it too. Vandiyatevan would have laughed out loud but for the excruciating pain. The impulse reduced but did not banish his fear. He strained his ears to hear the footsteps that were gaining in volume. They tantalized him by sounding alternately near and far. He stopped, focused his attention and stared in the direction of the sound.

'Ah! Light! There . . . ! Light! Brighter and nearer . . . Light and smoke. Someone is approaching with a torch. Perhaps Nandini was coming in search of him. That would be good. But what if it was somebody else? Best to hide and wait. After all, there is no dearth of hiding places.'

The torch made him see that he was in a large hall. Its huge pillars were carved with figures of hideous ghouls. A staircase came up into it, took a curve and then went upward. He saw that the torchlight came from below the staircase. Were the dungeons he had heard about situated below that dark palace? Was someone emerging from the dungeons? It could not be Nandini. Vandiyatevan sprang to hide behind a huge pillar. He had heard a great deal about the torture chambers in those dungeons. The very thought brought drops of sweat from every pore in his body. And Vandiyatevan, the daredevil, found himself going limp and shaking like a leaf.

Three figures came up the staircase. All humans. One held the torch. Another held a spear. The man in the middle had nothing in his hands. The moment he saw their faces, Vandiyatevan's fear vanished. He was overcome by an astonishment far greater than the fear he had felt earlier. The man who came first was none other than Vandiyatevan's dear friend Kandamaran. The figure in the middle aroused a strange sense of bemusement. For an instant, he thought it was Nandini, the young queen of Pazhuvur. But it was a man, the man he had glimpsed in the Kadambur palace, Prince Madhurantakan. He had never seen the third man who was surely a guard or an attendant.

Vandiyatevan's brain worked at top speed. All too soon, he understood the mystery of their passing through the underground staircase. The Pazhuvur queen had returned in her palanquin the day before. Pazhuvettaraiyar was back that evening. Both had entered the fort openly. But Madhurantakan's comings and goings had to be undercover activities. This subterranean passage was useful for this purpose. This was the mystery of the unilluminated palace.

After seeing Vandiyatevan near the Kollidam, Kandamaran must have joined Pazhuvettaraiyar at some appointed place. Pazhuvettaraiyar had made use of him for this hidden manoeuvre. He also remembered Kandamaran telling him that he too may land up in Tanjavur on some work. What would Kandamaran do if Vandiyatevan stepped out suddenly and stood before him? But he dismissed the thought. If he saw Vandiyatevan there, Kandamaran would have to kill him according to the vow he had taken. Or Vandiyatevan would have to kill his friend. Why create such a predicament?

The three men went up the staircase. The light began to dim. Vandiyatevan thought of following them but changed his mind almost immediately. It was certain that they were going to Chinna Pazhuvettaraiyar's palace. Why should he go there? Escape from the lion's den only to stick his head back into the lion's jaws? Nor was it advisable to return to Nandini's arbour. Periya Pazhuvettaraiyar would have reached it by now. What should he do? Why . . . he could go down the staircase . . .

The young warrior began to climb down the stairs.

41

The Subterranean Vault

Vandiyatevan walked down the dark underground stairs, placing one foot after another firmly and carefully. After a while, the stairs reached ground level, went up again and ended on flat ground. He concluded that the pathway had to be a wide one because he could stretch his hands on both sides without touching the walls. Then he hit the stairs again, this time curving upward. Good god! How much longer would he have to stumble through pitch darkness?

Ah! What was this? The darkness was yielding to some dingy light. Where did it come from? Was it moonlight piercing through an aperture in the ceiling? Or a high window? The spreading light of a hidden lamp?

No! No! What a miracle! But was the scene before him real at all? Or a figment of some disoriented fantasy?

Vandiyatevan found himself in a wide, subterranean rock-cut vault, with a flat ceiling low enough to hit the head while standing. Here, the pale light of the moon did not merely come through the roof or window. It was reflected by objects lying in piles both widespread and high. What kind of objects could refract light? Then he saw them. Crowns studded with diamonds and pearls. Necklaces, chokers, strings of pearls and ornaments with the nine gems. There! What did that cavernous cauldron hold? 'God! Pearls! Huge and heavy! Pearls as white as the buds of the punnai flower!' he exclaimed. 'That pot is filled with gold coins sparkling like the sun! And here lies a heap of gold bars! This must be the underground treasury of Tanjavur. No surprise that this dark palace and underground treasury should be located adjacent to the palace of Pazhuvettaraiyar, the Lord Chancellor of the Exchequer. What great good luck has landed me in this subterranean vault! Surely, the goddesses of wealth and good fortune have bestowed their grace upon me. I have learnt this rare and precious secret without any effort on my part. But how can I make use of it when all I want to do is to loiter around here? As long as I am here, I will not know hunger or thirst or even sleep. All the fruits of the Chozha army's victories of a hundred years are right here. The fabled wealth of the legends is here. A bounty greater than the mythical treasures of Kubhera, the god of wealth. Why should I leave this crypt at all?'

Vandiyatevan circled the chamber. He touched the crowns lying in the corner. He examined the gem-studded ornaments. Suddenly, he dropped a neckpiece to plunge his arms into the copper cauldron filled with pearls. He grabbed fistfuls of gold coins and let them drizzle down his fingers. Then he approached the corner where he saw something longish and gleaming. At first, he could not make out what it was and bent down to examine it more closely. Every hair on his body stood on end. He thought he was going mad. 'Ayo! God! A skeleton! The skeleton of a human body that had once been filled with blood, flesh, skin, hair, face, nose and eyes . . . Ah!

The skeleton moves. It comes alive! It makes a noise like a shower of gold coins . . . It is rising up to say something to me . . . Chee! Chee! Nothing but a bandicoot rushing out of it to run over my foot. The skeleton is still lying on the floor. But it is indeed saying something to me. It is warning me. *Run! Don't linger! Once, I too was a man of blood and flesh like you. Then I got trapped here. Now I lie here as a skeleton. Go! Run!* If I don't escape, I will face the same fate. I will be doomed.'

Vandiyatevan tried to find a way out of the vault. Darkness yawned at him from every corner. He sensed unfathomable depths below. As he wandered round and round, trying to find the staircase he had taken, he saw a heap of gold coins covered by cobwebs. It reminded him of how the ancients had compared the lust for land, women and gold to a spider's web. The fly gets trapped in the web to be slowly drawn in and swallowed by the spider. Man loses his way and is inescapably drawn into the snare. He cannot get out. In the end, he discovers that the three kinds of lust are one and the same.

On that very day, Vandiyatevan had experienced all three–the lust for land, women and gold. Nandini had tried to capture him in her web of seduction. She had also tempted him with the possibility of regaining his ancestral kingdom. He had managed to extricate himself from both temptations. And now, finally, this spine-chilling spectre, the greed for gold, was trying to devour him. Somehow, he must escape from this threat as well.

Why invite trouble? Kingdom, wealth, women–did he need them at all? The vast earth roofed by the sky was his palace. He belonged to every town and village. Every human being was his kin. He would travel from place to place. He would rejoice in everything he saw–fresh floods rising in the rivers, trees sprouting new leaves, mountain peaks, sky, clouds, oceans, waves . . . He would eat where he could, sleep where he liked. Ah! That was the true life of bliss. Why give up a life so easily attainable and opt for a life of troubles, intrigues, temptations, dangers . . . What he had to do now was to escape from the crypt, the dark palace and the Tanjavur Fort, and make sure that he never got into such dire straits again.

Ah! The sound of a door opening . . . Footsteps once again . . . It seemed there was to be no end to the marvels *and* the horrors of that night. This time the footsteps came from a great distance, as if they were approaching from two different directions. Vandiyatevan sharpened his ears. He stared hard as if he would tear the darkness apart. Soon, like a distant spectator, he witnessed what appeared to be an uncanny scene being played out on a high stage.

A torch appeared from the wings as it were, making two black, lanky figures visible. A second torch came from behind a lifted curtain on the opposite side, revealing two other black figures—one tall and regal, the other short and slender. The torches approached each other.

Vandiyatevan stared until his bulging eyes threatened to pop out. He could recognize the figures. On the left were Kandamaran and the attendant who had accompanied him earlier. On the right, he saw Periya Pazhuvettaraiyar and his young queen Nandini Devi.

Would the two groups come into some conflict or would they simply nod and move on? Vandiyatevan held his breath.

The two groups met. Both seemed to be taken aback by the encounter. But nothing untoward happened. Vandiyatevan could hear neither Pazhuvettaraiyar's question nor Kandamaran's reply. Pazhuvettaraiyar made a sign and pointed to the staircase in the secret passage. Kandamaran bowed respectfully to him before stepping into it. Then

Pazhuvettaraiyar gestured silently to the attendant. He did not reply but bowed, covering his mouth deferentially with his hand, before following Kandamaran. Pazhuvettaraiyar and the young queen took the path in the other direction.

Resembling shadow play and puppet theatre as it did, this entire sequence had a run time of just a few minutes. Vandiyatevan noticed that it happened beside the staircase where the steps went down to the secret passage. How lucky that he had not tarried anywhere as he roamed in the dark. He had been lucky to have escaped getting caught by the two groups. What next? Undoubtedly, Kandamaran was returning to the same path by which he had brought Madhurantakan. Vandiyatevan too had been on that passage. But he had wandered into the treasury. But now, if he followed Kandamaran, he would surely find the exit door. He could contrive to escape or ask Kandamaran for help. Worst case scenario, he could manage to overcome Kandamaran and the attendant by using force and make his escape. Either way, he simply had to follow Kandamaran.

At first, it looked as if the torchlight was coming close to the vault. Vandiyatevan held his breath even as the light moved away. By now, Vandiyatevan had noted the descending staircase. Moving silently, he went down the stairs only to find himself climbing up again. He had to remain out of sight while also ensuring that the torchlight did not go out of *his* sight. Without guidance, he would have never found his way on the path which went not merely up and down, but also curved, slid, circled and twisted itself in the darkness.

A grateful Vandiyatevan asked himself how he could repay his friend for the great favour he had done him, albeit unknowingly.

He certainly did not anticipate that the opportunity would occur quite so soon.

The tunnel came to an end before a huge wall. No outlet or door could be seen on that wall. But it had to be there!

The guard shifted the torch from his right hand to the left. He placed his right hand on the wall and twisted something on it. A thin crack appeared on the wall. It got wider and wider until it became wide enough for a man to pass through. The guard pointed a finger at it. Kandamaran said something to the guard and placed one foot across the crack with the other foot still within the passage.

His entire back was exposed now.

Ah! What was this? What was the guard doing? He was drawing a small, sharp dagger from his waist. He plunges it into Kandamaran's back. Scoundrel! A scoundrel who would stab a man from behind when his victim's back was turned to him.

Vandiyatevan took a giant leap forward. The guard turned when he heard the noise. The light of the torch fell on Vandiyatevan's face.

42

'Do You Call This Friendship?'

Vandiyatevan's first impulse was to save Kandamaran. But if he attended to Kandamaran first, he would have to undergo Kandamaran's fate. He had to deal with the brutish guard. So, he twisted his arm around the guard's head and struck at his torch with the other. The torch fell to the ground and began to spew more smoke than light. Vandiyatevan tightened his grip and used all his strength to push the guard down to the ground. As the guard slumped down, his head hit the granite wall. When Vandiyatevan held the torch above him, he looked dead. Still, as a precaution, Vandiyatevan took his shoulder cloth and bound his hands firmly with it. Performing these actions in a few seconds, he ran to Kandamaran and saw him sprawled half in and half out of the exit door, the dagger still stuck in his back. His spear lay beside him. Vandiyatevan went out, pulled Kandamaran through the door and took his spear. The door shut itself at once. The wall merged into the darkness, taking its secret with it.

The gusty wind blew over him. Vandiyatevan realized that he was outside the fort. There was little light as the moon was hidden by thick trees and massive fortifications. Vandiyatevan threw Kandamaran on his shoulder, picked up his friend's spear and took a step forward. He felt the ground giving way under him. Thrusting the spear on the ground to balance himself, he made a great effort to stand upright. He looked down and saw the waters shadowed by trees and ramparts. A hair's breadth escape from death. God had saved them. That scoundrel of a guard . . . ! But what was the use of cursing him? He was only executing his master's command. He must have wanted to kill Kandamaran at the exit door and toss the corpse into the river below. If Vandiyatevan's foot had slipped a fraction more, he and Kandamaran would both be in the waters by now. He might have made it somehow, but Kandamaran would have met his end.

Vandiyatevan had heard that the Vadavaru flowed close to the Tanjavur Fort. It was not in full spate at this time, but it could have been deep beside the fort. Vandiyatevan plunged his spear into it. Even when the spear was almost submerged, it did not touch the river bed. He had to find a way to escape and save Kandamaran too. He had no time to think of the barbarians who had left them in this situation.

Vandiyatevan walked beside the river, taking each step as firmly as he could until the fort's walls were left behind and he saw the woods stretching before him. Every step felt painful as if the ground was full of thorns, but he was heartened to hear Kandamaran groan now and then.

What was this? A tree had fallen into the river. It must have been a tall tree. The floods had torn its roots away, but the tree stretched halfway across the waters. Vandiyatevan tried his best to steady himself as he scrambled across the trunk. The tree was juddering as its leaves and branches were tossed by the racing currents. The winds were blowing at an incredible speed.

As he came to the other end of the tree, he immersed his spear into the waters again. Thank goodness. It was not so deep there. Vandiyatevan got down and managed to walk on the uneven river bed, combating the speeding currents and high winds with sheer willpower. His body was shaking badly. There were times when Kandamaran was in danger of sliding down his shoulders. Somehow, Vandiyatevan overcame all these hazards to make it to the shore. After stumbling along for some time, dripping wet from the waist, bearing Kandamaran's heavy muscular body on his shoulders, Vandiyatevan spied a tree whose foliage offered some cover and lowered his friend gently to the ground. He wanted to rest for a little while and check if Kandamaran was still alive. Why carry a corpse? Better to drop the body into the floods as the guard had planned to do. No! No! Kandamaran was alive. He was breathing rather heavily. His pulse was beating fast. His chest was heaving. What should he do now? Pull out the dagger from his back? If he did, Kandamaran would die due to excessive loss of blood. The wound had to be treated and bound quickly. He could not do it by himself and needed to enlist some help. Vandiyatevan remembered Sendan Amudan. His house and garden were on the banks of the Vadavaru, perhaps close by. Kandamaran stood a chance of surviving if he could be carried to Sendan Amudan's house. Vandiyatevan had to try.

When Vandiyatevan tried to hoist him up once again, he was surprised and delighted to see that Kandamaran's eyes were open.

'Kandamara! Do you recognize me?'

'Yes. Very well. You are Vandiyatevan. How can I not recognize you? How can I forget a dear friend like you? Are you not the best friend who stabs from behind?' Kandamaran said.

Vandiyatevan felt as if he was being horsewhipped. 'Ayo! Was it I who stabbed you from behind?' he began. He stopped abruptly as he remembered something.

'You did not stab me. Your dagger simply stroked my back. Scoundrel! It was for your sake that I came rushing down the underground passage so quickly. I hastened to reach you before Pazhuvettaraiyar's men could. I swore to find you and get you recruited in Chinna Pazhuvettaraiyar's security forces. I wanted to inform you about an imminent change in the Chozha government. How many times had we held hands and vowed to help one another? You have betrayed the friend who wanted to help you. Do you call this friendship? Is there anyone left in the world who can be trusted?' said Kandamaran and closed his eyes. His voluble and enraged outpouring drained all his energy and made him faint once again.

Tears sprang to Vandiyatevan's eyes as he muttered, 'No one to trust you say? Should you trust the Pazhuvettaraiyars then?' He hauled his friend up again and started walking with the thought that it was best to leave unsaid what he had wanted to say.

Suddenly, there came a burst of fragrance from night-blooming flowers. He had not been wrong in presuming that Amudan's house was close by. Though he reached the garden soon enough, what he saw was a garden that was nothing like what he had seen the day before. Now it looked like the grove Asokavanam, ravaged by Hanuman, the monkey god. Ah! Pazhuvettaraiyar's men must have come searching for him and razed it to the ground. Sendan Amudan and his mother had worked so hard to nurture this garden! Now devastated!

Vandiyatevan's empathy for the damaged garden was replaced by anxiety over his own dangerous plight. What if the spies and guards from the fort were waiting for him somewhere close by? He would have to take his chances in fighting with them. Thank god, his horse was still tethered to the tree. But could it have been left behind as bait? He would have to leave Kandamaran with the good people in the house, mount his horse and ride hell for leather. He would have to make the poor horse gallop at full speed until he reached Pazhaiyarai.

Vandiyatevan walked with extreme caution and reached the front door. Amudan was sleeping outside on the raised *pyol** near the door. He was startled to be awakened by a tap on the shoulder. Vandiyatevan covered his mouth with his hand and whispered, 'Tambi! You will have to help me. I am in grave danger. This is my dear friend, Kadambur Sambuvaraiyar's son, Kandamaran. Someone stabbed him and left him for dead. I carried him here.'

'O the devils! How gallant they must be to have stabbed him in the back,' Amudan said, and added, 'I will do the best I can for him. Since last evening, groups of men have been coming here to search for you. The garden has been ruined by them. Never mind. I will be glad if you can escape. Fortunately, they have left your horse. Take it and go at once.'

'That is my intention. But something must be done to save this man's life.'

'Don't worry. My mother is an expert in the art of healing. She knows very well how to treat wounds like these,' Amudan said and knocked gently on the door. The door opened at once. Amudan's mother was at the threshold.

---

* Raised platform at the entrance of the house in the verandah or porch.

The two men carried Kandamaran inside. In the light of a handheld lamp, Amudan spoke to his mother in signs. She appeared to understand him very well. She took one look at the dagger embedded in the flesh and went in to bring some herbs and rags. Then she looked at the two men standing by.

Sendan Amudan held Kandamaran tight. With great effort, Vandiyatevan yanked out the dagger that had been embedded in the flesh until then. Blood spurted out. Though unconscious, Kandamaran let out a scream. Vandiyatevan closed his mouth. Amudan pressed his hand on the wound. Amudan's mother placed some fresh herbs on the wound and bound it up. Kandamaran groaned again.

They heard the sounds of running feet. 'Go! Go! At once!' Amudan urged Vandiyatevan.

Vandiyatevan took the bloodstained dagger and spear. He started to leave but hung back at the door. 'Tambi! Do you trust me?' he asked.

'I trust in god. I have affection for you. Why do you ask?'

'You must do me a favour. I don't know the way in these parts. I must go to Pazhaiyarai quickly. To take an urgent message to Kundavai Devi. Can you come with me for a short distance to show me the way?'

Sendan Amudan spoke to his mother in gestures. She did not look surprised. She made signs telling him to go; she would look after the wounded man.

The two men left the house and mounted the horse with Amudan sitting behind the warrior. Vandiyatevan guided the horse to trot slowly and silently. After covering some distance, he tugged at the reins. The horse began to tear away.

When the horse left, five or six soldiers came to the house and banged on the door.

Amudan's mother opened the door and stood at the threshold.

'Who was screaming here?' one of the soldiers shouted.

Amudan's mother burbled some gibberish.

'What's the use of talking to this deaf mute? Let's go in and see.'

'But she's blocking the way.'

'Where has that boy with the flowers gone?'

'Push the dumbo aside and get in!'

Sendan Amudan's mother shouted again in a language of her own. She tried to push the man who was shoving her and shut the door. But three or four men held the door and prevented her from shutting it.

Amudan's mother shrieked even more as she suddenly let go of the door. Two or three men rolled to the ground. The others stepped on them as they entered the house.

One of them shouted, 'The man is here!'

'Got caught, did he?' said another.

'Tie him up, he may try to run,' said a third.

The dumb woman wailed.

One of the men shrieked, 'Blood everywhere!'

The dumb woman lifted the handheld lamp over the wounded man and babbled again.

'Dei! Looks like someone else.'

'Bb-eaea b-b-ae ae!' Amudan's mother moaned.

'Is this the man who arrived here yesterday?'

'Bb-eaea b-b-ae ae!'

'Where's your son?'

'Bb-eaea b-b-ae ae!'

'Dumbo! Stop it! Dei! Look at him properly. Do you recognize him?'

'It's not him!'

'It's him all right.'

'Not at all.'

'Bb-eaea b-b-ae ae!'

'Whoever he may be, he is still a stranger. Lift him up!'

'Bb-eaea b-b-ae ae!'

'Devil! Stop it!'

Four men lifted Kandamaran together.

'Bb-eaea b-b-ae ae! Bb-eaea b-b-ae ae!' Amudan's mother screamed unceasingly.

'Dei! Can you hear a horse?'

'Some of you can pick him up. The rest can run and see!'

'This man won't go anywhere! Run!'

Dropping Kandamaran to the ground, everyone ran out.

Amudan's mother moaned on and on, 'Bb-ea b-b-ae !' 'Bb-ea b-b-ae !'

43

Pazhaiyarai

Before Vandiyatevan overcomes all kinds of dangers and difficulties to land in Pazhaiyarai, we invite our readers to join us on a visit to that hallowed city.

Let us stand on the southern bank of the Arasalaru for an overview. God! Is this a city at all? Or is it an ornament encrusted with emeralds, rubies and sapphires adorning the beauteous forehead of the mother goddess of Tamizh?

Fresh waters are brimming in the rivers, streams, pools and fields, packed with flowers of many hues. The tennai and punnai trees spread their cool shades of green. The konrai trees are festooned with innumerable golden showers. Between them, the golden spires of the temples and the towering domes of the grand terraced mansions cast their scintillating light.

Goodness! How many towns are encompassed within this single city of Pazhaiyarai, the erstwhile Chozha capital?

Four Siva temples are located in the four cardinal directions. There are four colonies where the warriors serving in the Chozha army dwell with their families. The crown jewel of the city is the royal palace. A single mansion during the time of Vijayalaya Chozha, it has since then expanded into an architectural complex with a new palace built for each succeeding king, queen and princess. This many-splendoured marvel requires a thousand eyes to see and ten thousand bards to describe.

Two centuries later, if the poet Sekkizhar could describe Pazhayarai as 'the world-famous city of wide streets paved with cobblestones that shone like pearls, and crowded with chariots', one can imagine the magnificence of the city during the reign of Sundara Chozha.

And yet, sadly, on our first visit, we are not lucky enough to see this large and ancient city in all its spectacular pomp when Sundara Chozha ruled the empire from the Pazhaiyarai palace.

Once ill health constrained Sundara Chozha to move to Tanjavur, the feudal lords, ministers, generals and other government officers shifted to the new capital with their families. Pazhaiyarai could no longer attract visits from kings of other lands, foreign diplomats and royal envoys, all trailing their large retinues.

Half the warriors who lived in the four military colonies were now fighting in Ilankai. Others were located in Madurai and at the northern border. Only senior citizens, women and children were to be seen in those colonies now. And that part of the city which had been occupied by the Velakkara corps was completely deserted. Those houses were under lock and key, as the troopers had departed to Tanjavur.

Despite this, there was no dearth of high spirits and good cheer on the crowded streets of Pazhaiyarai. They were now frequented by temple architects, sculptors, Saiva monks, hymnodists, palace employees, temple priests and pilgrims who had come to worship and enjoy the festivals.

Today seems to be one such day of festive celebrations. Dressed in their best, men and women, boys and girls are sauntering down the streets. Ah! Now we know why. Today is Krishna Jayanti, and the people are romping, frolicking and splashing turmeric water everywhere as they celebrate the birthday of their beloved god Krishna. There are crowds at every street corner where shows of dance and music are being held. The actors are dressed as Krishna and the cowherds. There! Krishna is lifting the mountain! Indra, king of the gods, is bowing to him. And over here, the divine Brahma is praying to the blue god.

The festivities are at their height around the Vishnu temple in Nandipuram.

I've seen, I've seen, I've seen

I've seen what is sweet to the eye

Who is singing these lines? The voice sounds familiar! Why, it is our old friend Azhvarkadiyan Nambi himself! People have gathered around him—some are listening with rapt devotion while others are beginning to ridicule him. We wonder whether a few heads are going to get slammed by his staff all too soon.

There is some commotion in front of the temple. The chariots and palanquins parked by the roadside begin to move to the entrance. Some high-born ladies, obviously belonging to an aristocratic household, are emerging from the temple.

They are the queens and princesses from the Pazhaiyarai palace. Dowager queen Sembiyan Mahadevi, universally revered across the country, comes first. She is the daughter of the Mazhavaraiyar clan and was the queen consort of the Late King Gandaraditta Chozha, the devout Saiva savant. Even at this ripe old age and in a widow's garb, her face beams radiance. Behind her comes Queen Kalyani of the Vaidumbaraya tribe, the wife of Arinjaya Chozha. Her appearance defies description. What a beauty she must have been in her youth!

It was hardly surprising that her son, Sundara Chozha, should have inherited her stunning good looks. They are followed by Parantakan Devi of the Chera dynasty, another wife of Sundara Chozha. Behind them, we see Kundavai Devi, Vanathi and the girls we met near Arasalaru, looking like nymphs descended from the heavens.

From the time of Vijayalaya Chozha, the Chozha royals had worshipped Siva and Durga. But this did not make them shun Vishnu, which is why we see them here at the Vishnu temple on the day of Krishna's birth.

As she was about to enter the palanquin, Queen Sembiyan Mahadevi happened to hear Azhvarkadiyan's song. Perhaps he sang so loudly to make sure she heard him. She had him brought to her.

Azhvarkadiyan stood before her, the picture of humility.

'Tirumalai! You have not been around for some time. Were you on a pilgrimage?'

'Yes, Amma! I did go to Tirupati, Kanchi, Veeranarayanapuram and other places. I saw many strange things.'

'Come to the palace tomorrow and tell me about them.'

'Amma, I cannot. I have to leave again tonight.'

'In that case, come this evening.'

'Yes, Amma, your wish is my command.'

Kundavai Devi pointed to Azhvarkadiyan and said something to her companions. Their giggles rang out. Azhvarkadiyan glanced at them. Kundavai Devi's eyes transmitted a message to him. Azhvarkadiyan bowed his head in acknowledgement.

The palanquins and chariots hastened to the palace.

* * *

Sembiyan Mahadevi's palace was at the very centre of the Chozha palace complex. She was in the audience chamber, seated on a gem-studded throne of gold. Belonging to the tradition of the Saiva women saints Karaikkal Ammai and Tilakavati, she wore plain white silk with sacred ash and rudraksha beads as her sole adornments, proving by example that it was possible to lead the life of a renunciate in the midst of immeasurable wealth. Though she wore neither crown nor jewels, her majestic appearance and the inner light shining on her countenance were enough to show that she was born and married into royalty, and that she was the queen of queens. No wonder every member of the Chozha clan, without exception, revered and hailed her as a divinity, and never acted against her will.

And yet, it seemed that this immutable reverence had begun to develop a fault line. Flouting his mother's will and against her express wishes, her son Madhurantakan married into the Pazhuvettaraiyar clan. Moreover, rumours about his hankering for the Chozha throne had come to his mother's ears and gave her some anxiety.

In general, Sembiyan Mahadevi's palace courtyard and assembly hall bustled with sculptors and tevaram singers. Saiva monks and Tamizh poets came from far-off places and left the court laden with gifts. Priests too flocked there, bringing offerings from the Siva temples. On that day, several sculptors and Saiva devotees had come from various places, including Mazhapadi, with petitions for support to rebuild their temples with stone. They brought paintings and architectural models to showcase their plans visually.

After granting her support to the first two petitions for reconstruction, the maharani asked, 'Did you mention Mazhapadi?'

The man from Mazhapadi said, 'It is the place where the god himself called out to the poet Sundarar and had the poet sing about him.'

When the maharani asked for more details, the man said, 'Once, as Sundarar was about to cross a river during his pilgrimage, a voice called out, "Sundaram! Have you forgotten me?" The poet asked his disciples if there was any Siva temple close by. They replied, "Yes, behind those konrai trees." Sundarar found a small Siva shrine nestling among the konrai trees in full bloom. He had his fill of gazing at the god and sang with a melting heart. He wondered at Siva's compassion in calling out to him by name once before, only to shower his divine grace on the poet. And now, Sundarar's thoughts flowed into this song:

Lord of the golden form
A tiger skin at your waist
The glistening konrai flower
On your auburn locks
My king, my great gem,
The jewel of Mazhapadi!
Who would be in my mind
If not you?

The narrator continued, 'Your Highness! That temple still remains small and hidden behind the konrai trees. We pray that it may be restored.'

'Yes, it can be done,' said Sembiyan Mahadevi.

Azhvarkadiyan and another man in the gathering moved forward and watched the proceedings attentively.

44

'It Is All Her Doing!'

A descendant of the great sculptors of Mamallapuram now came forward. He had brought a miniature model of a stone temple he had visualized. The queen was fascinated by the novel architectural design. To the man standing next to Azhvarkadiyan, she said, 'Bhattar! See this! I really wish all the major Siva temples in the Tamizh realm could be rebuilt in this new style.'

'Amma, what can stop your wish from being fulfilled? This can be the model for restructuring temples where tevaram verses have been composed. As soon as they see them, the people will recognize those temples as having been glorified in poetry.'

'Yes. Yes! We must compile all the songs composed by Appar, Sambandar and Sundarar. Temples sanctified by their songs must be rebuilt in this design with their towers reaching the sky. These are my two greatest wishes. But I have my doubts about their coming true. If only my husband had not passed away before his time! If only he had lived for a few more years!'

'Why, Amma? Hasn't the emperor ordered that every wish of yours should be fulfilled to the letter? Both his sons are ready to obey you even before you give the command . . .'

'That may be so. But for some reason, I feel somewhat uneasy. I hear all kinds of rumours. I believe some people complain that my contributions to the temples empty the state treasury. *Why does Siva need so many temples?* they ask. I don't care about the others. But the prince in Kanchi too—'

Azhvarkadiyan stepped forward and interrupted the queen. 'Amma! I am one of those who ask this question.'

The maharani looked at him in surprise. The others stared at him, quite affronted by his unseemly intrusion.

Azhvarkadiyan continued in a voice quivering with indignation. 'Amma! My stomach burns at this injustice! You are the embodiment of righteousness. Should you permit such discrimination?'

Ishana Siva Bhattar, who was standing next to Tirumalai, now said, 'Maharani! Sometimes my brother talks nonsense. He gets these sudden bouts of frenzy. Please pardon him.'

In those days, Saivas and Vaishnavas did not necessarily belong to different communities. The same family could have some of its members devoted to Siva and others to Vishnu. Sometimes, the same priest officiated at both Siva and Vishnu shrines. Ishana Siva Bhattar was among such broad-minded men. Tirumalai was his cousin brother. Both had great affection for each other. Therefore, the elder brother asked for forgiveness on his younger brother's behalf.

The queen smiled and said, 'Tirumalai! Calm down. What is this injustice you speak of?'

'Amma! How many temples for Siva, the ghoulish pauper, begging for alms, skull in hand? So many of them are to be rebuilt with stones! Nothing for Vishnu, who protects and nurtures the whole world? At the least, can an old temple not be restored?' Tirumalai wailed.

Ishana Siva Bhattar said, 'Amma! The god whose dance redeems the whole universe needs a vast temple with high towers, surrounded by spacious chambers and equipped with a golden stage. Isn't a small booth more than sufficient for Vishnu, who is sunk in eternal slumber? All he wants is a dark, lightless cubicle. Why bother him with temples and restorations?'

'Anna! The god who sleeps is the god who measured the worlds. He is the god who pushed the demon king Mahabali into the underworld.'

'The same god who measured the world could not find the divine feet of our Siva despite digging right down to the underworld,' Ishana Siva Bhattar scoffed.

'If your Siva is so gigantic, why does he need a temple at all? When he enters it, his head will hit the roof and the whole temple will collapse.'

Sembiyan Mahadevi laughed and said, 'Do stop fighting. Tirumalai! Who said that no temple should be built for Vishnu? Which temple do you want to be restored? Why don't you say it in a civil manner?'

'Gracious lady! I was at Veeranarayanapuram, named after one of the titular names of your father-in-law, the world-renowned emperor Parantaka. There, the god Veeranarayana remains eternally wide-eyed and awake, and protects the vast Veeranarayana Lake. Its brick walls are crumbling. If the temple suffers any damage, the banks of the lake will crack open and hundreds of villages will be submerged in the flooding. The Veeranarayana temple must be rebuilt with stone.'

'All right. We will do it. Give me more details. Let the others leave now,' said the Chozha queen.

As soon as everyone left, Sembiyan Mahadevi lowered her voice and said, 'Tirumalai! Which places did you visit? What did you see? What did you hear? Did you not interrupt me because you have important news?'

'Yes, Amma! I have brought important information. But I would have waited to tell you at your convenience. I broke in because you began to say something about the prince in Kanchi. What if there was a spy among those people? So many mishaps are happening in the country. You can never guess when and what kind of treason will be committed, or who will turn traitor.'

The dowager queen heaved a great sigh. 'So it has come to this. Members of the same household, bound by ties of blood, have come to suspect one another. There was a time when Aditta Karikalan had complete faith in me! He had greater affection and respect for me than for his own mother. And now, even he has begun to doubt my intentions. Tirumalai! If only I had left the earth with my lord. If only he had not stopped me from accompanying him and left me with tasks to be done! How unfortunate I am!'

'Amma! Your husband was a prescient soul who knew the past, present and future. He sat on the Chozha throne in this kaliyuga with all the detached wisdom of the fabled king, Janaka.* It is the good fortune of this land that he asked you to stay back. It is your responsibility to ensure that this Chozha kingdom, whose greatness and glory have been fostered through a hundred years, is not destroyed by fratricidal war. Only you can prevent this catastrophe.'

* The Ramayana describes Janaka, King of the Videha kingdom and the foster father of the female protagonist Sita, as a *rajarishi*, a king as wise and dispassionate as a sage.

'I don't think so. How can I control others when my own son refuses to listen to me? You talked about spies. Who would send their spies here? Aditta Karikalan? Has he really come to mistrust me?'

'I heard it with my own ears, Amma! Otherwise, I never would have believed that Prince Karikalan could doubt you.'

'What did you hear, Tirumalai? What did you hear with your ears?'

'I heard them talking near a rock-cut temple in Mamallapuram.'

'Who were "they"?'

'Prince Karikalan, Tirukovilur Malayaman and Partibhendra Pallavan. I hid in a dark temple to eavesdrop on them. Malayaman and Partibhendran were seething in fury. They said that the two Pazhuvettaraiyars and your son have imprisoned the emperor. Malayaman said that you must be in league with them. The others agreed. Partibhendran said that Tanjavur must be invaded, the emperor freed and brought to Kanchi. The other two agreed to this proposal. The prince declared that before launching any war, a final attempt must be made to bring the emperor to Kanchi. The others agreed. They decided to draft a letter to the emperor and send it through an envoy. I also discovered the identity of that envoy. He is no ordinary messenger but an extremely intelligent, brave and powerful warrior, capable of working as both envoy and spy. A slippery customer indeed! He tried to extract information from me without disclosing a single thing about himself. The Kudantai astrologer tried his luck with him. To no avail. I hear that he did go to Tanjavur and deliver his missive to the emperor.'

'And then? What was the emperor's reply?'

'He said that he would give his answer on the next day. By then, the Pazhuvettaraiyars smelled a rat. But the young man broke through all the surveillance and managed to escape.'

'He must be remarkably resourceful. But what did you do after leaving Kanchi?'

'I was planning to come straight here. On the way, I stopped at the Veeranarayana temple. And there, by god's grace, I discovered a crucial secret.'

'Another secret?'

'Yes, Amma! I learnt about a grand dinner being hosted in Sambuvariyar's palace in Kadambur. Periya Pazhuvettaraiyar came and so did the young Pazhuvur queen's palanquin.'

'Tirumalai! It is all her doing. The danger facing the Chozha realm today is due to her exploits. Were you able to meet and talk to her?'

'No, Amma, no. At your command, I nurtured that snake as my own sister for so many years. My heart boils when I think of how diligently I unearthed the many hymns that I taught her! After becoming Pazhuvettaraiyar's queen, she refuses to even look at me.'

'Why waste time in regret? Human actions trigger results that differ very greatly from the intentions that prompted them. What else happened in Kadambur?'

'I went to Kadambur believing that it was Nandini who had travelled in the palanquin. I hoped to meet her somehow, or at least give her a message, a warning. I even took the risk of climbing over the ramparts of the fort. That was when I discovered that amazing and mysterious secret.'

'Tirumalai! This has become your habit. You keep on provoking the listener's curiosity but never get to the point. So, what *is* that secret?'

'Forgive me, Amma! I feel extremely reluctant to disclose it. It was not the young queen who was in that palanquin. We thought all along that Pazhuvettaraiyar takes his young queen with him everywhere. Big mistake!'

'Who else is he taking around with him? Is there no end to his lust for women?'

'The person inside the palanquin was not a woman.'

'Not a woman . . . ? What kind of man would stoop to hide in a covered palanquin?'

'Forgive me, Amma! The man hiding in the palanquin was your son, Madhurantakan.'

Sembiyan Mahadevi was stunned into silence. Then she murmured to herself, 'Lord! Such a huge punishment for the crime I committed . . .'

Azhvarkadiyan proceeded to tell her about the conspiracy at the midnight conference. The venerable lady was stricken by inexpressible grief. 'Ayo! My son! I tried to raise you to achieve the true wisdom of faith. And this is the result of my endeavours! Should it be you who brings infamy to the Chozha dynasty? Should it be you who inflicts this great calamity on the Chozha empire?'

She said to Azhvarkadiyan, 'Tirumalai, come and see me again before you go. I will consult Kundavai and see if I can come up with something to stop this calamity.'

'Amma, it is better that you don't discuss this with the princess.'

'Why? Do you have doubts about her too?'

'Amma, isn't it natural for me to have those doubts? After all, she is Aditta Karikalan's dear sister.'

'So what? Tirumalai! I may believe it if you say that the sun rises in the west and sets in the east. I may even believe you when you insist that Vishnu is a greater god than Siva.

But never will I doubt Kundavai in any way. As soon as she was born, the midwife placed her in my hands. From that day, I have raised her with greater love than if she had been born to me. She too has given me great respect and affection. Till today, she sees me as both her father and her mother.'

'Amma, may I ask you something? Did Kundavai Devi tell you about her visit to the astrologer in Kudantai?'

'No. So what?'

'Did she tell you about a young man of the Vaanan tribe she met there and again on the banks of the Arasalaru?'

'What do you intend to prove by asking such questions?'

'The princess is keeping a secret from you. That young man was Aditta Karikalan's messenger. It won't be wrong to call him a spy.'

'Tirumalai. Say what you will. If Kundavai holds something back from me, there will certainly be a sound reason for it. I will give up my life rather than entertain suspicions about her.'

'Ayyayyo! May it never come to that! May you be right in your trust. I will convey your wish to the princess. She has asked me to meet her,' Azhvarkadiyan said.

45

The Spy Who Committed a Crime

Twenty centuries ago, a Chozha king called Karikal Valavan built embankments on both sides of the Kaveri. They were carefully maintained for a very long time and kept the river under control. When the Chozhas lost their supremacy, the Pandya, Pallava, Kalappala and Vaanan dynasties came into power. Under their rule, the Kaveri often overflowed and flooded the land. When this happened on a massive scale, there were times when the river completely changed its course. The old river became a new river and then the new river went back to being the old river. Such unforeseen changes could turn the river bed into fertile agricultural land or create new waterways where the waves rolled on as they do on the sea.

One such rivulet had been formed behind the Chozha palaces in Pazhaiyarai. The Chozha kings deepened and widened it, and ensured that it always remained full. This waterway offered protection to the palaces, particularly the women's quarters. Entry was severely restricted, and only those who were closely connected to the palaces were allowed to take their boats across.

The women's quarters in the palaces had their gardens set alongside this stream, where they could wander freely at any time. And here they gathered to indulge in carefree banter, dance like peacocks or sing like the cuckoo. They also enjoyed themselves as they went swimming and boating.

In the Pazhaiyarai palace complex, Kundavai Devi's palace was next only to Sembiyan Mahadevi's in its majestic beauty. After all, it had been the palace of Sundara Chozha when he dwelt in Pazhaiyarai. After his departure, Kundavai became its sole and undisputed mistress.

It had a most attractive garden in the rear, where towering trees as well as flowering shrubs grew. It had several arbours overhung with blooming creepers.

Kundavai and her companions spent most of their evenings in the garden.

At times, they sat together and told stories. Or they went in twos and threes to exchange confidences. For some time now, it had become a habit for Kundavai and Vanathi to go off by themselves.

On that day, Kundavai and Vanathi were swaying on a swing of twisted creepers hanging on a big banyan branch. Peals of girlish laughter and jaunty avian trills filled the air. But Kundavai and Vanathi were in no mood for merriment. Nor did they seem to be pleased by the sounds of mirth. They talked but little.

A girl sang from one of the bowers. Since it was the day of Krishna's birth, she sang of the blue god's flute wafting across the moonlight. A woman expresses her pain through a song. From its perch on a branch, a parrot offers her some solace.

WOMAN:
Who is this wastrel playing the flute
In the tormenting light of the moon?
What does he gain by inflicting pain
On a waif bereft of her mate?
BIRD:
The music he makes with the flute on his lips
Brings joy to the earth and the sky.
A wonder to all in the wide world it is
That his notes could afflict you with pain!
WOMAN
I hail you, my dear, my sweet, blooming bird,
I bring flowers to garland you now,
At this time of woe, as my heart breaks in two,
You sought me to soothe me with songs.
BIRD:
O beauty! I'm here, to say how I fear
Our blue god is wasting away.
Since leaving your side he has ruefully sighed,
All the sweetness has fled from his life.

Kundavai, who had been attending to the latter half of the song, scoffed, 'What a god this Krishna has turned out to be for us in the Tamizh land! How do you get anything done if you keep on gobbling butter, playing the flute and flirting with girls?' Looking at the unresponsive Vanathi, she added, 'Why are you silent? Are you also beguiled by Krishna's flute?'

'Akka! What did you ask me?' Vanathi said.

'Vanathi! Where are you?'

'Here, with you.'

'Fibber! Why do you lie? You are not here at all. Shall I tell you where you are?'

'Tell me.'

'I know it only too well. Your mind is on the battlefield in Ilankai. You are wondering what kind of spell you can cast on my innocent brother there.'

'Half of what you say is true. My mind does go to Ilankai quite often. But I don't think of casting spells. I think of his wounds, where he sleeps, what he eats, his sufferings on the battlefield . . . I am assailed by guilt when I think of all the comforts I enjoy here, good food, fine clothes and a soft mattress to sleep on. If only I had wings, I would fly to Ilankai.'

'Fly there and do what? Add to his troubles?'

'Never. I will drive his chariot as Subhadra did for Arjuna, as Satyabhama did for Krishna. I will take on my breast the arrows aimed at him.'

'And he will simply stand by and watch you do that?'

'I will wait in the camp and treat his wounds when he returns from battle. I will cook for him, serve him, spread flowers on his bed, and play the veena to make him forget his aches and pains and sleep well.'

'Impossible. Chozha warriors do not take their women to the battlefield.'

'Why, Akka?'

'They are more afraid of women than of wounds.'

'Why? What will the women do to them?'

'The women may not do anything to them. But what if the foe gets mesmerized by the women and surrenders? Then how can our warriors display their skills? The Chozha warriors do not want to owe their victories to their womenfolk.'

'How can that be? Are the enemies so stupid as to fall for women?'

'Why not? Vanathi! Do you remember the young warrior we saw in the astrologer's house? And later, beside the Arasalaru?'

'Yes. Why?'

'Do you remember how he became completely intoxicated when he saw us?'

'I do. But you are wrong to say *us*. He was intoxicated when he saw *you*. He had no eyes to spare for anyone else.'

'Vanathi! You lie very convincingly. Are you mocking me?'

'No. Not at all. If I ask you something, will you answer truthfully?'

'Try.'

'Why did you think of that young warrior now?'

'You have become far too saucy! What's wrong in thinking of him?'

'I did not say anything was wrong. It is natural to remember him. I too am anxious about what may have befallen him.'

'Why should you worry about it?'

'Why not? Is it not natural to want to know what happened to someone we met and whom we recall frequently?'

'Natural? No. One must control the mind, not become a scatterbrain . . . Vanathi! Listen! Do you hear the *parai* drum? An announcement . . . ! What is it? Listen carefully!'

From a street far away came the rumbling of the parai drum alternating with a loud announcement. The women followed it closely. 'A spy from the enemy country entered the Tanjavur Fort under false pretences and escaped after gleaning information. He has inflicted two men with near-fatal wounds. He is a young man, strong and muscular. He is adept at tricks and stratagems. His name is Vallavaraiyan

Vandiyatevan. Anyone who gives him shelter will be sentenced to death. Anyone who captures him will be rewarded with a thousand gold coins. By order of Chinna Pazhuvettaraiyar, Kalantaka Kantan, commander of the Tanjavur Fort.'

The announcement was followed by thunderous drumming. Kundavai shivered, she knew not why.

Just then, a maid came running to say, 'Devi! A Vaishnava called Azhvarkadiyan has come to see you.'

'I am coming,' said Kundavai and got down from the swing.

46

The Mutterings of the People

Azhvarkadiyan left Sembiyan Mahadevi's presence and went to Princess Kundavai's palace.

The scenes he had witnessed earlier on the streets of Pazhaiyarai made him rejoice. The people were celebrating Krishna's birthday with great zest. No doubt at all that the Vaishnava faith was deeply ingrained in the Chozha country, and would continue to spread and flourish. There were many reasons for the Saiva cult to gain influence in the land. For over a hundred years, the Chozha kings had been building Siva temples everywhere. The tevaram songs of the three principal Saiva poets were propagated through those temples, where festivals were conducted with great pomp. Despite that, Vishnu's eminence had not diminished in any way. And Krishna, Vishnu's avatar in the fullness of his glory, had stolen the people's hearts. They were enthralled by Krishna's divine acts of play in Gokulam, Brindavanam and Mathura. Oh my god! How many music ensembles! How many street plays! Theatre troupes came pouring into the city from the surrounding villages with actors attired in the guise of the different characters—Vasudeva, Devaki, Krishna, Balarama and Kamsa.

Azhvarkadiyan stopped to watch a particular troupe whose singing, dancing and dialogue delivery were most striking. At that moment, the scene being played featured a conversation between the demonic Kamsa and the divine Krishna. Krishna was played by a child. He lisped his dialogues listing all the crimes committed by Kamsa and challenged him to a single combat. Kamsa replied in a voice of thunder, 'Dei! Krishna! Your magic tricks won't work with me. I am going to kill you right now. I am going to kill your brother Balarama. I will kill your father Vasudeva. See that Vaishnava standing over there with sandal paste and namam marks all over his body? I am going to kill him too!' The spectators began to laugh at Azhvarkadiyan. Even the actors playing Krishna and Balarama looked at him. Many more came to surround him, and began to jeer at him with guffaws and grimaces.

Tirumalai was infuriated. He thought of using his staff and teaching the hecklers a lesson. He particularly wanted to land a blow on Kamsa's head. But it would be useless. A wooden mask with fearful moustaches and hideous canine teeth covered the head of the actor playing Kamsa. So Azhvarkadiyan decided that on the whole, it would not be prudent to use a staff in such a big crowd. As he slipped away, he felt that there was something familiar about Kamsa's voice, even though it was deliberately raised to an ear-splitting blast. Where had he heard it before?

As he walked on, he noticed a sudden change in the people's mood. The crowds and the celebrations were diminishing. Why? Why was the crowd dispersing so quickly? All music, dance and instruments had ceased. Why were the people standing in little groups at street corners and talking furtively? Why were they hurrying away? Why were the doors banging shut?

The reason became clear soon enough. It was the same parai drum and announcement about the spy that had made Kundavai Devi shudder. People stared hard at those who walked alone. Some directed suspicious glances at Azhvarkadiyan before walking away quickly.

Azhvarkadiyan guessed the reason for this just as he knew why people were whispering in groups. The few words falling on his ears confirmed his surmise.

The people were grumbling about the despotic rule of the Pazhuvettaraiyars. It was natural for the citizens of Pazhaiyarai and its surrounding villages to be angry with the Pazhuvettaraiyars. Had they not taken their maharaja away to Tanjavur, their maharaja who had been extolled by the poets who said:

> Who can match
> Sundara Chozha of Pazhaiyarai
> In this ancient realm?

Since that time, hadn't Pazhaiyarai's fame decreased day by day? If only the emperor had been in the city on Krishna Jayanti, how much more splendid the celebrations would have been! After staging their plays across the city, all the theatre groups would have gathered in the palace courtyard. Actors, singers, bards and minstrels would have received gifts at the emperor's hands. The crowds would have been so gigantic as to suggest that the entire population of the empire had congregated in Pazhaiyarai. The shops and stalls would have had a 100 per cent increase in sales. At night, a magnificent procession would have been launched at the Vishnu temple, with spectacular displays of dance and music, martial arts and swordplay.

The citizens of Pazhaiyarai had been divested of all this glory by the Pazhuvettaraiyars.

Apart from this, the natives of Pazhaiyarai had another reason for their resentment. Their darling Prince Arulmozhi Varman had gone across the seas to fight in Ilankai. Fifteen thousand warriors from the four military colonies of Pazhaiyarai had accompanied him. They were fighting in an alien land of hills and forests to defend the honour and ensure the safety of the Tamizh realm. In an earlier war with Ilankai, Siriya Velar, the younger of the Kodumbalur feudal chieftains, had been speared to death as he fought on the frontlines. The remaining Chozha soldiers had died fighting to the end. Prince Arulmozhi had gone to Ilankai to appease the spirits of the dead by planting the flag of victory in Ilankai. And the Pazhuvettariyars were refusing to send the necessary military equipment and provisions to wage that war! The granaries of Tanjavur were overflowing with paddy. What was the purpose of storing all that grain if it was not to be used to sustain the soldiers? What was the use of all the staggering wealth lying in the state treasury, accumulated through a hundred years of warfare, if it could not aid the soldiers? What were the Pazhuvettaraiyars going to do with all of it? Take it with them to the underworld?

Azhvarkadiyan knew only too well that, for some time now, these dissatisfactions had given rise to grumblings among the people. It was natural for Pazhaiyarai citizens to feel particularly aggrieved. The wives and children of the fifteen thousand warriors who had gone to fight in Ilankai were still living in the city.

Therefore, the public proclamation issued by the Pazhuvettaraiyars, warning the people about a spy in their midst, served only to annoy them. It afforded them an opportunity to voice their own grievances against the Pazhuvur brothers. 'Spy . . . ! *Spy*? The tiger flag is flying from the southern cape to the North Pennai River. Which foreign king is powerful enough to send a spy here? If these Pazhuvettaraiyars wish to get rid of anyone, they call him a spy and finish him off! Or throw him into the dungeons! No need to follow due process or consult the local council if you label someone a spy. Still, why invite trouble? They have the authority to do right or wrong as they please.'

Azhvarkadiyan's keen ears and sharp mind grasped the sentiments that prompted the people to speak to one another under their breath. He could not help but wonder where this general state of disgruntlement was going to end.

Princess Kundavai was always eager to know about the affairs of the outside world and relished discussing them with Azhvarkadiyan, who told her about the incidents he witnessed while roaming across country and town. She also enjoyed listening to the songs he picked up from different places. So, whenever he came, she always welcomed him warmly and made enquiries about his well-being.

But on that day, Azhvarkadiyan noticed a change in the princess' expression and speech. Her face showed that her mind was elsewhere. Her speech betrayed an unusual jitteriness and some floundering.

'Tirumalai! What is the news? What made you come here?' she asked.

'Nothing special, Amma! I came here thinking you wanted to discuss the news and other matters as usual. Sorry. I will take leave of you.'

'No. No. Stay a while. I did invite you.'

'Amma, before I forget, may I say that Queen Sembiyan Mahadevi asked me to tell you that she wants you to go and see her as she has something important to tell you.'

'All right, I was going to see her anyway. Tell me about the places you visited this time.'

'I travelled from the southern cape to the Tirupati hills.'

'What are the people talking about in all these places?'

'They talk about the glory of the kings of the Chozha dynasty. They say that, soon, the Chozha empire will reach the shores of the River Ganga and stretch beyond, even up to the Himalayan range.'

'What else?'

'They applaud the great and brave deeds of the Pazhuvettaraiyar brothers. They say that the Chozha empire has reached this summit because the Pazhuvur lords–'

Kundavai broke in to say, 'Enough. What else do they say?'

'They speak of your brothers with great affection. In particular, their love and admiration for Prince Arulmozhi Varman is incalculable.'

'No surprise. Anything else?'

'They are wondering why the marriage of the emperor's daughter has not yet taken place. They even asked me for my opinion in this matter.'

'What was your reply?'

'I said that anyone worthy of marrying our princess has yet to be born.'

'Great! *Yet to be born?* I will turn into an old crone before he is born and becomes old enough to marry. Enough about me for now. Tirumalai! Anything else . . . ?'

'Many are astonished by the unexpected marriage of Prince Madhurantakan who had been talking about becoming a Saiva yogi.'

'How is your dear sister, who was to become a saint like Andal?'

'What does she lack, Amma? Periya Pazhuvettaraiyar's palace is under her despotic rule.'

'Only Pazhuvettaraiyar's palace? I had heard that she is the undisputed ruler of the Chozha empire.'

'Some people do say that. Amma, forget her. Why talk about her on this auspicious day? Since you mentioned Andal, I recall visiting the saint's birthplace, Srivilliputhur. I learnt a few songs composed by her father, Vishnu Chittar. This song is about Krishna's birthday. Listen!

On the day the lord is born
Dark hued, with rippling locks,
In the town of towered mansions
The courtyard is a messy sludge
Of powdered scents
and fragrant balms,
sprayed in celebrations.
In rapture do devotees,
Hail their child divine.

They run and trip, they slip and fall,
They embrace their kin in joy,
'Where's he?' they ask anxiously.
And rush to seek their lord.
The cowherds' town
Does now rejoice
With those who sing and drum,
And those who dance in glee,
To hail their lord divine.

'Today, our Pazhaiyarai city resounds with the same joyous tumult that pervaded Krishna's hometown on the day he was born.'

'True. But just a while ago, there was a tumult of a very different kind. What was that, Tirumalai?'

'Some spy who got away, they say. A prize is to be given to anyone who catches him. Amma, what do I know about such things?'

'No clue at all about who he may be?'

'I do have my suspicions, but it would be a risk to voice them. As it is, people were glaring at me as I made my way down the streets to be here. What if I am caught and thrown into the dungeon?'

'They'd need an extra pair of hands to catch you. Please share your thoughts with me. Surely you don't think I would betray you!'

'Krishna! Krishna! I saw a sturdy young man in Veeranarayana town. He said that he was going to Tanjavur. He did not tell me why, but he did question me at length.'

Kundavai sounded a little frantic when she asked, 'What did he look like?'

'He looked as if he belonged to some noble clan. He had an attractive face. He seemed to have both physical strength and mental resilience.'

'What did he ask you?'

'He asked me about the emperor's health, the line of succession and the prince in Ilankai. I learnt that he asked the same questions of the Kudantai astrologer.'

'Ah! So he went to the astrologer's house?'

'Now I remember. It seems he made a dramatic entry into the house when you were there. Fortunately, he did not recognize you.'

'My instincts have proved to be right.'

'What did you think, Amma?'

'I thought that the brash youth was asking for trouble.'

'You were right. I too suspect him to be a secret agent. The Pazhuvettaraiyars have announced a reward to anyone who captures him.'

'Tirumalai, will you do me a favour?'

'Order me, Amma!'

'If you ever happen to see that young man . . .'

'Shall I seize him and claim the reward?'

'No! No! Bring him to me. I have an important job for him.'

Azhvarkadiyan feigned surprise as he stared at Kundavai. Then he said, 'It won't be necessary, Amma! I won't have to bring him to you. He will keep on searching for you until he finds you.'

47

Ishana Siva Bhattar

After meeting the princess, Azhvarkadiyan went to see his cousin Ishana Siva Bhattar. His house was a few miles away from the palace and close to the Siva temple in the north. By this time, the Krishna Jayanti celebrations were more or less over. But that little jaunt was enough to give him an overall view of the sweep and splendour of Pazhaiyarai.

Passing through the military colonies, he saw several groups of women talking angrily in the street corners. Each one of them had garlanded their sons or husbands with vanji flowers and proudly sent them to the Ilankai war. From each household, men had sacrificed their lives in all the wars waged by the Chozha army. Now Azhvarkadiyan saw those women chuntering in discontent. He walked on, worrying about the disaster that this boded.

It was dark by the time he reached the temple. In times long ago, the Jains had forged hillocks around it, with grottos where Digambara monks engaged in meditation. Visiting the holy city to see the temple of his visions, Appar* was pained to find it hidden behind the mounds and lodged a complaint. The local king, a representative of the Pallavas, cleared some of the obstructions. Appar sang in a state of bliss. Later, the Chozha kings rebuilt that temple with stone. But the hillocks continued to wall it in, leaving a single doorway for entry.

When Azhvarkadiyan took a quick shortcut through this doorway to Ishana Siva Bhattar's house, he could see a few devotees standing before the sanctum. Among them were some dressed in the costumes of Krishna and Balarama. Before he could make a guess about how and why the men came to be there, Ishana Siva Bhattar came rushing out, grabbed Azhvarkadiyan and dragged him out of the temple.

'Anna! What is this?' Azhvarkadiyan asked.

'I will tell you, Tirumalai! From now on, our kinship stays outside the temple. You are a sinner. You blaspheme against Siva. I put up with a great deal from you. But I cannot tolerate what you said today in the presence of the Maharani. If you like, come home and fill your huge belly. But don't you dare to step inside the temple, understand? If you do, I will become an avenging spirit!' Pushing him by the neck, Ishana Siva Bhattar shoved Azhvarkadiyan out of the temple, banged the door shut and locked it from within.

'Anna! Anna!' Tirumalai shouted.

Ignoring his cries, Ishana Siva Bhattar drew the bolt from inside and marched away.

'I see!' Azhvarkadiyan murmured and stood still. Then he went round the temple twice or thrice, deliberately choosing

---

* One of the greatest Tamil Saiva poet-saints (circa 570–650 CE) also known as Tirunavukkarasar—king of the tongue, lord of language.

to go left, as circling the temple from the right would be an act of worship. He saw that all the Jain caves in the circular mounds were shut.

He went to Bhattar's house. Bhattar's wife was extremely fond of Tirumalai, who always made her laugh at his drollery. He diverted her with more jokes than ever, ate the offerings from the Siva temple until his belly was full and went to lie down on the raised pyol platform beside the entrance of the house.

That was when he remembered the scene he had witnessed by the Kudamurutti River.

Azhvarkadiyan had hidden himself behind a thick clump of bamboo when he heard the galloping hoof beats. The horse that came first looked as if it had broken away. It was dripping wet—with sweat or water, he could not guess. A stripling was bound to the horse's back. His face showed both fear and determination. Four or five horsemen followed him, spear in hand. They came nearer and nearer until they almost caught up with him. One of the men raised his spear over his head and aimed it at the boy. Another man stopped him.

The boy's horse plunged into a slope under the tangled bamboo clumps. His hair got caught in the curve of a low-hanging bamboo. The horse dragged him in front, the bamboo yanked him back. The boy was in a desperate situation by the time one of the horsemen caught the horse.

When the men realized who the rider was, they were startled and angry. 'Where is he?' 'Where is he?' Azhvarkadiyan could hear the men repeating this question. The boy sobbed and stuttered as he replied, 'He fell into the flood! Gone with the river!' The horsemen took the boy away.

Azhvarkadiyan could not quite comprehend what he had seen. But now the whole thing began to make sense. He also recalled the street theatre troupe. Particularly the voice and demeanour of the actor in Kamsa's guise with the wooden mask hiding his entire face. Now he could identify that voice.

After finishing the night puja at the temple, Ishana Siva Bhattar came home. He saw Azhvarkadiyan lying on the platform by the front door. 'Tirumalai! Tirumalai!' he called angrily. Tirumalai pretended to be fast asleep.

Bhattar banged the door open and went in. Azhvarkadiyan heard him fighting with his wife. He realized that the fight was about him.

The next morning, as soon as he got up, Ishana Siva Bhattar came to Tirumalai and asked, 'When do you plan to start tramping around again?'

'When your anger is appeased, Anna,' Azhvarkadiyan replied.

'Don't call me "Anna" ever again! From today, I am not your anna! You are not my tambi! You are a Siva-hater, a depraved scoundrel, an outcaste!'

Bhattar's wife came to Azhvarkadiyan's rescue. 'Why are you cursing him? What is he saying now that he has not said before? It is your devotion to Siva that has gone over the top.'

'Do you know what he said in the presence of the maharani yesterday? *Siva roams in the graveyard strewn with ash, why does he need a temple?* I felt as though molten lead was being poured into my ears. It seems that the maharani did not sleep at all last night.'

'He will not say such things again. I will talk to him and convince him to mend his ways. Kind words will surely bring about this change.'

'Kind words, did you say? Let him go to Rameswaram, where Rama got rid of his sins by worshipping Siva. Let him worship the same Siva and atone for his sins. I will have nothing to do with him until then.'

Azhvarkadiyan's lips trembled. He wanted to retaliate in kind, but he controlled himself and remained patient. He could not afford to ruin the task at hand.

Bhattar's wife interposed again. 'Why not? If we tell him to go to Rameswaram, he certainly will. Let us go with him. We have not had a child in all these years. Who knows what sins we committed in our previous birth? Tirumalai! Shall we all go to Rameswaram together?'

Ishana Siva Bhattar glared at them both and strode away.

A little later, he came back and spoke to Azhvarkadiyan in calm tones. 'Tambi! The elders say that anger is a sin. It is evil. I gave room to anger. You are not upset with me, are you?'

'Not at all,' Azhvarkadiyan said.

'In that case, wait for me right here. I will finish the noon puja and return. There are important matters about which I need to consult you. You will stay back, won't you? And not go anywhere else?'

'I won't go anywhere, Anna! I have no intention of leaving you.'

Bhattar left. 'And is that so indeed?' said Azhvarkadiyan to himself, repeatedly. Then he too left without informing his sister-in-law. He circled the temple several times. At the least sound, he quickly hid himself.

His anticipation was not in vain. Very slowly and cautiously, a door opened in one of the Jain mounds. Ishana Siva Bhattar looked around before stepping out. Another man followed him. His face could not be seen. His physical appearance suggested the actor who had worn the Kamsa costume. Azhvarkadiyan muttered to himself, 'Aha! So this is the reason for all those bursts of anger!'

Azhvarkadiyan surreptitiously followed the two men. They reached the wide stream where the waves billowed as on the sea. Azhvarkadiyan slid behind the thick trees on the shore and thrust his head out between two branches. A boat was bobbing on the waters with a boatman standing on the shore, looking as if it belonged to the palace.

The two men got into the boat. As the boat began to move, Bhattar's companion turned his head towards the shore. His face could be seen very clearly. Azhvarkadiyan was not surprised. It was the man he had expected to see, the gallant young man he had met in Veeranarayana town and the boat on the Kollidam River. Undoubtedly, he was also the man in the guise of Kamsa. Where was the boat taking the men? Azhvarkadiyan had to find out and see if he had guessed it right.

He headed to the street where several Chozha palaces towered into the sky. The last was the mansion of Aniruddha Brahmarayar, Sundara Chozha's chief minister. The chief minister had gone to the Pandya country to regularize administrative affairs. His family was in Tanjavur. Therefore, his Pazhaiyarai mansion was kept under lock and key.

Azhvarkadiyan reached that mansion. The guards stood to attention when they saw him. He ordered them to unlock the mansion, entered its precincts and had the entrance door locked behind him. He crossed the three courtyards in the building and came to the garden. A creeper-covered pergola cut through the trees and shrubs. Tirumalai followed this path and reached Kundavai's garden. He hid himself in a bower and looked around. His efforts were not wasted. A scene was being played before him, of the kind that had to be described by great poets like Kalidasa.

The boat came to a halt on the shore. Ishana Siva Bhattar and Vandiyatevan got out and climbed the steps on the jetty.

Kundavai Devi was seated in the garden on a marble bench. When the men came up the steps, she too got up from her seat.

Vandiyatevan looked at Kundavai.

He stood motionless and still, his eyes riveted on her face.

A flowering creeper extended a slender branch between them as if to bar the way.

A butterfly with iridescent wings fluttered by and hovered over the creeper.

Bending her head a little, Kundavai looked at the butterfly.

Vandiyatevan gazed unblinkingly at her blooming face.

On the river, the waves came to rest.

The birds stopped singing.

The earth ceased spinning.

The stars and the galaxies stood unmoving.

Aeons rolled by.

48

Swirling Pools and Darting Eyes

Adi Manithan, the first human being created by god, lived on a mountain slope. A cavern gave him shelter from the wind and the rain. The forest trees gave enough fruit to sate his hunger. The wild animals trembled when they saw him. Like the birds in the sky, he lived without a care. And yet, burning deep within was a constant craving–an imperceptible yearning. His mind was searching for something rare, some ravishment that he had never seen or experienced before. Something infused in his fantasies by day and dreams of the night. Restless and hankering, his heart wondered, 'When will I encounter that marvel which draws me like a magnet? When will I find that fruit of bliss created for me alone?'

When he created Adi Manithan, the primordial man, god also created *Adi Stri*, the primordial woman. She lived on the slope by the other side of the mountain. She too had food to satisfy her hunger, a pool to assuage her thirst and a cave to give her shelter. Outwardly, she lacked nothing. But a flame blazing within was drawing her towards something unknown and unknowable.

A towering mountain stood between the man and the woman, preventing them from meeting one another.

On a hot summer day, according to the laws of nature, a raging forest fire began to circle the mountain. It snaked upwards with alarming speed. Realizing that running into the forest spelt nothing but danger, the man and the woman sped to the heights. When they reached the topmost peak, the first man and first woman found themselves standing face to face. Their eyes met. Unable to blink or even to look away, they could not tear their locked eyes apart. They forgot about the forest fire. They forgot what it was that drove them up to the summit. They forgot all about hunger and thirst. Instinctively, they realized that the driving purpose of their entire lives had propelled them towards that singular encounter. They understood that they could fulfil each other's wants and needs. What one lacked or missed would be provided by the other. No more could any force drive them apart. No longer would they face the void in themselves or in the world around them.

Surveying the scene as it developed, Brahma, the god of creation, was completely satisfied to see his work getting off to a good start.

Personifying the Adi Manithan and the Adi Stri as they did in that moment of time, Vallavaraiyan Vandiyatevan and Kundavai Devi intuitively came to realize that they had been born and raised on earth for this very moment, for this singular encounter.

But unlike the primordial man and primordial woman, they led their lives in an urban milieu and polite society. They could not forget the difference in their status. Therefore, they could not allow their surging emotions to free their minds of all control. Again and again, they let their eyes meet momentarily, before turning away to gaze at the nearby flower, tree, butterfly, stream . . .

Only when Ishana Siva Bhattar cleared his throat did they recall that their rendezvous was to serve an important purpose.

Infusing sternness into her voice, Kundavai asked, 'Did you tell Ishana Siva Bhattar that you had to see me alone?'

Her severe, authoritarian tone made Vandiyatevan pull himself together. He said, 'I can answer that question only if I can be sure of your identity. I am afraid that Bhattar has brought me to the wrong place.'

'I too wonder if that is so. Whom did you wish to meet?'

'I told Ishana Siva Bhattar that I wanted to see the leading light of the time-honoured Chozha clan, the beloved daughter of King Sundara Chozha, the cherished younger sister of Prince Aditta Karikalan, the adored elder sister of Prince Arulmozhi Varman—Princess Kundavai Devi.'

Breaking into a smile, Kundavai said, 'It is I who happens to be struggling under the weight of all those glories.'

'You are also the lady I saw at the astrologer's house in Kudantai and beside Arasalaru . . .'

'Yes. Yes. It was I who behaved so rudely to you in those two places. You would not have expected to meet that uncivilized woman again and so soon.'

'It is not correct to say "meeting again".'

'Why?'

'One has to part in order to meet again. Not even for an instant have you left my heart.'

'I did not expect the people of Tondaimandalam to be so adroit in speech.'

'I guess you would claim credit for every achievement in every field for the Chozha land, with nothing to spare for others.'

'It is true. I plead guilty. You don't like our Chozha country?'

'Very much. But this land poses two great threats. It scares me even to think of them.'

'Spear and sword are dangerous weapons in the hands of the Chozha warriors. Outsiders must be wary of them when they visit us. Particularly those who are engaged in espionage . . .'

'Princess! I did not refer to those dangers. I carry my own sword and spear with me. I know how to use them.'

'Didn't I see your spear-wielding skills the other day? Your spear went right through the crocodile and so swiftly! A single throw was enough to bring all the stuffing out.'

'Lady! I did not know that the valiant women of the Chozha land were scared sick of dead crocodiles. I threw my spear believing the creature to be alive. Neither my spear nor I are at fault.'

'It is the stupid crocodile that is at fault. Why did it die without waiting for the valiant Vandiyatevan of the Vaanan clan to arrive with his spear? It deserves this humiliation . . . But what other threats did you mention?'

'The whirlpools in the rivers of the Chozha country during the first flood. Never trust them. They got me into a gut-wrenching struggle.'

'How did you fall into the whirlpool? You look like someone who wouldn't even dream of dipping a toe into the waters.'

'If you get into a wrestling match, can you avoid getting punched? Drowning in the river and suffocating in the whirlpool were part of the deal in carrying out this mission in the Chozha country. And that foolish boy who came with me absolutely refused to tell a little white lie. And this was the result . . .'

'You speak in riddles. It would be easier for me if you were more specific with the details.'

'I will. Chinna Pazhuvettaraiyar, the commander of the Tanjavur Fort, accused me, your brother Aditta Karikalan's envoy, of being a spy, and sent his men to capture me. I had no wish to be caught before I finished my job. So I left Tanjavur with a young boy to show me the way.'

'Where did you stay in Tanjavur?'

'Outside the fort, in the house of a mute woman who grows flowers.'

'Her name?'

'I don't know her name, but I know the name of her son—Sendan Amudan.'

'My guess proved to be right. Go on.'

'I took up that young man behind me on the horse and was on my way to Tanjavur when Pazhuvettaraiyar's men almost managed to catch up with me. When we reached the river Kudamurutti, I told the boy, "I will get off here, tambi. Keep going. They will continue to follow you, mistaking you for me. When they finally seize you and question you, tell them that I fell into the river and drowned." But that boy seemed to be a descendant of the fabled Harischandran, who never told a lie. "How can I say you drowned when you didn't?" he asked. So I bound him to the horse and jumped into the river. Ayyayyo! The whirlpools in the rivers of the Chozha land, especially close to the banks! I was almost undone. Finally, I grabbed the root of a tree by the shore and managed to crawl out alive. Devi! When I was trapped in one of those whirlpools, spinning round and round and losing my mind in breathless suffocation, what do you think I saw, and what do you suppose I thought?'

'How would I know? Perhaps you thought of Gajendra, the elephant who was miraculously saved from the pool . . .'

'No. I saw some fish trapped in the whirlpool just like me. They reminded me of the darting eyes of the women of the Chozha realm. A man may escape from a whirlpool, but no man trapped in the eyes of the women of the Chozha country can ever hope to be free.'

'Some men exult in finding fault with women. It is a habit with menfolk to blame women for their shortcomings.'

'What is wrong if I follow that universal trend?' Vandiyatevan asked.

The mellifluous notes of the flute flowed from the palace, mingled with the tinkling of *tandai* anklets and rumbling of the *maddalam* drum. The youthful voices of several girls sang the *aichiyar kuravai** verses from the *Silappathikaram*.

O friend!
If Mayavan the lord,
the dark and dusky lord,
who threw the demon calf
up into the boughs
to bring the fruit down,
comes here among our cows
Shall we hear him play
the sweet konrai flute?

O friend!
If Mayavan the lord
The dark and dusky lord
who slew the evil demon
Disguised as a tree

---

* The name of a chapter in the epic *Silappathikaram*. It is also the ritual dance of the cowherdesses described therein.

standing in our pastures–
comes here among our cows–
Shall we hear him play
the sweet mullai flute?

Until the song ended, Vandiyatevan and Kundavai remained bound by its spell and lost to the world. Then, once again the anklets and instruments began to resound, indicating that the dancing had commenced.

'So . . . Kuravai koothu in the palace . . . I saw a wholly different kind of kuravai koothu in the Kadambur palace,' Vandiyatevan said.

'Yes, my companions are learning kuravai koothu. Soon, they will start looking for me. What has brought you here?' Kundavai asked.

'Just this–a missive from your brother. I have escaped from many perils–from the maelstroms of whirlpools and women's eyes, to bring it safely to you,' said Vandiyatevan as he held out the palm leaf scroll.

49

Wonder of Wonders

Kundavai Devi took the scroll from Vandiyatevan. As she read it, her face, which had been drooping under knitted brows until then, brightened and bloomed.

Looking up at Vandiyatevan, she said, 'You have delivered the letter. What do you intend to do now?'

'My job is over. All I have to do now is to return home.'

'Your work is not over. It has just begun.'

'Devi! I don't understand.'

'Are you not going to do what the prince has written down in this scroll? He says that I can safely entrust you with any confidential mission.'

'I did agree to do that when I left the prince. But I beg of you, please do not entrust me with any important task.'

'I don't understand you. Is it the custom among the Vaanan tribe to backtrack after having reached an agreement?'

'It is not a custom with the Vaanan clan to boast about their past glory. Nor is it their custom to renege on their given word.'

'Then why do you hesitate? Is it your dislike of women in general, or is it that you don't like me?' said Princess Kundavai and smiled.

'Ah! What a question! Does the sea dislike the moon? Why then does it throw up a thousand waves to seize the moon? Who can say that the sky doesn't like the earth? Why then does it delight in gazing at the earth all night long with a thousand starry eyes? Can the cloud loathe the lightning? Why does it so tightly clasp to its breast the lightning that tears through it? Does the bee shun the flower? Then why does it endlessly circle the flower and swoon right into it? Can anyone believe that the wasp hates the lamp? Why then does it sink into the lamp to die? Devi! If I didn't like you, why does your sidelong glance stupefy me? Why does the little smile playing at the corner of your lips knock me senseless?' All these thoughts arose in Vandiyatevan's mind. But his tongue could not utter them.

'Ayya! You have not answered my question. Does your reluctance stem from the thought of an intrepid warrior of the Vaanan clan having to do a woman's bidding? Didn't the prince tell you about what he had said in this letter?' the princess asked again.

'Devi, I knew the prince's intention only too well when I left. But I think that I did not start on this journey at a propitious time. I have gained enemies all along the way. I turned a close friend into an enemy. Other foes are searching for me everywhere. In such a situation, how can I promise to carry out the task you give me? I have misgivings because I don't want your work to suffer,' Vandiyatevan said.

'Who are those enemies? May I know?' Kundavai asked in an anxious voice.

'The Pazhuvettaraiyars have sent their men everywhere to hunt me down. My best friend Kandamaran believes that I stabbed him in the back with the intent to kill. A Vaishnava named Azhvarkadiyan is scouring high and low for me. The young queen of Pazhuvur has sent a sorcerer after me. I don't know when I will get caught and by whom.'

Vandiyatevan recalled his experience with the sorcerer on the night he escaped drowning in the floods. Since it was dangerous to travel by day, he had hidden himself in the bamboo woods and plantain groves. He walked beside the river for a long time until he reached a broken-down mandapam late in the night. The full moon was turning night into day. Its brilliant light beamed through the mandapam as well. Vandiyatevan crossed the moonlit patch and found a dark corner inside. Just as he was about to fall asleep, he heard the hoot of an owl. He jumped up, remembering that he had heard the same call near Nandini's arbour. Two tiny spots of light glared at him from the darkness. As he took a few steps to get away, he heard footsteps. He grabbed a craggy, weatherbeaten pillar and stood behind it. Then the face of the intruder came into view. Vandiyatevan recognized him as the sorcerer who visited the Pazhuvur queen. The sorcerer walked to the pillar. Vandiyatevan thought that he would not be seen in the dark and the man would go past him. However, the man came in slow motion, like a stalking cat, pounced on Vandiyatevan with a spine-chilling cry and started strangling him. 'Bring it out. Give it to me. If you don't hand over the signet ring with the palm tree emblem, I will squeeze your neck until you die,' he shrieked.

Vandiyatevan felt as if his neck would break, his eyes would pop out. He was struggling to breathe. And yet, he managed to keep his mind under control. Holding the old pillar firmly with an arm, he raised one of his legs with all his strength and gave a hard kick. The sorcerer squealed and fell. Simultaneously, the old pillar came toppling down along with a shower of stones from the ceiling. A bat flapped its wings and flew out. Vandiyatevan followed the bat and ran pell-mell, stopping only to make sure that he was not being followed. And now, the memory of that night was enough to make him shudder all over.

Kundavai's question brought him out of the horrors of that night and restored his sanity. 'Ayya, how long has it been since you left Kanchi?'

'A week and a day,' he replied.

'It is a wonder of wonders that you have made so many enemies in so short a time. How did you work this miracle?'

'It is a long story, Devi.'

'Never mind. You will have to share it with me. I can assign the job to you only after learning all the details,' Kundavai said, and called Ishana Siva Bhattar to ask, 'What about the boatman?'

'He is stone deaf. He cannot hear even thunderclaps.'

'Excellent. Come, let us take the boat. I must hear his whole story.'

Vandiyatevan was ecstatic. Was it so easy to have the good fortune of riding on the same boat with the illustrious daughter of the Chozha clan? He must have performed penances in seven previous births to have obtained such a chance. Vandiyatevan decided that he would spin out his story for as long as he could. What was the hurry? Why should he not make the best use of this rare opportunity?

True, Vandiyatevan was in no hurry. But as the boat began to move, Kundavai's anxiety and impatience accelerated with every passing moment as he described the incidents at the Kadambur palace. She kept on hurrying him along with 'Then?' and 'What next?' Vandiyatevan tried his best to lengthen the tale. However, in due course, every tale, however long, has to come to an end. The boat returned to the jetty, just as Vandiyatevan finished his account.

When they disembarked from the boat and entered the garden once again, the sounds of anklets and musical instruments indicated that the kuravai koothu was still going on within the palace. The song was again from the *Silappathikaram*.

Mayavan, the great lord,
who bears the whole world
in his lotus-bloom navel;
whose lips, hands and feet
glow in ruby red;
Eyes are not eyes
that do not see
the dark-hued lord.
Eyes are not eyes
that blink at the sight
of the lord.

He who quelled the vile
and black-hearted Kamsa;
he who walked for peace,
with holy chants around him,
as the Pandavas' envoy;
the lord for whom our prayers
are raised in all directions;
Tongues are not tongues
That haven't praised the lord.
Tongues are not tongues
If they haven't hailed his name.
Narayana!

Vandiyatevan remarked, 'Kamsa might have been a vile and black-hearted villain. But he did me a great good turn yesterday.'

'How's that? How could Kamsa help you?' Kundavai asked him.

'It was Kamsa who helped me get into this city,' said Vandiyatevan and recounted the experience.

Vandiyatevan had guessed that Pazhuvettaraiyars' men would have reached Pazhaiyarai before him. They would be waiting at the city gates. The least suspicion would end in his arrest. How could he enter the city without being hauled in by them? Plagued by these apprehensions, Vandiyatevan halted by the Arasalaru at some distance from the city. A street theatre troupe passed him by. It comprised actors playing several characters like Kamsa, Balarama and Krishna. Kamsa wore a wooden mask over his head. Vandiyatevan had an idea. He struck up a conversation with the troupe saying, 'The actor playing Kamsa is not good enough in the role.' That offended actor began to bicker with him. Could Vandiyatevan ever let go of any fight that came his way? Announcing that he could act better than their man, he forcibly grabbed the man's headgear, thrust it over his own head and began to enact the role. His loud declamations and roistering swagger made the others applaud him and concede that he surpassed their actor in histrionics. The man who played Kamsa stomped away in anger. The troupe accepted Vandiyatevan's offer joyfully when he said, 'Never mind, I will go with you and act in your play.'

After all the play-acting and singing were over on the streets of Pazhaiyarai, Vandiyatevan went to meet Ishana Siva Bhattar at the temple as Aditta Karikalan had directed him. Bhattar had Vandiyatevan waiting in the Jain grotto as he informed Princess Kundavai and then took him across the stream to meet her.

After hearing this, Kundavai looked at Vandiyatevan in wonder and said, 'The Chozha clan is blessed with the boundless grace of the goddess of victory. She has sent you to me at this time of crisis.'

'My queen! You have not given me any task to perform as yet. I have not had the opportunity to show you what I can do.'

'Don't worry. I am going to entrust you with a mission that will reduce everything you have endured so far to trifles,' she said.

Vandiyatevan was overwhelmed with a gladness that suffused his body and soul. He geared himself up to cross the seven seas, fight a thousand lions, scale the Meru mountains and pluck the stars from the sky to fulfil the mission she would give him.

Kundavai walked to the marble pavilion in the garden. Bhattar and Vandiyatevan followed her. From a little shelf on the wall, Kundavai picked out a palm leaf strip and a stylus with a golden stem. On it, she wrote, *Ponniyin Selva! Come as soon as you see this letter. The person who brings it will give you all the details.* She etched the image of an aathi leaf below the words. Holding it out to Vandiyatevan, she said, 'You must take this message to Ilankai as quickly as possible. You must give it to Prince Arulmozhi Varman and bring him back with you forthwith.'

Waves of joy crashed over him. One of his two long-held ambitions had been fulfilled. He had met Princess Kundavai, the light of the Chozha clan. And thanks to her, his second wish was also going to come true. He was going to have the privilege of meeting Prince Arulmozhi Varman.

'Devi! You have given me a task after my own heart. I will take your missive and leave at once,' said he, and held out his hand to take the scroll.

When Kundavai handed him the scroll, Vandiyatevan's lucky hand felt the touch of her fingers as slender as kantal flowers. Vandiyatevan's body began to tingle all over. He felt as if his heart would explode. A thousand butterflies fluttered their wings in flight. Ten thousand cuckoos trilled their songs together. Mountains of polychromatic flowers rained and scattered around him.

Overwhelmed by euphoria, Vandiyatevan raised his head and looked at Kundavai. His heart swelled, aching to release his surging feelings. But how could mere lifeless words have the power to express them?

His eyes spoke for him. How can you describe the lyrical outpourings of those eyes unless you say that even Kalidasa and the Tamizh poets of the ancient anthology, the *Triple Nine Hundred*, could not match them?

At a little distance from the arbour, the dry leaves rustled in whispers.

Ishana Siva Bhattar cleared his throat.

Vandiyatevan came back to earth.

50

The Parantaka House of Healing

The next day dawned and the world shone bright. The red rays of the sun lit up the golden domes of the Pazhaiyarai palaces with all their dazzling refulgence. Right in front of Kundavai's palace stood a massive, caparisoned elephant with an ornamental seat on its back. Kundavai and Vanathi emerged from the palace and mounted it. The earth shook under its feet as the elephant made its way to the Parantaka House of Healing, located in the middle of the four military colonies of Pazhaiyarai. The mahout walked beside the animal to guide it along at a steady pace.

The elephant's bell brought the people out of their houses. Their faces lit up when they saw the two princesses. They put their palms together in welcome.

The elephant crossed the street and reached the military colonies where the streets showcased distinct and characteristic scenes of their own. Plump roosters were roaming and looking to pick fights. Sporting a set of thick, curved horns, the rams were nosing around to see if they could engage in combat. Pugnacious hounds were tied to the doorposts with leather leashes or twisted ropes. Little boys practised martial arts on the streets with their *silambam* rods slamming against one other.

The outer walls of the houses had pictures painted with red ochre. Most of them centre-staged scenes of war from the legends of the god Murugan or the lives of the Chozha kings. There were terrifying incidents of Muruga slicing off the sprouting heads of the demon Soora, and the goddess Durga slaying the buffalo demon. There were lifelike depictions of the acts of daredevilry performed by Chozha warriors on the battlefields of Tellaru, Tanjavur, Kudamookku, Arasalaru, Tirupurampiyam, Vellur, Takkolam and Sevur.

When the royal elephant appeared, the military colony erupted into an excited furore. Roosters beat their wings noisily and flew to the rooftops to crow. Little boys shouted to each other as they ran to knock on doors, announcing the news of the visitors' arrival. As the elephant ambled down the streets, women, children and senior citizens stood on their front steps to shout, 'Long live Princess Kundavai Devi!' 'Long live the daughter of Sundara Chozha!' Some of them began to follow the elephant. Soon, the crowd increased as did the cries of welcome.

The readers know by now that the family members of the soldiers fighting in the Ilankai war lived in the military colonies. Kundavai had established an infirmary for their welfare with her personal income from her landholdings. In keeping with the Chozha custom of revering ancestors, Princess Kundavai had named it after Emperor Parantaka, her great-grandfather, the most renowned among her forefathers. She made use of her frequent visits to supervise the infirmary to interact with the warriors' families and to enquire about their welfare.

The elephant halted in front of the healing house, folded its legs and crouched down on the ground. The two women got down.

As soon as the elephant moved away, the people, particularly the women and children, surrounded the princesses.

'Is this infirmary useful to you? Are the doctors taking good care of you and giving you the medicaments you require?' Kundavai asked them.

Many voices shouted, 'Yes, Amma! Yes!'

One of the women said, 'I was troubled by a cough for three months. It stopped after a week's medicines prescribed by the doctor here.'

'Amma! My son climbed a tree and broke his leg. The doctor bound it up and gave him medications for fifteen days. He has started jumping and playing again, even climbing trees as before,' said another.

A young girl said, 'My mother's eyesight started failing. She came to the infirmary for a month's treatment. Now she is able to see very well.'

'See, Vanathi! We cannot even begin to imagine how our ancestors discovered the different therapeutic herbs to treat varying afflictions.'

'Only by the power of the omniscient inner-eye could they have found these cures.'

'True indeed! But sadly they have not found cures for people like you who suffer from the maladies of the mind.'

'Akka! I have no such ailment. Please don't go on and on about it! My friends torment me about it all the time.'

'You deserve it. My brother had no care in the world. Haven't you played havoc with his mind? Each time he sends a message from Ilankai, he enquires about your health!'

Shouts of 'Make way for the physician!' had the guards regulating the crowds. The elderly chief physician of the healing house came to welcome the princesses.

'Ayya, you had said that there were unique herbs to be found in the Kodikkarai woods. I sent a young warrior to find them for you. Has he arrived?' Kundavai asked him.

'Yes, Amma. That smart young man is here. I am sending one of my sons with him. My son will return from Kodikkarai. But your man says he is ready to go to Ilankai island.'

'You would need herbs from Ilankai too?' Vanathi asked.

'Yes, Amma. It is said that when Hanuman brought the Sanjivini mountain to Ilankai, he crossed the ocean at Kodikkarai, where a few herbs from the mountain dropped down into the woods. Some of them continue to grow there even today. Since the whole mountain was taken to Ilankai, herbs of an even rarer kind can still be found on that island. If only I can get the herbs I require, I will certainly be able to cure the emperor.'

'By god's grace may it be so. Where are those young men now?' Kundavai asked.

'They are here, Amma, waiting to take their leave of you.'

The chief healer led the princesses into the healing house. They walked past the groups of patients waiting to be treated. Each one of them broke into bright smiles and warm greetings, expressing their gratitude to Kundavai Devi for establishing such a fine infirmary for them.

Two men were waiting in the chief physician's room. Kundavai smiled to see Vandiyatevan attired in a mode altogether different. Vanathi too recognized him. She whispered in Kundavai's ear, 'Akka! The man we saw in the astrologer's house . . .'

'I think so. Meeting the astrologer has led him to the physician. Like you, he too may be afflicted by some mental ailment,' said Kundavai, and turned to Vandiyatevan. 'Ayya! Is it you who agreed to go all the way to Ilankai to bring herbs for the emperor's well-being?'

Vandiyatevan's eyes spoke in a language of their own. But he opened his mouth to say, 'Yes, princess! I am the man who is going to Ilankai. I may perhaps see the prince there. Any message that I may convey to him?'

'If you see him, please tell him, without fail, that the Kodumbalur princess has not been keeping well. She has frequent fainting fits. If he wants to see her before she is wholly deprived of sense and sensibility, he must make his way here at once.'

'I will do so,' said Vandiyatevan and glanced at Vanathi.

Kundavai's words made Vanathi blush. This bashfulness made her appear all the more beautiful. Suppressing her shyness, she stammered, 'Ayya! I beg of you, say no such thing. Please tell the prince that, under Kundavai Devi's care, Vanathi is provided with every comfort and is doing very well.'

'I will,' said Vandiyatevan.

'What's this? You have said "I will" to both of us,' said Kundavai. 'Only one of these statements can be true.'

'So what, Amma? I will convey the statements of the defence and the prosecution. Let the prince make his own judgement,' Vandiyatevan said.

Vanathi interposed, 'But please don't attribute what one said to the other.'

Wishing to change the subject, Kundavai asked the healer, 'Ayya, have you obtained the letter of accreditation from the palace officer for these men?'

'Yes, Amma. One says, "All government officials must assist these two men who are going to find herbs for the treatment of the emperor's ailment." The other is a letter to the keeper of the lighthouse in Kodikkarai. I have given them both to these men.'

'Why the delay? They may leave at once,' Kundavai said.

'Yes, time to leave,' Vandiyatevan agreed. But it was not so easy to depart quickly.

The group headed out. The elephant stood ready for the princesses. Two mettlesome horses from the palace waited impatiently to fly away with Vandiyatevan and his companion.

But Vandiyatevan was assailed by endless doubts. Kundavai too felt repeatedly impelled to issue fresh warnings to the men about the dangers along their way.

Finally, the princesses mounted the elephant.

Vandiyatevan and his companion got on their horses.

It did not look as if the elephant would start moving anytime soon. Kundavai indicated that those who were leaving on the long journey should depart first. Vandiyatevan turned his horse half-heartedly. He directed a last eager glance at the princess and then whipped the horse as if he was angry with it. With offended pride, the horse galloped away. The doctor's son had to struggle to keep pace with him.

As the elephant headed back to the palace, Kundavai became lost in thoughts. 'Strange are the ways of the heart,' she mused. 'Having rejected great kings and mighty warriors, why does it take an interest in this young man, a wayfarer? Why is it so anxious that he should succeed in the task he has undertaken and return safe and sound?'

'Akka, what are you thinking?' Vanathi's voice brought Kundavai back to the world.

'Nothing, Vanathi. I was thinking about the arrogance of that young man. Now I feel that I should not have sent a message to my brother through a man like him.'

'Yes, Akka, he is a cunning fellow. I could even call him a bandit.'

'What do you mean "bandit"?'

'Ordinary bandits steal worthless things like gold and silver. But I am afraid that this young man will make away with the goddess of the Chozha clan. You will not allow that to happen, will you?' Vanathi said.

'You rascal! You think I am like you? Never,' Kundavai replied.

As they moved on, the princesses saw a group of women at a street corner. Ordering the elephant to stop, Kundavai asked them, 'Why are you standing here? Is there anything you want to tell me?'

One of the girls came forward and said, 'Amma, there is no news of our husbands from Ilankai. It seems the Tanjavur men have stopped all the food that was to be sent to them! How can they fight on an empty stomach?'

'There's no need at all for you to worry. All the food they need is being sent to them from the Mamallapuram port. Whatever the Tanjavur men may ordain, will your prince abandon his soldiers? Will he let the great warriors of the Tamizh land starve and do nothing about it?'

At any other time, Kundavai would have got down there and then and reassured the women even more. But her heart was restive now and she longed for solitude. The elephant made for the palace.

51

Mamallapuram*

We wish to take our readers to Mamallapuram at this moment in time, even though they may know it only too well.

It is now more than three hundred years since the Pallava kings, Mahendra and Mamalla Narasimha, turned the port city into a dream world of exquisite sculptures. At present, the city has lost much of its lustre. These ravages of time cannot but be disheartening. The mansions have cracked and disintegrated. The streets and the harbour have lost their bustling crowds. Trade has dwindled. The huge warehouses are missing. Mountainous heaps of cargo, for both import and export, are no longer piled high along the streets.

* Now a UNESCO world heritage site known as Mahabalipuram, this was the major port city of the Pallava kingdom, named after Narasimhavarman I, also known as Mamalla (the great wrestler). It is the site of royal monuments, exquisitely carved out of living rock, dated 7–8 CE.

In times long ago, it had been a natural port with the sea shaping a channel deep enough for ships to dock safely in the harbour. Now accumulated deposits of silt have made the waters shallow, allowing only small skiffs and boats to sail through. The huge ships must halt at a considerable distance from the shore. Small boats carry all the merchandise to be loaded on them.

However, as the centuries passed, Mamallapuram has also attained a few distinctions. The stone temple on the shore arrests our eye and mind. This is not a temple excavated from a single rock as in the age of Mahendra and Mamalla Narasimha but built with rocks brought here for the purpose. Its architectural design remains an indescribable marvel, like a crown on the head of the sea king.

A Vishnu temple stands in the middle of the town, housing the god reclining in slumber, constructed by Parameshvara Varman, a Pallava king who nurtured the cults of Siva and Vishnu like two eyes of his own. The poet Tirumangai Azhvar had visited this temple to sing verses overflowing with ardour. One of the verses shows that, during the poet's lifetime, the Pallava kingdom had expanded and retained its glory, and Mamallapuram had been a port of exceeding wealth.

In Mallai stand the stately ships
With treasure troves galore,
They swing and sway on gliding waves
Burdened by their store
Of high-piled heaps of shining gold,
And gems in colours nine,
And elephants of strength and girth
With trunks that twist and twirl.

To Mallai come the devotees
All staunch of faith and heart,
Going round the lord divine
Reclining on the shore.
O mind of mine! Go worship them
Who worship the great lord.

The sun set on the Pallava empire within a hundred years after Tirumangai Azhvar's time. Kanchi, famed as the centre of boundless learning, lost its glory. The economic prosperity of the Mamallapuram port, once packed with fleets of ships, also decreased.

But nothing could dim the undying glory brought to the Tamizh realm by the magnificent sculptures immortalizing the port city. The astounding variety of the carvings on the rock-cut monuments and chariots appeared as fresh and new as when they were created three hundred years ago. There were more sightseers for the sculptures than traders of mercantile goods.

* * *

A fine chariot drawn by two horses came smartly down the streets of Kanchi. The caparisoned steeds and the ornately carved vehicle, its gold-plated dome shining like another sun in the evening light, all proclaimed that its occupants belonged to a royal clan.

Within its spacious interior sat three men of royal blood. One of them was the dauntless warrior Aditta Karikalan, Sundara Chozha's firstborn son. He had entered the battlefield at a very young age, performed astonishing feats and was given the title 'the great lion who beheaded Veerapandiyan'. Sundara

Chozha, who fell ill soon after the death of Veerapandiyan and the annexation of the Pandya territories, had declared Aditta Karikalan as his heir apparent in order to establish his son's indubitable right to succeed him. This also gave Aditta Karikalan the authority to issue royal edicts and endow grants inscribed on stone tablets under his own name.

Soon, the crown prince went northward to free Tondaimandalam from Kannaradevan the Rashtrakuta king. His daring acts of bravery drove the Rashtrakuta army far beyond the North Pennai river. However, a full-fledged invasion of the north required a larger and stronger army. Therefore, Karikalan remained in Kanchi and busied himself in gathering troops, armaments and everything necessary for such an endeavour. The Pazhuvettaraiyars began to hinder his efforts. They insisted that any invasion of the north had to wait for the conclusion of the Ilankai war. Rumour had it that sufficient food was not being sent from the Chozha country to the soldiers in Ilankai. Aditta Karikalan's blood began to boil.

For three hundred years before and after our story took place, men as mighty as the heroes of epics and myths, as valiant as Bhima, Arjuna, Bhishma, Drona, Ghatotkacha and Abhimanyu, were born in the land of the Tamizh people. Their acts of courage astounded the world. Every victory on the battlefield strengthened their physical might. Old men possessed the power to raise mountains. Striplings could ride on the winds, reach the sky and scatter the stars.

On that day, two such redoubtable warriors were seated on the chariot beside Karikalan. One of them was Malayaman of Tirukovilur, Aditta Karikalan's grandfather. Sundara Chozha's second wife and royal consort, Vanamadevi, was his daughter. In age and wisdom, he resembled the patriarch Bhishma, the grandfather of the princes of the Kuru kingdom in the great epic. Though Aditta Karikalan was devoted to him, there were times when Malayaman's advice tested his patience.

The other man in the chariot was Partibhendran. A little older than Aditta Karikalan, he belonged to a branch of the old Pallava dynasty. Since he had no claim to any kingdom, he was keen to gain a reputation by proving his skills on the battlefield. In the war against Veerapandiyan, he had functioned as Aditta Karikalan's right-hand man. This made him Karikalan's intimate friend. From the day Veerapandiyan fell, the two men became inseparable.

The three men in the chariot were discussing the news from Tanjavur that had reached them as the word on the street.

Aditta Karikalan said, 'I cannot tolerate the arrogance of the Pazhuvettaraiyars any longer. How dare they accuse my envoy of being a spy! They have even announced a reward of a thousand gold coins for the man who captures him. How can I bear these insults? My sword is shrinking in shame. But you continue to advise me to be patient!'

Partibhendran said, 'I don't advise you to be patient. But I told you back then not to send Vandiyatevan on this important mission. I knew that he would make a mess of things with his impetuosity. Is it enough to know how to flash a sword and fling a spear? An envoy on a diplomatic mission must have an astute brain.'

Partibhendran did not like the prince's affection for Vandiyatevan. This made him constantly undermine Vandiyatevan and cavil at everything he did. It was no different this time.

'Have you started your usual baiting? You cannot pass the time without criticizing Vandiyatevan. Who can match him in sharpness of wit? He has fulfilled the task I gave him to personally hand the missive to the emperor. That must have infuriated the Pazhuvettaraiyars. How is it Vandiyatevan's fault?' Karikalan asked.

'He would not have stopped with the job you gave him. He would have interfered in things that did not concern him,' Partibhendran insisted.

'Keep quiet! *Thatha*!* Why are you silent? What do you think? Why not take a huge army, go to Tanjavur, free the emperor and bring him here? How long should we remain supine while the emperor is kept imprisoned by the Pazhuvettaraiyars? How long should we remain scared of them?'

As the chariot turned the corner and the sea came into view, Tirukovilur Malayaman, the seasoned veteran of sixty-four battles, cleared his throat to reply. Then, catching sight of the waves, he said, 'Let us first get down from this chariot, tambi. Let us go to our usual place and sit down. I have become old. It is not easy for me to talk in a moving chariot.'

---

* Grandfather.

52

The Dotard Ties the Knot!

The Mamallapuram beach is scattered with rocks, large and small. At high tide, the billowing waves crash over them, but when the sea recedes, they become dry and visible under the sun. None of those rocks were left untouched by the great sculptors of the Pallava age, who had let their imagination shape deathless scenes on each according to its size.

The three warriors got down from the chariot. Karikalan and Malayaman took their seat on two rocks facing one another as they would on a throne. Partibhendran stood close by. The incessant waves splashed them up to their knees. Sometimes, they bounced off the rocks, spattering froth on their faces like a shower of pearls. In the distance, a row of boats were tearing through the sea carrying goods to be loaded on the frigates waiting with their sails unfurled.

'My heart boils when I think of all the goods and provisions stocked up for the Rashtrakuta invasion, having to be sent to Ilankai,' Partibhendran said.

'Do we have a choice? The elite contingent of the Chozha army is fighting in Ilankai. They are gaining victory after victory. They have taken Anuradhapuram, which had been ruled by the native Sinhala kings for a thousand years. Do we let such bravehearts starve to death?' Aditta Karikalan retorted.

'Who says so? Provisions must be dispatched to them. But from the Chozha country through the Nagapattinam port. Or across the Setu bridge from Pandya country. Why is it necessary to send it from this arid Tondaimandalam? Moreover, this has delayed our invasion of the north,' Partibhendran said.

'My blood boils when I think of it. We can't figure out what those Pazhuvur bounders have in mind. How long can we put up with all this? Thatha! Why are you still keeping your mouth shut? Say something!' Karikalan growled.

'My child! The waves roar endlessly. Your friend Partibhendran is having a shouting match with them. How can I make myself heard in this din? I am old now and getting infirm . . .' Malayaman said.

'Partibhendra! Keep quiet. Let Thatha share his opinion.'

'See, I've sealed my mouth. Poor grandfather has taken so much trouble in his old age to climb down the hill fort and come here. Can I open my mouth before him? But look at this sea! It has no brains at all! It keeps on howling along! It seems to have no fear of our Malayaman king."

'Tambi! Partibhendra! There was a time when all the kings of the world trembled when they heard Malayaman's name. The kings of the Chalukya, Vaanan, Ganga and Kongu regions slithered into their holes as serpents do when they hear the crash of thunder. Even the sea king cringed in humility. Now that this body has become debilitated, all those men have started acting up again. Now, the Pazhuvettaraiyars too, who popped out from the west quite recently, are trying to quash me. Karikala! Did you not say just now that the Pazhuvettaraiyars' intentions are not clear to you? I will tell you.

Listen! They want to weaken you and your brother by dividing you. Arulmozhi must lose in Ilankai and face humiliation. And you should become angry with your brother. You must fight with each other. I must be made miserable by it. This is their hidden agenda.'

Karikalan cut in as Malayaman vented his fury. 'They are never going to succeed with this plan. No one can divide me from my brother. I would give my life for Arulmozhi. In fact, I am constantly teased by the thought–why not board the ship and sail to Ilankai? Who knows what difficulties he may be facing there? And here I am, luxuriating in the palace. My weapons are getting rusty and every moment seems like an age. Shall I board one of these ships setting sail for Ilankai?'

Partibhendran burst out, 'My king! Great idea! You are voicing the thoughts that have been seething within me all along. Come! Let us go. No use asking grandfather. He will only tell us to hang back and sit tight. Let's leave tomorrow, taking half the troops with us. Let us finish the war in Ilankai and sail straight to Nagapattinam. From there, we can go to Tanjavur and deal with the Pazhuvettaraiyars once and for all.'

'Karikala! See? What did I tell you? Did I not say that I will speak only if he keeps his mouth shut?'

'Here! I will shut up. Have your say,' said Partibhendran and raised his hand to clamp his mouth shut.

'Karikala, you are *the* warrior among warriors. Few born in this Tamizh land have been endowed with might such as yours. In all the battles I have seen, and I have seen many, I have never encountered any warrior who penetrated the enemy forces all by himself and fought as you did. You were not even sixteen when the Sevur battle took place. I have never seen anyone of that age darting through the enemy, or swinging the sword to the left and to the right with such dazzling speed as you did. That scene remains fresh in my mind; I see it before my eyes even now. Like you, your friend Partibhendran too is a great warrior. But you are both reckless and hot-tempered. This blurs your mind and diminishes your ability to reflect. You wish to do the very opposite of what you *should* do.'

'Thatha! You have given me the same advice many times before.'

'True. Are you saying that I am useless? Do you want me to return quietly to my home town?'

'No! No! Tell me what is to be done now.'

'You must bring your brother Arulmozhi here. Immediately. You and your brother should never be apart.'

'Thatha! What are you saying? If Arulmozhi comes here, what will happen to the war in Ilankai?'

'The Ilankai war has reached an impasse. Anuradhapuram has been captured. The rainy season will begin all too soon. Nothing can be done in the next four months. The only job to be done is to guard the captured regions and keep them under control. The army generals can take care of it. It is essential for Arulmozhi to be here now. Karikala! What is the use of hiding the truth? The Chozha empire and the dynasty founded by Vijayalaya Chozha are both in grave danger. You and those close to you must stay together and take great precautions for your safety. We must gather all our strength. You cannot predict when and what kind of calamity will strike you.'

'Grandfather! What is this? Are you trying to scare me? What do I fear as long as I have my sword in my hand? However great the approaching threat may be, I am capable of handling it single-handedly. I am not afraid of any danger.'

'My boy! Do I have to be told how dauntless you are? And yet, there are occasions to recall what the great poet Valluvar said:

> It is folly to fear what should not be feared.
> But the wise dread what ought to be dreaded.

You should be free from fear when you fight your enemies face-to-face on the battlefield. If a coward who fears them were to be born in my clan, I would cut him to pieces with this aged and enfeebled arm. But you must fear hidden conspiracies, plots and dangers that the eye cannot see, and take proper precautions according to each situation. If those who are born in royal clans and those who are heirs to the throne remain reckless, the country will be destroyed.'

'Thatha! What kind of hidden threats do you anticipate? We can be careful only if you explain things more clearly.'

'I am about to tell you. A midnight conference was held in Kadambur Sambuvaraiyar's palace some days ago. Periya Pazhuvettaraiyar attended it. So did Tennavan Mazhavaraiyar, Kundratur Kizhar, Vanangamudi Munaiyar, Anjadasinga Mutharaiyar and Irattaikudai Rajaliyar. These are the only names that reached my ears. There may have been more.'

'So what? They would have watched shows until midnight, eaten to bursting point, guzzled tons of liquor and fallen asleep. How does it affect us? What can these doddering fools and old codgers accomplish in their meetings?'

'What is the use of anything I may say when you have such a positive opinion about old codgers? After all, I am older than all of them!'

'Thatha, don't be angry. Would I rank you with those useless old men?'

'See, again you call them useless. Don't forget that their leader, the oldest codger among them all, got married recently. Understand this, no young man in the world is as dangerous as an old man who has tied the knot with a blooming young woman.'

This reference to old men marrying nubile young women brought a bizarre change of expression to Aditta Karikalan's face. His eyes turned red like the eyes of an evil spirit demanding blood sacrifice. His lips twitched, he ground his teeth.

Malayaman did not notice these changes, but Partibhendran did. He said, 'Why get into that marriage business? Ayya! What happened in Sambuvaraiyar's palace?'

'I was coming to that, but age makes me ramble. Karikala, listen! Partibhendra, you too must listen. That midnight conference was not confined to old men. Some young men were there too. One of them was Sambuvaraiyar's son Kandamaran. The other was . . .'

Seeing Malayaman hesitate, Aditta Karikalan prodded him, 'Thatha, who was the other?'

Malayaman answered, 'Your grand uncle Gandaraditta's son, your uncle, Madhurantakan.'

Aditta Karikalan and Partibhendran howled and screamed with laughter.

'What is this? Why do you laugh? Are you making fun of me?' Malayaman asked.

'No, Thatha! No! We laughed because you referred to Madhurantakan as a *young* man. Isn't he the oldest dodderer among them, ripe with all the wisdom of piety?' said Aditta Karikalan.

'Haven't you heard of a new spring in old age? Madhurantakan has regained his youth. Why, until recently, the man had announced that he was going to renounce the world and serve the lord. And now he has acquired wives, one, two, three, and still counting . . . ?'

'Let him. Let him marry as many times as he likes. So what?'

'Tambi, Madhurantakan's marriages are not ordinary marriages. They are diplomatic alliances promoting Pazhuvettaraiyar's secret plots.'

'Thatha, why are you talking in riddles? Come out with it! What in the world do the Pazhuvettaraiyars want? What is the reason for their going from town to town to hold conferences? How does Madhurantakan come into this picture?' Aditta Karikalan asked.

'What else? They want to divest you and your brother of your right to claim the throne. They want to crown Madhurantakan as the sovereign king of the Chozha empire. They have kept your father prisoner in the Tanjavur Fort only to gain his consent to their scheme,' Malayaman said.

53

Malayaman's Frenzy

Aditta Karikalan stopped short of fainting when he heard what Tirukovilur Malayaman had to say. For the ripe old warrior's wisdom matched his consummate skills, and those skills were compounded by experience. But for a while, he remained frozen in silence, unable to move. Partibhendran lost his voice. The sea had toned itself down. In the distance, the rhythmic calls of the boatmen who were loading the ships seemed to have ceased.

Embarrassed at having yielded to astonishment, Karikalan raised his head to look directly at his grandfather and said, 'Grandfather! I too am aware that this kind of tittle-tattle is rife among the people. I dismissed them all as false rumours. But you speak with absolute certainty. Do you really know this for a fact? Can such things happen?'

'Why not? Before your grandfather, it was your grand uncle Gandaraditta who ruled the land. Doesn't his son have a greater right to the kingdom than you do?'

'Never! That complete moron, born a man and not a woman by sheer accident, who cannot string four words together coherently, and has never touched a sword–*he* has the right to the throne? Or does it belong to Aditta Karikalan, who entered the battlefield at age twelve, the lion who beheaded Veerapandiyan, the warrior of warriors, a total stranger to defeat? Ayya! Has your brain gone rusty with old age?' Partibhendran howled.

Karikalan admonished him to stay silent before telling his grandfather, 'I don't care about losing the empire. I can establish ten empires with my sword. But is this fair? I would not have objected if Madhurantakan had been pronounced the heir apparent right in the beginning. But how can an official announcement made before the country and the people designating me as the crown prince with the right to rule, be revoked? Would you consent to this change?'

'No, and I will never give my consent. And if you agree to offer the kingdom to Madhurantakan, I will chop you to pieces with this sword of mine. Then I will slaughter your mother who bore you in her womb and gave birth to you. After that, I will stab myself and die for having given birth to your mother. As long as there is breath in my body, I will not allow the Chozha empire to be wrested away from you!' the old man roared. Lightning flashed in his eyes. His entire body shook in a frenzy.

'Well said, Thatha! Well said!' Partibhendran hollered with tears in his eyes and rushed to embrace Malayaman.

Karikalan looked at the deep sea. And then, turning to his grandfather, he said, 'Let us get the army together and leave at once. Let us do away with the Pazhuvettaraiyars and their associates–Mazhavaraiyar, Sambuvaraiyar, Mutharaiyar, Munaiyaraiyar, the whole lot once and for all. Let us seize the Tanjavur Fort, throw Madhurantakan into prison and set the emperor free. Your blessings will be enough for us to succeed. If Partibhendran and I stand side by side, who can defeat us?'

'True. You cannot be defeated on the battlefield. But what will you do if you are assaulted by political schemes and palace intrigues? As your army approaches Tanjavur, they will launch a smear campaign about the son coming to fight with his own father. They will put out the canard that the emperor has died of unbearable shame. There will be people to believe those stories. Child, what can you do in such a situation? You will lose heart. Can you bear to be accused of heading a mutiny against your own father?'

Aditta Karikalan covered his ears with his hands. 'I can't even bear to *hear* these words!'

'That is why I told you long ago that a huge threat looms over us.'

'What can we do, Thatha? What can we do?'

'First, you must send a dependable man to Ilankai to bring Arulmozhi here. Your brother will not leave the battlefield so easily or abandon his men. You must send someone who is capable of persuading him to change his mind.'

Partibhendran came forward and said, 'If you allow me, I will do it.'

'I leave the decision to Karikalan and you. However, unlike Vandiyatevan, the man who undertakes the job must not poke his nose into things that are of no concern to him.'

'See! What did I tell you?' Partibhendran crowed.

'Thatha, do you have any news of Vandiyatevan?'

'At first, I had my doubts about whether he had joined our enemies. But they were dispelled quickly.'

'See, Partibhendra?' Karikalan said.

'Don't be in such a hurry. Let him finish. Ayya, what made you doubt Vandiyatevan?'

'I learnt that he was in Sambuvaraiyar's palace at the time of the midnight conference. But I also learnt that he had nothing to do with the conspiracy.'

'Thatha, how did you learn all these things?'

'I did not get invited to the dinner at the Kadambur palace. That was enough to make me a little suspicious. I captured one of its attendees on his way home. It was from him that I learnt about everything that happened there. I believe Vandiyatevan is a friend of Sambuvaraiyar's son, Kandamaran.'

'Yes. Didn't they both serve in our army and the border patrol on the banks of the North Pennai? I know that they have been friends since then.'

'Anyhow, Vandiyatevan was in that palace on that night. But I could not be sure about whether he was involved in that conspiracy. Later, as soon as I found out that Vandiyatevan had stabbed Kandamaran in the back and escaped from the Tanjavur Fort–'

'Thatha, I will never believe this. Whatever his turn of mind may be, Vandiyatevan is not someone who will stab anyone in his back. He is certainly not a villain who would stab his friend.'

'What if he knew that the friend was involved in a plot against his master? What if that friend tried to involve him in that plot?'

'Whatever it may be, he would have fought him face to face. Never would he have stabbed him in the back.'

'I am amazed by your unassailable trust in your friend, Tambi! But whatever the truth may be, the Pazhuvettaraiyars have charged Vandiyatevan with that crime and are hunting him down. This is all I know. Therefore, there must have been some kind of skirmish between Vandiyatevan and Kandamaran. Does this not confirm that Vandiyatevan did not join the conspiracy?' Malayaman said.

'In this case, I don't require any proof at all. If Vandiyatevan joins our enemies, the earth will turn upside down. The seas will go dry. The skies will fall. The sun will rise in the night. The Chozha dynasty will be completely destroyed,' Aditta Karikalan said heatedly.

'I agree with the prince. Vandiyatevan will never turn into a traitor and join the enemies. The only fault I find with him is this. He becomes giddy whenever he sees a pretty face. Then his mind goes berserk.'

Aditta Karikalan smiled and said, 'It is because I am well aware of this trait that I asked him to go and see my sister after delivering the missive to the emperor. Once he sets his eyes on the princess, where is the possibility of escape? He will have to remain her slave!'

Malayaman asked, 'So that's what you have instructed Vandiyatevan to do! I didn't know. Any message from him after reaching Tanjavur? At least, a word from Princess Kundavai?'

'I expect it every moment. No news until now.'

'Once Arulmozhi comes here, we must fetch your sister too. Then all our worries will be over. All we have to do is consult her and follow her advice.'

'Thatha, where my sister is concerned, you seem to be worse than Vandiyatevan.'

'You are right, Karikala! From the time she was two years old, your sister has been a tyrant, ruling over your parents, your grandmother and me with a rod of iron, making us dance to her tune. Karikala, don't think that this praise for your sister demeans you. It should be a matter of pride for you. Anyone as richly endowed with intelligence—man or woman—is yet to be born. Don't you know the kind of man our Chief Minister, Aniruddha Brahmarayar happens to be? What more can I say when he himself seeks her counsel?' Malayaman intoned in rapture.

Bristling with envy, Partibhendran said, 'That's all very well. Nobody denies it! However, what if Vandiyatevan had been smitten by some other woman's face before meeting Princess Kundavai? Such as, let's say . . . the dazzling siren, the young queen of Pazhuvur . . . ?' he drawled.

He spoke the last words in a lowered voice so the old man did not hear them. But Aditta Karikalan did. He swung around to glare at Partibhendran with eyes that blazed fire. That glance petrified Partibhendran.

Rising from his seat, Malayaman said, 'Partibhendra! You are leaving for Ilankai tomorrow. You young folk will have much to talk over. I am an old man. I will take my own time to get back to the palace. And you boys should take yours before you return.'

Once Malayaman moved away from them, Partibhendran looked at Karikalan and said, 'My king! My master! Some deep distress preys upon you. Pain eats away at your heart. I know that it has something to do with that young queen. Your whole appearance changes when Pazhuvettaraiyar or his young queen are mentioned. Your eyes turn red and spout fire. How long are you going to let this anguish burn you up? A thousand times have you called me your dearest friend. Can't you open your heart to such a friend? Can't you share your pain with me? Can't you give me an opportunity to find a remedy for your misery? How long can I keep watching you suffer agonies in silence?'

Aditta Karikalan sighed heavily and said, 'My friend! Mine is an anguish that can never end. It can end only with my death. It has no remedy. It is not that it cannot be shared with you. I will tell you tonight. Let us go back to the palace now. It is not right to let Thatha return alone.'

With these words, Aditta Karikalan rose from his seat on the boulder.

54

More Lethal than Venom

The three warriors spent the night at one of the old palaces of the Pallava kings of the past. After dinner, Malayaman left to hear the tale of Aravan that was to be enacted in the vicinity of the five rock-cut chariots. Aditta Karikalan and Partibhendran went up to the palace terrace.

For some time, Aditta Karikalan stood gazing at Mamallapuram by night. A few dim lamps twinkled here and there. The streets were mostly silent. The doors of the temples were being shut after the midnight puja. The sea wailed a sad dirge. Near the five chariot sculptures, a storyteller and his team of musicians were performing the tale of Aravan. The torchlights turned his audience into a circle of shadows.

'See how the old man retains his vim and vigour! Attending storytelling sessions at this ripe old age! The men of those times were men indeed! Who has their physical stamina and mental fortitude these days?'

'My king, have you too started mooning about the old days? What is it that the men of the past have accomplished that we have not? I have not heard of heroic deeds performed by anyone in his youth that can possibly rival yours, not even in myths and epics,' Partibhendran said.

'Partibhendra, I know that you are totally honest; you say what you think. Otherwise, I would suspect you of being not my friend but my foe. You flatter me far too much. Nothing can guarantee a man's downfall more easily than flattery.'

'Ayya, flattery is praising someone with self-seeking motives for the attributes that he does not possess. It would be flattery if I were to say to Madhurantakan, who has turned himself into a slave of the Pazhuvettaraiyars, that he is a great warrior. If ever you see me do such a thing, please kill me at once with your sword. But there is nothing untrue in what I said about you. Which hero of old days has accomplished what you did as a youth? Perhaps we may compare you to Rajaditta, the "lionheart who perished on the elephant". But we cannot say he was greater than you.'

'Stop it, Partibha! Stop it! What am I before Rajaditta? Rajaditta, who reached the warrior's haven after massacring the Rashtrakuta army that came rushing like the tidal waves of the sea with his small troops. Should we dare to compare ourselves with him? But leave the Chozha clan aside. What about the mighty heroes of the Pallava dynasty, into which you were born? Can we ever hope to see a Mahendra Pallava or a Mamalla Narasimha in our country again? Mamalla Narasimha defeated Pulikesin, the king who ruled the vast lands between the Tungabhadra in the south and Narmada in the north, ravaged his capital Vatapi, and built a pillar of victory in that city! Where do you and I stand in comparison with him? Can anyone build a dream city like Mamallapuram in our times or the future for that matter? Ah! Look around you! Partibhendra! Look well at the spot where the storytelling is taking place. Could ordinary men have excavated those rocks and shaped them into chariots? I get gooseflesh when I think of how spectacular Mamallapuram must have appeared, three hundred and fifty years ago! Don't you feel the same? Don't you swell with pride when you think of your ancestors?'

'My king! Just a while ago, you said that I flatter you. You had forgotten that I also speak of the faults I find in you. You too have been afflicted by this craze for painting, sculpture and the arts. It was this madness that nullified all the victories of my ancestors. What did Mamalla do once he returned from Vatapi after building his victory pillar there? Why, he spent all his time carving stones and hammering rocks! The result? Soon, the Chalukyas regained their strength and brought a huge army to take revenge. They destroyed Kanchi and Uraiyur. They went right up to Madurai. If Nedumara Pandiyan had not stopped them in Nelveli, wouldn't the entire peninsular region still be under the Chalukyas?'

'No, Partibhendra, no. Nowhere in the world has any single dynasty reigned over its kingdom forever. There was an end even to the Ikshvaku dynasty to which Rama belonged. Once the Chalukyas fell, the Rashtrakutas took their place. The rise and fall of kingdoms is a natural occurrence, though some kingdoms retain their power for a long time before they disappear without a trace. Take my ancestors. Karikal Valavan and Killi Valavan were hailed for their might and magnificence. But what do we know about them today? We recognize their names because a few poets have sung about them. But we don't know if those verses record the truth or were merely the fervid fantasies of drunken bards. On the other hand, this city of sculptures created by Mahendra and Mamalla will continue to showcase their glory to the world for thousands of years. You and I have killed thousands on the war front. We have made rivers of blood flow. What else have we done to establish our names in the world?'

Partibhendran was dumbfounded by this outburst. He began to doubt if it was indeed Karikalan who was speaking. Then he heaved a big sigh and said, 'My king! What can I say if this is your view of war and valour? You are not in your right mind today. That is why you are talking in this vein. Ayya, can't you share your pain with me? Can't you open your heart to me?'

'Partibhendra! If I could tear my heart out, what do you think you will see?'

'That is what I want to know, swami!'

'Not the father and mother who gave me birth. Not my sister and brother dearer to me than my life. Not you or Vandiyatevan, my dearest friends. It holds a woman who is the personification of malice, an embodiment of sin. It is Nandini, the young queen of Pazhuvur, the woman who is more lethal than venom, who has taken possession of my heart and subjects me to cruel torture. Today, I am speaking of what I have never shared with anyone before.' Aditta Karikalan's words blazed fire.

'My king! I had rather guessed it may be so. Your face turns dark and your eyes become red whenever the young queen of Pazhuvur is mentioned. Enough to indicate the torments within. But how did this unbecoming craze infect you? Yours is a tradition and culture where every woman, unknown and unrelated to you, would be regarded as a mother. Pazhuvettaraiyar has bonds of kinship with your clan through the long years. He is old in years. He may be an enemy now, but it was not always so. Your father and grandfather have given him great respect and honour. However evil she may be, how can you allow yourself to yearn for the woman he has married according to the sacred rites?'

'No. I should not. Partibhendra, do you think I don't know this? I suffer agonies because I know it only too well. But you should know that this poisonous desire had seeped into my soul long before her marriage to Pazhuvettaraiyar. All my efforts could not uproot it. I speak as if it was all her fault. Only god knows whose fault it was. I should say that the fault and the blame lie with the god who created us. Or we should blame fate for having separated us after setting up our meeting.'

'Had you met Nandini before she became the queen of Pazhuvur? Where, when and how did you meet her?'

'It is a long story. Do you want to hear it now?'

'Absolutely. I cannot be at peace unless I do. You have asked me to leave for Ilankai tomorrow. I cannot carry out my duties there properly or be at peace unless I know what it is and try to offer some solace to you.'

'My friend! Solace! No solace is possible for me, not in this lifetime. It is doubtful if I can get any in my next life. I am sharing this with you only for you to be at peace. You need not go to Ilankai thinking that I am hiding something from you.'

Aditta Karikalan paused to steady his thoughts. Then he heaved a big sigh and began to speak.

55

Nandini's Beloved

'I met Nandini for the first time when I was twelve years old. One day my sister, brother and I were sailing a little boat on the stream behind the palace in Pazhaiyarai. When we got off the boat and headed back to the palace, we heard our grandaunt's voice in the garden. The three of us had grown up being greatly indulged by Queen Sembiyan Mahadevi. We went to the bower from where she had called us, to tell her about our games. We found three strangers with her. One of them was a little girl of our age. The others turned out to be her parents, who were saying something about the girl. Everyone turned to look at us when we entered the bower. But all I could see were the wide eyes of that little girl as she looked at us in surprise. I can see those eyes even now . . .'

Karikalan fell silent and looked up at the sky. Perhaps he saw a young girl's face through the translucent cloud curtains drifting above.

'Ayya, go on!' Partibhendran's voice brought Karikalan back to earth to continue his tale.

'It was Kundavai who described all the fun we had in sailing boats. After hearing her out, the queen said, "My darling! These people have come from Pandya country to Ishana Siva Bhattar's house. They will be here for some time. See this little girl? How bright she is! Her name is Nandini. Let her join your games sometimes. She will be a good companion to you."

'I saw that my sister did not like this. When the three of us reached the palace, Kundavai said to me, "Anna, that girl is so ugly! Why does her face make me think of an owl? Grandaunt says that we should play with her. But I can't stop myself from giggling when I see her dreadful face. What can I do?"

'When I heard this, I came to understand this great truth. Women are born jealous. However beautiful a girl may be, she cannot bear to admit that another girl may be beautiful too. It was well known that my sister was the greatest beauty in our clan. But even she couldn't bear to see another girl endowed with beauty. Why else should she have belittled her? I wouldn't let this pass. I teased my sister by insisting that the other girl *was* beautiful. We argued and even had fights about this. Our brother Arulmozhi was bewildered because he could not figure out why we were fighting. Soon, I accompanied my father to the war in the Pandya country. We defeated the Pandya troops and the army sent by the king of Ilankai to assist the Pandya king. Finally, Veerapandiyan disappeared. At that time, it was not clear whether he had died on the battlefield or gone into hiding. The Ilankai forces began to retreat. We chased them up to the Setu bridge. The survivors escaped by boarding ships.

'This time, my father wanted to teach a lesson to the kings of Ilankai, who were frequently sending troops to assist the Pandyas. He decided to send an army under the leadership of Siriya Velar, the younger brother of the Kodumbalur chieftain.

It took a while to gather the army and armaments for this purpose. We returned after sending them off to Ilankai and learning that our soldiers had safely landed in Mathottam.

'By the time I returned to Pazhaiyarai, more than two years had gone by. I had completely forgotten the priest's daughter who had come to our city from somewhere near Madurai. I found that both she and my sister had grown beyond recognition. I also saw that they had become good friends. Thanks to my sister, Nandini looked gorgeous, dressed as she was in fine clothes and jewels. But Nandini had become too shy to interact with me as she used to do earlier. I tried to dispel her shyness. In her company, I found a joy I never knew before, an experience that astonished me. Like the fresh floods rising in the Kaveri, a new emotion flooded my heart. But very soon, I discovered that no one liked this new development. Kundavai started showing her dislike for Nandini. One day, my grandaunt called me and advised me, "Nandini belongs to a priest's family. You are the son of an emperor. Both of you have grown up. It is not appropriate for you to have anything to do with her." I, who had revered my grandaunt as a divinity until then, felt affronted by her. In sheer defiance, I sought Nandini and spent my time with her. This did not last long. All of a sudden, I found that Nandini and her parents had returned to their home town in Pandya country. I was grief-stricken. I could not contain my anger. I kept my sorrow to myself and turned all my anger on my sister. Fortunately, in a few days, I was sent to the north with our army, to Tirumunaipadi and Tondaimandalam. It was here that you and I met and became inseparable.

'With Malayaman's help, you and I fought against the Rashtrakutas. We drove the enemy to the north of the river Palar and captured Kanchi city. Then we had bad news from

Ilankai. We learnt that our army had met with defeat and Siriya Velar was dead. Hearing this, Veerapandiyan, who had hidden himself in a desert cave until then, came out like a snake from its hole. He gathered an army again, seized Madurai and raised his flag with the fish emblem. Don't you remember the overwhelming rage with which we headed to Pazhaiyarai at once? My father, the emperor, found his health failing at that time. But he was still ready to go to war. I stopped him by taking this oath, "I will not return to the Chozha country until I defeat the Pandya forces, retake Madurai, and bring Veerapandiyan's head with me." You were with me then. My father sent us to the battlefield in the Pandya territory. He ordered us to fight under the command of the Kodumbalur chieftain, Bhooti Vikramakesari. Along the way, we met Pazhuvettaraiyar and learnt that he was disgruntled by the appointment of Periya Velar, the Kodumbalur chieftain, as army general instead of him.

'Seeing how eager we were to fight, General Bhooti Vikramakesari made us responsible for conducting the war. Friend! It wouldn't be wrong for you and me to take great pride in having performed phenomenal acts of valour. We trounced the Pandya army and seized Madurai. Not content with that, we wanted to massacre the Pandya forces to ensure that they would never be able to rise again. We ordered our soldiers to chase the runaways and slaughter them all. Taking a strong battalion, we two gave chase to the Pandya king. The pennant with the fish hoisted high above the company showed us the direction in which he was retreating. We caught up with him. His personal bodyguard stood like a protective bulwark around him. In their intrepidity, the royal bodyguards of the Pandya land are a cut above the Velakkara corps of the Chozhas. We fought with men who had sworn that they would never retreat; they would strive to save their king at the cost of their own lives and would behead themselves if they failed. They fulfilled their oath. We slew them all, each and every one of them. The corpses of the dead lay in mountainous heaps, but we could not find Veerapandiyan among them. We had been deceived by the flag carried on top of an elephant. Neither on the beast nor beside it, could the Pandya king be found. He was a past master at running away and hiding himself, wasn't he? We suspected this and divided our troops to launch an exhaustive search.

'You and the others went along the two banks of the Vaikai river. I did not remain idle. I headed south on the dry river bed. Here and there, the hoof marks of a single horse were imprinted on the sand. There were bloodstains too. I followed them and reached the tiny island in the middle of the river with a Vishnu shrine and one or two houses for the priests. The grove around them had a great number of trees whose flowers were used for worship and a small lotus pond filled with blooming flowers. Friend! You may perhaps remember that I had pointed to that grove and told our soldiers that they were strictly forbidden to enter its precincts. This was not only to avoid disturbing the temple rituals. The real reason was that the girl who had stolen my heart, the goddess enshrined within me, lived in one of those houses.

'Earlier, I had come upon Nandini there when I entered the grove by chance. Her appearance had changed. She wore her hair bundled at one side in the front, with a string of flowers circling it, as you see in the sculpted figures of the poet Andal. She wore a flower garland around her neck. When I asked her about this new look, she told me that when she was separated from me, she had vowed never to marry another man. Like Andal, she would marry the god Krishna.

Madness, I thought. A human marrying a god! But I didn't want to argue just then. Let the war end and then we will see, I thought. I asked her if she would want any help. "Please keep your soldiers away from here. My old blind parents live in the house. I have a strong brother, but he has gone on a pilgrimage to Tirupati," she said. I promised to do so. After that, I went to see her two or three times. The passion I had felt for her in the past now burned ten times more intensely. But I controlled myself. I had to finish the task I had undertaken. I had to return to Pazhaiyarai with Veerapandiyan's head. I decided that I would ask my father to reward me by permitting me to marry Nandini.

'Having made this decision, I felt unbounded anger and astonishment at seeing hoof prints leading into the grove. I followed them and found a horse tethered to a tree. The fugitive had to be in one of those houses. I went to Nandini's house and looked through the window. O friend! What I saw within is engraved in my heart with molten lead. Veerapandiyan was lying on an old rope cot. Nandini was giving him water to quench his thirst. Her face glowed with a luminescence as never before. Two drops of water stood in her eyes.

I kicked the door open. I leapt inside. Nandini saw me. She stopped binding the wounds and fell flat at my feet. She rose with her hands folded together in supplication and said, "Ayya! I beg of you! By the love you once bore me, please don't harm him. He is mortally wounded. Don't kill him with your hands!"

'Choking and stuttering, I managed to say, "What is your connection to this man? Why are you asking me to spare his life?"

'"He is my beloved. He is my god. He is the benevolent soul who has agreed to marry me."

'The little pity I had for the wounded Veerapandiyan drained away from me. What a revenge this sinner, this villain, had taken on me! Had he grabbed my entire kingdom, it would have meant nothing to me. But he had snatched the woman enshrined in my heart. How could I show him mercy?

'I kicked Nandini aside, leapt over her and, with a single slash of my sword, severed Veerapandiyan's head. It rolled down to the floor.

'I feel ashamed to think of that barbaric act now. I am engulfed by shame. But at that time, I was afflicted not only by the frenzy of war but also by the frenzy of rage. After killing Veerapandiyan in that state of manic delirium, I left the house. As I crossed the threshold, I turned back to look at Nandini, just once. She too looked at me unblinkingly. Never have I seen anything like it on this earth, not ever. In that single glance, all the fires of lust, rage, greed, delusion, attachment, arrogance and envy spiralled upwards in a conflagration. Since then, over and over again I have pondered on what that glance could have implied. In vain. You came searching for me with the other soldiers and found me there. All of you burst into cries of victory on seeing Veerapandiyan's headless body and his severed head dripping with blood and gore. But my heart was heavy with a burden that made me feel as though the colossal weight of the Vindhya mountains was bearing down on me.'

56

Incident in the Women's Quarters

Centuries ago, when Mahendra Pallava ruled Tondaimandalam with Kanchi as his capital, he built mandapams in several towns and made arrangements for the Mahabharata to be narrated therein—a tradition that continued long after his time.

The people flocked to those Mahabharata sessions held in closed or open-air pavilions. Meanwhile, the storytellers honed their performance skills to dramatize the main narrative as well as the stories within the story in an inspiring blend of verse, song and dialogue.

One of those stories described how, while on a pilgrimage, the Pandava Prince Arjuna met Chitrangi, the princess of Manipur. They fell in love and had a son, Aravan. Born to the great hero and the warlike princess of the mountains, Aravan grew to be an indomitable warrior. When he learnt about the imminent Kurukshetra war, the boy hastened to join the Pandava army. Before the war began, there was talk of making a propitiatory sacrifice of a youth endowed with perfect form and insurmountable valour. Aravan came forward and offered himself. His offer had to be accepted as there was no one in the Pandava army to outshine the gallant youth.

The story of Aravan, who sacrificed himself for the victory of his side, stole the hearts of the Tamizh people. They built shrines for him beside every Draupadi temple and held celebratory festivals.

When Aravan's story came to an end beside the five chariots of Mamallapuram, the crowds dispersed into the night shouting, 'Hail Sundara Chozha, king of the three worlds!' and 'Hail Prince Aditta Karikalan!'

As their cries came floating in the air, Aditta Karikalan said, 'The storytelling is over. Malayaman will be here soon.'

'Aravan's story is over, but not the story you have been telling me,' Partibhendran said.

'Look at Malayaman's fortitude. At this age, he is able to stay awake until midnight to listen to the story,' Karikalan said.

'What is so surprising about living to a ripe old age? Old men pass long hours listening to old tales because they cannot fall asleep.'

'Would you equate Tirukovilur Malayaman with other old men? How many battles he has seen? It is doubtful whether we will live to reach his age. Even if we do, we will not be as strong.'

'My king! There is a reason for men of the older generation to remain hale and hearty. They don't wear themselves out by getting infatuated with women. They don't lose their hearts to the daughter of a temple priest and waste their time in longing for her. If at all they do, they would grab the girl by the hair and drag her to their women's quarters before they did anything else.'

'Partibhendra, Nandini is not the daughter of a priest. There must be some secret about her birth.'

'What does it matter whether she is the daughter of a priest or the daughter of a king? Or an orphan for that matter? Look at Pazhuvettaraiyar, that other old codger! He saw her somewhere on the way. He dragged her to his palace and locked her up in the women's quarters along with his many other wives.'

'Friend! I become distraught when I think of it!'

'Think about what? About how that old man got caught in her web?'

'No. No. How did the girl who once said that she loved me, and subsequently came to love Veerapandiyan and tried to save his life, agree to marry that antiquated old man?'

'I don't find it strange; not at all. It is your action that amazes me. Veerapandiyan is the prime enemy of the Chozha clan, a coward who ran away when he was defeated and yet called himself Veerapandiyan, the brave king! And you left the woman who gave him shelter and begged for his life, free! Just like that! You should have either slain her there and then, or bound her arms and legs and thrown her into the prison house. But you did neither! You let her go . . . ! I still remember how you carried Veerapandiyan's body out of that house and threw it down. Maddened by victory, we raised hysterical shouts of joy. But we heard sobs from within the hut. "Who is that?" I asked. You replied, "Some women from the priest's family. They are all petrified. Don't go in." Delirious in triumph, we paid no attention to the sounds of weeping. We left with Veerapandiyan's head. You came with us. But you did not join in our revelry and celebrations. You seemed to have been drained of all zest. When I asked you about it, you gave some unconvincing reply. I suspected that you were badly wounded and were refusing to admit it,' Partibhendran recalled.

'There was no wound on my body. It was my heart that was wounded beyond healing. How can I forget Nandini standing before the cot where Veerapandiyan was lying and begging me for his life with folded hands? I am tortured by regrets. Why couldn't I have granted her wish? If I could have restored his life to Veerapandiyan by giving up my own, I would have done so. Since that was impossible, I blamed myself. I cursed myself. Partibhendra! We are infinitely proud of our might. In our arrogance, we believe that nothing is beyond us. We even believe those inscriptions which proclaim that the king is divine. But do we have the power to give life to a lifeless body? Did anyone of royal birth ever have that power? We can take life, but no human being has the power to restore life.'

'Thank god. For you to have had that power would have been terrible indeed. You would have restored his life to Veerapandiyan. He would have run off to hide in some mountain hole again. And perhaps the Pandya war would still be going on! And all this for a girl's fake tears!'

'Partibhendra, you are an unfortunate man who hates women. You know nothing about love. That is why you talk in this vein.'

'True. I have not been bewitched by a woman's eyes. But your dear friend Vandiyatevan is someone who is hypnotized by any female face enough to drool over it. That is why you have more affection for him than for me. Right?'

'Ah! So, back to grousing about Vandiyatevan. I wondered how you had forgotten him for so long.'

'You will always find it bitter to hear the truth about him. Let it go. What happened next? Did you never meet Nandini again? Did you ask her why she married Pazhuvettaraiyar after sobbing and weeping over Veerapandiyan?'

'On the night Veerapandiyan was killed and the furore over the victory ended, everyone went to the camp and fell asleep. But I couldn't sleep at all. Every nerve in my body ached to see her once again. I wanted to offer some solace and ask for forgiveness. I also wanted to pour out the rage that overwhelmed me. I could not be at peace, nor return to Chozha country if I did not meet her again. That is why, after midnight, when you were all asleep, I took my horse and went to the island on the Vaikai river. With a palpitating heart, my body trembling all over, I got down and tottered towards the Vishnu temple. All the huts beside it had been burnt down. A man and a woman were sitting next to the smoking remains and wailing in lament, the same elderly couple who had brought Nandini to Pazhaiyarai all those years ago. Their grief and fear mounted when they saw me. At first, they couldn't speak at all. I comforted them and made gentle enquiries. They had gone to visit their daughter, who lived in a village on the opposite side of the river, to be with her when she gave birth to her child. Wilful and obstinate as ever, Nandini had refused to accompany them. Unable to convince her to change her mind, they went away, leaving her behind. As they were returning, they saw a few ruffians throwing a bound and gagged girl into the burning pyre. Fearing to go anywhere near them and reflecting that such horrors were part of life in wartime, they hurried home only to find the huts burnt down and Nandini missing. They ended their account with loud wails, "Prince! Where is our child? Where is our darling daughter?"'

'I had known that they were not Nandini's birth parents. And this confirmed it. Would her real parents have left her behind alone? I felt no pity or sympathy for them. The anguish I felt over Nandini's fate choked my throat. "Go and throw yourselves on the pyre in which your daughter was burnt!" I cursed them and returned to the camp before dawn. You were all sleeping soundly. You knew nothing of the trip I'd made.'

'Yes, prince! We didn't know. It amazes me that you should have kept all this to yourself for such a long time. I never imagined that you had so little faith in friendship. If I had been in your position, I would not have hidden such a secret from you,' Partibhendran said.

'Partibhendra, you are not in my position. Nor could anyone else in the world have been in that position. Who can say how you would have behaved, had you been in my place?'

'Let us not argue about the past. What happened next? When did you see Nandini again? Before, or after she became the Pazhuvur queen?'

'If I had seen her before, she would not have become the queen of Pazhuvur. Neither you nor I was in town when Pazhuvettaraiyar got married. You will remember how disgusted we were when the news reached us. Soon after that wedding, I was installed as the crown prince. My father, grandaunt and the other elders had conducted that ceremony to make sure that there was no room for doubt about the line of succession. Perhaps they feared that someone would advise Madhurantakan to stake his claim. "From now on, you will be responsible for the well-being of the Chozha kingdom," my father said with all his heart. Ministers, army generals and the people of the land raised shouts of victory. These circumstances made me forget all thoughts of Nandini. After the ceremonies were over, I saw her again.'

'I was wearing the ancient crown of the heir apparent when the emperor took me to the women's quarters in the palace to be blessed by my mother, grandaunt and other family elders. My brother, the chief minister and the Pazhuvettaraiyars followed us. My sister too was there with her companions, all arrayed in dazzling silks and jewels, with their faces bright and joyful as they waited to greet me. But my eyes saw only one—Nandini's. How did the goddess who reigned in my heart, the girl who had been burnt to cinders, appear in the women's quarters in the palace? Dressed in splendour, how could she take the leading place among them all, like an empress among the queens? How could her beauty have increased tenfold? Oh, the enchanting smile on her face! In a few seconds, my heart built innumerable castles in the air. Was the day I was proclaimed crown prince going to be the luckiest day of my life? By some powerful, phenomenal magic, was I going to attain the queen of my heart as my queen consort? As I was lost in these thoughts, my mother Vanamadevi came forward. "My child!" and kissed my forehead. Simultaneously, something unexpected occurred. My father shrieked and collapsed. Pandemonium broke out. I was one of those who tried to make the emperor regain consciousness.

'All the women left the room except for my mother and Sembiyan Mahadevi. My father recovered in a short while. I took my sister Kundavai aside and asked her how Nandini came to be there. Kundavai told me that Nandini had married Periya Pazhuvettaraiyar and was now the young queen of Pazhuvur. A sharp spear punctured my heart. I have been wounded in battles times past counting. But the wound I received when Kundavai said that Nandini was the young queen of Pazhuvur has never healed.'

As he spoke these words, Aditta Karikalan clutched at his breast as if his heart was still throbbing in pain.

57

The Ravishing Enchantress

Partibhendran had been listening to Aditta Karikalan's story without much sympathy. But now he found himself deeply moved.

'My king! I never thought that love for a woman could generate such anguish. We did not know that you were racked by misery on the day you became the crown prince. So we were surprised by your listlessness. I remember how we tried to cheer you up with jests and banter.'

'You tried to enthuse me with jokes and pleasantries. You talked about all the great deeds I was going to perform during my reign. On that day, your fantasies expanded the Chozha kingdom from Ilankai to the Himalayas. You crossed the oceans and seized kingdoms in foreign lands. I remember it all, and also how those wisecracks pained me.

'Later, one day, Nandini invited me to the Pazhuvur palace. I was conflicted. I hardly knew what I should do. Finally, I decided to go. I had to clear my doubts. I wanted to know the truth about her birth. I even wondered if my father's swooning had anything to do with seeing Nandini in the women's quarters. You will also remember that, though he made a quick recovery, his health was never the same again. I had this feeling that Nandini would be able to unravel some mystery . . .

'I guess I knew that these were really only pretexts I thought up to deceive myself. The real reason was her irresistible magnetic power. Pazhuvettaraiyar was not in town. There was no one to stop me when I entered his palace. Nor did anyone know of my old friendship with Nandini. Everyone thought that the newly designated crown prince was coming to take the blessings of the Pazhuvur queens. I met Nandini in a bower in the palace garden. Partibhendra! You have heard of mariners' tales, haven't you? About maelstroms in the sea, where the currents have illimitable power and speed? Any ship sucked into those currents would be shattered to shards in no time at all. In Nandini's presence, mine was the plight of a ship trapped in the vortex of a whirlpool. My body, mind and heart were shattering into a thousand fragments. I was surprised by the words that came out of my mouth on their own. While my heart asked, "Ayo! What in hell is making me say these things?" my tongue continued to babble.'

'At first, Nandini expressed her joy at my being designated "crown prince".'

'"Nothing to be happy about," I replied.'

'"Why?" she asked me.'

'"What kind of a question is this? How can I be happy? You have done this terrible thing," I said.'

'She pretended not to know what I meant. Our talk ran on. I accused her of throwing me over and opting for Veerapandiyan instead. I ridiculed the marriage she had entered into with old man Pazhuvettaraiyar.'

'"Prince! First, you killed my love. Then, before my very eyes, you killed the man who loved me. It looks as though you will not be content unless you kill me too. It irks you to see me alive. All right. Kill me and fulfil your wish," said she and held out a small knife she had kept tucked at her waist.'

'"Why should I kill you? It is you who is torturing the life out of me," I said.'

'Finally, my mouth spoke the words that make me cringe whenever I recall them. "Things have not gone out of hand even now. Say the word. Say you will leave this old man and come with me. I will give up this kingdom for you. Let us take a ship and sail away to some distant land."'

'Nandini broke into diabolic laughter. Even now, my hair stands on end when I remember it.'

'"What should we do after crossing the seas and reaching that distant land? Chop wood? Work in a plantain grove?"

'"Such things won't be to your taste, not now anyway. After all, having been raised in a priest's house, you have become the Pazhuvur queen."

'"I am not going to stop here, oh no! I intend to sit on the throne as the empress of the Chozha kingdom. Tell me if you are willing to put me there. Tell me if you would like to kill the two Pazhuvettaraiyars, throw the emperor into prison, become the Chozha emperor and enthrone me as your queen consort."'

'"Ayo! What fiendish things you say!"'

'"Was it not fiendish to kill the wounded Pandya king before my eyes?"'

'Rage consumed me. I hurled raving insults before I left. But she did not let me go so easily.'

'"Prince! If you ever change your mind, come to me. Come when your heart allows you to make me your empress."'

'That was the last time I saw her,' Aditta Karikalan said.

Partibhendran was flabbergasted. He finally managed to say, 'My king! Can such a devil exist among us on the earth? It was fortunate that you did not meet her again.'

'It is true that I did not go back to see her. But she has not relinquished her hold over me. Day and night, she haunts me, she tortures me. She lives in my memory during the day and in my dreams during the night. Sometimes, she appears with a seductive smile to embrace me and kiss me. At other times, she rushes in with a sharp knife to stab me. Or she comes sobbing in a flood of tears, while at a different time, she turns up howling and tearing at her cheeks, her unbound hair flying all about her. She comes screaming with maniacal laughter or to give me solace with an aura of serenity. God! I cannot describe how the wretch batters me. Do you remember what Thatha said this evening? He came up with several reasons for me to avoid going to Tanjavur. But the real reason for my wish to bring my father to Kanchi rather than for me to go to Tanjavur is Nandini.'

'My king! Are you really avoiding Tanjavur out of some preposterous fear of a *girl*? What on earth can she do to you? Do you think she would poison you?'

'No, Partibhendra! *No*! You have still not understood me. I am not afraid of her killing me. I am afraid that she may bend me to her will. If that enchantress tells me, "Throw your father into prison!" "Banish your sister from the country!" "Kill this old man and put me on the throne!", I am afraid that I might be tempted to comply. Either Nandini, or I, or both of us, must die. I will never know peace in this lifetime unless one of these things takes place.'

'All this is nothing but nonsense! Why should you die? Give me leave. I will go to Ilankai later. I will make straight for Tanjavur and return after killing her. What do I care if I'm cursed for the sin of killing a woman?'

'I will consider you to be my worst enemy if you attempt such a thing. If Nandini has to be killed, I will kill her with my own hands. I cannot bear it if anybody else harms so much as a nail on her little finger. Friend! Forget Nandini. Forget everything I told you about her. Go to Ilankai tomorrow as grandfather has advised. Bring my brother Arulmozhi by any means whatsoever. We will ask him to stay here. Let grandfather and grandson mull over things and do what they will. You and I will go to Ilankai. From there, we sail to the south seas with a vast army to conquer Kadaram, Pushpakam and Savakam. Then we may go westward and put up the tiger flag and establish the valour of the Tamizh people in Arabia, Persia and Egypt. Partibhendra! Do you know that the concept of a woman's virtue as we understand it in this country does not exist in those lands? The king can pick any girl he likes and have her confined in the palace.'

Malayaman arrived before Partibhendran could respond to this remark.

'No story in the world can be as wonderful as the story of Aravan, not even in the countries you spoke of just now. But why are you still wide awake and chatting away? Partibhendra, don't you remember that you have to leave for Ilankai tomorrow?' Malayaman said.

'That is exactly why we are wide awake, and going over my assignment,' Partibhendran replied.

End of Part 1

To be continued

Acknowledgements

May I thank from the heart:

- Penguin Random House India, for asking me to translate *Ponniyin Selvan*, which I would have never dared to do without the support they provided.
- Deepthi Talwar, for editing the translation with lynx-eyed professionalism and the empathy of an ally.
- Aparna Abhijit, for her patience and efficiency in copy-editing.
- Mihir Joglekar and Gunjan Ahlawat, for indulging my fancies as they came up with striking cover illustrations and designs.
- Arundhathi Subramaniam, poet, for translating a crucial poem in the text written by Kalki Krishnamurthy.
- Gopal Gandhi, writer/translator, for allowing me to use his translations of Tirukkural verses quoted in the book.
- T.K. Neelakantan, Tamizh scholar/writer, for his valuable comments and word-for-word translations of the poems quoted in the text.
- Professor Whitney Cox, University of Chicago, who helped me more than he knew.

– My uncle K. Rajendran, former editor, *Kalki* magazine, for his patience in reading *Ponniyin Selvan* aloud, a life-changing experience for me, then a nine-year-old.
– My sister Rukmini Ramachandran, for teaching me how to use tech tools more effectively in my work and taking charge wherever I couldn't follow her.
– E. Ravikumar, for always being there to help.
– My husband V. Ramnarayan, for going over some ticklish portions with his insider's knowledge as a translator, and his unfailing support in this task, as in everything I do; daughter Akhila Ramnarayan, for being ready to answer any SOS and subjecting my translator's preface to her exacting scrutiny; son Abhinav Ramnarayan, for hounding me to send the drafts as he couldn't wait for the book to be released (what can be more encouraging?).
– Two members of my family who are no more–my mother Anandhi, who taught me to sing all the songs in *Ponniyin Selvan*, and grandmother Rukmini, whose love and adoration for her husband shone in every word she spoke about him as her memories brought him to life.

Scan QR code to access the
Penguin Random House India website